The Hobbit is a tale of high adventure, undertaken by a company of dwarves, in search of dragon-guarded gold. A reluctant partner in this perilous quest is Bilbo Baggins, a comfort-loving, unambitious hobbit, who surprises even himself by his resourcefulness and his skill as a burglar.

Encounters with trolls, goblins, dwarves, elves and giant spiders, conversations with the dragon, Smaug the Magnificent, and a rather unwilling presence at the Battle of the Five Armies are some of the adventures that befall Bilbo. But there are lighter moments as well: good fellowship, welcome meals, laughter and song.

Bilbo Baggins has taken his place among the ranks of the immortals of children's fiction. Written for Professor Tolkien's own children, *The Hobbit* met with instant acclaim when published. It is a complete and marvellous tale in itself, but it also forms a prelude to *The Lord of the Rings*.

'One of the most influential books of our generation'
The Times

Works by J.R.R. Tolkien

THE HOBBIT
LEAF BY NIGGLE
ON FAIRY-STORIES
FARMER GILES OF HAM
THE HOMECOMING OF BEORHTNOTH
THE LORD OF THE RINGS
THE ADVENTURES OF TOM BOMBADIL
THE ROAD GOES EVER ON (WITH DONALD SWANN)
SMITH OF WOOTTON MAJOR

Works published posthumously

SIR GAWAIN AND THE GREEN KNIGHT, PEARL AND SIR ORFEO*
THE FATHER CHRISTMAS LETTERS
THE SILMARILLION*
PICTURES BY J.R.R. TOLKIEN*
UNFINISHED TALES*
THE LETTERS OF J.R.R. TOLKIEN*
FINN AND HENGEST
MR BLISS
THE MONSTERS AND THE CRITICS & OTHER ESSAYS*
ROVERANDOM
THE CHILDREN OF HÚRIN*
THE LEGEND OF SIGURD AND GUDRÚN*
THE FALL OF ARTHUR*
BEOWULF: A TRANSLATION AND COMMENTARY*
THE STORY OF KULLERVO
THE LAY OF AOTROU AND ITROUN
BEREN AND LÚTHIEN*
THE FALL OF GONDOLIN*

The History of Middle-earth – by Christopher Tolkien

I THE BOOK OF LOST TALES, PART ONE
II THE BOOK OF LOST TALES, PART TWO
III THE LAYS OF BELERIAND
IV THE SHAPING OF MIDDLE-EARTH
V THE LOST ROAD AND OTHER WRITINGS
VI THE RETURN OF THE SHADOW
VII THE TREASON OF ISENGARD
VIII THE WAR OF THE RING
IX SAURON DEFEATED
X MORGOTH'S RING
XI THE WAR OF THE JEWELS
XII THE PEOPLES OF MIDDLE-EARTH

* Edited by Christopher Tolkien

THE HOBBIT

OR
THERE AND BACK AGAIN

BY

J.R.R. TOLKIEN

HarperCollins*Publishers*

HarperCollins*Publishers* Ltd
1 London Bridge Street
London SE1 9GF

HarperCollins*Publishers*
1st Floor, Watermarque Building, Ringsend Road
Dublin 4, Ireland

www.tolkien.co.uk

www.tolkienestate.com

This paperback edition 2006
143

This new reset edition is based on the edition first published in 1995

First published by HarperCollins*Publishers* 1991
Fifth edition (reset) 1995

First published in Great Britain by George Allen & Unwin 1937
Second edition 1951
Third edition 1966
Fourth edition 1978

ISBN 978-0-261-10221-7

Set in Monotype Plantin

A CIP catalogue record for this book is available
from the British Library

Printed and bound in the UK using 100% Renewable Electricity
by CPI Group (UK) Ltd, Croydon CR0 4YY

MIX
Paper from
responsible sources
FSC™ C007454

This book is produced from independently certified FSC™ paper
to ensure responsible forest management.

For more information visit: www.harpercollins.co.uk/green

CONTENTS

ILLUSTRATIONS

NOTE ON THE TEXT

The Hobbit was first published in September 1937. Its 1951 second edition (fifth impression) contains a significantly revised portion of Chapter V, "Riddles in the Dark," which brings the story of The Hobbit more in line with its sequel, The Lord of the Rings, then in progress. Tolkien made some further revisions to the American edition published by Ballantine Books in February 1966, and to the British third edition (sixteenth impression) published by George Allen & Unwin later that same year.

For the 1995 British hardcover edition, published by HarperCollins, the text of The Hobbit was entered into word-processing files, and a number of further corrections of misprints and errors were made. Since then, various editions of The Hobbit have been generated from that computerized text file. For the present text, that file has been compared again, line by line, with the earlier editions, and a number of further corrections have been made to present a text that, as closely as possible, represents Tolkien's final intended form.

Readers interested in details of the changes made at various times to the text of The Hobbit are referred to Appendix A, "Textual and Revisional Notes," of The Annotated Hobbit (1988), and J. R. R. Tolkien: A Descriptive Bibliography by Wayne G. Hammond, with the assistance of Douglas A. Anderson (1993).

Douglas A. Anderson
May 2001

East lie the
where is ?

The
Lonely
Mountain
ᛁ·ᛏ·ᛒ·ᛏ·

Here of old was T
King under the ᚷ

Far
to the North
are
the Grey Mountains
&
the Withered Heath
whence came the

Great Worms.

Thror's Map

West lies ᚷ

ills

M.

Here was Girion
lord in Dale

the Running River

here is
the gateway
of the Long
Lake

n

ain

The Desolation
of Smaug

In Esgaroth upon
the Long Lake
dwell Men

Here flows the
Forest River

ood the Great
there are Spiders.

Elvenking

ᚦᛗ·ᚻᚠᛒᛒᛁᛏ

ᚠᚱ

ᚦᛗᚱᛗ·ᚠᛏᛗ·ᛒᚠᛤᛂ·ᚠᚷᚠᛁᛏ

This is a story of long ago. At that time the languages and letters were quite different from ours of today. English is used to represent the languages. But two points may be noted. (1) In English the only correct plural of *dwarf* is *dwarfs*, and the adjective is *dwarfish*. In this story *dwarves* and *dwarvish* are used*, but only when speaking of the ancient people to whom Thorin Oakenshield and his companions belonged. (2) *Orc* is not an English word. It occurs in one or two places but is usually translated *goblin* (or *hobgoblin* for the larger kinds). *Orc* is the hobbits' form of the name given at that time to these creatures, and it is not connected at all with our *orc*, *ork*, applied to sea-animals of dolphin-kind.

Runes were old letters originally used for cutting or scratching on wood, stone, or metal, and so were thin and angular. At the time of this tale only the Dwarves made regular use of them, especially for private or secret records. Their runes are in this book represented by English runes, which are known now to few people. If the runes on Thror's Map are compared

---

* The reason for this use is given in *The Lord of the Rings*, III, 1136.

with the transcriptions into modern letters (on pp. 25 and 62–3), the alphabet, adapted to modern English, can be discovered and the above runic title also read. On the Map all the normal runes are found, except ᛣ for X. I and U are used for J and V. There was no rune for Q (use CW); nor for Z (the dwarf-rune ᛉ may be used if required). It will be found, however, that some single runes stand for two modern letters: *th, ng, ee*; other runes of the same kind (ᛠ *ea* and ᛥ *st*) were also sometimes used. The secret door was marked D ᛥ. From the side a hand pointed to this, and under it was written: ᚠᛁᚾᛗ·ᛈᚱᛏ·ᚾᛁᚷᚾ· ᚦᛗ·ᛗᚨᚱ·ᚠᛏᛥ·ᚠᚱᚷ·ᛗᚠᛗ·ᛈᚠᚱᚲ·ᚠᛒᚱᛗᚠ�747: ᛈ·ᛈ. The last two runes are the initials of Thror and Thrain. The moon-runes read by Elrond were:

ᛋᛏᚠᚨᛗ·ᛒᛗ·ᚠᛗ·ᚷᚱᛗᚨ·ᛋᛏᚨᛗ·ᚠᛈᛗᛏ·ᚦᛗ·ᛈᚱᚾᛋᚾ·ᚾᛏᛈᚾᛋ·ᚠᛏ
ᛥ·ᚦᛗ·ᛋᛗᛏᛏᛁᛉ·ᛋᚾᛏ·ᛈᛁᛈ·ᚦᛗ·ᛏᚠᛋᛏ·ᛏᛁᚷᚨᛏ·ᛒᛈ·ᛥᚾᚱᛁᛏᛋ·ᛗᚠᛘ·
ᛈᛁᛏᛏ·ᛋᚾᛁᛏᛗ·ᚾᚲᛈᛏ·ᚦᛗ·ᚨᛗᚨᚾᚠᚠᛗ.

On the Map the compass points are marked in runes, with East at the top, as usual in dwarf-maps, and so read clockwise: E(ast), S(outh), W(est), N(orth).

Chapter I

AN UNEXPECTED PARTY

In a hole in the ground there lived a hobbit. Not a nasty, dirty, wet hole, filled with the ends of worms and an oozy smell, nor yet a dry, bare, sandy hole with nothing in it to sit down on or to eat: it was a hobbit-hole, and that means comfort.

It had a perfectly round door like a porthole, painted green, with a shiny yellow brass knob in the exact middle. The door opened on to a tube-shaped hall like a tunnel: a very comfortable tunnel without smoke, with panelled walls, and floors tiled and carpeted, provided with polished chairs, and lots and lots of pegs for hats and coats—the hobbit was fond of visitors. The tunnel wound on and on, going fairly but not quite straight into the side of the hill— The Hill, as all the people for many miles round called it—and many little round doors opened out of it, first on one side and then on another. No going upstairs for the hobbit: bedrooms, bathrooms, cellars, pantries (lots of these), wardrobes (he had whole rooms devoted to clothes), kitchens, dining-rooms, all were on the same floor, and indeed on the same passage. The best rooms were all on the left-hand side (going in), for these were the only ones to have windows, deep-set round windows looking over his garden, and meadows beyond, sloping down to the river.

This hobbit was a very well-to-do hobbit, and his name was Baggins. The Bagginses had lived in the neighbourhood of The Hill for time out of mind, and people considered them very respectable, not only because most of them were rich, but also because they never had any adventures or did anything unexpected: you could tell what a Baggins would say on any question without the bother of asking him. This is a story of how a Baggins had an adventure, and found himself doing and saying things altogether unexpected. He may have lost the neighbours' respect, but he gained—well, you will see whether he gained anything in the end.

The mother of our particular hobbit—what is a hobbit? I suppose hobbits need some description nowadays, since they have become rare and shy of the Big People, as they call us. They are (or were) a little people, about half our height, and smaller than the bearded Dwarves. Hobbits have no beards. There is little or no magic about them, except the ordinary everyday sort which helps them to disappear quietly and quickly when large stupid folk like you and me come blundering along, making a noise like elephants which they can hear a mile off. They are inclined to be fat in the stomach; they dress in bright colours (chiefly green and yellow); wear no shoes, because their feet grow natural leathery soles and thick warm brown hair like the stuff on their heads (which is curly); have long clever brown fingers, good-natured faces, and laugh deep fruity laughs (especially after dinner, which they have twice a day when they can get it). Now you know enough to go on with. As I was saying, the mother of this hobbit—of Bilbo

Baggins, that is—was the famous Belladonna Took, one of the three remarkable daughters of the Old Took, head of the hobbits who lived across The Water, the small river that ran at the foot of The Hill. It was often said (in other families) that long ago one of the Took ancestors must have taken a fairy wife. That was, of course, absurd, but certainly there was still something not entirely hobbitlike about them, and once in a while members of the Took-clan would go and have adventures. They discreetly disappeared, and the family hushed it up; but the fact remained that the Tooks were not as respectable as the Bagginses, though they were undoubtedly richer.

Not that Belladonna Took ever had any adventures after she became Mrs. Bungo Baggins. Bungo, that was Bilbo's father, built the most luxurious hobbit-hole for her (and partly with her money) that was to be found either under The Hill or over The Hill or across The Water, and there they remained to the end of their days. Still it is probable that Bilbo, her only son, although he looked and behaved exactly like a second edition of his solid and comfortable father, got something a bit queer in his make-up from the Took side, something that only waited for a chance to come out. The chance never arrived, until Bilbo Baggins was grown up, being about fifty years old or so, and living in the beautiful hobbit-hole built by his father, which I have just described for you, until he had in fact apparently settled down immovably.

By some curious chance one morning long ago in the quiet of the world, when there was less noise and more green, and the hobbits were still numerous and prosperous, and Bilbo Baggins was standing at his

door after breakfast smoking an enormous long
wooden pipe that reached nearly down to his woolly
toes (neatly brushed)—Gandalf came by. Gandalf! If
you had heard only a quarter of what I have heard
about him, and I have only heard very little of all
there is to hear, you would be prepared for any sort
of remarkable tale. Tales and adventures sprouted up
all over the place wherever he went, in the most
extraordinary fashion. He had not been down that
way under The Hill for ages and ages, not since his
friend the Old Took died, in fact, and the hobbits
had almost forgotten what he looked like. He had
been away over The Hill and across The Water on
businesses of his own since they were all small
hobbit-boys and hobbit-girls.

All that the unsuspecting Bilbo saw that morning
was an old man with a staff. He had a tall pointed
blue hat, a long grey cloak, a silver scarf over which
his long white beard hung down below his waist, and
immense black boots.

"Good Morning!" said Bilbo, and he meant it. The
sun was shining, and the grass was very green. But
Gandalf looked at him from under long bushy eyebrows that stuck out further than the brim of his
shady hat.

"What do you mean?" he said. "Do you wish me a
good morning, or mean that it is a good morning
whether I want it or not; or that you feel good this
morning; or that it is a morning to be good on?"

"All of them at once," said Bilbo. "And a very fine
morning for a pipe of tobacco out of doors, into the
bargain. If you have a pipe about you, sit down and
have a fill of mine! There's no hurry, we have all the

day before us!" Then Bilbo sat down on a seat by his door, crossed his legs, and blew out a beautiful grey ring of smoke that sailed up into the air without breaking and floated away over The Hill.

"Very pretty!" said Gandalf. "But I have no time to blow smoke-rings this morning. I am looking for someone to share in an adventure that I am arranging, and it's very difficult to find anyone."

"I should think so—in these parts! We are plain quiet folk and have no use for adventures. Nasty disturbing uncomfortable things! Make you late for dinner! I can't think what anybody sees in them," said our Mr. Baggins, and stuck one thumb behind his braces, and blew out another even bigger smokering. Then he took out his morning letters, and began to read, pretending to take no more notice of the old man. He had decided that he was not quite his sort, and wanted him to go away. But the old man did not move. He stood leaning on his stick and gazing at the hobbit without saying anything, till Bilbo got quite uncomfortable and even a little cross.

"Good morning!" he said at last. "We don't want any adventures here, thank you! You might try over The Hill or across The Water." By this he meant that the conversation was at an end.

"What a lot of things you do use *Good morning* for!" said Gandalf. "Now you mean that you want to get rid of me, and that it won't be good till I move off."

"Not at all, not at all, my dear sir! Let me see, I don't think I know your name?"

"Yes, yes, my dear sir—and I do know your name, Mr. Bilbo Baggins. And you do know my name, though you don't remember that I belong to it. I am Gandalf, and Gandalf means me! To think that I should have lived to be good-morninged by Belladonna Took's son, as if I was selling buttons at the door!"

"Gandalf, Gandalf! Good gracious me! Not the wandering wizard that gave Old Took a pair of magic diamond studs that fastened themselves and never came undone till ordered? Not the fellow who used to tell such wonderful tales at parties, about dragons and goblins and giants and the rescue of princesses and the unexpected luck of widows' sons? Not the man that used to make such particularly excellent fireworks! I remember those! Old Took used to have them on Midsummer's Eve. Splendid! They used to go up like great lilies and snapdragons and laburnums of fire and hang in the twilight all evening!" You will notice already that Mr. Baggins was not quite so prosy as he liked to believe, also that he was very fond of flowers. "Dear me!" he went on. "Not the Gandalf who was responsible for so many quiet lads and lasses going off into the Blue for mad adventures? Anything from climbing trees to visiting elves—or sailing in ships, sailing to other shores! Bless me, life used to be quite inter—I mean, you used to upset things badly in these parts once upon a time. I beg your pardon, but I had no idea you were still in business."

"Where else should I be?" said the wizard. "All the same I am pleased to find you remember something about me. You seem to remember my fireworks kindly, at any rate, and that is not without hope. Indeed for your old grandfather Took's sake, and for the sake of poor Belladonna, I will give you what you asked for."

"I beg your pardon, I haven't asked for anything!"

"Yes, you have! Twice now. My pardon. I give it you. In fact I will go so far as to send you on this adventure. Very amusing for me, very good for you—and profitable too, very likely, if you ever get over it."

"Sorry! I don't want any adventures, thank you. Not today. Good morning! But please come to tea—any time you like! Why not tomorrow? Come tomorrow! Good bye!" With that the hobbit turned and scuttled inside his round green door, and shut it as quickly as he dared, not to seem rude. Wizards after all are wizards.

"What on earth did I ask him to tea for!" he said to himself, as he went to the pantry. He had only just had breakfast, but he thought a cake or two and a drink of something would do him good after his fright.

Gandalf in the meantime was still standing outside the door, and laughing long but quietly. After a while he stepped up, and with the spike on his staff scratched a queer sign on the hobbit's beautiful green front-door. Then he strode away, just about the time when Bilbo was finishing his second cake and beginning to think that he had escaped adventures very well.

The next day he had almost forgotten about Gandalf. He did not remember things very well, unless he put them down on his Engagement Tablet: like this: *Gandalf Tea Wednesday*. Yesterday he had been too flustered to do anything of the kind.

Just before tea-time there came a tremendous ring on the front-door bell, and then he remembered! He rushed and put on the kettle, and put out another cup and saucer, and an extra cake or two, and ran to the door.

"I am so sorry to keep you waiting!" he was going to say, when he saw that it was not Gandalf at all. It was a dwarf with a blue beard tucked into a golden belt, and very bright eyes under his dark-green hood. As soon as the door was opened, he pushed inside, just as if he had been expected.

He hung his hooded cloak on the nearest peg, and "Dwalin at your service!" he said with a low bow.

"Bilbo Baggins at yours!" said the hobbit, too surprised to ask any questions for the moment. When the silence that followed had become uncomfortable, he added: "I am just about to take tea; pray come and have some with me." A little stiff perhaps, but he meant it kindly. And what would you do, if an uninvited dwarf came and hung his things up in your hall without a word of explanation?

They had not been at table long, in fact they had hardly reached the third cake, when there came another even louder ring at the bell.

"Excuse me!" said the hobbit, and off he went to the door.

"So you have got here at last!" That was what he was going to say to Gandalf this time. But it was not Gandalf. Instead there was a very old-looking dwarf on the step with a white beard and a scarlet hood; and he too hopped inside as soon as the door was open, just as if he had been invited.

"I see they have begun to arrive already," he said when he caught sight of Dwalin's green hood hanging up. He hung his red one next to it, and

"Balin at your service!" he said with his hand on his breast.

"Thank you!" said Bilbo with a gasp. It was not the correct thing to say, but *they have begun to arrive* had flustered him badly. He liked visitors, but he liked to know them before they arrived, and he preferred to ask them himself. He had a horrible thought that the cakes might run short, and then he—as the host: he knew his duty and stuck to it however painful—he might have to go without.

"Come along in, and have some tea!" he managed to say after taking a deep breath.

"A little beer would suit me better, if it is all the same to you, my good sir," said Balin with the white beard. "But I don't mind some cake—seed-cake, if you have any."

"Lots!" Bilbo found himself answering, to his own surprise; and he found himself scuttling off, too, to the cellar to fill a pint beer-mug, and then to a pantry to fetch two beautiful round seed-cakes which he had baked that afternoon for his after-supper morsel.

When he got back Balin and Dwalin were talking at the table like old friends (as a matter of fact they were brothers). Bilbo plumped down the beer and the cake in front of them, when loud came a ring at the bell again, and then another ring.

"Gandalf for certain this time," he thought as he puffed along the passage. But it was not. It was two more dwarves, both with blue hoods, silver belts, and yellow beards; and each of them carried a bag of tools and a spade. In they hopped, as soon as the door began to open—Bilbo was hardly surprised at all.

"What can I do for you, my dwarves?" he said.

"Kili at your service!" said the one. "And Fili!" added the other; and they both swept off their blue hoods and bowed.

"At yours and your family's!" replied Bilbo, remembering his manners this time.

"Dwalin and Balin here already, I see," said Kili. "Let us join the throng!"

"Throng!" thought Mr. Baggins. "I don't like the sound of that. I really must sit down for a minute and collect my wits, and have a drink." He had only just had a sip—in the corner, while the four dwarves sat round the table, and talked about mines and gold and troubles with the goblins, and the depredations of dragons, and lots of other things which he did not understand, and did not want to, for they sounded much too adventurous— when, *ding-dong-a-ling-dang*, his bell rang again, as if some naughty little hobbit-boy was trying to pull the handle off.

"Someone at the door!" he said, blinking.

"Some four, I should say by the sound," said Fili. "Besides, we saw them coming along behind us in the distance."

The poor little hobbit sat down in the hall and put his head in his hands, and wondered what had happened, and what was going to happen, and whether they would all stay to supper. Then the bell rang again louder than ever, and he had to run to the door. It was not four after all, it was five. Another dwarf had come along while he was wondering in the hall. He had hardly turned the knob, before they were all inside, bowing and saying "at your service" one after another. Dori, Nori, Ori, Oin, and Gloin were their names; and very soon two purple hoods, a grey hood, a brown hood, and a white hood were hanging on the pegs, and off they marched with their broad hands stuck in their gold and silver belts to join the others. Already it had almost become a throng. Some called for ale, and some for porter, and one for coffee, and all of them for cakes; so the hobbit was kept very busy for a while.

A big jug of coffee had just been set in the hearth, the seed-cakes were gone, and the dwarves were starting on a round of buttered scones, when there came—a loud knock. Not a ring, but a hard rat-tat on the hobbit's beautiful green door. Somebody was banging with a stick!

Bilbo rushed along the passage, very angry, and altogether bewildered and bewuthered—this was the most awkward Wednesday he ever remembered. He pulled open the door with a jerk, and they all fell in, one on top of the other. More dwarves, four more! And there was Gandalf behind, leaning on his staff and laughing. He had made quite a dent on the beautiful door; he had also, by the way, knocked out the secret mark that he had put there the morning before.

"Carefully! Carefully!" he said. "It is not like you, Bilbo, to keep friends waiting on the mat, and then open the door like a pop-gun! Let me introduce Bifur, Bofur, Bombur, and especially Thorin!"

"At your service!" said Bifur, Bofur, and Bombur standing in a row. Then they hung up two yellow hoods and a pale green one; and also a sky-blue one with a long silver tassel. This last belonged to Thorin, an enormously important dwarf, in fact no other than the great Thorin Oakenshield himself, who was not at all pleased at falling flat on Bilbo's mat with Bifur, Bofur, and Bombur on top of him. For one thing Bombur was immensely fat and heavy. Thorin indeed was very haughty, and said nothing about *service*; but poor Mr. Baggins said he was sorry so many times, that at last he grunted "pray don't mention it," and stopped frowning.

"Now we are all here!" said Gandalf, looking at the row of thirteen hoods—the best detachable party hoods—and his own hat hanging on the pegs. "Quite a merry gathering! I hope there is something left for the late-comers to eat and drink! What's that? Tea! No thank you! A little red wine, I think for me."

"And for me," said Thorin.

"And raspberry jam and apple-tart," said Bifur.

"And mince-pies and cheese," said Bofur.

"And pork-pie and salad," said Bombur.

"And more cakes—and ale—and coffee, if you don't mind," called the other dwarves through the door.

"Put on a few eggs, there's a good fellow!" Gandalf called after him, as the hobbit stumped off to the pantries. "And just bring out the cold chicken and pickles!"

"Seems to know as much about the inside of my larders as I do myself!" thought Mr. Baggins, who was feeling positively flummoxed, and was beginning to wonder whether a most wretched adventure had not come right into his house. By the time he had got all the bottles and dishes and knives and forks and glasses and plates and spoons and things piled up on big trays, he was getting very hot, and red in the face, and annoyed.

"Confusticate and bebother these dwarves!" he said aloud. "Why don't they come and lend a hand?" Lo and behold! there stood Balin and Dwalin at the door of the kitchen, and Fili and Kili behind them, and before he could say *knife* they had whisked the trays and a couple of small tables into the parlour and set out everything afresh.

Gandalf sat at the head of the party with the thirteen dwarves all round: and Bilbo sat on a stool at the fireside, nibbling at a biscuit (his appetite was quite taken away), and trying to look as if this was all perfectly ordinary and not in the least an adventure. The dwarves ate and ate, and talked and talked, and time got on. At last they pushed their chairs back, and Bilbo made a move to collect the plates and glasses.

"I suppose you will all stay to supper?" he said in his politest unpressing tones.

"Of course!" said Thorin. "And after. We shan't get through the business till late, and we must have some music first. Now to clear up!"

Thereupon the twelve dwarves—not Thorin, he was too important, and stayed talking to Gandalf—jumped to their feet, and made tall piles of all the things. Off they went, not waiting for trays, balancing columns of plates, each with a bottle on the top, with one hand, while the hobbit ran after them almost squeaking with fright: "please be careful!" and "please, don't trouble! I can manage." But the dwarves only started to sing:

> *Chip the glasses and crack the plates!*
> *Blunt the knives and bend the forks!*
> *That's what Bilbo Baggins hates—*
> *Smash the bottles and burn the corks!*
>
> *Cut the cloth and tread on the fat!*
> *Pour the milk on the pantry floor!*
> *Leave the bones on the bedroom mat!*
> *Splash the wine on every door!*
>
> *Dump the crocks in a boiling bowl;*
> *Pound them up with a thumping pole;*
> *And when you've finished, if any are whole,*
> *Send them down the hall to roll!*
>
> *That's what Bilbo Baggins hates!*
> *So, carefully! carefully with the plates!*

And of course they did none of these dreadful things, and everything was cleaned and put away safe as quick as lightning, while the hobbit was turning round and round in the middle of the kitchen trying to see what they were doing. Then they went back, and found Thorin with his feet on the fender smoking a pipe. He was blowing the most enormous smoke-rings, and wherever he told one to go, it went—up the chimney, or behind the clock on the mantelpiece, or under the table, or round and round the ceiling; but wherever it went it was not quick enough to escape Gandalf. Pop! he sent a smaller smoke-ring from his short clay-pipe straight through each one of Thorin's. Then Gandalf's smoke-ring would go green and come back to hover over the wizard's head. He had a cloud of them about him already, and in the dim light it made him look strange and sorcerous. Bilbo stood still and watched—he loved smoke-rings—and then he blushed to think how proud he had been yesterday morning of the smoke-rings he had sent up the wind over The Hill.

"Now for some music!" said Thorin. "Bring out the instruments!"

Kili and Fili rushed for their bags and brought back little fiddles; Dori, Nori, and Ori brought out flutes from somewhere inside their coats; Bombur produced a drum from the hall; Bifur and Bofur went out too, and came back with clarinets that they had left among the walking-sticks. Dwalin and Balin said: "Excuse me, I left mine in the porch!" "Just bring mine in with you!" said Thorin. They came back with viols as big as themselves, and with Thorin's harp wrapped in a green cloth. It was a beautiful golden harp, and when Thorin struck it the music began all at once, so sudden and sweet that Bilbo forgot everything else, and was swept away into dark lands under strange moons, far over The Water and very far from his hobbit-hole under The Hill.

The dark came into the room from the little window that opened in the side of The Hill; the fire-light flickered—it was April—and still they played on, while the shadow of Gandalf's beard wagged against the wall.

The dark filled all the room, and the fire died down, and the shadows were lost, and still they played on. And suddenly first one and then another began to sing as they played, deep-throated singing of the dwarves in the deep places of their ancient homes; and this is like a fragment of their song, if it can be like their song without their music.

> *Far over the misty mountains cold*
> *To dungeons deep and caverns old*
> *We must away ere break of day*
> *To seek the pale enchanted gold.*
>
> *The dwarves of yore made mighty spells,*
> *While hammers fell like ringing bells*
> *In places deep, where dark things sleep,*
> *In hollow halls beneath the fells.*
>
> *For ancient king and elvish lord*
> *There many a gleaming golden hoard*
> *They shaped and wrought, and light they caught*
> *To hide in gems on hilt of sword.*
>
> *On silver necklaces they strung*
> *The flowering stars, on crowns they hung*
> *The dragon-fire, in twisted wire*
> *They meshed the light of moon and sun.*
>
> *Far over the misty mountains cold*
> *To dungeons deep and caverns old*
> *We must away, ere break of day,*
> *To claim our long-forgotten gold.*
>
> *Goblets they carved there for themselves*
> *And harps of gold; where no man delves*
> *There lay they long, and many a song*
> *Was sung unheard by men or elves.*

The pines were roaring on the height,
The winds were moaning in the night.
The fire was red, it flaming spread;
The trees like torches blazed with light.

The bells were ringing in the dale
And men looked up with faces pale;
The dragon's ire more fierce than fire
Laid low their towers and houses frail.

The mountain smoked beneath the moon;
The dwarves, they heard the tramp of doom.
They fled their hall to dying fall
Beneath his feet, beneath the moon.

Far over the misty mountains grim
To dungeons deep and caverns dim
We must away, ere break of day,
To win our harps and gold from him!

As they sang the hobbit felt the love of beautiful things made by hands and by cunning and by magic moving through him, a fierce and a jealous love, the desire of the hearts of dwarves. Then something Tookish woke up inside him, and he wished to go and see the great mountains, and hear the pine-trees and the waterfalls, and explore the caves, and wear a sword instead of a walking-stick. He looked out of the window. The stars were out in a dark sky above the trees. He thought of the jewels of the dwarves shining in dark caverns. Suddenly in the wood beyond The Water a flame leapt up—probably somebody lighting

a wood-fire—and he thought of plundering dragons
settling on his quiet Hill and kindling it all to flames.
He shuddered; and very quickly he was plain Mr.
Baggins of Bag-End, Under-Hill, again.

He got up trembling. He had less than half a mind
to fetch the lamp, and more than half a mind to
pretend to, and go and hide behind the beer-barrels
in the cellar, and not come out again until all the
dwarves had gone away. Suddenly he found that the
music and the singing had stopped, and they were all
looking at him with eyes shining in the dark.

"Where are you going?" said Thorin, in a tone that
seemed to show that he guessed both halves of the
hobbit's mind.

"What about a little light?" said Bilbo apologetically.

"We like the dark," said all the dwarves. "Dark for
dark business! There are many hours before dawn."

"Of course!" said Bilbo, and sat down in a hurry.
He missed the stool and sat in the fender, knocking
over the poker and shovel with a crash.

"Hush!" said Gandalf. "Let Thorin speak!" And
this is how Thorin began.

"Gandalf, dwarves and Mr. Baggins! We are met
together in the house of our friend and fellow conspirator, this most excellent and audacious hobbit—
may the hair on his toes never fall out! all praise to
his wine and ale!—" He paused for breath and for a
polite remark from the hobbit, but the compliments
were quite lost on poor Bilbo Baggins, who was
wagging his mouth in protest at being called *audacious* and worst of all *fellow conspirator*, though no
noise came out, he was so flummoxed. So Thorin
went on:

"We are met to discuss our plans, our ways, means, policy and devices. We shall soon before the break of day start on our long journey, a journey from which some of us, or perhaps all of us (except our friend and counsellor, the ingenious wizard Gandalf) may never return. It is a solemn moment. Our object is, I take it, well known to us all. To the estimable Mr. Baggins, and perhaps to one or two of the younger dwarves (I think I should be right in naming Kili and Fili, for instance), the exact situation at the moment may require a little brief explanation—"

This was Thorin's style. He was an important dwarf. If he had been allowed, he would probably have gone on like this until he was out of breath, without telling any one there anything that was not known already. But he was rudely interrupted. Poor Bilbo couldn't bear it any longer. At *may never return* he began to feel a shriek coming up inside, and very soon it burst out like the whistle of an engine coming out of a tunnel. All the dwarves sprang up, knocking over the table. Gandalf struck a blue light on the end of his magic staff, and in its firework glare the poor little hobbit could be seen kneeling on the hearth-rug, shaking like a jelly that was melting. Then he fell flat on the floor, and kept on calling out "struck by lightning, struck by lightning!" over and over again; and that was all they could get out of him for a long time. So they took him and laid him out of the way on the drawing-room sofa with a drink at his elbow, and they went back to their dark business.

"Excitable little fellow," said Gandalf, as they sat down again. "Gets funny queer fits, but he is one of the best, one of the best—as fierce as a dragon in a pinch."

If you have ever seen a dragon in a pinch, you will realize that this was only poetical exaggeration applied to any hobbit, even to Old Took's great-grand-uncle Bullroarer, who was so huge (for a hobbit) that he could ride a horse. He charged the ranks of the goblins of Mount Gram in the Battle of the Green Fields, and knocked their king Golfimbul's head clean off with a wooden club. It sailed a hundred yards through the air and went down a rabbit-hole, and in this way the battle was won and the game of Golf invented at the same moment.

In the meanwhile, however, Bullroarer's gentler descendant was reviving in the drawing-room. After a while and a drink he crept nervously to the door of the parlour. This is what he heard, Gloin speaking: "Humph!" (or some snort more or less like that). "Will he do, do you think? It is all very well for Gandalf to talk about this hobbit being fierce, but one shriek like that in a moment of excitement would be enough to wake the dragon and all his relatives, and kill the lot of us. I think it sounded more like fright than excitement! In fact, if it had not been for the sign on the door, I should have been sure we had come to the wrong house. As soon as I clapped eyes on the little fellow bobbing and puffing on the mat, I had my doubts. He looks more like a grocer than a burglar!"

Then Mr. Baggins turned the handle and went in. The Took side had won. He suddenly felt he would go without bed and breakfast to be thought fierce. As for *little fellow bobbing on the mat* it almost made him really fierce. Many a time afterwards the Baggins part regretted what he did now, and he said to himself: "Bilbo, you were a fool; you walked right in and put your foot in it."

"Pardon me," he said, "if I have overheard words that you were saying. I don't pretend to understand what you are talking about, or your reference to burglars, but I think I am right in believing" (this is what he called being on his dignity) "that you think I am no good. I will show you. I have no signs on my door—it was painted a week ago—, and I am quite sure you have come to the wrong house. As soon as I saw your funny faces on the door-step, I had my doubts. But treat it as the right one. Tell me what you want done, and I will try it, if I have to walk from here to the East of East and fight the wild Were-worms in the Last Desert. I had a great-great-great-grand-uncle once, Bullroarer Took, and—"

"Yes, yes, but that was long ago," said Gloin. "I was talking about *you*. And I assure you there is a mark on this door—the usual one in the trade, or used to be. *Burglar wants a good job, plenty of Excitement and reasonable Reward*, that's how it is usually read. You can say *Expert Treasure-hunter* instead of *Burglar* if you like. Some of them do. It's all the same to us. Gandalf told us that there was a man of the sort in these parts looking for a Job at once, and that he had arranged for a meeting here this Wednesday tea-time."

"Of course there is a mark," said Gandalf. "I put it there myself. For very good reasons. You asked me to find the fourteenth man for your expedition, and I chose Mr. Baggins. Just let any one say I chose the wrong man or the wrong house, and you can stop at thirteen and have all the bad luck you like, or go back to digging coal."

He scowled so angrily at Gloin that the dwarf huddled back in his chair; and when Bilbo tried to open his mouth to ask a question, he turned and frowned at him and stuck out his bushy eyebrows, till Bilbo shut his mouth tight with a snap. "That's right," said Gandalf. "Let's have no more argument. I have chosen Mr. Baggins and that ought to be enough for all of you. If I say he is a Burglar, a Burglar he is, or will be when the time comes. There is a lot more in him than you guess, and a deal more than he has any idea of himself. You may (possibly) all live to thank me yet. Now Bilbo, my boy, fetch the lamp, and let's have a little light on this!"

On the table in the light of a big lamp with a red shade he spread a piece of parchment rather like a map.

"This was made by Thror, your grandfather, Thorin," he said in answer to the dwarves' excited questions. "It is a plan of the Mountain."

"I don't see that this will help us much," said Thorin disappointedly after a glance. "I remember the Mountain well enough and the lands about it. And I know where Mirkwood is, and the Withered Heath where the great dragons bred."

"There is a dragon marked in red on the Mountain," said Balin, "but it will be easy enough to find him without that, if ever we arrive there."

"There is one point that you haven't noticed," said the wizard, "and that is the secret entrance. You see that rune on the West side, and the hand pointing to it from the other runes? That marks a hidden passage to the Lower Halls." (Look at the map at the beginning of this book, and you will see there the runes.)

"It may have been secret once," said Thorin, "but how do we know that it is secret any longer? Old Smaug has lived there long enough now to find out anything there is to know about those caves."

"He may—but he can't have used it for years and years."

"Why?"

"Because it is too small. 'Five feet high the door and three may walk abreast' say the runes, but Smaug could not creep into a hole that size, not even when he was a young dragon, certainly not after devouring so many of the dwarves and men of Dale."

"It seems a great big hole to me," squeaked Bilbo (who had no experience of dragons and only of hobbit-holes). He was getting excited and interested again, so that he forgot to keep his mouth shut. He loved maps, and in his hall there hung a large one of the Country Round with all his favourite walks marked on it in red ink. "How could such a large door be kept secret from everybody outside, apart from the dragon?" he asked. He was only a little hobbit you must remember.

"In lots of ways," said Gandalf. "But in what way this one has been hidden we don't know without going to see. From what it says on the map I should guess there is a closed door which has been made to look exactly like the side of the Mountain. That is the usual dwarves' method—I think that is right, isn't it?"

"Quite right," said Thorin.

"Also," went on Gandalf, "I forgot to mention that with the map went a key, a small and curious key. Here it is!" he said, and handed to Thorin a key with a long barrel and intricate wards, made of silver. "Keep it safe!"

"Indeed I will," said Thorin, and he fastened it upon a fine chain that hung about his neck and under his jacket. "Now things begin to look more hopeful. This news alters them much for the better. So far we have had no clear idea what to do. We thought of going East, as quiet and careful as we could, as far as the Long Lake. After that the trouble would begin—."

"A long time before that, if I know anything about the roads East," interrupted Gandalf.

"We might go from there up along the River Running," went on Thorin taking no notice, "and so to the ruins of Dale—the old town in the valley there, under the shadow of the Mountain. But we none of us liked the idea of the Front Gate. The river runs right out of it through the great cliff at the South of the Mountain, and out of it comes the dragon too— far too often, unless he has changed his habits."

"That would be no good," said the wizard, "not without a mighty Warrior, even a Hero. I tried to find one; but warriors are busy fighting one another in distant lands, and in this neighbourhood heroes are scarce, or simply not to be found. Swords in these parts are mostly blunt, and axes are used for trees, and shields as cradles or dish-covers; and dragons are comfortably far-off (and therefore legendary). That is why I settled on *burglary*—especially when I remembered the existence of a Side-door.

And here is our little Bilbo Baggins, *the* burglar, the chosen and selected burglar. So now let's get on and make some plans."

"Very well then," said Thorin, "supposing the burglar-expert gives us some ideas or suggestions." He turned with mock-politeness to Bilbo.

"First I should like to know a bit more about things," said he, feeling all confused and a bit shaky inside, but so far still Tookishly determined to go on with things. "I mean about the gold and the dragon, and all that, and how it got there, and who it belongs to, and so on and further."

"Bless me!" said Thorin, "haven't you got a map? and didn't you hear our song? and haven't we been talking about all this for hours?"

"All the same, I should like it all plain and clear," said he obstinately, putting on his business manner (usually reserved for people who tried to borrow money off him), and doing his best to appear wise and prudent and professional and live up to Gandalf's recommendation. "Also I should like to know about risks, out-of-pocket expenses, time required and remuneration, and so forth"—by which he meant: "What am I going to get out of it? and am I going to come back alive?"

"O very well," said Thorin. "Long ago in my grandfather Thror's time our family was driven out of the far North, and came back with all their wealth and their tools to this Mountain on the map. It had been discovered by my far ancestor, Thrain the Old, but now they mined and they tunnelled and they made huger halls and greater workshops— and in addition I believe they found a good deal of gold and a great many jewels too. Anyway they grew immensely rich and famous, and my grandfather was King under the Mountain again, and treated with great reverence by the mortal men, who lived to the South, and were gradually spreading up the Running River as far as the valley overshadowed by the Mountain. They built the merry town of Dale there in those days. Kings used to send for our smiths, and reward even the least skillful most richly. Fathers would beg us to take their sons as apprentices, and pay us handsomely, especially in food-supplies, which we never bothered to grow or find for ourselves. Altogether those were good days for us, and the poorest of us had money to spend and to lend, and leisure to make beautiful things just for the fun of it, not to speak of the most marvellous and magical toys, the like of which is not to be found in the world now-a-days. So my grandfather's halls became full of armour and jewels and carvings and cups, and the toy market of Dale was the wonder of the North.

"Undoubtedly that was what brought the dragon. Dragons steal gold and jewels, you know, from men and elves and dwarves, wherever they can find them; and they guard their plunder as long as they live (which is practically for ever, unless they are killed), and never enjoy a brass ring of it. Indeed they hardly know a good bit of work from a bad, though they usually have a good notion of the current market value; and they can't make a thing for themselves, not even mend a little loose scale of their armour. There were lots of dragons in the North in those days, and gold was probably getting scarce up there,

with the dwarves flying south or getting killed, and all
the general waste and destruction that dragons make
going from bad to worse. There was a most specially
greedy, strong and wicked worm called Smaug. One
day he flew up into the air and came south. The first
we heard of it was a noise like a hurricane coming
from the North, and the pine-trees on the Mountain
creaking and cracking in the wind. Some of the
dwarves who happened to be outside (I was one
luckily—a fine adventurous lad in those days, always
wandering about, and it saved my life that day)—
well, from a good way off we saw the dragon settle
on our mountain in a spout of flame. Then he came
down the slopes and when he reached the woods
they all went up in fire. By that time all the bells were
ringing in Dale and the warriors were arming. The
dwarves rushed out of their great gate; but there was
the dragon waiting for them. None escaped that way.
The river rushed up in steam and a fog fell on Dale,
and in the fog the dragon came on them and
destroyed most of the warriors—the usual unhappy
story, it was only too common in those days. Then
he went back and crept in through the Front Gate
and routed out all the halls, and lanes, and tunnels,
alleys, cellars, mansions and passages. After that
there were no dwarves left alive inside, and he took
all their wealth for himself. Probably, for that is the
dragons' way, he has piled it all up in a great heap
far inside, and sleeps on it for a bed. Later he used
to crawl out of the great gate and come by night to
Dale, and carry away people, especially maidens, to
eat, until Dale was ruined, and all the people dead or
gone. What goes on there now I don't know for

certain, but I don't suppose any one lives nearer to the Mountain than the far edge of the Long Lake now-a-days.

"The few of us that were well outside sat and wept in hiding, and cursed Smaug; and there we were unexpectedly joined by my father and my grand-father with singed beards. They looked very grim but they said very little. When I asked how they had got away, they told me to hold my tongue, and said that one day in the proper time I should know. After that we went away, and we have had to earn our livings as best we could up and down the lands, often enough sinking as low as blacksmith-work or even coalmining. But we have never forgotten our stolen treasure. And even now, when I will allow we have a good bit laid by and are not so badly off"—here Thorin stroked the gold chain round his neck—"we still mean to get it back, and to bring our curses home to Smaug—if we can.

"I have often wondered about my father's and my grand-father's escape. I see now they must have had a private Side-door which only they knew about. But apparently they made a map, and I should like to know how Gandalf got hold of it, and why it did not come down to me, the rightful heir."

"I did not 'get hold of it,' I was given it," said the wizard. "Your grandfather Thror was killed, you remember, in the mines of Moria by Azog the Goblin."

"Curse his name, yes," said Thorin.

"And Thrain your father went away on the twenty-first of April, a hundred years ago last Thursday, and has never been seen by you since—"

"True, true," said Thorin.

"Well, your father gave me this to give to you; and if I have chosen my own time and way for handing it over, you can hardly blame me, considering the trouble I had to find you. Your father could not remember his own name when he gave me the paper, and he never told me yours; so on the whole I think I ought to be praised and thanked! Here it is," said he handing the map to Thorin.

"I don't understand," said Thorin, and Bilbo felt he would have liked to say the same. The explanation did not seem to explain.

"Your grandfather," said the wizard slowly and grimly, "gave the map to his son for safety before he went to the mines of Moria. Your father went away to try his luck with the map after your grandfather was killed; and lots of adventures of a most unpleasant sort he had, but he never got near the Mountain. How he got there I don't know, but I found him a prisoner in the dungeons of the Necromancer."

"Whatever were you doing there?" asked Thorin with a shudder, and all the dwarves shivered.

"Never you mind. I was finding things out, as usual; and a nasty dangerous business it was. Even I, Gandalf, only just escaped. I tried to save your father, but it was too late. He was witless and wandering, and had forgotten almost everything except the map and the key."

"We have long ago paid the goblins of Moria," said Thorin; "we must give a thought to the Necromancer."

"Don't be absurd! He is an enemy far beyond the powers of all the dwarves put together, if they could all be collected again from the four corners of the world. The one thing your father wished was for his son to read the map and use the key. The dragon and the Mountain are more than big enough tasks for you!"

"Hear, hear!" said Bilbo, and accidentally said it aloud.

"Hear what?" they all said turning suddenly towards him, and he was so flustered that he answered "Hear what I have got to say!"

"What's that?" they asked.

"Well, I should say that you ought to go East and have a look round. After all there is the Side-door, and dragons must sleep sometimes, I suppose. If you sit on the door-step long enough, I daresay you will think of something. And well, don't you know, I think we have talked long enough for one night, if you see what I mean. What about bed, and an early start, and all that? I will give you a good breakfast before you go."

"Before *we* go, I suppose you mean," said Thorin. "Aren't you the burglar? And isn't sitting on the door-step your job, not to speak of getting inside the door? But I agree about bed and breakfast. I like six eggs with my ham, when starting on a journey: fried not poached, and mind you don't break 'em."

After all the others had ordered their breakfasts without so much as a please (which annoyed Bilbo very much), they all got up. The hobbit had to find room for them all, and filled all his spare-rooms and made beds on chairs and sofas, before he got them all stowed and went to his own little bed very tired and not altogether happy. One thing he did make his mind up about was not to bother to get up very early and cook everybody else's wretched breakfast. The Tookishness was wearing off, and he was not now quite so sure that he was going on any journey in the morning.

As he lay in bed he could hear Thorin still humming to himself in the best bedroom next to him:

> Far over the misty mountains cold
> To dungeons deep and caverns old
> We must away, ere break of day,
> To find our long-forgotten gold.

Bilbo went to sleep with that in his ears, and it gave him very uncomfortable dreams. It was long after the break of day, when he woke up.

Chapter II

ROAST MUTTON

Up jumped Bilbo, and putting on his dressing-gown went into the dining-room. There he saw nobody, but all the signs of a large and hurried breakfast. There was a fearful mess in the room, and piles of unwashed crocks in the kitchen. Nearly every pot and pan he possessed seemed to have been used. The washing-up was so dismally real that Bilbo was forced to believe the party of the night before had not been part of his bad dreams, as he had rather hoped. Indeed he was really relieved after all to think that they had all gone without him, and without bothering to wake him up ("but with never a thank-you" he thought); and yet in a way he could not help feeling just a trifle disappointed. The feeling surprised him.

"Don't be a fool, Bilbo Baggins!" he said to himself, "thinking of dragons and all that outlandish nonsense at your age!" So he put on an apron, lit fires, boiled water, and washed up. Then he had a nice little breakfast in the kitchen before turning out the dining-room. By that time the sun was shining; and the front door was open, letting in a warm spring breeze. Bilbo began to whistle loudly and to forget about the night before. In fact he was just sitting down to a nice little second breakfast in the dining-room by the open window, when in walked Gandalf.

"My dear fellow," said he, "whenever *are* you

going to come? What about *an early start*?—and here you are having breakfast, or whatever you call it, at half past ten! They left you the message, because they could not wait."

"What message?" said poor Mr. Baggins all in a fluster.

"Great Elephants!" said Gandalf, "you are not at all yourself this morning—you have never dusted the mantelpiece!"

"What's that got to do with it? I have had enough to do with washing up for fourteen!"

"If you had dusted the mantelpiece, you would have found this just under the clock," said Gandalf, handing Bilbo a note (written, of course, on his own note-paper).

This is what he read:

"Thorin and Company to Burglar Bilbo greeting! For your hospitality our sincerest thanks, and for your offer of professional assistance our grateful acceptance. Terms: cash on delivery, up to and not exceeding one fourteenth of total profits (if any); all travelling expenses guaranteed in any event; funeral expenses to be defrayed by us or our representatives, if occasion arises and the matter is not otherwise arranged for.

"Thinking it unnecessary to disturb your esteemed repose, we have proceeded in advance to make requisite preparations, and shall await your respected person at the Green Dragon Inn, Bywater, at 11 a.m. sharp. Trusting that you will be *punctual*,
　　　"*We have the honour to remain*
　　　　"*Yours deeply*
　　　　　"*Thorin & Co.*"

"That leaves you just ten minutes. You will have to run," said Gandalf.

"But—," said Bilbo.

"No time for it," said the wizard.

"But—," said Bilbo again.

"No time for that either! Off you go!"

To the end of his days Bilbo could never remember how he found himself outside, without a hat, a walking-stick or any money, or anything that he usually took when he went out; leaving his second breakfast half-finished and quite unwashed-up, pushing his keys into Gandalf's hands, and running as fast as his furry feet could carry him down the lane, past the great Mill, across The Water, and then on for a mile or more.

Very puffed he was, when he got to Bywater just on the stroke of eleven, and found he had come without a pocket-handkerchief!

"Bravo!" said Balin who was standing at the inn door looking out for him.

Just then all the others came round the corner of the road from the village. They were on ponies, and each pony was slung about with all kinds of baggages, packages, parcels, and paraphernalia. There was a very small pony, apparently for Bilbo.

"Up you two get, and off we go!" said Thorin.

"I'm awfully sorry," said Bilbo, "but I have come without my hat, and I have left my pocket-handkerchief behind, and I haven't got any money. I didn't get your note until after 10.45 to be precise."

"Don't be precise," said Dwalin, "and don't worry! You will have to manage without pocket-handkerchiefs, and a good many other things, before you get to the journey's end. As for a hat, I have got a spare hood and cloak in my luggage."

That's how they all came to start, jogging off from the inn one fine morning just before May, on laden ponies; and Bilbo was wearing a dark-green hood (a little weather-stained) and a dark-green cloak borrowed from Dwalin. They were too large for him, and he looked rather comic. What his father Bungo would have thought of him, I daren't think. His only comfort was he couldn't be mistaken for a dwarf, as he had no beard.

They had not been riding very long, when up came Gandalf very splendid on a white horse. He had brought a lot of pocket-handkerchiefs, and Bilbo's pipe and tobacco. So after that the party went along very merrily, and they told stories or sang songs as they rode forward all day, except of course when they stopped for meals. These didn't come quite as often as Bilbo would have liked them, but still he began to feel that adventures were not so bad after all.

At first they had passed through hobbit-lands, a wide respectable country inhabited by decent folk, with good roads, an inn or two, and now and then a dwarf or a farmer ambling by on business. Then they came to lands where people spoke strangely, and sang songs Bilbo had never heard before. Now they had gone on far into the Lone-lands, where there were no people left, no inns, and the roads grew steadily worse. Not far ahead were dreary hills, rising higher and higher, dark with trees. On some of them were old castles with an evil look, as if they had been built by wicked people. Everything seemed gloomy, for the weather that day had taken a nasty turn. Mostly it had been as good as May can be, can be, even in merry tales, but now it was cold and wet. In the Lone-lands they had been obliged to camp when they could, but at least it had been dry.

"To think it will soon be June!" grumbled Bilbo, as he splashed along behind the others in a very muddy track. It was after tea-time; it was pouring with rain, and had been all day; his hood was dripping into his eyes, his cloak was full of water; the pony was tired and stumbled on stones; the others were too grumpy to talk. "And I'm sure the rain has got into the dry clothes and into the food-bags," thought Bilbo. "Bother burgling and everything to do with it! I wish I was at home in my nice hole by the fire, with the kettle just beginning to sing!" It was not the last time that he wished that!

Still the dwarves jogged on, never turning round or taking any notice of the hobbit. Somewhere behind the grey clouds the sun must have gone down, for it began to get dark as they went down into a deep valley with a river at the bottom. Wind got up, and willows along its banks bent and sighed. Fortunately the road went over an ancient stone bridge, for the river, swollen with the rains, came rushing down from the hills and mountains in the north.

It was nearly night when they had crossed over. The wind broke up the grey clouds, and a wandering moon appeared above the hills between the flying rags. Then they stopped, and Thorin muttered something about supper, "and where shall we get a dry patch to sleep on?"

Not until then did they notice that Gandalf was missing. So far he had come all the way with them, never saying if he was in the adventure or merely keeping them company for a while. He had eaten most, talked most, and laughed most. But now he simply was not there at all!

"Just when a wizard would have been most useful, too," groaned Dori and Nori (who shared the hobbit's views about regular meals, plenty and often).

They decided in the end that they would have to camp where they were. They moved to a clump of trees, and though it was drier under them, the wind shook the rain off the leaves, and the drip, drip, was most annoying. Also the mischief seemed to have got into the fire. Dwarves can make a fire almost anywhere out of almost anything, wind or no wind; but they could not do it that night, not even Oin and Gloin, who were specially good at it.

Then one of the ponies took fright at nothing and bolted. He got into the river before they could catch him; and before they could get him out again, Fili and Kili were nearly drowned, and all the baggage that he carried was washed away off him. Of course it was mostly food, and there was mighty little left for supper, and less for breakfast.

There they all sat glum and wet and muttering, while Oin and Gloin went on trying to light the fire, and quarrelling about it. Bilbo was sadly reflecting that adventures are not all pony-rides in May-sunshine, when Balin, who was always their look-out man, said: "There's a light over there!" There was a hill some way off with trees on it, pretty thick in parts. Out of the dark mass of the trees they could now see a light shining, a reddish comfortable-looking light, as it might be a fire or torches twinkling.

When they had looked at it for some while, they fell to arguing. Some said "no" and some said "yes". Some said they could but go and see, and anything was better than little supper, less breakfast, and wet clothes all the night.

Others said: "These parts are none too well known, and are too near the mountains. Travellers seldom come this way now. The old maps are no use: things have changed for the worse and the road is unguarded. They have seldom even heard of the king round here, and the less inquisitive you are as you go along, the less trouble you are likely to find." Some said: "After all there are fourteen of us." Others said: "Where has Gandalf got to?" This remark was repeated by everybody. Then the rain began to pour down worse than ever, and Oin and Gloin began to fight.

That settled it. "After all we have got a burglar with us," they said; and so they made off, leading their ponies (with all due and proper caution) in the direction of the light. They came to the hill and were soon in the wood. Up the hill they went; but there was no proper path to be seen, such as might lead to a house or a farm; and do what they could they made a deal of rustling and crackling and creaking (and a good deal of grumbling and dratting), as they went through the trees in the pitch dark.

Suddenly the red light shone out very bright through the tree-trunks not far ahead.

"Now it is the burglar's turn," they said, meaning Bilbo. "You must go on and find out all about that light, and what it is for, and if all is perfectly safe and canny," said Thorin to the hobbit. "Now scuttle off, and come back quick, if all is well. If not, come back if you can! If you can't, hoot twice like a barn-owl and once like a screech-owl, and we will do what we can."

Off Bilbo had to go, before he could explain that he could not hoot even once like any kind of owl any more than fly like a bat. But at any rate hobbits can move quietly in woods, absolutely quietly. They take a pride in it, and Bilbo had sniffed more than once at what he called "all this dwarvish racket," as they went along, though I don't suppose you or I would have noticed anything at all on a windy night, not if the whole cavalcade had passed two feet off. As for Bilbo walking primly towards the red light, I don't suppose even a weasel would have stirred a whisker at it. So, naturally, he got right up to the fire—for fire it was—without disturbing anyone. And this is what he saw.

Three very large persons sitting round a very large fire of beech-logs. They were toasting mutton on long spits of wood, and licking the gravy off their fingers. There was a fine toothsome smell. Also there was a barrel of good drink at hand, and they were drinking out of jugs. But they were trolls. Obviously trolls. Even Bilbo, in spite of his sheltered life, could see that: from the great heavy faces of them, and their size, and the shape of their legs, not to mention their language, which was not drawing-room fashion at all, at all.

"Mutton yesterday, mutton today, and blimey, if it don't look like mutton again tomorrer," said one of the trolls.

"Never a blinking bit of manflesh have we had for long enough," said a second. "What the 'ell William was a-thinkin' of to bring us into these parts at all, beats me—and the drink runnin' short, what's more," he said jogging the elbow of William, who was taking a pull at his jug.

William choked. "Shut yer mouth!" he said as soon as he could. "Yer can't expect folk to stop here for ever just to be et by you and Bert. You've et a village and a half between yer, since we come down from the mountains. How much more d'yer want? And time's been up our way, when yer'd have said 'thank yer Bill' for a nice bit o' fat valley mutton like what this is." He took a big bite off a sheep's leg he was roasting, and wiped his lips on his sleeve.

Yes, I am afraid trolls do behave like that, even those with only one head each. After hearing all this Bilbo ought to have done something at once. Either he should have gone back quietly and warned his friends that there were three fair-sized trolls at hand in a nasty mood, quite likely to try roasted dwarf, or even pony, for a change; or else he should have done a bit of good quick burgling. A really first-class and legendary burglar would at this point have picked the trolls' pockets—it is nearly always worth while, if you can manage it—, pinched the very mutton off the spits, purloined the beer, and walked off without their noticing him. Others more practical but with less professional pride would perhaps have stuck a dagger into each of them before they observed it. Then the night could have been spent cheerily.

Bilbo knew it. He had read of a good many things he had never seen or done. He was very much alarmed, as well as disgusted; he wished himself a hundred miles away, and yet—and yet somehow he could not go straight back to Thorin and Company emptyhanded. So he stood and hesitated in the shadows. Of the various burglarious proceedings he had heard of picking the trolls' pockets seemed the least difficult, so at last he crept behind a tree just behind William.

Bert and Tom went off to the barrel. William was having another drink. Then Bilbo plucked up courage and put his little hand in William's enormous pocket. There was a purse in it, as big as a bag to Bilbo. "Ha!" thought he, warming to his new work as he lifted it carefully out, "this is a beginning!"

It was! Trolls' purses are the mischief, and this was no exception. "'Ere, 'oo are you?" it squeaked, as it left the pocket; and William turned round at once and grabbed Bilbo by the neck, before he could duck behind the tree.

"Blimey, Bert, look what I've copped!" said William.

"What is it?" said the others coming up.

"Lumme, if I knows! What are yer?"

"Bilbo Baggins, a bur—a hobbit," said poor Bilbo, shaking all over, and wondering how to make owl-noises before they throttled him.

"A burrahobbit?" said they a bit startled. Trolls are slow in the uptake, and mighty suspicious about anything new to them.

"What's a burrahobbit got to do with my pocket, anyways?" said William.

"And can yer cook 'em?" said Tom.

"Yer can try," said Bert, picking up a skewer.

"He wouldn't make above a mouthful," said William, who had already had a fine supper, "not when he was skinned and boned."

"P'raps there are more like him round about, and we might make a pie," said Bert. "Here you, are there any more of your sort a-sneakin' in these here woods, yer nassty little rabbit," said he looking at the hobbit's furry feet; and he picked him up by the toes and shook him.

"Yes, lots," said Bilbo, before he remembered not to give his friends away. "No none at all, not one," he said immediately afterwards.

"What d'yer mean?" said Bert, holding him right way up, by the hair this time.

"What I say," said Bilbo gasping. "And please don't cook me, kind sirs! I am a good cook myself, and cook better than I cook, if you see what I mean. I'll cook beautifully for you, a perfectly beautiful breakfast for you, if only you won't have me for supper."

"Poor little blighter," said William. He had already had as much supper as he could hold; also he had had lots of beer. "Poor little blighter! Let him go!"

"Not till he says what he means by *lots* and *none at all*," said Bert. "I don't want to have me throat cut in me sleep! Hold his toes in the fire, till he talks!"

"I won't have it," said William. "I caught him anyway."

"You're a fat fool, William," said Bert, "as I've said afore this evening."

"And you're a lout!"

"And I won't take that from you, Bill Huggins," says Bert, and puts his fist in William's eye.

Then there was a gorgeous row. Bilbo had just enough wits left, when Bert dropped him on the ground, to scramble out of the way of their feet, before they were fighting like dogs, and calling one another all sorts of perfectly true and applicable names in very loud voices. Soon they were locked in one another's arms, and rolling nearly into the fire kicking and thumping, while Tom whacked at them both with a branch to bring them to their senses—and that of course only made them madder than ever.

That would have been the time for Bilbo to have left. But his poor little feet had been very squashed in Bert's big paw, and he had no breath in his body, and his head was going round; so there he lay for a while panting, just outside the circle of firelight.

Right in the middle of the fight up came Balin. The dwarves had heard noises from a distance, and after waiting for some time for Bilbo to come back, or to hoot like an owl, they started off one by one to creep towards the light as quietly as they could. No sooner did Tom see Balin come into the light than he gave an awful howl. Trolls simply detest the very sight of dwarves (uncooked). Bert and Bill stopped fighting immediately, and "a sack, Tom, quick!" they said. Before Balin, who was wondering where in all this commotion Bilbo was, knew what was happening, a sack was over his head, and he was down.

"There's more to come yet," said Tom, "or I'm mighty mistook. Lots and none at all, it is," said he. "No burrahobbits, but lots of these here dwarves. That's about the shape of it!"

"I reckon you're right," said Bert, "and we'd best get out of the light."

And so they did. With sacks in their hands, that they used for carrying off mutton and other plunder, they waited in the shadows. As each dwarf came up and looked at the fire, and the spilled jugs, and the gnawed mutton, in surprise, pop! went a nasty smelly sack over his head, and he was down. Soon Dwalin lay by Balin, and Fili and Kili together, and Dori and Nori and Ori all in a heap, and Oin and Gloin and Bifur and Bofur and Bombur piled uncomfortably near the fire.

"That'll teach 'em," said Tom; for Bifur and Bombur had given a lot of trouble, and fought like mad, as dwarves will when cornered.

Thorin came last—and he was not caught unawares. He came expecting mischief, and didn't need to see his friends' legs sticking out of sacks to tell him that things were not all well. He stood outside in the shadows some way off, and said: "What's all this trouble? Who has been knocking my people about?"

"It's trolls!" said Bilbo from behind a tree. They had forgotten all about him. "They're hiding in the bushes with sacks," said he.

"O! are they?" said Thorin, and he jumped forward to the fire, before they could leap on him. He caught up a big branch all on fire at one end; and Bert got that end in his eye before he could step aside. That put him out of the battle for a bit. Bilbo did his best. He caught hold of Tom's leg—as well as he could, it was thick as a young tree-trunk—but he was sent spinning up into the top of some bushes, when Tom kicked the sparks up in Thorin's face.

The Trolls.

Tom got the branch in his teeth for that, and lost one of the front ones. It made him howl, I can tell you. But just at that moment William came up behind and popped a sack right over Thorin's head and down to his toes. And so the fight ended. A nice pickle they were all in now: all neatly tied up in sacks, with three angry trolls (and two with burns and bashes to remember) sitting by them, arguing whether they should roast them slowly, or mince them fine and boil them, or just sit on them one by one and squash them into jelly; and Bilbo up in a bush, with his clothes and his skin torn, not daring to move for fear they should hear him.

It was just then that Gandalf came back. But no one saw him. The trolls had just decided to roast the dwarves now and eat them later—that was Bert's idea, and after a lot of argument they had all agreed to it.

"No good roasting 'em now, it'd take all night," said a voice. Bert thought it was William's.

"Don't start the argument all over again, Bill," he said, "or it *will* take all night."

"Who's a-arguing?" said William, who thought it was Bert that had spoken.

"You are," said Bert.

"You're a liar," said William; and so the argument began all over again. In the end they decided to mince them fine and boil them. So they got a great black pot, and they took out their knives.

"No good boiling 'em! We ain't got no water, and it's a long way to the well and all," said a voice. Bert and William thought it was Tom's.

"Shut up!" said they, "or we'll never have done. And yer can fetch the water yerself, if yer say any more."

"Shut up yerself!" said Tom, who thought it was William's voice. "Who's arguing but you, I'd like to know."

"You're a booby," said William.

"Booby yerself!" said Tom.

And so the argument began all over again, and went on hotter than ever, until at last they decided to sit on the sacks one by one and squash them, and boil them next time.

"Who shall we sit on first?" said the voice.

"Better sit on the last fellow first," said Bert, whose eye had been damaged by Thorin. He thought Tom was talking.

"Don't talk to yerself!" said Tom. "But if you wants to sit on the last one, sit on him. Which is he?"

"The one with the yellow stockings," said Bert.

"Nonsense, the one with the grey stockings," said a voice like William's.

"I made sure it was yellow," said Bert.

"Yellow it was," said William.

"Then what did yer say it was grey for?" said Bert.

"I never did. Tom said it."

"That I never did!" said Tom. "It was you."

"Two to one, so shut yer mouth!" said Bert.

"Who are you a-talkin' to?" said William.

"Now stop it!" said Tom and Bert together. "The night's gettin' on, and dawn comes early. Let's get on with it!"

"Dawn take you all, and be stone to you!" said a voice that sounded like William's. But it wasn't. For just at that moment the light came over the hill, and there was a mighty twitter in the branches. William never spoke for he stood turned to stone as he stooped; and Bert and Tom were stuck like rocks as they looked at him. And there they stand to this day, all alone, unless the birds perch on them; for trolls, as you probably know, must be underground before dawn, or they go back to the stuff of the mountains they are made of, and never move again. That is what had happened to Bert and Tom and William.

"Excellent!" said Gandalf, as he stepped from behind a tree, and helped Bilbo to climb down out of a thorn-bush. Then Bilbo understood. It was the wizard's voice that had kept the trolls bickering and quarrelling, until the light came and made an end of them.

The next thing was to untie the sacks and let out the dwarves. They were nearly suffocated, and very annoyed: they had not at all enjoyed lying there listening to the trolls making plans for roasting them and squashing them and mincing them. They had to hear Bilbo's account of what had happened to him twice over, before they were satisfied.

"Silly time to go practising pinching and pocket-picking," said Bombur, "when what we wanted was fire and food!"

"And that's just what you wouldn't have got of those fellows without a struggle, in any case," said Gandalf. "Anyhow you are wasting time now. Don't you realize that the trolls must have a cave or a hole dug somewhere near to hide from the sun in? We must look into it!"

They searched about, and soon found the marks of trolls' stony boots going away through the trees. They followed the tracks up the hill, until hidden by bushes they came on a big door of stone leading to a cave. But they could not open it, not though they all pushed while Gandalf tried various incantations.

"Would this be any good?" asked Bilbo, when they were getting tired and angry. "I found it on the ground where the trolls had their fight." He held out a largish key, though no doubt William had thought it very small and secret. It must have fallen out of his pocket, very luckily, before he was turned to stone.

"Why on earth didn't you mention it before?" they cried. Gandalf grabbed it and fitted it into the key-hole. Then the stone door swung back with one big push, and they all went inside. There were bones on the floor and a nasty smell was in the air; but there was a good deal of food jumbled carelessly on shelves and on the ground, among an untidy litter of plunder, of all sorts from brass buttons to pots full of gold coins standing in a corner. There were lots of clothes, too, hanging on the walls—too small for trolls, I am afraid they belonged to victims—and among them were several swords of various makes, shapes, and sizes. Two caught their eyes particularly, because of their beautiful scabbards and jewelled hilts.

Gandalf and Thorin each took one of these; and Bilbo took a knife in a leather sheath. It would have made only a tiny pocket-knife for a troll, but it was as good as a short sword for the hobbit.

"These look like good blades," said the wizard, half drawing them and looking at them curiously. "They were not made by any troll, nor by any smith among men in these parts and days; but when we can read the runes on them, we shall know more about them."

"Let's get out of this horrible smell!" said Fili. So they carried out the pots of coins, and such food as was untouched and looked fit to eat, also one barrel of ale which was still full. By that time they felt like breakfast, and being very hungry they did not turn their noses up at what they had got from the trolls' larder. Their own provisions were very scanty. Now they had bread and cheese, and plenty of ale, and bacon to toast in the embers of the fire.

After that they slept, for their night had been disturbed; and they did nothing more till the afternoon. Then they brought up their ponies, and carried away the pots of gold, and buried them very secretly not far from the track by the river, putting a great many spells over them, just in case they ever had the chance to come back and recover them. When that was done, they all mounted once more, and jogged along again on the path towards the East.

"Where did you go to, if I may ask?" said Thorin to Gandalf as they rode along.

"To look ahead," said he.

"And what brought you back in the nick of time?"

"Looking behind," said he.

"Exactly!" said Thorin; "but could you be more plain?"

"I went on to spy out our road. It will soon become dangerous and difficult. Also I was anxious about replenishing our small stock of provisions. I had not gone very far, however, when I met a couple of friends of mine from Rivendell."

"Where's that?" asked Bilbo.

"Don't interrupt!" said Gandalf. "You will get there in a few days now, if we're lucky, and find out all about it. As I was saying I met two of Elrond's people. They were hurrying along for fear of the trolls. It was they who told me that three of them had come down from the mountains and settled in the woods not far from the road: they had frightened everyone away from the district, and they waylaid strangers.

"I immediately had a feeling that I was wanted back. Looking behind I saw a fire in the distance and made for it. So now you know. Please be more careful, next time, or we shall never get anywhere!"

"Thank you!" said Thorin.

Chapter III

A SHORT REST

They did not sing or tell stories that day, even though
the weather improved; nor the next day, nor the day
after. They had begun to feel that danger was not far
away on either side. They camped under the stars, and
their horses had more to eat than they had; for there
was plenty of grass, but there was not much in their
bags, even with what they had got from the trolls. One
morning they forded a river at a wide shallow place
full of the noise of stones and foam. The far bank was
steep and slippery. When they got to the top of it,
leading their ponies, they saw that the great mountains
had marched down very near to them. Already they
seemed only a day's easy journey from the feet of the
nearest. Dark and drear it looked, though there were
patches of sunlight on its brown sides, and behind its
shoulders the tips of snow-peaks gleamed.

"Is that *The* Mountain?" asked Bilbo in a solemn
voice, looking at it with round eyes. He had never
seen a thing that looked so big before.

"Of course not!" said Balin. "That is only the
beginning of the Misty Mountains, and we have got
to get through, or over, or under those somehow,
before we can come into Wilderland beyond. And it
is a deal of a way even from the other side of them to
the Lonely Mountain in the East where Smaug lies
on our treasure."

"O!" said Bilbo, and just at that moment he felt more tired than he ever remembered feeling before. He was thinking once again of his comfortable chair before the fire in his favourite sitting-room in his hobbit-hole, and of the kettle singing. Not for the last time!

Now Gandalf led the way. "We must not miss the road, or we shall be done for," he said. "We need food, for one thing, *and* rest in reasonable safety— also it is very necessary to tackle the Misty Mountains by the proper path, or else you will get lost in them, and have to come back and start at the beginning again (if you ever get back at all)."

They asked him where he was making for, and he answered: "You are come to the very edge of the Wild, as some of you may know. Hidden somewhere ahead of us is the fair valley of Rivendell where Elrond lives in the Last Homely House. I sent a message by my friends, and we are expected."

That sounded nice and comforting, but they had not got there yet, and it was not so easy as it sounds to find the Last Homely House west of the Mountains. There seemed to be no trees and no valleys and no hills to break the ground in front of them, only one vast slope going slowly up and up to meet the feet of the nearest mountain, a wide land the colour of heather and crumbling rock, with patches and slashes of grass-green and moss-green showing where water might be.

Morning passed, afternoon came; but in all the silent waste there was no sign of any dwelling. They were growing anxious, for they saw now that the house might be hidden almost anywhere between them and the mountains. They came on unexpected valleys, narrow with steep sides, that opened suddenly at their feet, and they looked down surprised to see trees below them and running water at the bottom. There were gullies that they could almost leap over, but very deep with waterfalls in them. There were dark ravines that one could neither jump over nor climb into. There were bogs, some of them green pleasant places to look at, with flowers growing bright and tall; but a pony that walked there with a pack on its back would never have come out again.

It was indeed a much wider land from the ford to the mountains than ever you would have guessed. Bilbo was astonished. The only path was marked with white stones, some of which were small, and others were half covered with moss or heather. Altogether it was a very slow business following the track, even guided by Gandalf, who seemed to know his way about pretty well.

His head and beard wagged this way and that as he looked for the stones, and they followed his lead, but they seemed no nearer to the end of the search when the day began to fail. Tea-time had long gone by, and it seemed supper-time would soon do the same. There were moths fluttering about, and the light became very dim, for the moon had not risen. Bilbo's pony began to stumble over roots and stones. They came to the edge of a steep fall in the ground so suddenly that Gandalf's horse nearly slipped down the slope.

"Here it is at last!" he called, and the others gathered round him and looked over the edge. They saw a valley far below. They could hear the voice of hurrying water in a rocky bed at the bottom; the scent of

trees was in the air; and there was a light on the
valley-side across the water.

Bilbo never forgot the way they slithered and
slipped in the dusk down the steep zig-zag path into
the secret valley of Rivendell. The air grew warmer
as they got lower, and the smell of the pine-trees
made him drowsy, so that every now and again he
nodded and nearly fell off, or bumped his nose on
the pony's neck. Their spirits rose as they went down
and down. The trees changed to beech and oak, and
there was a comfortable feeling in the twilight. The
last green had almost faded out of the grass, when
they came at length to an open glade not far above
the banks of the stream.

"Hmmm! it smells like elves!" thought Bilbo, and
he looked up at the stars. They were burning bright
and blue. Just then there came a burst of song like
laughter in the trees:

> *O! What are you doing,*
> *And where are you going?*
> *Your ponies need shoeing!*
> *The river is flowing!*
> *O! tra-la-la-lally*
> *here down in the valley!*

> *O! What are you seeking,*
> *And where are you making?*
> *The faggots are reeking,*
> *The bannocks are baking!*
> *O! tril-lil-lil-lolly*
> *the valley is jolly,*
> *ha! ha!*

O! Where are you going
With beards all a-wagging?
No knowing, no knowing
What brings Mister Baggins
   And Balin and Dwalin
      down into the valley
         in June
         ha! ha!

O! Will you be staying,
Or will you be flying?
Your ponies are straying!
The daylight is dying!
To fly would be folly,
To stay would be jolly
   And listen and hark
      Till the end of the dark
         to our tune
         ha! ha!

So they laughed and sang in the trees; and pretty fair nonsense I daresay you think it. Not that they would care; they would only laugh all the more if you told them so. They were elves of course. Soon Bilbo caught glimpses of them as the darkness deepened. He loved elves, though he seldom met them; but he was a little frightened of them too. Dwarves don't get on well with them. Even decent enough dwarves like Thorin and his friends think them foolish (which is a very foolish thing to think), or get annoyed with them. For some elves tease them and laugh at them, and most of all at their beards.

"Well, well!" said a voice. "Just look! Bilbo the hobbit on a pony, my dear! Isn't it delicious!"

"Most astonishing wonderful!"

Then off they went into another song as ridiculous as the one I have written down in full. At last one, a tall young fellow, came out from the trees and bowed to Gandalf and to Thorin.

"Welcome to the valley!" he said.

"Thank you!" said Thorin a bit gruffly; but Gandalf was already off his horse and among the elves, talking merrily with them.

"You are a little out of your way," said the elf: "that is, if you are making for the only path across the water and to the house beyond. We will set you right, but you had best get on foot, until you are over the bridge. Are you going to stay a bit and sing with us, or will you go straight on? Supper is preparing over there," he said. "I can smell the wood-fires for the cooking."

Tired as he was, Bilbo would have liked to stay a while. Elvish singing is not a thing to miss, in June under the stars, not if you care for such things. Also he would have liked to have a few private words with these people that seemed to know his names and all about him, although he had never seen them before. He thought their opinion of his adventure might be interesting. Elves know a lot and are wondrous folk for news, and know what is going on among the peoples of the land, as quick as water flows, or quicker.

But the dwarves were all for supper as soon as possible just then, and would not stay. On they all went, leading their ponies, till they were brought to a good path and so at last to the very brink of the river.

It was flowing fast and noisily, as mountain-streams do of a summer evening, when sun has been all day on the snow far up above. There was only a narrow bridge of stone without a parapet, as narrow as a pony could well walk on; and over that they had to go, slow and careful, one by one, each leading his pony by the bridle. The elves had brought bright lanterns to the shore, and they sang a merry song as the party went across.

"Don't dip your beard in the foam, father!" they cried to Thorin, who was bent almost on to his hands and knees. "It is long enough without watering it."

"Mind Bilbo doesn't eat all the cakes!" they called. "He is too fat to get through key-holes yet!"

"Hush, hush! Good People! and good night!" said Gandalf, who came last. "Valleys have ears, and some elves have over merry tongues. Good night!"

And so at last they all came to the Last Homely House, and found its doors flung wide.

Now it is a strange thing, but things that are good to have and days that are good to spend are soon told about, and not much to listen to; while things that are uncomfortable, palpitating, and even gruesome, may make a good tale, and take a deal of telling anyway. They stayed long in that good house, fourteen days at least, and they found it hard to leave. Bilbo would gladly have stopped there for ever and ever—even supposing a wish would have taken him right back to his hobbit-hole without trouble. Yet there is little to tell about their stay.

The master of the house was an elf-friend—one of those people whose fathers came into the strange stories before the beginning of History, the wars of the evil goblins and the elves and the first men in the North. In those days of our tale there were still some people who had both elves and heroes of the North for ancestors, and Elrond the master of the house was their chief.

He was as noble and as fair in face as an elf-lord, as strong as a warrior, as wise as a wizard, as venerable as a king of dwarves, and as kind as summer. He comes into many tales, but his part in the story of Bilbo's great adventure is only a small one, though important, as you will see, if we ever get to the end of it. His house was perfect, whether you liked food, or sleep, or work, or story-telling, or singing, or just sitting and thinking best, or a pleasant mixture of them all. Evil things did not come into that valley.

I wish I had time to tell you even a few of the tales or one or two of the songs that they heard in that house. All of them, the ponies as well, grew refreshed and strong in a few days there. Their clothes were mended as well as their bruises, their tempers and their hopes. Their bags were filled with food and provisions light to carry but strong to bring them over the mountain passes. Their plans were improved with the best advice. So the time came to midsummer eve, and they were to go on again with the early sun on midsummer morning.

Elrond knew all about runes of every kind. That day he looked at the swords they had brought from the trolls' lair, and he said: "These are not troll-make. They are old swords, very old swords of the High Elves of the West, my kin. They were made in Gondolin for the Goblin-wars. They must have come from a dragon's hoard or goblin plunder, for dragons and goblins destroyed that city many ages ago. This, Thorin, the runes name Orcrist, the Goblin-cleaver in the ancient tongue of Gondolin; it was a famous blade. This, Gandalf, was Glamdring, Foe-hammer that the king of Gondolin once wore. Keep them well!"

"Whence did the trolls get them, I wonder?" said Thorin looking at his sword with new interest.

"I could not say," said Elrond, "but one may guess that your trolls had plundered other plunderers, or come on the remnants of old robberies in some hold in the mountains. I have heard that there are still forgotten treasures of old to be found in the deserted caverns of the mines of Moria, since the dwarf and goblin war."

Thorin pondered these words. "I will keep this sword in honour," he said. "May it soon cleave goblins once again!"

"A wish that is likely to be granted soon enough in the mountains!" said Elrond. "But show me now your map!"

He took it and gazed long at it, and he shook his head; for if he did not altogether approve of dwarves and their love of gold, he hated dragons and their cruel wickedness, and he grieved to remember the ruin of the town of Dale and its merry bells, and the burned banks of the bright River Running. The moon was shining in a broad silver crescent. He held up the map and the white light shone through it. "What is this?" he said. "There are moon-letters here, beside the plain runes which say 'five feet high the door and three may walk abreast.'"

"What are moon-letters?" asked the hobbit full of excitement. He loved maps, as I have told you before; and he also liked runes and letters and cunning handwriting, though when he wrote himself it was a bit thin and spidery.

"Moon-letters are rune-letters, but you cannot see them," said Elrond, "not when you look straight at them. They can only be seen when the moon shines behind them, and what is more, with the more cunning sort it must be a moon of the same shape and season as the day when they were written. The dwarves invented them and wrote them with silver pens, as your friends could tell you. These must have been written on a midsummer's eve in a crescent moon, a long while ago."

"What do they say?" asked Gandalf and Thorin together, a bit vexed perhaps that even Elrond should have found this out first, though really there had not been a chance before, and there would not have been another until goodness knows when.

"Stand by the grey stone when the thrush knocks," read Elrond, "and the setting sun with the last light of Durin's Day will shine upon the key-hole."

"Durin, Durin!" said Thorin. "He was the father of the fathers of the eldest race of Dwarves, the Longbeards, and my first ancestor: I am his heir."

"Then what is Durin's Day?" asked Elrond.

"The first day of the dwarves' New Year," said Thorin, "is as all should know the first day of the last moon of Autumn on the threshold of Winter. We still call it Durin's Day when the last moon of Autumn and the sun are in the sky together. But this will not help us much, I fear, for it passes our skill in these days to guess when such a time will come again."

"That remains to be seen," said Gandalf. "Is there any more writing?"

"None to be seen by this moon," said Elrond, and he gave the map back to Thorin; and then they went down to the water to see the elves dance and sing upon the midsummer's eve.

The next morning was a midsummer's morning as fair and fresh as could be dreamed: blue sky and never a cloud, and the sun dancing on the water. Now they rode away amid songs of farewell and good speed, with their hearts ready for more adventure, and with a knowledge of the road they must follow over the Misty Mountains to the land beyond.

Chapter IV

OVER HILL AND UNDER HILL

There were many paths that led up into those mountains, and many passes over them. But most of the paths were cheats and deceptions and led nowhere or to bad ends; and most of the passes were infested by evil things and dreadful dangers. The dwarves and the hobbit, helped by the wise advice of Elrond and the knowledge and memory of Gandalf, took the right road to the right pass.

Long days after they had climbed out of the valley and left the Last Homely House miles behind, they were still going up and up and up. It was a hard path and a dangerous path, a crooked way and a lonely and a long. Now they could look back over the lands they had left, laid out behind them far below. Far, far away in the West, where things were blue and faint, Bilbo knew there lay his own country of safe and comfortable things, and his little hobbit-hole. He shivered. It was getting bitter cold up here, and the wind came shrill among the rocks. Boulders, too, at times came galloping down the mountainsides, let loose by mid-day sun upon the snow, and passed among them (which was lucky), or over their heads (which was alarming). The nights were comfortless and chill, and they did not dare to sing or talk too loud, for the echoes were uncanny, and the silence seemed to dislike being broken—except by the noise of water and the wail of wind and the crack of stone.

"The summer is getting on down below," thought Bilbo, "and haymaking is going on and picnics. They will be harvesting and blackberrying, before we even begin to go down the other side at this rate." And the others were thinking equally gloomy thoughts, although when they had said good-bye to Elrond in the high hope of a midsummer morning, they had spoken gaily of the passage of the mountains, and of riding swift across the lands beyond. They had thought of coming to the secret door in the Lonely Mountain, perhaps that very next last moon of Autumn—"and perhaps it will be Durin's Day" they had said. Only Gandalf had shaken his head and said nothing. Dwarves had not passed that way for many years, but Gandalf had, and he knew how evil and danger had grown and thriven in the Wild, since the dragons had driven men from the lands, and the goblins had spread in secret after the battle of the Mines of Moria. Even the good plans of wise wizards like Gandalf and of good friends like Elrond go astray sometimes when you are off on dangerous adventures over the Edge of the Wild; and Gandalf was a wise enough wizard to know it.

He knew that something unexpected might happen, and he hardly dared to hope that they would pass without fearful adventure over those great tall mountains with lonely peaks and valleys where no king ruled. They did not. All was well, until one day they met a thunderstorm—more than a thunderstorm, a thunder-battle. You know how terrific a really big thunderstorm can be down in the land and in a river-valley; especially at times when two great thunderstorms meet and clash. More terrible still are thunder and lightning in the mountains at night, when storms come up from East and West and make war. The lightning splinters on the peaks, and rocks shiver, and great crashes split the air and go rolling and tumbling into every cave and hollow; and the darkness is filled with overwhelming noise and sudden light.

Bilbo had never seen or imagined anything of the kind. They were high up in a narrow place, with a dreadful fall into a dim valley at one side of them. There they were sheltering under a hanging rock for the night, and he lay beneath a blanket and shook from head to toe. When he peeped out in the lightning-flashes, he saw that across the valley the stone-giants were out, and were hurling rocks at one another for a game, and catching them, and tossing them down into the darkness where they smashed among the trees far below, or splintered into little bits with a bang. Then came a wind and a rain, and the wind whipped the rain and the hail about in every direction, so that an overhanging rock was no protection at all. Soon they were getting drenched and their ponies were standing with their heads down and their tails between their legs, and some of them were whinnying with fright. They could hear the giants guffawing and shouting all over the mountainsides.

"This won't do at all!" said Thorin. "If we don't get blown off, or drowned, or struck by lightning, we shall be picked up by some giant and kicked sky-high for a football."

The Mountain-path

"Well, if you know of anywhere better, take us there!" said Gandalf, who was feeling very grumpy, and was far from happy about the giants himself.

The end of their argument was that they sent Fili and Kili to look for a better shelter. They had very sharp eyes, and being the youngest of the dwarves by some fifty years they usually got these sort of jobs (when everybody could see that it was absolutely no use sending Bilbo). There is nothing like looking, if you want to find something (or so Thorin said to the young dwarves). You certainly usually find something, if you look, but it is not always quite the something you were after. So it proved on this occasion.

Soon Fili and Kili came crawling back, holding on to the rocks in the wind. "We have found a dry cave," they said, "not far round the next corner; and ponies and all could get inside."

"Have you *thoroughly* explored it?" said the wizard, who knew that caves up in the mountains were seldom unoccupied.

"Yes, yes!" they said, though everybody knew they could not have been long about it; they had come back too quick. "It isn't all that big, and it does not go far back."

That, of course, is the dangerous part about caves: you don't know how far they go back, sometimes, or where a passage behind may lead to, or what is waiting for you inside. But now Fili and Kili's news seemed good enough. So they all got up and prepared to move. The wind was howling and the thunder still growling, and they had a business getting themselves and their ponies along. Still it was not very far to go, and before long they came to a big rock standing out into the path. If you stepped behind, you found a low arch in the side of the mountain. There was just room to get the ponies through with a squeeze, when they had been unpacked and unsaddled. As they passed under the arch, it was good to hear the wind and the rain outside instead of all about them, and to feel safe from the giants and their rocks. But the wizard was taking no risks. He lit up his wand—as he did that day in Bilbo's dining-room that seemed so long ago, if you remember—, and by its light they explored the cave from end to end.

It seemed quite a fair size, but not too large and mysterious. It had a dry floor and some comfortable nooks. At one end there was room for the ponies; and there they stood (mighty glad of the change) steaming, and champing in their nosebags. Oin and Gloin wanted to light a fire at the door to dry their clothes, but Gandalf would not hear of it. So they spread out their wet things on the floor, and got dry ones out of their bundles; then they made their blankets comfortable, got out their pipes and blew smoke rings, which Gandalf turned into different colours and set dancing up by the roof to amuse them. They talked and talked, and forgot about the storm, and discussed what each would do with his share of the treasure (when they got it, which at the moment did not seem so impossible); and so they dropped off to sleep one by one. And that was the last time that they used the ponies, packages, baggages, tools and paraphernalia that they had brought with them.

It turned out a good thing that night that they had brought little Bilbo with them, after all. For, somehow, he could not go to sleep for a long while; and when he did sleep, he had very nasty dreams. He dreamed that a crack in the wall at the back of the cave got bigger and bigger, and opened wider and wider, and he was very afraid but could not call out or do anything but lie and look. Then he dreamed that the floor of the cave was giving way, and he was slipping—beginning to fall down, down, goodness knows where to.

At that he woke up with a horrible start, and found that part of his dream was true. A crack had opened at the back of the cave, and was already a wide passage. He was just in time to see the last of the ponies' tails disappearing into it. Of course he gave a very loud yell, as loud a yell as a hobbit can give, which is surprising for their size.

Out jumped the goblins, big goblins, great ugly-looking goblins, lots of goblins, before you could say *rocks and blocks*. There were six to each dwarf, at least, and two even for Bilbo; and they were all grabbed and carried through the crack, before you could say *tinder and flint*. But not Gandalf. Bilbo's yell had done that much good. It had wakened him up wide in a splintered second, and when goblins came to grab him, there was a terrific flash like lightning in the cave, a smell like gunpowder, and several of them fell dead.

The crack closed with a snap, and Bilbo and the dwarves were on the wrong side of it! Where was Gandalf? Of that neither they nor the goblins had any idea, and the goblins did not wait to find out. They seized Bilbo and the dwarves and hurried them along. It was deep, deep, dark, such as only goblins that have taken to living in the heart of the mountains can see through. The passages there were crossed and tangled in all directions, but the goblins knew their

way, as well as you do to the nearest post-office; and
the way went down and down, and it was most horribly stuffy. The goblins were very rough, and pinched
unmercifully, and chuckled and laughed in their horrible stony voices; and Bilbo was more unhappy even
than when the troll had picked him up by his toes. He
wished again and again for his nice bright hobbit-
hole. Not for the last time.

Now there came a glimmer of a red light before
them. The goblins began to sing, or croak, keeping
time with the flap of their flat feet on the stone, and
shaking their prisoners as well.

> *Clap! Snap! the black crack!*
> *Grip, grab! Pinch, nab!*
> *And down down to Goblin-town*
>   *You go, my lad!*

> *Clash, crash! Crush, smash!*
> *Hammer and tongs! Knocker and gongs!*
> *Pound, pound, far underground!*
>   *Ho, ho! my lad!*

> *Swish, smack! Whip crack!*
> *Batter and beat! Yammer and bleat!*
> *Work, work! Nor dare to shirk,*
> *While Goblins quaff, and Goblins laugh,*
> *Round and round far underground*
>   *Below, my lad!*

It sounded truly terrifying. The walls echoed to the
clap, snap! and the *crush, smash!* and to the ugly
laughter of their *ho, ho! my lad!* The general meaning

of the song was only too plain; for now the goblins
took out whips and whipped them with a *swish*,
smack!, and set them running as fast as they could in
front of them; and more than one of the dwarves
were already yammering and bleating like anything,
when they stumbled into a big cavern.

It was lit by a great red fire in the middle, and by
torches along the walls, and it was full of goblins.
They all laughed and stamped and clapped their
hands, when the dwarves (with poor little Bilbo at the
back and nearest to the whips) came running in,
while the goblin-drivers whooped and cracked their
whips behind. The ponies were already there huddled
in a corner; and there were all the baggages and
packages lying broken open, and being rummaged by
goblins, and smelt by goblins, and fingered by
goblins, and quarrelled over by goblins.

I am afraid that was the last they ever saw of those
excellent little ponies, including a jolly sturdy little
white fellow that Elrond had lent to Gandalf, since his
horse was not suitable for the mountain-paths. For
goblins eat horses and ponies and donkeys (and other
much more dreadful things), and they are always
hungry. Just now however the prisoners were thinking
only of themselves. The goblins chained their hands
behind their backs and linked them all together in a
line, and dragged them to the far end of the cavern
with little Bilbo tugging at the end of the row.

There in the shadows on a large flat stone sat a
tremendous goblin with a huge head, and armed
goblins were standing round him carrying the axes and
the bent swords that they use. Now goblins are cruel,
wicked, and bad-hearted. They make no beautiful

things, but they make many clever ones. They can
tunnel and mine as well as any but the most skilled
dwarves, when they take the trouble, though they are
usually untidy and dirty. Hammers, axes, swords,
daggers, pickaxes, tongs, and also instruments of
torture, they make very well, or get other people to
make to their design, prisoners and slaves that have
to work till they die for want of air and light. It is
not unlikely that they invented some of the machines
that have since troubled the world, especially the
ingenious devices for killing large numbers of people
at once, for wheels and engines and explosions
always delighted them, and also not working with
their own hands more than they could help; but in
those days and those wild parts they had not
advanced (as it is called) so far. They did not hate
dwarves especially, no more than they hated everybody and everything, and particularly the orderly
and prosperous; in some parts wicked dwarves had
even made alliances with them. But they had a
special grudge against Thorin's people, because of
the war which you have heard mentioned, but which
does not come into this tale; and anyway goblins
don't care who they catch, as long as it is done
smart and secret, and the prisoners are not able to
defend themselves.

   "Who are these miserable persons?" said the Great
Goblin.

   "Dwarves, and this!" said one of the drivers, pulling
at Bilbo's chain so that he fell forward onto his knees.
"We found them sheltering in our Front Porch."

   "What do you mean by it?" said the Great Goblin
turning to Thorin. "Up to no good, I'll warrant!

Spying on the private business of my people, I guess! Thieves, I shouldn't be surprised to learn! Murderers and friends of Elves, not unlikely! Come! What have you got to say?"

"Thorin the dwarf at your service!" he replied—it was merely a polite nothing. "Of the things which you suspect and imagine we had no idea at all. We sheltered from a storm in what seemed a convenient cave and unused; nothing was further from our thoughts than inconveniencing goblins in any way whatever." That was true enough!

"Um!" said the Great Goblin. "So you say! Might I ask what you were doing up in the mountains at all, and where you were coming from, and where you were going to? In fact I should like to know all about you. Not that it will do you much good, Thorin Oakenshield, I know too much about your folk already; but let's have the truth, or I will prepare something particularly uncomfortable for you!"

"We were on a journey to visit our relatives, our nephews and nieces, and first, second, and third cousins, and the other descendants of our grandfathers, who live on the East side of these truly hospitable mountains," said Thorin, not quite knowing what to say all at once in a moment, when obviously the exact truth would not do at all.

"He is a liar, O truly tremendous one!" said one of the drivers. "Several of our people were struck by lightning in the cave, when we invited these creatures to come below; and they are as dead as stones. Also he has not explained this!" He held out the sword which Thorin had worn, the sword which came from the Trolls' lair.

The Great Goblin gave a truly awful howl of rage when he looked at it, and all his soldiers gnashed their teeth, clashed their shields, and stamped. They knew the sword at once. It had killed hundreds of goblins in its time, when the fair elves of Gondolin hunted them in the hills or did battle before their walls. They had called it Orcrist, Goblin-cleaver, but the goblins called it simply Biter. They hated it and hated worse any one that carried it.

"Murderers and elf-friends!" the Great Goblin shouted. "Slash them! Beat them! Bite them! Gnash them! Take them away to dark holes full of snakes, and never let them see the light again!" He was in such a rage that he jumped off his seat and himself rushed at Thorin with his mouth open.

Just at that moment all the lights in the cavern went out, and the great fire went off poof! into a tower of blue glowing smoke, right up to the roof, that scattered piercing white sparks all among the goblins.

The yells and yammering, croaking, jibbering and jabbering; howls, growls and curses; shrieking and skriking, that followed were beyond description. Several hundred wild cats and wolves being roasted slowly alive together would not have compared with it. The sparks were burning holes in the goblins, and the smoke that now fell from the roof made the air too thick for even their eyes to see through. Soon they were falling over one another and rolling in heaps on the floor, biting and kicking and fighting as if they had all gone mad.

Suddenly a sword flashed in its own light. Bilbo saw it go right through the Great Goblin as he stood dumbfounded in the middle of his rage. He fell dead, and the goblin soldiers fled before the sword shrieking into the darkness.

The sword went back into its sheath. "Follow me quick!" said a voice fierce and quiet; and before Bilbo understood what had happened he was trotting along again, as fast as he could trot, at the end of the line, down more dark passages with the yells of the goblin-hall growing fainter behind him. A pale light was leading them on.

"Quicker, quicker!" said the voice. "The torches will soon be relit."

"Half a minute!" said Dori, who was at the back next to Bilbo, and a decent fellow. He made the hobbit scramble on his shoulders as best he could with his tied hands, and then off they all went at a run, with a clink-clink of chains, and many a stumble, since they had no hands to steady themselves with. Not for a long while did they stop, and by that time they must have been right down in the very mountain's heart.

Then Gandalf lit up his wand. Of course it was Gandalf; but just then they were too busy to ask how he got there. He took out his sword again, and again it flashed in the dark by itself. It burned with a rage that made it gleam if goblins were about; now it was bright as blue flame for delight in the killing of the great lord of the cave. It made no trouble whatever of cutting through the goblin-chains and setting all the prisoners free as quickly as possible. This sword's name was Glamdring the Foe-hammer, if you remember. The goblins just called it Beater, and hated it worse than Biter if possible. Orcrist, too, had been saved; for

Gandalf had brought it along as well, snatching it from one of the terrified guards. Gandalf thought of most things; and though he could not do everything, he could do a great deal for friends in a tight corner.

"Are we all here?" said he, handing his sword back to Thorin with a bow. "Let me see: one—that's Thorin; two, three, four, five, six, seven, eight, nine, ten, eleven; where are Fili and Kili? Here they are! twelve, thirteen—and here's Mr. Baggins: fourteen! Well, well! it might be worse, and then again it might be a good deal better. No ponies, and no food, and no knowing quite where we are, and hordes of angry goblins just behind! On we go!"

On they went. Gandalf was quite right: they began to hear goblin noises and horrible cries far behind in the passages they had come through. That sent them on faster than ever, and as poor Bilbo could not possibly go half as fast—for dwarves can roll along at a tremendous pace, I can tell you, when they have to— they took it in turn to carry him on their backs.

Still goblins go faster than dwarves, and these goblins knew the way better (they had made the paths themselves), and were madly angry; so that do what they could the dwarves heard the cries and howls getting closer and closer. Soon they could hear even the flap of the goblin feet, many many feet which seemed only just round the last corner. The blink of red torches could be seen behind them in the tunnel they were following; and they were getting deadly tired.

"Why, O why did I ever leave my hobbit-hole!" said poor Mr. Baggins bumping up and down on Bombur's back.

"Why, O why did I ever bring a wretched little hobbit on a treasure hunt!" said poor Bombur, who was fat, and staggered along with the sweat dripping down his nose in his heat and terror.

At this point Gandalf fell behind, and Thorin with him. They turned a sharp corner. "About turn!" he shouted. "Draw your sword Thorin!"

There was nothing else to be done; and the goblins did not like it. They came scurrying round the corner in full cry, and found Goblin-cleaver, and Foe-hammer shining cold and bright right in their astonished eyes. The ones in front dropped their torches and gave one yell before they were killed. The ones behind yelled still more, and leaped back knocking over those that were running after them. "Biter and Beater!" they shrieked; and soon they were all in confusion, and most of them were hustling back the way they had come.

It was quite a long while before any of them dared to turn that corner. By that time the dwarves had gone on again, a long, long, way on into the dark tunnels of the goblins' realm. When the goblins discovered that, they put out their torches and they slipped on soft shoes, and they chose out their very quickest runners with the sharpest ears and eyes. These ran forward, as swift as weasels in the dark, and with hardly any more noise than bats.

That is why neither Bilbo, nor the dwarves, nor even Gandalf heard them coming. Nor did they see them. But they were seen by the goblins that ran silently up behind, for Gandalf was letting his wand give out a faint light to help the dwarves as they went along.

Quite suddenly Dori, now at the back again carrying Bilbo, was grabbed from behind in the dark. He shouted and fell; and the hobbit rolled off his shoulders into the blackness, bumped his head on hard rock, and remembered nothing more.

Chapter V

RIDDLES IN THE DARK

When Bilbo opened his eyes, he wondered if he had; for it was just as dark as with them shut. No one was anywhere near him. Just imagine his fright! He could hear nothing, see nothing, and he could feel nothing except the stone of the floor.

Very slowly he got up and groped about on all fours, till he touched the wall of the tunnel; but neither up nor down it could he find anything: nothing at all, no sign of goblins, no sign of dwarves. His head was swimming, and he was far from certain even of the direction they had been going in when he had his fall. He guessed as well as he could, and crawled along for a good way, till suddenly his hand met what felt like a tiny ring of cold metal lying on the floor of the tunnel. It was a turning point in his career, but he did not know it. He put the ring in his pocket almost without thinking; certainly it did not seem of any particular use at the moment. He did not go much further, but sat down on the cold floor and gave himself up to complete miserableness, for a long while. He thought of himself frying bacon and eggs in his own kitchen at home—for he could feel inside that it was high time for some meal or other; but that only made him miserabler.

He could not think what to do; nor could he think what had happened; or why he had been left behind;

or why, if he had been left behind, the goblins had not caught him; or even why his head was so sore. The truth was he had been lying quiet, out of sight and out of mind, in a very dark corner for a long while.

After some time he felt for his pipe. It was not broken, and that was something. Then he felt for his pouch, and there was some tobacco in it, and that was something more. Then he felt for matches and he could not find any at all, and that shattered his hopes completely. Just as well for him, as he agreed when he came to his senses. Goodness knows what the striking of matches and the smell of tobacco would have brought on him out of dark holes in that horrible place. Still at the moment he felt very crushed. But in slapping all his pockets and feeling all round himself for matches his hand came on the hilt of his little sword—the little dagger that he got from the trolls, and that he had quite forgotten; nor fortunately had the goblins noticed it, as he wore it inside his breeches.

Now he drew it out. It shone pale and dim before his eyes. "So it is an elvish blade, too," he thought; "and goblins are not very near, and yet not far enough."

But somehow he was comforted. It was rather splendid to be wearing a blade made in Gondolin for the goblin-wars of which so many songs had sung; and also he had noticed that such weapons made a great impression on goblins that came upon them suddenly.

"Go back?" he thought. "No good at all! Go sideways? Impossible! Go forward? Only thing to do! On we go!" So up he got, and trotted along with his little sword held in front of him and one hand feeling the wall, and his heart all of a patter and a pitter.

Now certainly Bilbo was in what is called a tight place. But you must remember it was not quite so tight for him as it would have been for me or for you. Hobbits are not quite like ordinary people; and after all if their holes are nice cheery places and properly aired, quite different from the tunnels of the goblins, still they are more used to tunnelling than we are, and they do not easily lose their sense of direction underground—not when their heads have recovered from being bumped. Also they can move very quietly, and hide easily, and recover wonderfully from falls and bruises, and they have a fund of wisdom and wise sayings that men have mostly never heard or have forgotten long ago.

I should not have liked to have been in Mr. Baggins' place, all the same. The tunnel seemed to have no end. All he knew was that it was still going down pretty steadily and keeping in the same direction in spite of a twist and a turn or two. There were passages leading off to the side every now and then, as he knew by the glimmer of his sword, or could feel with his hand on the wall. Of these he took no notice, except to hurry past for fear of goblins or half-imagined dark things coming out of them. On and on he went, and down and down; and still he heard no sound of anything except the occasional whirr of a bat by his ears, which startled him at first, till it became too frequent to bother about. I do not know how long he kept on like this, hating to go on, not daring to stop, on, on, until he was tireder than tired. It seemed like all the way to tomorrow and over it to the days beyond.

Suddenly without any warning he trotted splash into water! Ugh! it was icy cold. That pulled him up sharp and short. He did not know whether it was just a pool in the path, or the edge of an underground stream that crossed the passage, or the brink of a deep dark subterranean lake. The sword was hardly shining at all. He stopped, and he could hear, when he listened hard, drops drip-drip-dripping from an unseen roof into the water below; but there seemed no other sort of sound.

"So it is a pool or a lake, and not an underground river," he thought. Still he did not dare to wade out into the darkness. He could not swim; and he thought, too, of nasty slimy things, with big bulging blind eyes, wriggling in the water. There are strange things living in the pools and lakes in the hearts of mountains: fish whose fathers swam in, goodness only knows how many years ago, and never swam out again, while their eyes grew bigger and bigger and bigger from trying to see in the blackness; also there are other things more slimy than fish. Even in the tunnels and caves the goblins have made for themselves there are other things living unbeknown to them that have sneaked in from outside to lie up in the dark. Some of these caves, too, go back in their beginnings to ages before the goblins, who only widened them and joined them up with passages, and the original owners are still there in odd corners, slinking and nosing about.

Deep down here by the dark water lived old Gollum, a small slimy creature. I don't know where

he came from, nor who or what he was. He was
Gollum—as dark as darkness, except for two big
round pale eyes in his thin face. He had a little boat,
and he rowed about quite quietly on the lake; for
lake it was, wide and deep and deadly cold. He
paddled it with large feet dangling over the side, but
never a ripple did he make. Not he. He was looking
out of his pale lamp-like eyes for blind fish, which
he grabbed with his long fingers as quick as thinking. He liked meat too. Goblin he thought good,
when he could get it; but he took care they never
found him out. He just throttled them from behind,
if they ever came down alone anywhere near the
edge of the water, while he was prowling about.
They very seldom did, for they had a feeling that
something unpleasant was lurking down there,
down at the very roots of the mountain. They had
come on the lake, when they were tunnelling down
long ago, and they found they could go no further;
so there their road ended in that direction, and
there was no reason to go that way—unless the
Great Goblin sent them. Sometimes he took a fancy
for fish from the lake, and sometimes neither goblin
nor fish came back.

Actually Gollum lived on a slimy island of rock in
the middle of the lake. He was watching Bilbo now
from the distance with his pale eyes like telescopes.
Bilbo could not see him, but he was wondering a lot
about Bilbo, for he could see that he was no goblin
at all.

Gollum got into his boat and shot off from the
island, while Bilbo was sitting on the brink altogether
flummoxed and at the end of his way and his wits.

Suddenly up came Gollum and whispered and hissed:

"Bless us and splash us, my precioussss! I guess it's a choice feast; at least a tasty morsel it'd make us, gollum!" And when he said *gollum* he made a horrible swallowing noise in his throat. That is how he got his name, though he always called himself 'my precious'.

The hobbit jumped nearly out of his skin when the hiss came in his ears, and he suddenly saw the pale eyes sticking out at him.

"Who are you?" he said, thrusting his dagger in front of him.

"What iss he, my preciouss?" whispered Gollum (who always spoke to himself through never having anyone else to speak to). This is what he had come to find out, for he was not really very hungry at the moment, only curious; otherwise he would have grabbed first and whispered afterwards.

"I am Mr. Bilbo Baggins. I have lost the dwarves and I have lost the wizard, and I don't know where I am; and I don't want to know, if only I can get away."

"What's he got in his handses?" said Gollum, looking at the sword, which he did not quite like.

"A sword, a blade which came out of Gondolin!"

"Sssss" said Gollum, and became quite polite. "Praps ye sits here and chats with it a bitsy, my preciousss. It likes riddles, praps it does, does it?" He was anxious to appear friendly, at any rate for the moment, and until he found out more about the sword and the hobbit, whether he was quite alone really, whether he was good to eat, and whether Gollum was really hungry. Riddles were all he could think of. Asking them, and sometimes guessing them, had been the only game he had ever played with other funny creatures sitting in their holes in the long, long ago, before he lost all his friends and was driven away, alone, and crept down, down, into the dark under the mountains.

"Very well," said Bilbo, who was anxious to agree, until he found out more about the creature, whether he was quite alone, whether he was fierce or hungry, and whether he was a friend of the goblins.

"You ask first," he said, because he had not had time to think of a riddle.

So Gollum hissed:

> *What has roots as nobody sees,*
> *Is taller than trees,*
> *Up, up it goes,*
> *And yet never grows?*

"Easy!" said Bilbo. "Mountain, I suppose."

"Does it guess easy? It must have a competition with us, my preciouss! If precious asks, and it doesn't answer, we eats it, my preciouss. If it asks us, and we doesn't answer, then we does what it wants, eh? We shows it the way out, yes!"

"All right!" said Bilbo, not daring to disagree, and nearly bursting his brain to think of riddles that could save him from being eaten.

> *Thirty white horses on a red hill,*
> *First they champ,*
> *Then they stamp,*
> *Then they stand still.*

That was all he could think of to ask—the idea of eating was rather on his mind. It was rather an old one, too, and Gollum knew the answer as well as you do.

"Chestnuts, chestnuts," he hissed. "Teeth! teeth! my preciousss; but we has only six!" Then he asked his second:

> *Voiceless it cries,*
> *Wingless flutters,*
> *Toothless bites,*
> *Mouthless mutters.*

"Half a moment!" cried Bilbo, who was still thinking uncomfortably about eating. Fortunately he had once heard something rather like this before, and getting his wits back he thought of the answer. "Wind, wind of course," he said, and he was so pleased that he made up one on the spot. "This'll puzzle the nasty little underground creature," he thought:

> *An eye in a blue face*
> *Saw an eye in a green face.*
> *"That eye is like to this eye"*
> *Said the first eye,*
> *"But in low place*
> *Not in high place."*

"Ss, ss, ss," said Gollum. He had been underground a long long time, and was forgetting this sort of thing. But just as Bilbo was beginning to hope that the wretch would not be able to answer, Gollum brought up memories of ages and ages and

ages before, when he lived with his grandmother in
a hole in a bank by a river, "Sss, sss, my preciouss,"
he said. "Sun on the daisies it means, it does."

But these ordinary above ground everyday sort of
riddles were tiring for him. Also they reminded him
of days when he had been less lonely and sneaky and
nasty, and that put him out of temper. What is more
they made him hungry; so this time he tried something a bit more difficult and more unpleasant:

> *It cannot be seen, cannot be felt,*
> *Cannot be heard, cannot be smelt.*
> *It lies behind stars and under hills,*
> *And empty holes it fills.*
> *It comes first and follows after,*
> *Ends life, kills laughter.*

Unfortunately for Gollum Bilbo had heard that
sort of thing before; and the answer was all round
him any way. "Dark!" he said without even scratching his head or putting on his thinking cap.

> *A box without hinges, key, or lid,*
> *Yet golden treasure inside is hid,*

he asked to gain time, until he could think of a really
hard one. This he thought a dreadfully easy chestnut,
though he had not asked it in the usual words. But it
proved a nasty poser for Gollum. He hissed to
himself, and still he did not answer; he whispered
and spluttered.

After some while Bilbo became impatient. "Well,
what is it?" he said. "The answer's not a kettle boiling

over, as you seem to think from the noise you are making."

"Give us a chance; let it give us a chance, my preciouss—ss—ss."

"Well," said Bilbo after giving him a long chance, "what about your guess?"

But suddenly Gollum remembered thieving from nests long ago, and sitting under the river bank teaching his grandmother, teaching his grandmother to suck— "Eggses!" he hissed. "Eggses it is!" Then he asked:

> *Alive without breath,*
> *As cold as death;*
> *Never thirsty, ever drinking,*
> *All in mail never clinking.*

He also in his turn thought this was a dreadfully easy one, because he was always thinking of the answer. But he could not remember anything better at the moment, he was so flustered by the egg-question. All the same it was a poser for poor Bilbo, who never had anything to do with the water if he could help it. I imagine you know the answer, of course, or can guess it as easy as winking, since you are sitting comfortably at home and have not the danger of being eaten to disturb your thinking. Bilbo sat and cleared his throat once or twice, but no answer came.

After a while Gollum began to hiss with pleasure to himself: "Is it nice, my preciousss? Is it juicy? Is it scrumptiously crunchable?" He began to peer at Bilbo out of the darkness.

"Half a moment," said the hobbit shivering. "I gave you a good long chance just now."

"It must make haste, haste!" said Gollum, beginning to climb out of his boat on to the shore to get at Bilbo. But when he put his long webby foot in the water, a fish jumped out in a fright and fell on Bilbo's toes.

"Ugh!" he said, "it is cold and clammy!"—and so he guessed. "Fish! fish!" he cried. "It is fish!"

Gollum was dreadfully disappointed; but Bilbo asked another riddle as quick as ever he could, so that Gollum had to get back into his boat and think.

No-legs lay on one-leg, two-legs sat near on three-legs, four-legs got some.

It was not really the right time for this riddle, but Bilbo was in a hurry. Gollum might have had some trouble guessing it, if he had asked it at another time. As it was, talking of fish, "no-legs" was not so very difficult, and after that the rest was easy. "Fish on a little table, man at table sitting on a stool, the cat has the bones" that of course is the answer, and Gollum soon gave it. Then he thought the time had come to ask something hard and horrible. This is what he said:

> *This thing all things devours:*
> *Birds, beasts, trees, flowers;*
> *Gnaws iron, bites steel;*
> *Grinds hard stones to meal;*
> *Slays king, ruins town,*
> *And beats high mountain down.*

Poor Bilbo sat in the dark thinking of all the horrible names of all the giants and ogres he had ever heard told of in tales, but not one of them had done all these things. He had a feeling that the answer was quite different and that he ought to know it, but he could not think of it. He began to get frightened, and that is bad for thinking. Gollum began to get out of his boat. He flapped into the water and paddled to the bank; Bilbo could see his eyes coming towards him. His tongue seemed to stick in his mouth; he wanted to shout out: "Give me more time! Give me time!" But all that came out with a sudden squeal was:

"Time! Time!"

Bilbo was saved by pure luck. For that of course was the answer.

Gollum was disappointed once more; and now he was getting angry, and also tired of the game. It had made him very hungry indeed. This time he did not go back to the boat. He sat down in the dark by Bilbo. That made the hobbit most dreadfully uncomfortable and scattered his wits.

"It's got to ask uss a quesstion, my preciouss, yes, yess, yesss. Jusst one more question to guess, yes, yess," said Gollum.

But Bilbo simply could not think of any question with that nasty wet cold thing sitting next to him, and pawing and poking him. He scratched himself, he pinched himself; still he could not think of anything.

"Ask us! ask us!" said Gollum.

Bilbo pinched himself and slapped himself; he gripped on his little sword; he even felt in his pocket with his other hand. There he found the ring he had picked up in the passage and forgotten about.

"What have I got in my pocket?" he said aloud.

He was talking to himself, but Gollum thought it was a riddle, and he was frightfully upset.

"Not fair! not fair!" he hissed. "It isn't fair, my precious, is it, to ask us what it's got in its nassty little pocketses?"

Bilbo seeing what had happened and having nothing better to ask stuck to his question, "What have I got in my pocket?" he said louder.

"S-s-s-s-s," hissed Gollum. "It must give us three guesseses, my preciouss, three guesseses."

"Very well! Guess away!" said Bilbo.

"Handses!" said Gollum.

"Wrong," said Bilbo, who had luckily just taken his hand out again. "Guess again!"

"S-s-s-s-s," said Gollum more upset than ever. He thought of all the things he kept in his own pockets: fish-bones, goblins' teeth, wet shells, a bit of bat-wing, a sharp stone to sharpen his fangs on, and other nasty things. He tried to think what other people kept in their pockets.

"Knife!" he said at last.

"Wrong!" said Bilbo, who had lost his some time ago. "Last guess!"

Now Gollum was in a much worse state than when Bilbo had asked him the egg-question. He hissed and spluttered and rocked himself backwards and for-wards, and slapped his feet on the floor, and wriggled and squirmed; but still he did not dare to waste his last guess.

"Come on!" said Bilbo. "I am waiting!" He tried to sound bold and cheerful, but he did not feel at all sure how the game was going to end, whether Gollum guessed right or not.

"Time's up!" he said.

"String, or nothing!" shrieked Gollum, which was not quite fair—working in two guesses at once.

"Both wrong," cried Bilbo very much relieved; and he jumped at once to his feet, put his back to the nearest wall, and held out his little sword. He knew, of course, that the riddle-game was sacred and of immense antiquity, and even wicked creatures were afraid to cheat when they played at it. But he felt he could not trust this slimy thing to keep any promise at a pinch. Any excuse would do for him to slide out of it. And after all that last question had not been a genuine riddle according to the ancient laws.

But at any rate Gollum did not at once attack him. He could see the sword in Bilbo's hand. He sat still, shivering and whispering. At last Bilbo could wait no longer.

"Well?" he said. "What about your promise? I want to go. You must show me the way."

"Did we say so, precious? Show the nassty little Baggins the way out, yes, yes. But what has it got in its pocketses, eh? Not string, precious, but not nothing. Oh no! gollum!"

"Never you mind," said Bilbo. "A promise is a promise."

"Cross it is, impatient, precious," hissed Gollum. "But it must wait, yes it must. We can't go up the tunnels so hasty. We must go and get some things first, yes, things to help us."

"Well, hurry up!" said Bilbo, relieved to think of Gollum going away. He thought he was just making an excuse and did not mean to come back. What was Gollum talking about? What useful thing could he keep out on the dark lake? But he was wrong. Gollum did mean to come back. He was angry now and hungry. And he was a miserable wicked creature, and already he had a plan.

Not far away was his island, of which Bilbo knew nothing, and there in his hiding-place he kept a few wretched oddments, and one very beautiful thing, very beautiful, very wonderful. He had a ring, a golden ring, a precious ring.

"My birthday-present!" he whispered to himself, as he had often done in the endless dark days. "That's what we wants now, yes; we wants it!"

He wanted it because it was a ring of power, and if you slipped that ring on your finger, you were invisible; only in the full sunlight could you be seen, and then only by your shadow, and that would be shaky and faint.

"My birthday-present! It came to me on my birthday, my precious." So he had always said to himself. But who knows how Gollum came by that present, ages ago in the old days when such rings were still at large in the world? Perhaps even the Master who ruled them could not have said. Gollum used to wear it at first, till it tired him; and then he kept it in a pouch next his skin, till it galled him; and now usually he hid it in a hole in the rock on his island, and was always going back to look at it. And still sometimes he put it on, when he could not bear to be parted from it any longer, or when he was very, very, hungry, and tired of fish. Then he would creep along dark passages looking for stray goblins. He might even venture into places where the torches were lit and made his eyes blink and smart; for he would be safe. Oh yes, quite safe. No one would see him, no one would notice him, till he had his fingers on their throat. Only a few hours ago he had worn it, and caught a small goblin-imp. How it squeaked! He still had a bone or two left to gnaw, but he wanted something softer.

"Quite safe, yes," he whispered to himself. "It won't see us, will it, my precious? No. It won't see us, and its nasty little sword will be useless, yes quite."

That is what was in his wicked little mind, as he slipped suddenly from Bilbo's side, and flapped back to his boat, and went off into the dark. Bilbo thought he had heard the last of him. Still he waited a while; for he had no idea how to find his way out alone.

Suddenly he heard a screech. It sent a shiver down his back. Gollum was cursing and wailing away in the gloom, not very far off by the sound of it. He was on his island, scrabbling here and there, searching and seeking in vain.

"Where iss it? Where iss it?" Bilbo heard him crying. "Losst it is, my precious, lost, lost! Curse us and crush us, my precious is lost!"

"What's the matter?" Bilbo called. "What have you lost?"

"It mustn't ask us," shrieked Gollum. "Not its business, no, gollum! It's losst, gollum, gollum, gollum."

"Well, so am I," cried Bilbo, "and I want to get unlost. And I won the game, and you promised. So come along! Come and let me out, and then go on with your looking!" Utterly miserable as Gollum sounded, Bilbo could not find much pity in his heart, and he had a feeling that anything Gollum wanted so much could hardly be something good. "Come along!" he shouted.

"No, not yet, precious!" Gollum answered. "We must search for it, it's lost, gollum."

"But you never guessed my last question, and you promised," said Bilbo.

"Never guessed!" said Gollum. Then suddenly out of the gloom came a sharp hiss. "What has it got in its pocketses? Tell us that. It must tell first."

As far as Bilbo knew, there was no particular reason why he should not tell. Gollum's mind had jumped to a guess quicker than his; naturally, for Gollum had brooded for ages on this one thing, and he was always afraid of its being stolen. But Bilbo was annoyed at the delay. After all, he had won the game, pretty fairly, at a horrible risk. "Answers were to be guessed not given," he said.

"But it wasn't a fair question," said Gollum. "Not a riddle, precious, no."

"Oh well, if it's a matter of ordinary questions," Bilbo replied, "then I asked one first. What have you lost? Tell me that!"

"What has it got in its pocketses?" The sound came hissing louder and sharper, and as he looked towards it, to his alarm Bilbo now saw two small points of light peering at him. As suspicion grew in Gollum's mind, the light of his eyes burned with a pale flame.

"What have you lost?" Bilbo persisted.

But now the light in Gollum's eyes had become a green fire, and it was coming swiftly nearer. Gollum was in his boat again, paddling wildly back to the dark shore; and such a rage of loss and suspicion was in his heart that no sword had any more terror for him.

Bilbo could not guess what had maddened the wretched creature, but he saw that all was up, and that Gollum meant to murder him at any rate. Just in time he turned and ran blindly back up the dark passage down which he had come, keeping close to the wall and feeling it with his left hand.

"What has it got in its pocketses?" he heard the hiss loud behind him, and the splash as Gollum leapt from his boat. "What have I, I wonder?" he said to himself, as he panted and stumbled along. He put his left hand in his pocket. The ring felt very cold as it quietly slipped on to his groping forefinger.

The hiss was close behind him. He turned now and saw Gollum's eyes like small green lamps coming up the slope. Terrified he tried to run faster, but suddenly he struck his toes on a snag in the floor, and fell flat with his little sword under him.

In a moment Gollum was on him. But before Bilbo could do anything, recover his breath, pick himself up, or wave his sword, Gollum passed by, taking no notice of him, cursing and whispering as he ran.

What could it mean? Gollum could see in the dark. Bilbo could see the light of his eyes palely shining even from behind. Painfully he got up, and sheathed his sword, which was now glowing faintly again, then very cautiously he followed. There seemed nothing else to do. It was no good crawling back down to Gollum's water. Perhaps if he followed him, Gollum might lead him to some way of escape without meaning to.

"Curse it! curse it! curse it!" hissed Gollum. "Curse the Baggins! It's gone! What has it got in its pocketses? Oh we guess, we guess, my precious. He's found it, yes he must have. My birthday-present."

Bilbo pricked up his ears. He was at last beginning to guess himself. He hurried a little, getting as close as he dared behind Gollum, who was still going quickly, not looking back, but turning his head from side to side, as Bilbo could see from the faint glimmer on the walls.

"My birthday-present! Curse it! How did we lose it, my precious? Yes, that's it. When we came this way last, when we twisted that nassty young squeaker. That's it. Curse it! It slipped from us, after all these ages and ages! It's gone, gollum."

Suddenly Gollum sat down and began to weep, a whistling and gurgling sound horrible to listen to. Bilbo halted and flattened himself against the tunnel-wall. After a while Gollum stopped weeping and began to talk. He seemed to be having an argument with himself.

"It's no good going back there to search, no. We doesn't remember all the places we've visited. And it's no use. The Baggins has got it in its pocketses; the nassty noser has found it, we says."

"We guesses, precious, only guesses. We can't know till we find the nassty creature and squeezes it. But it doesn't know what the present can do, does it? It'll just keep it in its pocketses. It doesn't know, and it can't go far. It's lost itself, the nassty nosey thing. It doesn't know the way out. It said so."

"It said so, yes; but it's tricksy. It doesn't say what it means. It won't say what it's got in its pocketses. It knows. It knows a way in, it must know a way out, yes. It's off to the back-door. To the back-door, that's it."

"The goblinses will catch it then. It can't get out that way, precious."

"Ssss, sss, gollum! Goblinses! Yes, but if it's got the present, our precious present, then goblinses will get it, gollum! They'll find it, they'll find out what it does. We shan't ever be safe again, never, gollum! One of the goblinses will put it on, and then no one will see him. He'll be there but not seen. Not even our clever eyeses will notice him; and he'll come creepsy and tricksy and catch us, gollum, gollum!"

"Then let's stop talking, precious, and make haste. If the Baggins has gone that way, we must go quick and see. Go! Not far now. Make haste!"

With a spring Gollum got up and started shambling off at a great pace. Bilbo hurried after him, still cautiously, though his chief fear now was of tripping on another snag and falling with a noise. His head was in a whirl of hope and wonder. It seemed that the ring he had was a magic ring: it made you invisible! He had heard of such things, of course, in old old tales; but it was hard to believe that he really had found one, by accident. Still there it was: Gollum with his bright eyes had passed him by, only a yard to one side.

On they went, Gollum flip-flapping ahead, hissing and cursing; Bilbo behind going as softly as a hobbit can. Soon they came to places where, as Bilbo had noticed on the way down, side-passages opened, this way and that. Gollum began at once to count them.

"One left, yes. One right, yes. Two right, yes, yes. Two left, yes, yes." And so on and on.

As the count grew he slowed down, and he began to get shaky and weepy; for he was leaving the water further and further behind, and he was getting afraid. Goblins might be about, and he had lost his ring. At last he stopped by a low opening, on their left as they went up.

"Seven right, yes. Six left, yes!" he whispered. "This is it. This is the way to the back-door, yes. Here's the passage!"

He peered in, and shrank back. "But we dursn't go in, precious, no we dursn't. Goblinses down there. Lots of goblinses. We smells them. Ssss!"

"What shall we do? Curse them and crush them! We must wait here, precious, wait a bit and see."

So they came to a dead stop. Gollum had brought Bilbo to the way out after all, but Bilbo could not get in! There was Gollum sitting humped up right in the opening, and his eyes gleamed cold in his head, as he swayed it from side to side between his knees.

Bilbo crept away from the wall more quietly than a mouse; but Gollum stiffened at once, and sniffed, and his eyes went green. He hissed softly but menacingly. He could not see the hobbit, but now he was on the alert, and he had other senses that the darkness had sharpened: hearing and smell. He seemed to be crouched right down with his flat hands splayed on the floor, and his head thrust out, nose almost to the stone. Though he was only a black shadow in the gleam of his own eyes, Bilbo could see or feel that he was tense as a bowstring, gathered for a spring.

Bilbo almost stopped breathing, and went stiff himself. He was desperate. He must get away, out of this horrible darkness, while he had any strength

left. He must fight. He must stab the foul thing, put
its eyes out, kill it. It meant to kill him. No, not a
fair fight. He was invisible now. Gollum had no
sword. Gollum had not actually threatened to kill
him, or tried to yet. And he was miserable, alone,
lost. A sudden understanding, a pity mixed with
horror, welled up in Bilbo's heart: a glimpse of
endless unmarked days without light or hope of
betterment, hard stone, cold fish, sneaking and
whispering. All these thoughts passed in a flash of a
second. He trembled. And then quite suddenly in
another flash, as if lifted by a new strength and
resolve, he leaped.

No great leap for a man, but a leap in the dark.
Straight over Gollum's head he jumped, seven feet
forward and three in the air; indeed, had he known it,
he only just missed cracking his skull on the low arch
of the passage.

Gollum threw himself backwards, and grabbed as
the hobbit flew over him, but too late: his hands
snapped on thin air, and Bilbo, falling fair on his
sturdy feet, sped off down the new tunnel. He did
not turn to see what Gollum was doing. There was a
hissing and cursing almost at his heels at first, then it
stopped. All at once there came a blood-curdling
shriek, filled with hatred and despair. Gollum was
defeated. He dared go no further. He had lost: lost
his prey, and lost, too, the only thing he had ever
cared for, his precious. The cry brought Bilbo's heart
to his mouth, but still he held on. Now faint as an
echo, but menacing, the voice came behind:

"Thief, thief, thief! Baggins! We hates it, we hates
it, we hates it for ever!"

Then there was a silence. But that too seemed menacing to Bilbo. "If goblins are so near that he smelt them," he thought, "then they'll have heard his shrieking and cursing. Careful now, or this way will lead you to worse things."

The passage was low and roughly made. It was not too difficult for the hobbit, except when, in spite of all care, he stubbed his poor toes again, several times, on nasty jagged stones in the floor. "A bit low for goblins, at least for the big ones," thought Bilbo, not knowing that even the big ones, the orcs of the mountains, go along at a great speed stooping low with their hands almost on the ground.

Soon the passage that had been sloping down began to go up again, and after a while it climbed steeply. That slowed Bilbo down. But at last the slope stopped, the passage turned a corner and dipped down again, and there, at the bottom of a short incline, he saw, filtering round another corner—a glimpse of light. Not red light, as of fire or lantern, but a pale out-of-doors sort of light. Then Bilbo began to run.

Scuttling as fast as his legs would carry him he turned the last corner and came suddenly right into an open space, where the light, after all that time in the dark, seemed dazzlingly bright. Really it was only a leak of sunshine in through a doorway, where a great door, a stone door, was left standing open.

Bilbo blinked, and then suddenly he saw the goblins: goblins in full armour with drawn swords sitting just inside the door, and watching it with wide eyes, and watching the passage that led to it. They were aroused, alert, ready for anything.

They saw him sooner than he saw them. Yes, they saw him. Whether it was an accident, or a last trick of the ring before it took a new master, it was not on his finger. With yells of delight the goblins rushed upon him.

A pang of fear and loss, like an echo of Gollum's misery, smote Bilbo, and forgetting even to draw his sword he struck his hands into his pockets. And there was the ring still, in his left pocket, and it slipped on his finger. The goblins stopped short. They could not see a sign of him. He had vanished. They yelled twice as loud as before, but not so delightedly.

"Where is it?" they cried.

"Go back up the passage!" some shouted.

"This way!" some yelled. "That way!" others yelled.

"Look out for the door," bellowed the captain.

Whistles blew, armour clashed, swords rattled, goblins cursed and swore and ran hither and thither, falling over one another and getting very angry. There was a terrible outcry, to-do, and disturbance.

Bilbo was dreadfully frightened, but he had the sense to understand what had happened and to sneak behind a big barrel which held drink for the goblin-guards, and so get out of the way and avoid being bumped into, trampled to death, or caught by feel.

"I must get to the door, I must get to the door!" he kept on saying to himself, but it was a long time before he ventured to try. Then it was like a horrible game of blind-man's-buff. The place was full of goblins running about, and the poor little hobbit dodged this way and that, was knocked over by a goblin who could not make out what he had bumped into, scrambled away on all fours, slipped between the legs of the captain just in time, got up, and ran for the door.

It was still ajar, but a goblin had pushed it nearly to. Bilbo struggled but he could not move it. He tried to squeeze through the crack. He squeezed and squeezed, and he stuck! It was awful. His buttons had got wedged on the edge of the door and the door-post. He could see outside into the open air: there were a few steps running down into a narrow valley between tall mountains; the sun came out from behind a cloud and shone bright on the outside of the door—but he could not get through.

Suddenly one of the goblins inside shouted: "There is a shadow by the door. Something is outside!"

Bilbo's heart jumped into his mouth. He gave a terrific squirm. Buttons burst off in all directions. He was through, with a torn coat and waistcoat, leaping down the steps like a goat, while bewildered goblins were still picking up his nice brass buttons on the doorstep.

Of course they soon came down after him, hooting and hallooing, and hunting among the trees. But they don't like the sun: it makes their legs wobble and their heads giddy. They could not find Bilbo with the ring on, slipping in and out of the shadow of the trees, running quick and quiet, and keeping out of the sun; so soon they went back grumbling and cursing to guard the door. Bilbo had escaped.

Chapter VI

OUT OF THE FRYING-PAN
INTO THE FIRE

Bilbo had escaped the goblins, but he did not know where he was. He had lost hood, cloak, food, pony, his buttons and his friends. He wandered on and on, till the sun began to sink westwards—*behind the mountains*. Their shadows fell across Bilbo's path, and he looked back. Then he looked forward and could see before him only ridges and slopes falling towards lowlands and plains glimpsed occasionally between the trees.

"Good heavens!" he exclaimed. "I seem to have got right to the other side of the Misty Mountains, right to the edge of the Land Beyond! Where and O where can Gandalf and the dwarves have got to? I only hope to goodness they are not still back there in the power of the goblins!"

He still wandered on, out of the little high valley, over its edge, and down the slopes beyond; but all the while a very uncomfortable thought was growing inside him. He wondered whether he ought not, now he had the magic ring, to go back into the horrible, horrible, tunnels and look for his friends. He had just made up his mind that it was his duty, that he must turn back—and very miserable he felt about it—when he heard voices.

He stopped and listened. It did not sound like goblins; so he crept forward carefully. He was on a stony path winding downwards with a rocky wall on the left hand; on the other side the ground sloped away and there were dells below the level of the path overhung with bushes and low trees. In one of these dells under the bushes people were talking.

He crept still nearer, and suddenly he saw peering between two big boulders a head with a red hood on: it was Balin doing look-out. He could have clapped and shouted for joy, but he did not. He had still got the ring on, for fear of meeting something unexpected and unpleasant, and he saw that Balin was looking straight at him without noticing him.

"I will give them all a surprise," he thought, as he crawled into the bushes at the edge of the dell. Gandalf was arguing with the dwarves. They were discussing all that had happened to them in the tunnels, and wondering and debating what they were to do now. The dwarves were grumbling, and Gandalf was saying that they could not possibly go on with their journey leaving Mr. Baggins in the hands of the goblins, without trying to find out if he was alive or dead, and without trying to rescue him.

"After all he is my friend," said the wizard, "and not a bad little chap. I feel responsible for him. I wish to goodness you had not lost him."

The dwarves wanted to know why he had ever been brought at all, why he could not stick to his friends and come along with them, and why the wizard had not chosen someone with more sense. "He has been more trouble than use so far," said one. "If we have got to go back now into those abominable tunnels to look for him, then drat him, I say."

Gandalf answered angrily: "I brought him, and I don't bring things that are of no use. Either you help me to look for him, or I go and leave you here to get out of the mess as best you can yourselves. If we can only find him again, you will thank me before all is over. Whatever did you want to go and drop him for, Dori?"

"You would have dropped him," said Dori, "if a goblin had suddenly grabbed your legs from behind in the dark, tripped up your feet, and kicked you in the back!"

"Then why didn't you pick him up again?"

"Good heavens! Can you ask! Goblins fighting and biting in the dark, everybody falling over bodies and hitting one another! You nearly chopped off my head with Glamdring, and Thorin was stabbing here there and everywhere with Orcrist. All of a sudden you gave one of your blinding flashes, and we saw the goblins running back yelping. You shouted 'follow me everybody!' and everybody ought to have followed. We thought everybody had. There was no time to count, as you know quite well, till we had dashed through the gate-guards, out of the lower door, and helter-skelter down here. And here we are—without the burglar, confusticate him!"

"And here's the burglar!" said Bilbo stepping down into the middle of them, and slipping off the ring.

Bless me, how they jumped! Then they shouted with surprise and delight. Gandalf was as astonished as any of them, but probably more pleased than all the others. He called to Balin and told him what he thought of a look-out man who let people walk right into them like that without warning. It is a fact that

Bilbo's reputation went up a very great deal with the dwarves after this. If they had still doubted that he was really a first-class burglar, in spite of Gandalf's words, they doubted no longer. Balin was the most puzzled of all; but everyone said it was a very clever bit of work.

Indeed Bilbo was so pleased with their praise that he just chuckled inside and said nothing whatever about the ring; and when they asked him how he did it, he said: "Oh, just crept along, you know—very carefully and quietly."

"Well, it is the first time that even a mouse has crept along carefully and quietly under my very nose and not been spotted," said Balin, "and I take off my hood to you." Which he did.

"Balin at your service," said he.

"Your servant, Mr. Baggins," said Bilbo.

Then they wanted to know all about his adventures after they had lost him, and he sat down and told them everything—except about the finding of the ring ("not just now" he thought). They were particularly interested in the riddle-competition, and shuddered most appreciatively at his description of Gollum.

"And then I couldn't think of any other question with him sitting beside me," ended Bilbo; "so I said 'what's in my pocket?' And he couldn't guess in three goes. So I said: 'what about your promise? Show me the way out!' But he came at me to kill me, and I ran, and fell over, and he missed me in the dark. Then I followed him, because I heard him talking to himself. He thought I really knew the way out, and so he was making for it. And then he sat down in the entrance, and I could not get by. So I jumped over him and escaped, and ran down to the gate."

"What about the guards?" they asked. "Weren't there any?"

"O yes! lots of them; but I dodged 'em. I got stuck in the door, which was only open a crack, and I lost lots of buttons," he said sadly looking at his torn clothes. "But I squeezed through all right—and here I am."

The dwarves looked at him with quite a new respect, when he talked about dodging guards, jumping over Gollum, and squeezing through, as if it was not very difficult or very alarming.

"What did I tell you?" said Gandalf laughing. "Mr. Baggins has more about him than you guess." He gave Bilbo a queer look from under his bushy eyebrows, as he said this, and the hobbit wondered if he guessed at the part of his tale that he had left out.

Then he had questions of his own to ask, for if Gandalf had explained it all by now to the dwarves, Bilbo had not heard it. He wanted to know how the wizard had turned up again, and where they had all got to now.

The wizard, to tell the truth, never minded explaining his cleverness more than once, so now he told Bilbo that both he and Elrond had been well aware of the presence of evil goblins in that part of the mountains. But their main gate used to come out on a different pass, one more easy to travel by, so that they often caught people benighted near their gates. Evidently people had given up going that way, and the goblins must have opened their new entrance at the top of the pass the dwarves had taken, quite recently, because it had been found quite safe up to now.

"I must see if I can't find a more or less decent giant to block it up again," said Gandalf, "or soon there will be no getting over the mountains at all."

As soon as Gandalf had heard Bilbo's yell he realized what had happened. In the flash which killed the goblins that were grabbing him he had nipped inside the crack, just as it snapped to. He followed after the drivers and prisoners right to the edge of the great hall, and there he sat down and worked up the best magic he could in the shadows.

"A very ticklish business, it was," he said. "Touch and go!"

But, of course, Gandalf had made a special study of bewitchments with fire and lights (even the hobbit had never forgotten the magic fireworks at Old Took's midsummer-eve parties, as you remember). The rest we all know—except that Gandalf knew all about the back-door, as the goblins called the lower gate, where Bilbo lost his buttons. As a matter of fact it was well known to anybody who was acquainted with this part of the mountains; but it took a wizard to keep his head in the tunnels and guide them in the right direction.

"They made that gate ages ago," he said, "partly for a way of escape, if they needed one; partly as a way out into the lands beyond, where they still come in the dark and do great damage. They guard it always and no one has ever managed to block it up. They will guard it doubly after this," he laughed.

All the others laughed too. After all they had lost a good deal, but they had killed the Great Goblin and a great many others besides, and they had all escaped, so they might be said to have had the best of it so far.

But the wizard called them to their senses. "We must be getting on at once, now we are a little rested," he said. "They will be out after us in hundreds when night comes on; and already shadows are lengthening. They can smell our footsteps for hours and hours after we have passed. We must be miles on before dusk. There will be a bit of moon, if it keeps fine, and that is lucky. Not that they mind the moon much, but it will give us a little light to steer by."

"O yes!" he said in answer to more questions from the hobbit. "You lose track of time inside goblin-tunnels. Today's Thursday, and it was Monday night or Tuesday morning that we were captured. We have gone miles and miles, and come right down through the heart of the mountains, and are now on the other side—quite a short cut. But we are not at the point to which our pass would have brought us; we are too far to the North, and have some awkward country ahead. And we are still pretty high up. Let's get on!"

"I am dreadfully hungry," groaned Bilbo, who was suddenly aware that he had not had a meal since the night before the night before last. Just think of that for a hobbit! His stomach felt all empty and loose and his legs all wobbly, now that the excitement was over.

"Can't help it," said Gandalf, "unless you like to go back and ask the goblins nicely to let you have your pony back and your luggage."

"No thank you!" said Bilbo.

"Very well then, we must just tighten our belts and

trudge on—or we shall be made into supper, and that will be much worse than having none ourselves."

As they went on Bilbo looked from side to side for something to eat; but the blackberries were still only in flower, and of course there were no nuts, not even hawthorn-berries. He nibbled a bit of sorrel, and he drank from a small mountain-stream that crossed the path, and he ate three wild strawberries that he found on its bank, but it was not much good.

They still went on and on. The rough path disappeared. The bushes, and the long grasses between the boulders, the patches of rabbit-cropped turf, the thyme and the sage and the marjoram, and the yellow rockroses all vanished, and they found themselves at the top of a wide steep slope of fallen stones, the remains of a landslide. When they began to go down this, rubbish and small pebbles rolled away from their feet; soon larger bits of split stone went clattering down and started other pieces below them slithering and rolling; then lumps of rock were disturbed and bounded off, crashing down with a dust and a noise. Before long the whole slope above them and below them seemed on the move, and they were sliding away, huddled all together, in a fearful confusion of slipping, rattling, cracking slabs and stones.

It was the trees at the bottom that saved them. They slid into the edge of a climbing wood of pines that here stood right up the mountain slope from the deeper darker forests of the valleys below. Some caught hold of the trunks and swung themselves into lower branches, some (like the little hobbit) got behind a tree to shelter from the onslaught of the rocks. Soon the danger was over, the slide had stopped, and the last faint crashes could be heard as the largest of the disturbed stones went bounding and spinning among the bracken and the pine-roots far below.

"Well! that has got us on a bit," said Gandalf; "and even goblins tracking us will have a job to come down here quietly."

"I daresay," grumbled Bombur; "but they won't find it difficult to send stones bouncing down on our heads." The dwarves (and Bilbo) were feeling far from happy, and were rubbing their bruised and damaged legs and feet.

"Nonsense! We are going to turn aside here out of the path of the slide. We must be quick! Look at the light!"

The sun had long gone behind the mountains. Already the shadows were deepening about them, though far away through the trees and over the black tops of those growing lower down they could still see the evening lights on the plains beyond. They limped along now as fast as they were able down the gentle slopes of a pine forest in a slanting path leading steadily southwards. At times they were pushing through a sea of bracken with tall fronds rising right above the hobbit's head; at times they were marching along quiet as quiet over a floor of pine-needles; and all the while the forest-gloom got heavier and the forest-silence deeper. There was no wind that evening to bring even a sea-sighing into the branches of the trees.

"Must we go any further?" asked Bilbo, when it was so dark that he could only just see Thorin's beard wagging beside him, and so quiet that he could hear the dwarves' breathing like a loud noise. "My toes are all bruised and bent, and my legs ache, and my stomach is wagging like an empty sack."

"A bit further," said Gandalf.

After what seemed ages further they came suddenly to an opening where no trees grew. The moon was up and was shining into the clearing. Somehow it struck all of them as not at all a nice place, although there was nothing wrong to see.

All of a sudden they heard a howl away down hill, a long shuddering howl. It was answered by another away to the right and a good deal nearer to them; then by another not far away to the left. It was wolves howling at the moon, wolves gathering together!

There were no wolves living near Mr. Baggins' hole at home, but he knew that noise. He had had it described to him often enough in tales. One of his elder cousins (on the Took side), who had been a great traveller, used to imitate it to frighten him. To hear it out in the forest under the moon was too much for Bilbo. Even magic rings are not much use against wolves—especially against the evil packs that lived under the shadow of the goblin-infested mountains, over the Edge of the Wild on the borders of the unknown. Wolves of that sort smell keener than goblins, and do not need to see you to catch you!

"What shall we do, what shall we do!" he cried. "Escaping goblins to be caught by wolves!" he said, and it became a proverb, though we now say "out of the frying-pan into the fire" in the same sort of uncomfortable situations.

"Up the trees quick!" cried Gandalf; and they ran to the trees at the edge of the glade, hunting for those that had branches fairly low, or were slender enough to swarm up. They found them as quick as ever they could, you can guess; and up they went as high as ever they could trust the branches. You would have laughed (from a safe distance), if you had seen the dwarves sitting up in the trees with their beards dangling down, like old gentlemen gone cracked and playing at being boys. Fili and Kili were at the top of a tall larch like an enormous Christmas tree. Dori, Nori, Ori, Oin, and Gloin were more comfortable in a huge pine with regular branches sticking out at intervals like the spokes of a wheel. Bifur, Bofur, Bombur, and Thorin were in another. Dwalin and Balin had swarmed up a tall slender fir with few branches and were trying to find a place to sit in the greenery of the topmost boughs. Gandalf, who was a good deal taller than the others, had found a tree into which they could not climb, a large pine standing at the very edge of the glade. He was quite hidden in its boughs, but you could see his eyes gleaming in the moon as he peeped out.

And Bilbo? He could not get into any tree, and was scuttling about from trunk to trunk, like a rabbit that has lost its hole and has a dog after it.

"You've left the burglar behind again!" said Nori to Dori looking down.

"I can't be always carrying burglars on my back," said Dori, "down tunnels and up trees! What do you think I am? A porter?"

"He'll be eaten if we don't do something," said Thorin, for there were howls all round them now, getting nearer and nearer. "Dori!" he called, for Dori was lowest down in the easiest tree, "be quick, and give Mr. Baggins a hand up!"

Dori was really a decent fellow in spite of his grumbling. Poor Bilbo could not reach his hand even when he climbed down to the bottom branch and hung his arm down as far as ever he could. So Dori actually climbed out of the tree and let Bilbo scramble up and stand on his back.

Just at that moment the wolves trotted howling into the clearing. All of a sudden there were hundreds of eyes looking at them. Still Dori did not let Bilbo down. He waited till he had clambered off his shoulders into the branches, and then he jumped for the branches himself. Only just in time! A wolf snapped at his cloak as he swung up, and nearly got him. In a minute there was a whole pack of them yelping all round the tree and leaping up at the trunk, with eyes blazing and tongues hanging out.

But even the wild Wargs (for so the evil wolves over the Edge of the Wild were named) cannot climb trees. For a time they were safe. Luckily it was warm and not windy. Trees are not very comfortable to sit in for long at any time; but in the cold and the wind, with wolves all round below waiting for you, they can be perfectly miserable places.

This glade in the ring of trees was evidently a meeting-place of the wolves. More and more kept coming in. They left guards at the foot of the tree in which Dori and Bilbo were, and then went snuffling about till they had smelt out every tree that had anyone in it. These they guarded too, while all the rest (hundreds and hundreds it seemed) went and sat in a great circle in the glade; and in the middle of the circle was a great grey wolf. He spoke to them in the dreadful language of the Wargs. Gandalf understood it. Bilbo did not, but it sounded terrible to him, and as if all their talk was about cruel and wicked things, as it was. Every now and then all the Wargs in the circle would answer their grey chief all together, and their dreadful clamour almost made the hobbit fall out of his pine-tree.

I will tell you what Gandalf heard, though Bilbo did not understand it. The Wargs and the goblins often helped one another in wicked deeds. Goblins do not usually venture very far from their mountains, unless they are driven out and are looking for new homes, or are marching to war (which I am glad to say has not happened for a long while). But in those days they sometimes used to go on raids, especially to get food or slaves to work for them. Then they often got the Wargs to help and shared the plunder with them. Sometimes they rode on wolves like men do on horses. Now it seemed that a great goblin-raid had been planned for that very night. The Wargs had come to meet the goblins and the goblins were late. The reason, no doubt, was the death of the Great Goblin, and all the excitement caused by the dwarves and Bilbo and the wizard, for whom they were probably still hunting.

In spite of the dangers of this far land bold men had of late been making their way back into it from the South, cutting down trees, and building themselves places to live in among the more pleasant woods in the valleys and along the river-shores. There were many of them, and they were brave and well-armed, and even the Wargs dared not attack them if there were many together, or in the bright day. But now they had planned with the goblins' help to come by night upon some of the villages nearest the mountains. If their plan had been carried out, there would have been none left there next day; all would have been killed except the few the goblins kept from the wolves and carried back as prisoners to their caves.

This was dreadful talk to listen to, not only because of the brave woodmen and their wives and children, but also because of the danger which now threatened Gandalf and his friends. The Wargs were angry and puzzled at finding them here in their very meeting-place. They thought they were friends of the woodmen, and were come to spy on them, and would take news of their plans down into the valleys, and then the goblins and the wolves would have to fight a terrible battle instead of capturing prisoners and devouring people waked suddenly from their sleep. So the Wargs had no intention of going away and letting the people up the trees escape, at any rate not until morning. And long before that, they said, goblin soldiers would be coming down from the mountains; and goblins can climb trees, or cut them down.

Now you can understand why Gandalf, listening to their growling and yelping, began to be dreadfully afraid, wizard though he was, and to feel that they were in a very bad place, and had not yet escaped at all. All the same he was not going to let them have it all their own way, though he could not do very much stuck up in a tall tree with wolves all round on the ground below. He gathered the huge pine-cones from the branches of the tree. Then he set one alight with bright blue fire, and threw it whizzing down among the circle of the wolves. It struck one on the back, and immediately his shaggy coat caught fire, and he was leaping to and fro yelping horribly. Then another came and another, one in blue flames, one in red, another in green. They burst on the ground in the middle of the circle and went off in coloured sparks and smoke. A specially large one hit the chief wolf on the nose, and he leaped in the air ten feet, and then rushed round and round the circle biting and snapping even at the other wolves in his anger and fright.

The dwarves and Bilbo shouted and cheered. The rage of the wolves was terrible to see, and the commotion they made filled all the forest. Wolves are afraid of fire at all times, but this was a most horrible and uncanny fire. If a spark got in their coats it stuck and burned into them, and unless they rolled over quick they were soon all in flames. Very soon all about the glade wolves were rolling over and over to put out the sparks on their backs, while those that were burning were running about howling and setting others alight, till their own friends chased them away and they fled off down the slopes crying and yammering and looking for water.

"What is all this uproar in the forest tonight?" said the Lord of the Eagles. He was sitting, black in the moonlight, on the top of a lonely pinnacle of rock at the eastern edge of the mountains. "I hear wolves' voices! Are the goblins at mischief in the woods?"

He swept up into the air, and immediately two of his guards from the rocks at either hand leaped up to follow him. They circled up in the sky and looked down upon the ring of the Wargs, a tiny spot far far below. But eagles have keen eyes and can see small things at a great distance. The Lord of the Eagles of the Misty Mountains had eyes that could look at the sun unblinking, and could see a rabbit moving on the ground a mile below even in the moonlight. So though he could not see the people in the trees, he could make out the commotion among the wolves and see the tiny flashes of fire, and hear the howling and yelping come up faint from far beneath him. Also he could see the glint of the moon on goblin spears and helmets, as long lines of the wicked folk crept down the hillsides from their gate and wound into the wood.

Eagles are not kindly birds. Some are cowardly and cruel. But the ancient race of the northern mountains were the greatest of all birds; they were proud and strong and noble-hearted. They did not love goblins, or fear them. When they took any notice of them at all (which was seldom, for they did not eat such creatures), they swooped on them and drove them shrieking back to their caves, and stopped whatever wickedness they were doing. The goblins hated the eagles and feared them, but could not reach their lofty seats, or drive them from the mountains.

Tonight the Lord of the Eagles was filled with curiosity to know what was afoot; so he summoned many other eagles to him, and they flew away from the mountains, and slowly circling ever round and round they came down, down, down towards the ring of the wolves and the meeting-place of the goblins.

A very good thing too! Dreadful things had been going on down there. The wolves that had caught fire and fled into the forest had set it alight in several places. It was high summer, and on this eastern side of the mountains there had been little rain for some time. Yellowing bracken, fallen branches, deep-piled pine-needles, and here and there dead trees, were soon in flames. All round the clearing of the Wargs fire was leaping. But the wolf-guards did not leave the trees. Maddened and angry they were leaping and howling round the trunks, and cursing the dwarves in their horrible language, with their tongues hanging out, and their eyes shining as red and fierce as the flames.

Then suddenly goblins came running up yelling. They thought a battle with the woodmen was going on; but they soon learned what had really happened. Some of them actually sat down and laughed. Others waved their spears and clashed the shafts against their shields. Goblins are not afraid of fire, and they soon had a plan which seemed to them most amusing.

Some got all the wolves together in a pack. Some stacked fern and brushwood round the tree-trunks. Others rushed round and stamped and beat, and beat and stamped, until nearly all the flames were put out—but they did not put out the fire nearest to the trees where the dwarves were. That fire they fed with leaves and dead branches and bracken. Soon they had a ring of smoke and flame all round the dwarves, a ring which they kept from spreading outwards; but it closed slowly in, till the running fire was licking the fuel piled under the trees. Smoke was in Bilbo's eyes, he could feel the heat of the flames; and through the reek he could see the goblins dancing round and round in a circle like people round a midsummer bonfire. Outside the ring of dancing warriors with spears and axes stood the wolves at a respectful distance, watching and waiting.

He could hear the goblins beginning a horrible song:

> Fifteen birds in five fir-trees,
> their feathers were fanned in a fiery breeze!
> But, funny little birds, they had no wings!
> O what shall we do with the funny little things?
> Roast 'em alive, or stew them in a pot;
> fry them, boil them and eat them hot?

Then they stopped and shouted out: "Fly away little birds! Fly away if you can! Come down little birds, or you will get roasted in your nests! Sing, sing little birds! Why don't you sing?"

"Go away! little boys!" shouted Gandalf in answer. "It isn't bird-nesting time. Also naughty little boys that play with fire get punished." He said it to make them angry, and to show them he was not frightened of them—though of course he was, wizard though he was. But they took no notice, and they went on singing.

> Burn, burn tree and fern!
> Shrivel and scorch! A fizzling torch
> To light the night for our delight,
>   Ya hey!

Bake and toast 'em, fry and roast 'em!
till beards blaze, and eyes glaze;
till hair smells and skins crack,
fat melts, and bones black
   in cinders lie
   beneath the sky!
   So dwarves shall die,
and light the night for our delight,
   Ya hey!
   Ya-harri-hey!
   Ya hoy!

And with that *Ya hoy*! the flames were under Gandalf's tree. In a moment it spread to the others. The bark caught fire, the lower branches cracked.

Then Gandalf climbed to the top of his tree. The sudden splendour flashed from his wand like lightning, as he got ready to spring down from on high right among the spears of the goblins. That would have been the end of him, though he would probably have killed many of them as he came hurtling down like a thunderbolt. But he never leaped.

Just at that moment the Lord of the Eagles swept down from above, seized him in his talons, and was gone.

There was a howl of anger and surprise from the goblins. Loud cried the Lord of the Eagles, to whom Gandalf had now spoken. Back swept the great birds that were with him, and down they came like huge black shadows. The wolves yammered and gnashed their teeth; the goblins yelled and stamped with rage, and flung their heavy spears in the air in vain. Over them swooped the eagles; the dark rush of their beating wings smote them to the floor or drove them far away; their talons tore at goblin faces. Other birds flew to the tree-tops and seized the dwarves, who were scrambling up now as far as they ever dared to go.

Poor little Bilbo was very nearly left behind again! He just managed to catch hold of Dori's legs, as Dori was borne off last of all; and up they went together above the tumult and the burning, Bilbo swinging in the air with his arms nearly breaking.

Now far below the goblins and the wolves were scattering far and wide in the woods. A few eagles were still circling and sweeping above the battle-ground. The flames about the trees sprang suddenly up above the highest branches. They went up in crackling fire. There was a sudden flurry of sparks and smoke. Bilbo had escaped only just in time!

Soon the light of the burning was faint below, a red twinkle on the black floor; and they were high up in the sky, rising all the time in strong sweeping circles. Bilbo never forgot that flight, clinging onto Dori's ankles. He moaned "my arms, my arms!"; but Dori groaned "my poor legs, my poor legs!"

At the best of times heights made Bilbo giddy. He used to turn queer if he looked over the edge of quite a little cliff; and he had never liked ladders, let alone trees (never having had to escape from wolves before). So you can imagine how his head swam now, when he looked down between his dangling toes and saw the dark lands opening wide underneath him, touched here and there with the light of the moon on a hill-side rock or a stream in the plains.

The pale peaks of the mountains were coming nearer, moonlit spikes of rock sticking out of black shadows. Summer or not, it seemed very cold. He shut his eyes and wondered if he could hold on any longer. Then he imagined what would happen if he did not. He felt sick.

The flight ended only just in time for him, just before his arms gave way. He loosed Dori's ankles with a gasp and fell onto the rough platform of an eagle's eyrie. There he lay without speaking, and his thoughts were a mixture of surprise at being saved from the fire, and fear lest he fall off that narrow place into the deep shadows on either side. He was feeling very queer indeed in his head by this time after the dreadful adventures of the last three days with next to nothing to eat, and he found himself saying aloud: "Now I know what a piece of bacon feels like when it is suddenly picked out of the pan on a fork and put back on the shelf!"

"No you don't!" he heard Dori answering, "because the bacon knows that it will get back in the pan sooner or later; and it is to be hoped we shan't. Also eagles aren't forks!"

"O no! Not a bit like storks—forks, I mean," said Bilbo sitting up and looking anxiously at the eagle who was perched close by. He wondered what other nonsense he had been saying, and if the eagle would think it rude. You ought not to be rude to an eagle, when you are only the size of a hobbit, and are up in his eyrie at night!

The eagle only sharpened his beak on a stone and trimmed his feathers and took no notice.

Soon another eagle flew up. "The Lord of the

Eagles bids you to bring your prisoners to the Great Shelf," he cried and was off again. The other seized Dori in his claws and flew away with him into the night leaving Bilbo all alone. He had just strength to wonder what the messenger had meant by 'prisoners,' and to begin to think of being torn up for supper like a rabbit, when his own turn came.

The eagle came back, seized him in his talons by the back of his coat, and swooped off. This time he flew only a short way. Very soon Bilbo was laid down, trembling with fear, on a wide shelf of rock on the mountain-side. There was no path down on to it save by flying; and no path down off it except by jumping over a precipice. There he found all the others sitting with their backs to the mountain wall. The Lord of the Eagles also was there and was speaking to Gandalf.

It seemed that Bilbo was not going to be eaten after all. The wizard and the eagle-lord appeared to know one another slightly, and even to be on friendly terms. As a matter of fact Gandalf, who had often been in the mountains, had once rendered a service to the eagles and healed their lord from an arrow-wound. So you see 'prisoners' had meant 'prisoners rescued from the goblins' only, and not captives of the eagles. As Bilbo listened to the talk of Gandalf he realized that at last they were going to escape really and truly from the dreadful mountains. He was discussing plans with the Great Eagle for carrying the dwarves and himself and Bilbo far away and setting them down well on their journey across the plains below.

The Lord of the Eagles would not take them any-where near where men lived. "They would shoot at

The Misty Mountains looking West from the Eyrie towards Goblin Gate us with their great bows of yew," he said, "for they would think we were after their sheep. And at other times they would be right. No! we are glad to cheat the goblins of their sport, and glad to repay our thanks to you, but we will not risk ourselves for dwarves in the southward plains."

"Very well," said Gandalf. "Take us where and as far as you will! We are already deeply obliged to you. But in the meantime we are famished with hunger."

"I am nearly dead of it," said Bilbo in a weak little voice that nobody heard.

"That can perhaps be mended," said the Lord of the Eagles.

Later on you might have seen a bright fire on the shelf of rock and the figures of the dwarves round it cooking and making a fine roasting smell. The eagles had brought up dry boughs for fuel, and they had brought rabbits, hares, and a small sheep. The dwarves managed all the preparations. Bilbo was too weak to help, and anyway he was not much good at skinning rabbits or cutting up meat, being used to having it delivered by the butcher all ready to cook. Gandalf, too, was lying down after doing his part in setting the fire going, since Oin and Gloin had lost their tinder-boxes. (Dwarves have never taken to matches even yet.)

So ended the adventures of the Misty Mountains. Soon Bilbo's stomach was feeling full and comfortable again, and he felt he could sleep contentedly, though really he would have liked a loaf and butter better than bits of meat toasted on sticks. He slept curled up on the hard rock more soundly than ever he had done on his feather-bed in his own little hole at home. But all night he dreamed of his own house and wandered in his sleep into all his different rooms looking for something that he could not find nor remember what it looked like.

Chapter VII

QUEER LODGINGS

The next morning Bilbo woke up with the early sun in his eyes. He jumped up to look at the time and to go and put his kettle on—and found he was not home at all. So he sat down and wished in vain for a wash and a brush. He did not get either, nor tea nor toast nor bacon for his breakfast, only cold mutton and rabbit. And after that he had to get ready for a fresh start.

This time he was allowed to climb on to an eagle's back and cling between his wings. The air rushed over him and he shut his eyes. The dwarves were crying farewells and promising to repay the Lord of the Eagles if ever they could, as off rose fifteen great birds from the mountain's side. The sun was still close to the eastern edge of things. The morning was cool, and mists were in the valleys and hollows and twined here and there about the peaks and pinnacles of the hills. Bilbo opened an eye to peep and saw that the birds were already high up and the world was far away, and the mountains were falling back behind them into the distance. He shut his eyes again and held on tighter.

"Don't pinch!" said his eagle. "You need not be frightened like a rabbit, even if you look rather like one. It is a fair morning with little wind. What is finer than flying?"

Bilbo would have liked to say: "A warm bath and late breakfast on the lawn afterwards;" but he thought it better to say nothing at all, and to let go his clutch just a tiny bit.

After a good while the eagles must have seen the point they were making for, even from their great height, for they began to go down circling round in great spirals. They did this for a long while, and at last the hobbit opened his eyes again. The earth was much nearer, and below them were trees that looked like oaks and elms, and wide grass lands, and a river running through it all. But cropping out of the ground, right in the path of the stream which looped itself about it, was a great rock, almost a hill of stone, like a last outpost of the distant mountains, or a huge piece cast miles into the plain by some giant among giants.

Quickly now to the top of this rock the eagles swooped one by one and set down their passengers.

"Farewell!" they cried, "wherever you fare, till your eyries receive you at the journey's end!" That is the polite thing to say among eagles.

"May the wind under your wings bear you where the sun sails and the moon walks," answered Gandalf, who knew the correct reply.

And so they parted. And though the Lord of the Eagles became in after days the King of All Birds and wore a golden crown, and his fifteen chieftains golden collars (made of the gold that the dwarves gave them), Bilbo never saw them again—except high and far off in the battle of Five Armies. But as that comes in at the end of this tale we will say no more about it just now.

There was a flat space on the top of the hill of stone and a well worn path with many steps leading down it to the river, across which a ford of huge flat stones led to the grass-land beyond the stream. There was a little cave (a wholesome one with a pebbly floor) at the foot of the steps and near the end of the stony ford. Here the party gathered and discussed what was to be done.

"I always meant to see you all safe (if possible) over the mountains," said the wizard, "and now by good management *and* good luck I have done it. Indeed we are now a good deal further east than I ever meant to come with you, for after all this is not my adventure. I may look in on it again before it is all over, but in the meanwhile I have some other pressing business to attend to."

The dwarves groaned and looked most distressed, and Bilbo wept. They had begun to think Gandalf was going to come all the way and would always be there to help them out of difficulties. "I am not going to disappear this very instant," said he. "I can give you a day or two more. Probably I can help you out of your present plight, and I need a little help myself. We have no food, and no baggage, and no ponies to ride; and you don't know where you are. Now I can tell you that. You are still some miles north of the path which we should have been following, if we had not left the mountain pass in a hurry. Very few people live in these parts, unless they have come here since I was last down this way, which is some years ago. But there is *somebody* that I know of, who lives not far away. That Somebody made the steps on the great rock—the Carrock I believe he calls it. He does not come here often, certainly not in the daytime, and it is no good waiting for him. In fact it would be very dangerous. We must go and find him; and if all goes well at our meeting, I think I shall be off and wish you like the eagles 'farewell wherever you fare!'"

They begged him not to leave them. They offered him dragon-gold and silver and jewels, but he would not change his mind. "We shall see, we shall see!" he said, "and I think I have earned already some of your dragon-gold—when you have got it."

After that they stopped pleading. Then they took off their clothes and bathed in the river, which was shallow and clear and stony at the ford. When they had dried in the sun, which was now strong and warm, they were refreshed, if still sore and a little hungry. Soon they crossed the ford (carrying the hobbit), and then began to march through the long green grass and down the lines of the wide-armed oaks and the tall elms.

"And why is it called the Carrock?" asked Bilbo as he went along at the wizard's side.

"He called it the Carrock, because carrock is his word for it. He calls things like that carrocks, and this one is *the* Carrock because it is the only one near his home and he knows it well."

"Who calls it? Who knows it?"

"The Somebody I spoke of—a very great person. You must all be very polite when I introduce you. I shall introduce you slowly, two by two, I think; and you *must* be careful not to annoy him, or heaven knows what will happen. He can be appalling when he is angry, though he is kind enough if humoured. Still I warn you he gets angry easily."

The dwarves all gathered round when they heard the wizard talking like this to Bilbo. "Is that the person you are taking us to now?" they asked. "Couldn't you find someone more easy-tempered? Hadn't you better explain it all a bit clearer?"—and so on.

"Yes it certainly is! No I could not! And I was explaining very carefully," answered the wizard crossly. "If you must know more, his name is Beorn. He is very strong, and he is a skin-changer."

"What! a furrier, a man that calls rabbits conies, when he doesn't turn their skins into squirrels?" asked Bilbo.

"Good gracious heavens, no, no, NO, NO!" said Gandalf. "Don't be a fool Mr. Baggins if you can help it; and in the name of all wonder don't mention the word furrier again as long as you are within a hundred miles of his house, nor rug, cape, tippet, muff, nor any other such unfortunate word! He is a skin-changer. He changes his skin: sometimes he is a huge black bear, sometimes he is a great strong black-haired man with huge arms and a great beard. I cannot tell you much more, though that ought to be enough. Some say that he is a bear descended from the great and ancient bears of the mountains that lived there before the giants came. Others say that he is a man descended from the first men who lived before Smaug or the other dragons came into this part of the world, and before the goblins came into the hills out of the North. I cannot say, though I fancy the last is the true tale. He is not the sort of person to ask questions of.

"At any rate he is under no enchantment but his own. He lives in an oak-wood and has a great wooden house; and as a man he keeps cattle and horses which are nearly as marvellous as himself. They work for him and talk to him. He does not eat them; neither does he hunt or eat wild animals. He keeps hives and hives of great fierce bees, and lives most on cream and honey. As a bear he ranges far and wide. I once saw him sitting all alone on the top of the Carrock at night watching the moon sinking towards the Misty Mountains, and I heard him growl in the tongue of bears: 'The day will come when they will perish and I shall go back!' That is why I believe he once came from the mountains himself."

Bilbo and the dwarves had now plenty to think about, and they asked no more questions. They still had a long way to walk before them. Up slope and down dale they plodded. It grew very hot. Sometimes they rested under the trees, and then Bilbo felt so hungry that he would have eaten acorns, if any had been ripe enough yet to have fallen to the ground.

It was the middle of the afternoon before they noticed that great patches of flowers had begun to spring up, all the same kinds growing together as if they had been planted. Especially there was clover, waving patches of cockscomb clover, and purple clover, and wide stretches of short white sweet honey-smelling clover. There was a buzzing and a whirring and a droning in the air. Bees were busy everywhere. And such bees! Bilbo had never seen anything like them.

"If one was to sting me," he thought, "I should swell up as big again as I am!"

They were bigger than hornets. The drones were bigger than your thumb, a good deal, and the bands of yellow on their deep black bodies shone like fiery gold.

"We are getting near," said Gandalf. "We are on the edge of his bee-pastures."

After a while they came to a belt of tall and very ancient oaks, and beyond these to a high thorn-hedge through which you could neither see nor scramble.

"You had better wait here," said the wizard to the dwarves; "and when I call or whistle begin to come after me—you will see the way I go—but only in pairs, mind, about five minutes between each pair of you. Bombur is fattest and will do for two, he had better come alone and last. Come on Mr. Baggins! There is a gate somewhere round this way." And with that he went off along the hedge taking the frightened hobbit with him.

They soon came to a wooden gate, high and broad, beyond which they could see gardens and a cluster of low wooden buildings, some thatched and made of unshaped logs: barns, stables, sheds, and a long low wooden house. Inside on the southward side of the great hedge were rows and rows of hives with bell-shaped tops made of straw. The noise of the giant bees flying to and fro and crawling in and out filled all the air.

The wizard and the hobbit pushed open the heavy creaking gate and went down a wide track towards the house. Some horses, very sleek and well-groomed, trotted up across the grass and looked at them intently with very intelligent faces; then off they galloped to the buildings.

"They have gone to tell him of the arrival of strangers," said Gandalf.

Soon they reached a courtyard, three walls of which were formed by the wooden house and its two long wings. In the middle there was lying a great oak-trunk with many lopped branches beside it. Standing near was a huge man with a thick black beard and hair, and great bare arms and legs with knotted muscles. He was clothed in a tunic of wool down to his knees, and was leaning on a large axe. The horses were standing by him with their noses at his shoulder.

"Ugh! here they are!" he said to the horses. "They don't look dangerous. You can be off!" He laughed a great rolling laugh, put down his axe and came forward.

"Who are you and what do you want?" he asked gruffly, standing in front of them and towering tall above Gandalf. As for Bilbo he could easily have trotted through his legs without ducking his head to miss the fringe of the man's brown tunic.

"I am Gandalf," said the wizard.

"Never heard of him," growled the man. "And what's this little fellow?" he said, stooping down to frown at the hobbit with his bushy black eyebrows.

"That is Mr. Baggins, a hobbit of good family and unimpeachable reputation," said Gandalf. Bilbo bowed. He had no hat to take off, and was painfully conscious of his many missing buttons. "I am a wizard," continued Gandalf. "I have heard of you, if you have not heard of me; but perhaps you have heard of my good cousin Radagast who lives near the Southern borders of Mirkwood?"

"Yes; not a bad fellow as wizards go, I believe. I used to see him now and again," said Beorn. "Well, now I know who you are, or who you say you are. What do you want?"

"To tell you the truth, we have lost our luggage and nearly lost our way, and are rather in need of help, or at least of advice. I may say we have had rather a bad time with goblins in the mountains."

"Goblins?" said the big man less gruffly. "O ho, so you've been having trouble with *them* have you? What did you go near them for?"

"We did not mean to. They surprised us at night in a pass which we had to cross; we were coming out of the Lands over West into these countries—it is a long tale."

"Then you had better come inside and tell me some of it, if it won't take all day," said the man leading the way through a dark door that opened out of the courtyard into the house.

Following him they found themselves in a wide hall with a fire-place in the middle. Though it was summer there was a wood-fire burning and the smoke was rising to the blackened rafters in search of the way out through an opening in the roof. They passed through this dim hall, lit only by the fire and the hole above it, and came through another smaller door into a sort of veranda propped on wooden posts made of single tree-trunks. It faced south and was still warm and filled with the light of the westering sun which slanted into it, and

fell golden on the garden full of flowers that came right up to the steps.

Here they sat on wooden benches while Gandalf began his tale, and Bilbo swung his dangling legs and looked at the flowers in the garden, wondering what their names could be, as he had never seen half of them before.

"I was coming over the mountains with a friend or two..." said the wizard.

"Or two? I can only see one, and a little one at that," said Beorn.

"Well to tell you the truth, I did not like to bother you with a lot of us, until I found out if you were busy. I will give a call, if I may."

"Go on, call away!"

So Gandalf gave a long shrill whistle, and presently Thorin and Dori came round the house by the garden path and stood bowing low before them.

"One or three you meant, I see!" said Beorn. "But these aren't hobbits, they are dwarves!"

"Thorin Oakenshield, at your service! Dori at your service!" said the two dwarves bowing again.

"I don't need your service, thank you," said Beorn, "but I expect you need mine. I am not over fond of dwarves; but if it is true you are Thorin (son of Thrain, son of Thror, I believe), and that your companion is respectable, and that you are enemies of goblins and are not up to any mischief in my lands—what are you up to, by the way?"

"They are on their way to visit the land of their fathers, away east beyond Mirkwood," put in Gandalf, "and it is entirely an accident that we are in your lands at all. We were crossing by the High Pass that should have brought us to the road that lies to the south of your country, when we were attacked by the evil goblins—as I was about to tell you."

"Go on telling, then!" said Beorn, who was never very polite.

"There was a terrible storm; the stone-giants were out hurling rocks, and at the head of the pass we took refuge in a cave, the hobbit and I and several of our companions..."

"Do you call two several?"

"Well, no. As a matter of fact there were more than two."

"Where are they? Killed, eaten, gone home?"

"Well, no. They don't seem all to have come when I whistled. Shy, I expect. You see, we are very much afraid that we are rather a lot for you to entertain."

"Go on, whistle again! I am in for a party, it seems, and one or two more won't make much difference," growled Beorn.

Gandalf whistled again; but Nori and Ori were there almost before he had stopped, for, if you remember, Gandalf had told them to come in pairs every five minutes.

"Hullo!" said Beorn. "You came pretty quick—where were you hiding? Come on my jack-in-the-boxes!"

"Nori at your service, Ori at..." they began; but Beorn interrupted them.

"Thank you! When I want your help I will ask for it. Sit down, and let's get on with this tale, or it will be supper-time before it is ended."

"As soon as we were asleep," went on Gandalf, "a crack at the back of the cave opened; goblins came out and grabbed the hobbit and the dwarves and our troop of ponies—"

"Troop of ponies? What were you—a travelling circus? Or were you carrying lots of goods? Or do you always call six a troop?"

"O no! As a matter of fact there were more than six ponies, for there were more than six of us—and well, here are two more!" Just at that moment Balin and Dwalin appeared and bowed so low that their beards swept the stone floor. The big man was frowning at first, but they did their best to be frightfully polite, and kept on nodding and bending and bowing and waving their hoods before their knees (in proper dwarf-fashion), till he stopped frowning and burst into a chuckling laugh: they looked so comical.

"Troop, was right," he said. "A fine comic one. Come in my merry men, and what are *your* names? I don't want your service just now, only your names; and then sit down and stop wagging!"

"Balin and Dwalin," they said not daring to be offended, and sat flop on the floor looking rather surprised.

"Now go on again!" said Beorn to the wizard.

"Where was I? O yes—I was *not* grabbed. I killed a goblin or two with a flash—"

"Good!" growled Beorn. "It is some good being a wizard, then."

"—and slipped inside the crack before it closed. I followed down into the main hall, which was crowded with goblins. The Great Goblin was there with thirty or forty armed guards. I thought to myself 'even if they were not all chained together, what can a dozen do against so many?'"

"A dozen! That's the first time I've heard eight called a dozen. Or have you still got some more jacks that haven't yet come out of their boxes?"

"Well, yes, there seem to be a couple more here now—Fili and Kili, I believe," said Gandalf, as these two now appeared and stood smiling and bowing.

"That's enough!" said Beorn. "Sit down and be quiet! Now go on, Gandalf!"

So Gandalf went on with the tale, until he came to the fight in the dark, the discovery of the lower gate, and their horror when they found that Mr. Baggins had been mislaid. "We counted ourselves and found that there was no hobbit. There were only fourteen of us left!"

"Fourteen! That's the first time I've heard one from ten leave fourteen. You mean nine, or else you haven't told me yet all the names of your party."

"Well, of course you haven't seen Oin and Gloin yet. And, bless me! here they are. I hope you will forgive them for bothering you."

"O let 'em all come! Hurry up! Come along, you two, and sit down! But look here, Gandalf, even now we have only got yourself and ten dwarves and the hobbit that was lost. That only makes eleven (plus one mislaid) and not fourteen, unless wizards count differently to other people. But now please get on with the tale." Beorn did not show it more than he could help, but really he had begun to get very interested. You see, in the old days he had known the very part of the mountains that Gandalf was describing. He nodded and he growled, when he heard of the hobbit's reappearance and of their scramble down the stone-slide and of the wolf-ring in the woods.

When Gandalf came to their climbing into trees with the wolves all underneath, he got up and strode about and muttered: "I wish I had been there! I would have given them more than fireworks!"

"Well," said Gandalf very glad to see that his tale was making a good impression, "I did the best I could. There we were with the wolves going mad underneath us and the forest beginning to blaze in places, when the goblins came down from the hills and discovered us. They yelled with delight and sang songs making fun of us. *Fifteen birds in five fir-trees ...*"

"Good heavens!" growled Beorn. "Don't pretend that goblins can't count. They can. Twelve isn't fifteen and they know it."

"And so do I. There were Bifur and Bofur as well. I haven't ventured to introduce them before, but here they are."

In came Bifur and Bofur. "And me!" gasped Bombur puffing up behind. He was fat, and also angry at being left till last. He refused to wait five minutes, and followed immediately after the other two.

"Well, now there *are* fifteen of you; and since goblins can count, I suppose that is all that there were up the trees. Now perhaps we can finish this story without any more interruptions." Mr. Baggins saw then how clever Gandalf had been. The interruptions had really made Beorn more interested in the story, and the story had kept him from sending the dwarves off at once like suspicious beggars. He never invited people into his house, if he could help it. He had very few friends and they lived a good way away; and he never invited more than a couple of these to his house at a time. Now he had got fifteen strangers sitting in his porch!

By the time the wizard had finished his tale and had told of the eagles' rescue and of how they had all been brought to the Carrock, the sun had fallen behind the peaks of the Misty Mountains and the shadows were long in Beorn's garden.

"A very good tale!" said he. "The best I have heard for a long while. If all beggars could tell such a good one, they might find me kinder. You may be making it all up, of course, but you deserve a supper for the story all the same. Let's have something to eat!"

"Yes please!" they all said together. "Thank you very much!"

Inside the hall it was now quite dark. Beorn clapped his hands, and in trotted four beautiful white ponies and several large long-bodied grey dogs. Beorn said something to them in a queer language like animal noises turned into talk. They went out again and soon came back carrying torches in their mouths, which they lit at the fire and stuck in low brackets on the pillars of the hall about the central hearth. The dogs could stand on their hind-legs when they wished, and carry things with their fore-feet. Quickly they got out boards and trestles from the side walls and set them up near the fire.

Then baa—baa—baa! was heard, and in came some snow-white sheep led by a large coal-black ram. One bore a white cloth embroidered at the edges with figures of animals; others bore on their broad backs trays with bowls and platters and knives and wooden spoons, which the dogs took and quickly laid

on the trestle-tables. These were very low, low
enough even for Bilbo to sit at comfortably. Beside
them a pony pushed two low-seated benches with
wide rush-bottoms and little short thick legs for
Gandalf and Thorin, while at the far end he put
Beorn's big black chair of the same sort (in which he
sat with his great legs stuck far out under the table).
These were all the chairs he had in his hall, and he
probably had them low like the tables for the conven-
ience of the wonderful animals that waited on him.
What did the rest sit on? They were not forgotten.
The other ponies came in rolling round drum-shaped
sections of logs, smoothed and polished, and low
enough even for Bilbo; so soon they were all seated
at Beorn's table, and the hall had not seen such a
gathering for many a year.

There they had a supper, or a dinner, such as they
had not had since they left the Last Homely House
in the West and said good-bye to Elrond. The light
of the torches and the fire flickered about them, and
on the table were two tall red beeswax candles. All
the time they ate, Beorn in his deep rolling voice told
tales of the wild lands on this side of the mountains,
and especially of the dark and dangerous wood, that
lay outstretched far to North and South a day's ride
before them, barring their way to the East, the terrible forest of Mirkwood.

The dwarves listened and shook their beards, for
they knew that they must soon venture into that
forest and that after the mountains it was the worst
of the perils they had to pass before they came to the
dragon's stronghold. When dinner was over they
began to tell tales of their own, but Beorn seemed to

be growing drowsy and paid little heed to them. They spoke most of gold and silver and jewels and the making of things by smith-craft, and Beorn did not appear to care for such things: there were no things of gold or silver in his hall, and few save the knives were made of metal at all.

They sat long at the table with their wooden drinking-bowls filled with mead. The dark night came on outside. The fires in the middle of the hall were built with fresh logs and the torches were put out, and still they sat in the light of the dancing flames with the pillars of the house standing tall behind them, and dark at the top like trees of the forest. Whether it was magic or not, it seemed to Bilbo that he heard a sound like wind in the branches stirring in the rafters, and the hoot of owls. Soon he began to nod with sleep and the voices seemed to grow far away, until he woke with a start.

The great door had creaked and slammed. Beorn was gone. The dwarves were sitting cross-legged on the floor round the fire, and presently they began to sing. Some of the verses were like this, but there were many more, and their singing went on for a long while:

> The wind was on the withered heath,
> but in the forest stirred no leaf:
> there shadows lay by night and day,
> and dark things silent crept beneath.

> The wind came down from mountains cold,
> and like a tide it roared and rolled;
> the branches groaned, the forest moaned,
> and leaves were laid upon the mould.

The wind went on from West to East;
all movement in the forest ceased,
but shrill and harsh across the marsh
its whistling voices were released.

The grasses hissed, their tassels bent,
the reeds were rattling—on it went
o'er shaken pool under heavens cool
where racing clouds were torn and rent.

It passed the lonely Mountain bare
and swept above the dragon's lair:
there black and dark lay boulders stark
and flying smoke was in the air.

It left the world and took its flight
over the wide seas of the night.
The moon set sail upon the gale,
and stars were fanned to leaping light.

Bilbo began to nod again. Suddenly up stood Gandalf.

"It is time for us to sleep," he said, "—for us, but not I think for Beorn. In this hall we can rest sound and safe, but I warn you all not to forget what Beorn said before he left us: you must not stray outside until the sun is up, on your peril."

Bilbo found that beds had already been laid at the side of the hall, on a sort of raised platform between the pillars and the outer wall. For him there was a little mattress of straw and woollen blankets. He snuggled into them very gladly, summertime though it was. The fire burned low and he fell asleep. Yet in the night he woke: the fire had now sunk to a few embers; the dwarves and Gandalf were all asleep, to judge by their breathing; a splash of white on the floor came from the high moon, which was peering down through the smoke-hole in the roof.

There was a growling sound outside, and a noise as of some great animal scuffling at the door. Bilbo wondered what it was, and whether it could be Beorn in enchanted shape, and if he would come in as a bear and kill them. He dived under the blankets and hid his head, and fell asleep again at last in spite of his fears.

It was full morning when he awoke. One of the dwarves had fallen over him in the shadows where he lay, and had rolled down with a bump from the platform on to the floor. It was Bofur, and he was grumbling about it, when Bilbo opened his eyes.

"Get up lazybones," he said, "or there will be no breakfast left for you."

Up jumped Bilbo. "Breakfast!" he cried. "Where is breakfast?"

"Mostly inside us," answered the other dwarves who were moving about the hall; "but what is left is out on the veranda. We have been about looking for Beorn ever since the sun got up; but there is no sign of him anywhere, though we found breakfast laid as soon as we went out."

"Where is Gandalf?" asked Bilbo, moving off to find something to eat as quick as he could.

"O! out and about somewhere," they told him. But he saw no sign of the wizard all that day until the evening. Just before sunset he walked into the hall, where the hobbit and the dwarves were having supper, waited on by Beorn's wonderful animals, as they had been all day. Of Beorn they had seen and heard nothing since the night before, and they were getting puzzled.

"Where is our host, and where have *you* been all day yourself?" they all cried.

"One question at a time—and none till after supper! I haven't had a bite since breakfast."

At last Gandalf pushed away his plate and jug—he had eaten two whole loaves (with masses of butter and honey and clotted cream) and drunk at least a quart of mead—and he took out his pipe. "I will answer the second question first," he said, "—but bless me! this is a splendid place for smoke rings!" Indeed for a long time they could get nothing more out of him, he was so busy sending smoke rings dodging round the pillars of the hall, changing them into all sorts of different shapes and colours, and setting them at last chasing one another out of the hole in the roof. They must have looked very queer from outside, popping out into the air one after another, green, blue, red, silver-grey, yellow, white; big ones, little ones; little ones dodging through big ones and joining into figure-eights, and going off like a flock of birds into the distance.

"I have been picking out bear-tracks," he said at last. "There must have been a regular bears' meeting outside here last night. I soon saw that Beorn could not have made them all: there were far too many of them, and they were of various sizes too. I should say there were little bears, large bears, ordinary bears, and gigantic big bears, all dancing outside from dark to nearly dawn. They came from almost every direction, except from the west over the river, from the Mountains. In that direction only one set of footprints led—none coming, only ones going away from here. I followed these as far as the Carrock. There they disappeared into the river, but the water was too deep and strong beyond the rock for me to cross. It is easy enough, as you remember, to get from this bank to the Carrock by the ford, but on the other side is a cliff standing up from a swirling channel. I had to walk miles before I found a place where the river was wide and shallow enough for me to wade and swim, and then miles back again to pick up the tracks again. By that time it was too late for me to follow them far. They went straight off in the direction of the pine-woods on the east side of the Misty Mountains, where we had our pleasant little party with the Wargs the night before last. And now I think I have answered your first question, too," ended Gandalf, and he sat a long while silent.

Bilbo thought he knew what the wizard meant. "What shall we do," he cried, "if he leads all the Wargs and the goblins down here? We shall all be caught and killed! I thought you said he was not a friend of theirs."

"So I did. And don't be silly! You had better go to bed, your wits are sleepy."

The hobbit felt quite crushed, and as there seemed nothing else to do he did go to bed; and while the dwarves were still singing songs he dropped asleep, still puzzling his little head about Beorn, till he dreamed a dream of hundreds of black bears dancing slow heavy dances round and round in the moonlight in the courtyard. Then he woke up when everyone else was asleep, and he heard the same scraping, scuffling, snuffling, and growling as before.

Next morning they were all wakened by Beorn himself. "So here you all are still!" he said. He picked up the hobbit and laughed: "Not eaten up by Wargs or goblins or wicked bears yet I see"; and he poked Mr. Baggins' waistcoat most disrespectfully. "Little bunny is getting nice and fat again on bread and honey," he chuckled. "Come and have some more!"

So they all went to breakfast with him. Beorn was most jolly for a change; indeed he seemed to be in a splendidly good humour and set them all laughing with his funny stories; nor did they have to wonder long where he had been or why he was so nice to them, for he told them himself. He had been over the river and right back up into the mountains—from which you can guess that he could travel quickly, in bear's shape at any rate. From the burnt wolf-glade he had soon found out that part of their story was true; but he had found more than that: he had caught a Warg and a goblin wandering in the woods. From these he had got news: the goblin patrols were still hunting with Wargs for the dwarves, and they were fiercely angry because of the death of the Great Goblin, and also because of the burning of the chief wolf's nose and the death from the wizard's fire of many of his chief servants. So much they told him when he forced them, but he guessed there was more wickedness than this afoot, and that a great raid of the whole goblin army with their wolf-allies into the lands shadowed by the mountains might soon be made to find the dwarves, or to take vengeance on the men and creatures that lived there, and who they thought must be sheltering them.

"It was a good story, that of yours," said Beorn, "but I like it still better now I am sure it is true. You must forgive my not taking your word. If you lived near the edge of Mirkwood, you would take the word of no one that you did not know as well as your brother or better. As it is, I can only say that I have hurried home as fast as I could to see that you were safe, and to offer you any help that I can. I shall think more kindly of dwarves after this. Killed the Great Goblin, killed the Great Goblin!" he chuckled fiercely to himself.

"What did you do with the goblin and the Warg?" asked Bilbo suddenly.

"Come and see!" said Beorn, and they followed round the house. A goblin's head was stuck outside the gate and a warg-skin was nailed to a tree just beyond. Beorn was a fierce enemy. But now he was their friend, and Gandalf thought it wise to tell him their whole story and the reason of their journey, so that they could get the most help he could offer.

This is what he promised to do for them. He would provide ponies for each of them, and a horse for Gandalf, for their journey to the forest, and he would lade them with food to last them for weeks with care, and packed so as to be as easy as possible to carry—nuts, flour, sealed jars of dried fruits, and red earthenware pots of honey, and twice-baked cakes that would keep good a long time, and on a little of which they could march far. The making of these was one of his secrets; but honey was in them, as in most of his foods, and they were good to eat, though they made one thirsty. Water, he said, they would not need to carry this side of the forest, for there were streams and springs along the road. "But your way through Mirkwood is dark, dangerous and difficult," he said. "Water is not easy to find there, nor food. The time is not yet come for nuts (though it may be past and gone indeed before you get to the other side), and nuts are about all that grows there fit for food; in there the wild things are dark, queer, and savage. I will provide you with skins for carrying water, and I will give you some bows and arrows. But I doubt very much whether anything you find in Mirkwood will be wholesome to eat or to drink. There is one stream there, I know, black and strong which crosses the path. That you should neither drink of, nor bathe in; for I have heard that it carries enchantment and a great drowsiness and forgetfulness. And in the dim shadows of that place I don't think you will shoot anything, wholesome or unwholesome, without straying from the path. That you MUST NOT do, for any reason.

"That is all the advice I can give you. Beyond the edge of the forest I cannot help you much; you must depend on your luck and your courage and the food I send with you. At the gate of the forest I must ask you to send back my horse and my ponies. But I wish you all speed, and my house is open to you, if ever you come back this way again."

They thanked him, of course, with many bows and sweepings of their hoods and with many an "at your service, O master of the wide wooden halls!" But their

spirits sank at his grave words, and they all felt that
the adventure was far more dangerous than they had
thought, while all the time, even if they passed all the
perils of the road, the dragon was waiting at the end.

All that morning they were busy with preparations.
Soon after midday they ate with Beorn for the last
time, and after the meal they mounted the steeds he
was lending them, and bidding him many farewells
they rode off through his gate at a good pace.

As soon as they left his high hedges at the east of
his fenced lands they turned north and then bore to
the north-west. By his advice they were no longer
making for the main forest-road to the south of his
land. Had they followed the pass, their path would
have led them down a stream from the mountains
that joined the great river miles south of the
Carrock. At that point there was a deep ford which
they might have passed, if they had still had their
ponies, and beyond that a track led to the skirts of
the wood and to the entrance of the old forest road.
But Beorn had warned them that that way was now
often used by the goblins, while the forest-road itself,
he had heard, was overgrown and disused at the
eastern end and led to impassable marshes where the
paths had long been lost. Its eastern opening had
also always been far to the south of the Lonely
Mountain, and would have left them still with a long
and difficult northward march when they got to the
other side. North of the Carrock the edge of
Mirkwood drew closer to the borders of the Great
River, and though here the Mountains too drew
down nearer, Beorn advised them to take this way;
for at a place a few days' ride due north of the

Carrock was the gate of a little-known pathway through Mirkwood that led almost straight towards the Lonely Mountain.

"The goblins," Beorn had said, "will not dare to cross the Great River for a hundred miles north of the Carrock nor to come near my house—it is well protected at night!—but I should ride fast; for if they make their raid soon they will cross the river to the south and scour all the edge of the forest so as to cut you off, and Wargs run swifter than ponies. Still you are safer going north, even though you seem to be going back nearer to their strongholds; for that is what they will least expect, and they will have the longer ride to catch you. Be off now as quick as you may!"

That is why they were now riding in silence, galloping wherever the ground was grassy and smooth, with the mountains dark on their left, and in the distance the line of the river with its trees drawing ever closer. The sun had only just turned west when they started, and till evening it lay golden on the land about them. It was difficult to think of pursuing goblins behind, and when they had put many miles between them and Beorn's house they began to talk and to sing again and to forget the dark forest-path that lay in front. But in the evening when the dusk came on and the peaks of the mountains glowered against the sunset they made a camp and set a guard, and most of them slept uneasily with dreams in which there came the howl of hunting wolves and the cries of goblins.

Still the next morning dawned bright and fair again. There was an autumn-like mist white upon the ground and the air was chill, but soon the sun rose red in the East and the mists vanished, and while the shadows were still long they were off again. So they rode now for two more days, and all the while they saw nothing save grass and flowers and birds and scattered trees, and occasionally small herds of red deer browsing or sitting at noon in the shade. Sometimes Bilbo saw the horns of the harts sticking up out of the long grass, and at first he thought they were the dead branches of trees. That third evening they were so eager to press on, for Beorn had said that they should reach the forest-gate early on the fourth-day, that they rode still forward after dusk and into the night beneath the moon. As the light faded Bilbo thought he saw away to the right, or to the left, the shadowy form of a great bear prowling along in the same direction. But if he dared to mention it to Gandalf, the wizard only said: "Hush! Take no notice!"

Next day they started before dawn, though their night had been short. As soon as it was light they could see the forest coming as it were to meet them, or waiting for them like a black and frowning wall before them. The land began to slope up and up, and it seemed to the hobbit that a silence began to draw in upon them. Birds began to sing less. There were no more deer; not even rabbits were to be seen. By the afternoon they had reached the eaves of Mirkwood, and were resting almost beneath the great overhanging boughs of its outer trees. Their trunks were huge and gnarled, their branches twisted, their leaves were dark and long. Ivy grew on them and trailed along the ground.

"Well, here is Mirkwood!" said Gandalf. "The greatest of the forests of the Northern world. I hope you like the look of it. Now you must send back these excellent ponies you have borrowed."

The dwarves were inclined to grumble at this, but the wizard told them they were fools. "Beorn is not as far off as you seem to think, and you had better keep your promises anyway, for he is a bad enemy. Mr. Baggins' eyes are sharper than yours, if you have not seen each night after dark a great bear going along with us or sitting far off in the moon watching our camps. Not only to guard you and guide you, but to keep an eye on the ponies too. Beorn may be your friend, but he loves his animals as his children. You do not guess what kindness he has shown you in letting dwarves ride them so far and so fast, nor what would happen to you, if you tried to take them into the forest."

"What about the horse, then?" said Thorin. "You don't mention sending that back."

"I don't, because I am not sending it."

"What about *your* promise then?"

"I will look after that. I am not sending the horse back, I am riding it!"

Then they knew that Gandalf was going to leave them at the very edge of Mirkwood, and they were in despair. But nothing they could say would change his mind.

"Now we had this all out before, when we landed on the Carrock," he said. "It is no use arguing. I have, as I told you, some pressing business away south; and I am already late through bothering with you people. We may meet again before all is over,

and then again of course we may not. That depends
on your luck and on your courage and sense; and I
am sending Mr. Baggins with you. I have told you
before that he has more about him than you guess,
and you will find that out before long. So cheer up
Bilbo and don't look so glum. Cheer up Thorin and
Company! This is your expedition after all. Think of
the treasure at the end, and forget the forest and the
dragon, at any rate until tomorrow morning!"

When tomorrow morning came he still said the
same. So now there was nothing left to do but to fill
their water-skins at a clear spring they found close to
the forest-gate, and unpack the ponies. They distributed the packages as fairly as they could, though
Bilbo thought his lot was wearisomely heavy, and did
not at all like the idea of trudging for miles and miles
with all that on his back.

"Don't you worry!" said Thorin. "It will get lighter
all too soon. Before long I expect we shall all wish our
packs heavier, when the food begins to run short."

Then at last they said good-bye to their ponies and
turned their heads for home. Off they trotted gaily,
seeming very glad to put their tails towards the
shadow of Mirkwood. As they went away Bilbo could
have sworn that a thing like a bear left the shadow of
the trees and shambled off quickly after them.

Now Gandalf too said farewell. Bilbo sat on the
ground feeling very unhappy and wishing he was
beside the wizard on his tall horse. He had gone just
inside the forest after breakfast (a very poor one),
and it had seemed as dark in there in the morning as
at night, and very secret: "a sort of watching and
waiting feeling," he said to himself.

"Good-bye!" said Gandalf to Thorin. "And good-bye to you all, good-bye! Straight through the forest is your way now. Don't stray off the track!—if you do, it is a thousand to one you will never find it again and never get out of Mirkwood; and then I don't suppose I, or any one else, will ever see you again."

"Do we really have to go through?" groaned the hobbit.

"Yes, you do!" said the wizard, "if you want to get to the other side. You must either go through or give up your quest. And I am not going to allow you to back out now, Mr. Baggins. I am ashamed of you for thinking of it. You have got to look after all these dwarves for me," he laughed.

"No! no!" said Bilbo. "I didn't mean that. I meant, is there no way round?"

"There is, if you care to go two hundred miles or so out of your way north, and twice that south. But you wouldn't get a safe path even then. There are no safe paths in this part of the world. Remember you are over the Edge of the Wild now, and in for all sorts of fun wherever you go. Before you could get round Mirkwood in the North you would be right among the slopes of the Grey Mountains, and they are simply stiff with goblins, hobgoblins, and orcs of the worst description. Before you could get round it in the South, you would get into the land of the Necromancer; and even you, Bilbo, won't need me to tell you tales of that black sorcerer. I don't advise you to go anywhere near the places overlooked by his dark tower! Stick to the forest-track, keep your spirits up, hope for the best, and with a tremendous slice of luck you *may* come out one day and see the Long

Marshes lying below you, and beyond them, high in the East, the Lonely Mountain where dear old Smaug lives, though I hope he is not expecting you."

"Very comforting you are to be sure," growled Thorin. "Good-bye! If you won't come with us, you had better get off without any more talk!"

"Good-bye then, and really good-bye!" said Gandalf, and he turned his horse and rode down into the West. But he could not resist the temptation to have the last word. Before he had passed quite out of hearing he turned and put his hands to his mouth and called to them. They heard his voice come faintly: "Good-bye! Be good, take care of yourselves—and DON'T LEAVE THE PATH!"

Then he galloped away and was soon lost to sight. "O good-bye and go away!" grunted the dwarves, all the more angry because they were really filled with dismay at losing him. Now began the most dangerous part of all the journey. They each shouldered the heavy pack and the water-skin which was their share, and turned from the light that lay on the lands outside and plunged into the forest.

Chapter VIII

FLIES AND SPIDERS

They walked in single file. The entrance to the path was like a sort of arch leading into a gloomy tunnel made by two great trees that leant together, too old and strangled with ivy and hung with lichen to bear more than a few blackened leaves. The path itself was narrow and wound in and out among the trunks. Soon the light at the gate was like a little bright hole far behind, and the quiet was so deep that their feet seemed to thump along while all the trees leaned over them and listened.

As their eyes became used to the dimness they could see a little way to either side in a sort of darkened green glimmer. Occasionally a slender beam of sun that had the luck to slip in through some opening in the leaves far above, and still more luck in not being caught in the tangled boughs and matted twigs beneath, stabbed down thin and bright before them. But this was seldom, and it soon ceased altogether.

There were black squirrels in the wood. As Bilbo's sharp inquisitive eyes got used to seeing things he could catch glimpses of them whisking off the path and scuttling behind tree-trunks. There were queer noises too, grunts, scufflings, and hurryings in the undergrowth, and among the leaves that lay piled endlessly thick in places on the forest-floor; but what made the noises he could not see. The nastiest things they saw were the cobwebs: dark dense cobwebs with threads extraordinarily thick, often stretched from tree to tree, or tangled in the lower branches on either side of them. There were none stretched across the path, but whether because some magic kept it clear, or for what other reason they could not guess.

It was not long before they grew to hate the forest as heartily as they had hated the tunnels of the goblins, and it seemed to offer even less hope of any ending. But they had to go on and on, long after they were sick for a sight of the sun and of the sky, and longed for the feel of wind on their faces. There was no movement of air down under the forest-roof, and it was everlastingly still and dark and stuffy. Even the dwarves felt it, who were used to tunnelling, and lived at times for long whiles without the light of the sun; but the hobbit, who liked holes to make a house in but not to spend summer days in, felt that he was being slowly suffocated.

The nights were the worst. It then became pitch-dark—not what you call pitch-dark, but really pitch: so black that you really could see nothing. Bilbo tried flapping his hand in front of his nose, but he could not see it at all. Well, perhaps it is not true to say that they could see nothing: they could see eyes. They slept all closely huddled together, and took it in turns to watch; and when it was Bilbo's turn he would see gleams in the darkness round them, and sometimes pairs of yellow or red or green eyes would stare at him from a little distance, and then slowly fade and disappear and slowly shine out again in another place. And sometimes they would gleam down from the branches just above him; and that was most terrifying.

But the eyes that he liked the least were horrible pale bulbous sort of eyes. "Insect eyes," he thought, "not animal eyes, only they are much too big."

Although it was not yet very cold, they tried lighting watch-fires at night, but they soon gave that up. It seemed to bring hundreds and hundreds of eyes all round them, though the creatures, whatever they were, were careful never to let their bodies show in the little flicker of the flames. Worse still it brought thousands of dark-grey and black moths, some nearly as big as your hand, flapping and whirring round their ears. They could not stand that, nor the huge bats, black as a top-hat, either; so they gave up fires and sat at night and dozed in the enormous uncanny darkness.

All this went on for what seemed to the hobbit ages upon ages; and he was always hungry, for they were extremely careful with their provisions. Even so, as days followed days, and still the forest seemed just the same, they began to get anxious. The food would not last for ever: it was in fact already beginning to get low. They tried shooting at the squirrels, and they wasted many arrows before they managed to bring one down on the path. But when they roasted it, it proved horrible to taste, and they shot no more squirrels.

They were thirsty too, for they had none too much water, and in all the time they had seen neither spring nor stream. This was their state when one day they found their path blocked by a running water. It flowed fast and strong but not very wide right across the way, and it was black, or looked it in the gloom. It was well that Beorn had warned them against it, or they would have drunk from it, whatever its colour, and filled some of their emptied skins at its bank. As it was they only thought of how to cross it without wetting themselves in its water. There had been a bridge of wood across, but it had rotted and fallen leaving only the broken posts near the bank.

Bilbo kneeling on the brink and peering forward cried: "There is a boat against the far bank! Now why couldn't it have been this side!"

"How far away do you think it is?" asked Thorin, for by now they knew Bilbo had the sharpest eyes among them.

"Not at all far. I shouldn't think above twelve yards."

"Twelve yards! I should have thought it was thirty at least, but my eyes don't see as well as they used a hundred years ago. Still twelve yards is as good as a mile. We can't jump it, and we daren't try to wade or swim."

"Can any of you throw a rope?"

"What's the good of that? The boat is sure to be tied up, even if we could hook it, which I doubt."

"I don't believe it is tied," said Bilbo, "though of course I can't be sure in this light; but it looks to me as if it was just drawn up on the bank, which is low just there where the path goes down into the water."

"Dori is the strongest, but Fili is the youngest and still has the best sight," said Thorin. "Come here Fili, and see if you can see the boat Mr. Baggins is talking about."

Fili thought he could; so when he had stared a long while to get an idea of the direction, the others brought him a rope. They had several with them, and on the end of the longest they fastened one of the large iron hooks they had used for catching their packs to the straps about their shoulders. Fili took this in his hand, balanced it for a moment, and then flung it across the stream.

Splash it fell in the water! "Not far enough!" said Bilbo who was peering forward. "A couple of feet and you would have dropped it on to the boat. Try again. I don't suppose the magic is strong enough to hurt you, if you just touch a bit of wet rope."

Fili picked up the hook when he had drawn it back, rather doubtfully all the same. This time he threw it with great strength.

"Steady!" said Bilbo, "you have thrown it right into the wood on the other side now. Draw it back gently." Fili hauled the rope back slowly, and after a while Bilbo said: "Carefully! It is lying on the boat; let's hope the hook will catch."

It did. The rope went taut, and Fili pulled in vain. Kili came to his help, and then Oin and Gloin. They tugged and tugged, and suddenly they all fell over on their backs. Bilbo was on the look out, however, caught the rope, and with a piece of stick fended off the little black boat as it came rushing across the stream. "Help!" he shouted, and Balin was just in time to seize the boat before it floated off down the current.

"It was tied after all," said he, looking at the snapped painter that was still dangling from it. "That was a good pull, my lads; and a good job that our rope was the stronger."

"Who'll cross first?" asked Bilbo.

"I shall," said Thorin, "and you will come with me, and Fili and Balin. That's as many as the boat will hold at a time. After that Kili and Oin and Gloin and Dori; next Ori and Nori, Bifur and Bofur; and last Dwalin and Bombur."

"I'm always last and I don't like it," said Bombur. "It's somebody else's turn today."

"You should not be so fat. As you are, you must be with the last and lightest boatload. Don't start grumbling against orders, or something bad will happen to you."

"There aren't any oars. How are you going to push the boat back to the far bank?" asked the hobbit.

"Give me another length of rope and another hook," said Fili, and when they had got it ready, he cast it into the darkness ahead and as high as he could throw it. Since it did not fall down again, they saw that it must have stuck in the branches. "Get in now," said Fili, "and one of you haul on the rope that is stuck in a tree on the other side. One of the others must keep hold of the hook we used at first, and when we are safe on the other side he can hook it on, and you can draw the boat back."

In this way they were all soon on the far bank safe across the enchanted stream. Dwalin had just scrambled out with the coiled rope on his arm, and Bombur (still grumbling) was getting ready to follow, when something bad did happen. There was a flying sound of hooves on the path ahead. Out of the gloom came suddenly the shape of a flying deer. It charged into the dwarves and bowled them over, then gathered itself for a leap. High it sprang and cleared the water with a mighty jump. But it did not reach the other side in safety. Thorin was the only

one who had kept his feet and his wits. As soon as
they had landed he had bent his bow and fitted an
arrow in case any hidden guardian of the boat
appeared. Now he sent a swift and sure shot into the
leaping beast. As it reached the further bank it stumbled. The shadows swallowed it up, but they heard
the sound of hooves quickly falter and then go still.

Before they could shout in praise of the shot,
however, a dreadful wail from Bilbo put all thoughts
of venison out of their minds. "Bombur has fallen in!
Bombur is drowning!" he cried. It was only too true.
Bombur had only one foot on the land when the hart
bore down on him, and sprang over him. He had
stumbled, thrusting the boat away from the bank,
and then toppled back into the dark water, his hands
slipping off the slimy roots at the edge, while the boat
span slowly off and disappeared.

They could still see his hood above the water when
they ran to the bank. Quickly, they flung a rope with
a hook towards him. His hand caught it, and they
pulled him to the shore. He was drenched from hair
to boots, of course, but that was not the worst. When
they laid him on the bank he was already fast asleep,
with one hand clutching the rope so tight that they
could not get it from his grasp; and fast asleep he
remained in spite of all they could do.

They were still standing over him, cursing their ill
luck, and Bombur's clumsiness, and lamenting the
loss of the boat which made it impossible for them to
go back and look for the hart, when they became
aware of the dim blowing of horns in the wood and
the sound as of dogs baying far off. Then they all fell
silent; and as they sat it seemed they could hear the

noise of a great hunt going by to the north of the path, though they saw no sign of it.

There they sat for a long while and did not dare to make a move. Bombur slept on with a smile on his fat face, as if he no longer cared for all the troubles that vexed them. Suddenly on the path ahead appeared some white deer, a hind and fawns as snowy white as the hart had been dark. They glimmered in the shadows. Before Thorin could cry out three of the dwarves had leaped to their feet and loosed off arrows from their bows. None seemed to find their mark. The deer turned and vanished in the trees as silently as they had come, and in vain the dwarves shot their arrows after them.

"Stop! stop!" shouted Thorin; but it was too late, the excited dwarves had wasted their last arrows, and now the bows that Beorn had given them were useless.

They were a gloomy party that night, and the gloom gathered still deeper on them in the following days. They had crossed the enchanted stream; but beyond it the path seemed to straggle on just as before, and in the forest they could see no change. Yet if they had known more about it and considered the meaning of the hunt and the white deer that had appeared upon their path, they would have known that they were at last drawing towards the eastern edge, and would soon have come, if they could have kept up their courage and their hope, to thinner trees and places where the sunlight came again.

But they did not know this, and they were burdened with the heavy body of Bombur, which they had to carry along with them as best they could, taking the wearisome task in turns of four each while the others shared their packs. If these had not become all too light in the last few days, they would never have managed it; but a slumbering and smiling Bombur was a poor exchange for packs filled with food however heavy. In a few days a time came when there was practically nothing left to eat or to drink. Nothing wholesome could they see growing in the wood, only funguses and herbs with pale leaves and unpleasant smell.

About four days from the enchanted stream they came to a part where most of the trees were beeches. They were at first inclined to be cheered by the change, for here there was no undergrowth and the shadow was not so deep. There was a greenish light about them, and in places they could see some distance to either side of the path. Yet the light only showed them endless lines of straight grey trunks like the pillars of some huge twilight hall. There was a breath of air and a noise of wind, but it had a sad sound. A few leaves came rustling down to remind them that outside autumn was coming on. Their feet ruffled among the dead leaves of countless other autumns that drifted over the banks of the path from the deep red carpets of the forest.

Still Bombur slept and they grew very weary. At times they heard disquieting laughter. Sometimes there was singing in the distance too. The laughter was the laughter of fair voices not of goblins, and the singing was beautiful, but it sounded eerie and strange, and they were not comforted, rather they hurried on from those parts with what strength they had left.

Two days later they found their path going downwards, and before long they were in a valley filled almost entirely with a mighty growth of oaks.

"Is there no end to this accursed forest?" said Thorin. "Somebody must climb a tree and see if he can get his head above the roof and have a look round. The only way is to choose the tallest tree that overhangs the path."

Of course "somebody" meant Bilbo. They chose him, because to be of any use the climber must get his head above the topmost leaves, and so he must be light enough for the highest and slenderest branches to bear him. Poor Mr. Baggins had never had much practice in climbing trees, but they hoisted him up into the lowest branches of an enormous oak that grew right out into the path, and up he had to go as best he could. He pushed his way through the tangled twigs with many a slap in the eye; he was greened and grimed from the old bark of the greater boughs; more than once he slipped and caught himself just in time; and at last, after a dreadful struggle in a difficult place where there seemed to be no convenient branches at all, he got near the top. All the time he was wondering whether there were spiders in the tree, and how he was going to get down again (except by falling).

In the end he poked his head above the roof of leaves, and then he found spiders all right. But they were only small ones of ordinary size, and they were after the butterflies. Bilbo's eyes were nearly blinded by the light. He could hear the dwarves shouting up at him from far below, but he could not answer, only hold on and blink. The sun was shining brilliantly,

and it was a long while before he could bear it. When
he could, he saw all round him a sea of dark green,
ruffled here and there by the breeze; and there were
everywhere hundreds of butterflies. I expect they
were a kind of "purple emperor", a butterfly that
loves the tops of oak-woods, but these were not
purple at all, they were a dark dark velvety black
without any markings to be seen.

He looked at the "black emperors" for a long time,
and enjoyed the feel of the breeze in his hair and on
his face; but at length the cries of the dwarves, who
were now simply stamping with impatience down
below, reminded him of his real business. It was no
good. Gaze as much as he might, he could see no
end to the trees and the leaves in any direction. His
heart, that had been lightened by the sight of the sun
and the feel of the wind, sank back into his toes:
there was no food to go back to down below.

Actually, as I have told you, they were not far off
the edge of the forest; and if Bilbo had had the sense
to see it, the tree that he had climbed, though it was
tall in itself, was standing near the bottom of a wide
valley, so that from its top the trees seemed to swell
up all round like the edges of a great bowl, and he
could not expect to see how far the forest lasted. Still
he did not see this, and he climbed down full of
despair. He got to the bottom again at last, scratched,
hot, and miserable, and he could not see anything in
the gloom below when he got there. His report soon
made the others as miserable as he was.

"The forest goes on for ever and ever and ever in
all directions! Whatever shall we do? And what is the
use of sending a hobbit!" they cried, as if it was his

fault. They did not care tuppence about the butterflies, and were only made more angry when he told
them of the beautiful breeze, which they were too
heavy to climb up and feel.

That night they ate their very last scraps and crumbs
of food; and next morning when they woke the first
thing they noticed was that they were still gnawingly
hungry, and the next thing was that it was raining
and that here and there the drip of it was dropping
heavily on the forest floor. That only reminded them
that they were also parchingly thirsty, without doing
anything to relieve them: you cannot quench a terrible thirst by standing under giant oaks and waiting
for a chance drip to fall on your tongue. The only
scrap of comfort there was came unexpectedly from
Bombur.

He woke up suddenly and sat up scratching his
head. He could not make out where he was at all, nor
why he felt so hungry; for he had forgotten everything that had happened since they started their
journey that May morning long ago. The last thing
that he remembered was the party at the hobbit's
house, and they had great difficulty in making him
believe their tale of all the many adventures they had
had since.

When he heard that there was nothing to eat, he
sat down and wept, for he felt very weak and wobbly
in the legs. "Why ever did I wake up!" he cried. "I
was having such beautiful dreams. I dreamed I was
walking in a forest rather like this one, only lit with
torches on the trees and lamps swinging from the
branches and fires burning on the ground; and there

was a great feast going on, going on for ever. A woodland king was there with a crown of leaves, and there was a merry singing, and I could not count or describe the things there were to eat and drink."

"You need not try," said Thorin. "In fact if you can't talk about something else, you had better be silent. We are quite annoyed enough with you as it is. If you hadn't waked up, we should have left you to your idiotic dreams in the forest; you are no joke to carry even after weeks of short commons."

There was nothing now to be done but to tighten the belts round their empty stomachs, and hoist their empty sacks and packs, and trudge along the track without any great hope of ever getting to the end before they lay down and died of starvation. This they did all that day, going very slowly and wearily; while Bombur kept on wailing that his legs would not carry him and that he wanted to lie down and sleep.

"No you don't!" they said. "Let your legs take their share, we have carried you far enough."

All the same he suddenly refused to go a step further and flung himself on the ground. "Go on, if you must," he said. "I'm just going to lie here and sleep and dream of food, if I can't get it any other way. I hope I never wake up again."

At that very moment Balin, who was a little way ahead, called out: "What was that? I thought I saw a twinkle of light in the forest."

They all looked, and a longish way off, it seemed, they saw a red twinkle in the dark; then another and another sprang out beside it. Even Bombur got up, and they hurried along then, not caring if it was trolls or goblins. The light was in front of them and to the left of the path, and when at last they had drawn level with it, it seemed plain that torches and fires were burning under the trees, but a good way off their track.

"It looks as if my dreams were coming true," gasped Bombur puffing up behind. He wanted to rush straight off into the wood after the lights. But the others remembered only too well the warnings of the wizard and of Beorn.

"A feast would be no good, if we never got back alive from it," said Thorin.

"But without a feast we shan't remain alive much longer anyway," said Bombur, and Bilbo heartily agreed with him. They argued about it backwards and forwards for a long while, until they agreed at length to send out a couple of spies, to creep near the lights and find out more about them. But then they could not agree on who was to be sent: no one seemed anxious to run the chance of being lost and never finding his friends again. In the end, in spite of warnings, hunger decided them, because Bombur kept on describing all the good things that were being eaten, according to his dream, in the woodland feast; so they all left the path and plunged into the forest together.

After a good deal of creeping and crawling they peered round the trunks and looked into a clearing where some trees had been felled and the ground levelled. There were many people there, elvish-looking folk, all dressed in green and brown and sitting on sawn rings of the felled trees in a great circle. There was a fire in their midst and there were torches fastened to some of the trees round about; but most splendid sight of all: they were eating and drinking and laughing merrily.

The smell of the roast meats was so enchanting that, without waiting to consult one another, every one of them got up and scrambled forwards into the ring with the one idea of begging for some food. No sooner had the first stepped into the clearing than all the lights went out as if by magic. Somebody kicked the fire and it went up in rockets of glittering sparks and vanished. They were lost in a completely lightless dark and they could not even find one another, not for a long time at any rate. After blundering frantically in the gloom, falling over logs, bumping crash into trees, and shouting and calling till they must have waked everything in the forest for miles, at last they managed to gather themselves in a bundle and count themselves by touch. By that time they had, of course, quite forgotten in what direction the path lay, and they were all hopelessly lost, at least till morning.

There was nothing for it but to settle down for the night where they were; they did not even dare to search on the ground for scraps of food for fear of becoming separated again. But they had not been lying long, and Bilbo was only just getting drowsy, when Dori, whose turn it was to watch first, said in a loud whisper:

"The lights are coming out again over there, and there are more than ever of them."

Up they all jumped. There, sure enough, not far away were scores of twinkling lights, and they heard the voices and the laughter quite plainly. They crept slowly towards them, in a single line, each touching the back of the one in front. When they got near

Thorin said: "No rushing forward this time! No one is to stir from hiding till I say. I shall send Mr. Baggins alone first to talk to them. They won't be frightened of him—('What about me of them?' thought Bilbo)—and any way I hope they won't do anything nasty to him."

When they got to the edge of the circle of lights they pushed Bilbo suddenly from behind. Before he had time to slip on his ring, he stumbled forward into the full blaze of the fire and torches. It was no good. Out went all the lights again and complete darkness fell.

If it had been difficult collecting themselves before, it was far worse this time. And they simply could not find the hobbit. Every time they counted themselves it only made thirteen. They shouted and called: "Bilbo Baggins! Hobbit! You dratted hobbit! Hi! hobbit, confusticate you, where are you?" and other things of that sort, but there was no answer.

They were just giving up hope, when Dori stumbled across him by sheer luck. In the dark he fell over what he thought was a log, and he found it was the hobbit curled up fast asleep. It took a deal of shaking to wake him, and when he was awake he was not pleased at all.

"I was having such a lovely dream," he grumbled, "all about having a most gorgeous dinner."

"Good heavens! he has gone like Bombur," they said. "Don't tell us about dreams. Dream-dinners aren't any good, and we can't share them."

"They are the best I am likely to get in this beastly place," he muttered, as he lay down beside the dwarves and tried to go back to sleep and find his dream again.

But that was not the last of the lights in the forest. Later when the night must have been getting old, Kili who was watching then, came and roused them all again, saying:

"There's a regular blaze of light begun not far away—hundreds of torches and many fires must have been lit suddenly and by magic. And hark to the singing and the harps!"

After lying and listening for a while, they found they could not resist the desire to go nearer and try once more to get help. Up they got again; and this time the result was disastrous. The feast that they now saw was greater and more magnificent than before; and at the head of a long line of feasters sat a woodland king with a crown of leaves upon his golden hair, very much as Bombur had described the figure in his dream. The elvish folk were passing bowls from hand to hand and across the fires, and some were harping and many were singing. Their gleaming hair was twined with flowers; green and white gems glinted on their collars and their belts; and their faces and their songs were filled with mirth. Loud and clear and fair were those songs, and out stepped Thorin in to their midst.

Dead silence fell in the middle of a word. Out went all light. The fires leaped up in black smokes. Ashes and cinders were in the eyes of the dwarves, and the wood was filled again with their clamour and their cries.

Bilbo found himself running round and round (as he thought) and calling and calling: "Dori, Nori, Ori, Oin, Gloin, Fili, Kili, Bombur, Bifur, Bofur, Dwalin, Balin, Thorin Oakenshield," while people he could

not see or feel were doing the same all round him
(with an occasional "Bilbo!" thrown in). But the cries
of the others got steadily further and fainter, and
though after a while it seemed to him they changed
to yells and cries for help in the far distance, all noise
at last died right away, and he was left alone in complete silence and darkness.

That was one of his most miserable moments. But he
soon made up his mind that it was no good trying to
do anything till day came with some little light, and
quite useless to go blundering about tiring himself
out with no hope of any breakfast to revive him. So
he sat himself down with his back to a tree, and not
for the last time fell to thinking of his far-distant
hobbit-hole with its beautiful pantries. He was deep
in thoughts of bacon and eggs and toast and butter
when he felt something touch him. Something like a
strong sticky string was against his left hand, and
when he tried to move he found that his legs were
already wrapped in the same stuff, so that when he
got up he fell over.

Then the great spider, who had been busy tying
him up while he dozed, came from behind him and
came at him. He could only see the thing's eyes, but
he could feel its hairy legs as it struggled to wind its
abominable threads round and round him. It was
lucky that he had come to his senses in time. Soon he
would not have been able to move at all. As it was,
he had a desperate fight before he got free. He beat
the creature off with his hands—it was trying to
poison him to keep him quiet, as small spiders do to
flies—until he remembered his sword and drew it

out. Then the spider jumped back, and he had time
to cut his legs loose. After that it was his turn to
attack. The spider evidently was not used to things
that carried such stings at their sides, or it would
have hurried away quicker. Bilbo came at it before it
could disappear and stuck it with his sword right in
the eyes. Then it went mad and leaped and danced
and flung out its legs in horrible jerks, until he killed
it with another stroke; and then he fell down and
remembered nothing more for a long while.

There was the usual dim grey light of the forest-
day about him when he came to his senses. The
spider lay dead beside him, and his sword-blade was
stained black. Somehow the killing of the giant
spider, all alone by himself in the dark without the
help of the wizard or the dwarves or of anyone else,
made a great difference to Mr. Baggins. He felt a different person, and much fiercer and bolder in spite
of an empty stomach, as he wiped his sword on the
grass and put it back into its sheath.

"I will give you a name," he said to it, "and I shall
call you *Sting*."

After that he set out to explore. The forest was
grim and silent, but obviously he had first of all to
look for his friends, who were not likely to be very far
off, unless they had been made prisoners by the elves
(or worse things). Bilbo felt that it was unsafe to
shout, and he stood a long while wondering in what
direction the path lay, and in what direction he
should go first to look for the dwarves.

"O! why did we not remember Beorn's advice, and
Gandalf's!" he lamented. "What a mess we are in now!
We! I only wish it was *we*: it is horrible being all alone."

In the end he made as good a guess as he could at the direction from which the cries for help had come in the night—and by luck (he was born with a good share of it) he guessed more or less right, as you will see. Having made up his mind he crept along as cleverly as he could. Hobbits are clever at quietness, especially in woods, as I have already told you; also Bilbo had slipped on his ring before he started. That is why the spiders neither saw nor heard him coming.

He had picked his way stealthily for some distance, when he noticed a place of dense black shadow ahead of him, black even for that forest, like a patch of midnight that had never been cleared away. As he drew nearer, he saw that it was made by spider-webs one behind and over and tangled with another. Suddenly he saw, too, that there were spiders huge and horrible sitting in the branches above him, and ring or no ring he trembled with fear lest they should discover him. Standing behind a tree he watched a group of them for some time, and then in the silence and stillness of the wood he realised that these loathsome creatures were speaking one to another. Their voices were a sort of thin creaking and hissing, but he could make out many of the words that they said. They were talking about the dwarves!

"It was a sharp struggle, but worth it," said one. "What nasty thick skins they have to be sure, but I'll wager there is good juice inside."

"Aye, they'll make fine eating, when they've hung a bit," said another.

"Don't hang 'em too long," said a third. "They're not as fat as they might be. Been feeding none too well of late, I should guess."

"Kill 'em, I say," hissed a fourth; "kill 'em now and hang 'em dead for a while."

"They're dead now, I'll warrant," said the first.

"That they are not. I saw one a-struggling just now. Just coming round again, I should say, after a bee-autiful sleep. I'll show you."

With that one of the fat spiders ran along a rope till it came to a dozen bundles hanging in a row from a high branch. Bilbo was horrified, now that he noticed them for the first time dangling in the shadows, to see a dwarvish foot sticking out of the bottoms of some of the bundles, or here and there the tip of a nose, or a bit of beard or of a hood.

To the fattest of these bundles the spider went— "It is poor old Bombur, I'll bet," thought Bilbo—and nipped hard at the nose that stuck out. There was a muffled yelp inside, and a toe shot up and kicked the spider straight and hard. There was life in Bombur still. There was a noise like the kicking of a flabby football, and the enraged spider fell off the branch, only catching itself with its own thread just in time.

The others laughed. "You were quite right," they said, "the meat's alive and kicking!"

"I'll soon put an end to that," hissed the angry spider climbing back onto the branch.

Bilbo saw that the moment had come when he must do something. He could not get up at the brutes and he had nothing to shoot with; but looking about he saw that in this place there were many stones lying in what appeared to be a now dry little watercourse. Bilbo was a pretty fair shot with a stone, and it did not take him long to find a nice smooth egg-shaped one that fitted his hand cosily. As a boy he used to practise throwing stones at things, until rabbits and squirrels, and even birds, got out of his way as quick as lightning if they saw him stoop; and even grown-up he had still spent a deal of his time at quoits, dart-throwing, shooting at the wand, bowls, ninepins and other quiet games of the aiming and throwing sort—indeed he could do lots of things, besides blowing smoke-rings, asking riddles and cooking, that I haven't had time to tell you about. There is no time now. While he was picking up stones, the spider had reached Bombur, and soon he would have been dead. At that moment Bilbo threw. The stone struck the spider plunk on the head, and it dropped sense-less off the tree, flop to the ground, with all its legs curled up.

The next stone went whizzing through a big web, snapping its cords, and taking off the spider sitting in the middle of it, whack, dead. After that there was a deal of commotion in the spider-colony, and they forgot the dwarves for a bit, I can tell you. They could not see Bilbo, but they could make a good guess at the direction from which the stones were coming. As quick as lightning they came running and swinging towards the hobbit, flinging out their long threads in all directions, till the air seemed full of waving snares.

Bilbo, however, soon slipped away to a different place. The idea came to him to lead the furious spiders further and further away from the dwarves, if he could; to make them curious, excited and angry all at once. When about fifty had gone off to the place where he had stood before, he threw some more

stones at these, and at others that had stopped
behind; then dancing among the trees he began to
sing a song to infuriate them and bring them all after
him, and also to let the dwarves hear his voice.

This is what he sang:

> *Old fat spider spinning in a tree!*
> *Old fat spider can't see me!*
> > *Attercop! Attercop!*
> > > *Won't you stop,*
> *Stop your spinning and look for me?*

> *Old Tomnoddy, all big body,*
> *Old Tomnoddy can't spy me!*
> > *Attercop! Attercop!*
> > > *Down you drop!*
> *You'll never catch me up your tree!*

Not very good perhaps, but then you must remember that he had to make it up himself, on the spur of
a very awkward moment. It did what he wanted any
way. As he sang he threw some more stones and
stamped. Practically all the spiders in the place came
after him: some dropped to the ground, others raced
along the branches, swung from tree to tree, or cast
new ropes across the dark spaces. They made for his
noise far quicker than he had expected. They were
frightfully angry. Quite apart from the stones no
spider has ever liked being called Attercop, and
Tomnoddy of course is insulting to anybody.

Off Bilbo scuttled to a fresh place, but several of
the spiders had run now to different points in the
glade where they lived, and were busy spinning webs

across all the spaces between the tree-stems. Very
soon the hobbit would be caught in a thick fence of
them all round him—that at least was the spiders'
idea. Standing now in the middle of the hunting and
spinning insects Bilbo plucked up his courage and
began a new song:

> *Lazy Lob and crazy Cob*
> *are weaving webs to wind me.*
> *I am far more sweet than other meat,*
> *but still they cannot find me!*
>
> *Here am I, naughty little fly;*
> *you are fat and lazy.*
> *You cannot trap me, though you try,*
> *in your cobwebs crazy.*

With that he turned and found that the last space
between two tall trees had been closed with a web—but
luckily not a proper web, only great strands of double-
thick spider-rope run hastily backwards and forwards
from trunk to trunk. Out came his little sword. He
slashed the threads to pieces and went off singing.

The spiders saw the sword, though I don't suppose
they knew what it was, and at once the whole lot of
them came hurrying after the hobbit along the
ground and the branches, hairy legs waving, nippers
and spinners snapping, eyes popping, full of froth
and rage. They followed him into the forest until
Bilbo had gone as far as he dared. Then quieter than
a mouse he stole back.

He had precious little time, he knew, before the
spiders were disgusted and came back to their trees

where the dwarves were hung. In the meanwhile he had to rescue them. The worst part of the job was getting up on to the long branch where the bundles were dangling. I don't suppose he would have managed it, if a spider had not luckily left a rope hanging down; with its help, though it stuck to his hand and hurt him, he scrambled up—only to meet an old slow wicked fat-bodied spider who had remained behind to guard the prisoners, and had been busy pinching them to see which was the juiciest to eat. It had thought of starting the feast while the others were away, but Mr. Baggins was in a hurry, and before the spider knew what was happening it felt his sting and rolled off the branch dead.

Bilbo's next job was to loose a dwarf. What was he to do? If he cut the string which hung him up, the wretched dwarf would tumble thump to the ground a good way below. Wriggling along the branch (which made all the poor dwarves dance and dangle like ripe fruit) he reached the first bundle.

"Fili or Kili," he thought by the tip of a blue hood sticking out at the top. "Most likely Fili," he thought by the tip of a long nose poking out of the winding threads. He managed by leaning over to cut most of the strong sticky threads that bound him round, and then, sure enough, with a kick and a struggle most of Fili emerged. I am afraid Bilbo actually laughed at the sight of him jerking his stiff arms and legs as he danced on the spider-string under his armpits, just like one of those funny toys bobbing on a wire.

Somehow or other Fili was got on to the branch, and then he did his best to help the hobbit, although he was feeling very sick and ill from spider-poison, and from hanging most of the night and the next day wound round and round with only his nose to breathe through. It took him ages to get the beastly stuff out of his eyes and eyebrows, and as for his beard, he had to cut most of it off. Well, between them they started to haul up first one dwarf and then another and slash them free. None of them were better off than Fili, and some of them were worse. Some had hardly been able to breathe at all (long noses are sometimes useful you see) and some had been more poisoned.

In this way they rescued Kili, Bifur, Bofur, Dori and Nori. Poor old Bombur was so exhausted—he was the fattest and had been constantly pinched and poked—that he just rolled off the branch and fell plop on to the ground, fortunately on to leaves, and lay there. But there were still five dwarves hanging at the end of the branch when the spiders began to come back, more full of rage than ever.

Bilbo immediately went to the end of the branch nearest the tree-trunk and kept back those that crawled up. He had taken off his ring when he rescued Fili and forgotten to put it on again, so now they all began to splutter and hiss:

"Now we see you, you nasty little creature! We will eat you and leave your bones and skin hanging on a tree. Ugh! he's got a sting has he? Well, we'll get him all the same, and then we'll hang him head downwards for a day or two."

While this was going on, the other dwarves were working at the rest of the captives, and cutting at the threads with their knives. Soon all would be free, though it was not clear what would happen after that.

The spiders had caught them pretty easily the night before, but that had been unawares and in the dark. This time there looked like being a horrible battle.

Suddenly Bilbo noticed that some of the spiders had gathered round old Bombur on the floor, and had tied him up again and were dragging him away. He gave a shout and slashed at the spiders in front of him. They quickly gave way, and he scrambled and fell down the tree right into the middle of those on the ground. His little sword was something new in the way of stings for them. How it darted to and fro! It shone with delight as he stabbed at them. Half a dozen were killed before the rest drew off and left Bombur to Bilbo.

"Come down! Come down!" he shouted to the dwarves on the branch. "Don't stay up there and be netted!" For he saw spiders swarming up all the neighbouring trees, and crawling along the boughs above the heads of the dwarves.

Down the dwarves scrambled or jumped or dropped, eleven all in a heap, most of them very shaky and little use on their legs. There they were at last, twelve of them counting poor old Bombur, who was being propped up on either side by his cousin Bifur, and his brother Bofur; and Bilbo was dancing about and waving his Sting; and hundreds of angry spiders were goggling at them all round and about and above. It looked pretty hopeless.

Then the battle began. Some of the dwarves had knives, and some had sticks, and all of them could get at stones; and Bilbo had his elvish dagger. Again and again the spiders were beaten off, and many of them were killed. But it could not go on for long.

Bilbo was nearly tired out; only four of the dwarves were able to stand firmly, and soon they would all be overpowered like weary flies. Already the spiders were beginning to weave their webs all round them again from tree to tree.

In the end Bilbo could think of no plan except to let the dwarves into the secret of his ring. He was rather sorry about it, but it could not be helped.

"I am going to disappear," he said. "I shall draw the spiders off, if I can; and you must keep together and make in the opposite direction. To the left there, that is more or less the way towards the place where we last saw the elf-fires."

It was difficult to get them to understand, what with their dizzy heads, and the shouts, and the whacking of sticks and the throwing of stones; but at last Bilbo felt he could delay no longer—the spiders were drawing their circle ever closer. He suddenly slipped on his ring, and to the great astonishment of the dwarves he vanished.

Soon there came the sound of "Lazy Lob" and "Attercop" from among the trees away on the right. That upset the spiders greatly. They stopped advancing, and some went off in the direction of the voice. "Attercop" made them so angry that they lost their wits. Then Balin, who had grasped Bilbo's plan better than the rest, led an attack. The dwarves huddled together in a knot, and sending a shower of stones they drove at the spiders on the left, and burst through the ring. Away behind them now the shouting and singing suddenly stopped.

Hoping desperately that Bilbo had not been caught the dwarves went on. Not fast enough, though. They were sick and weary, and they could not go much better than a hobble and a wobble, though many of the spiders were close behind. Every now and then they had to turn and fight the creatures that were overtaking them; and already some spiders were in the trees above them and throwing down their long clinging threads.

Things were looking pretty bad again, when suddenly Bilbo reappeared, and charged into the astonished spiders unexpectedly from the side.

"Go on! Go on!" he shouted. "I will do the stinging!"

And he did. He darted backwards and forwards, slashing at spider-threads, hacking at their legs, and stabbing at their fat bodies if they came too near. The spiders swelled with rage, and spluttered and frothed, and hissed out horrible curses; but they had become mortally afraid of Sting, and dared not come very near, now that it had come back. So curse as they would, their prey moved slowly but steadily away. It was a most terrible business, and seemed to take hours. But at last, just when Bilbo felt that he could not lift his hand for a single stroke more, the spiders suddenly gave it up, and followed them no more, but went back disappointed to their dark colony.

The dwarves then noticed that they had come to the edge of a ring where elf-fires had been. Whether it was one of those they had seen the night before, they could not tell. But it seemed that some good magic lingered in such spots, which the spiders did not like. At any rate here the light was greener, and the boughs less thick and threatening, and they had a chance to rest and draw breath.

There they lay for some time, puffing and panting. But very soon they began to ask questions. They had to have the whole vanishing business carefully explained, and the finding of the ring interested them so much that for a while they forgot their own troubles. Balin in particular insisted on having the Gollum story, riddles and all, told all over again, with the ring in its proper place. But after a time the light began to fail, and then other questions were asked. Where were they, and where was their path, and where was there any food, and what were they going to do next? These questions they asked over and over again, and it was from little Bilbo that they seemed to expect to get the answers. From which you can see that they had changed their opinion of Mr. Baggins very much, and had begun to have a great respect for him (as Gandalf had said they would). Indeed they really expected him to think of some wonderful plan for helping them, and were not merely grumbling. They knew only too well that they would soon all have been dead, if it had not been for the hobbit; and they thanked him many times. Some of them even got up and bowed right to the ground before him, though they fell over with the effort, and could not get on their legs again for some time. Knowing the truth about the vanishing did not lessen their opinion of Bilbo at all; for they saw that he had some wits, as well as luck and a magic ring—and all three are very useful possessions. In fact they praised him so much that Bilbo began to feel there really was something of a bold adventurer about himself after all, though he would have felt a lot bolder still, if there had been anything to eat.

But there was nothing, nothing at all; and none of them were fit to go and look for anything, or to search for the lost path. The lost path! No other idea would come into Bilbo's tired head. He just sat staring in front of him at the endless trees; and after a while they all fell silent again. All except Balin. Long after the others had stopped talking and shut their eyes, he kept on muttering and chuckling to himself.

"Gollum! Well I'm blest! So that's how he sneaked past me, is it? Now I know! Just crept quietly along did you, Mr. Baggins? Buttons all over the doorstep! Good old Bilbo—Bilbo—Bilbo—bo—bo—bo—" And then he fell asleep, and there was complete silence for a long while.

All of a sudden Dwalin opened an eye, and looked round at them. "Where is Thorin?" he asked.

It was a terrible shock. Of course there were only thirteen of them, twelve dwarves and the hobbit. Where indeed was Thorin? They wondered what evil fate had befallen him, magic or dark monsters; and shuddered as they lay lost in the forest. There they dropped off one by one into uncomfortable sleep full of horrible dreams, as evening wore to black night; and there we must leave them for the present, too sick and weary to set guards or to take turns at watching.

Thorin had been caught much faster than they had. You remember Bilbo falling like a log into sleep, as he stepped into a circle of light? The next time it had been Thorin who stepped forward, and as the lights went out he fell like a stone enchanted. All the noise of the dwarves lost in the night, their cries as the spiders caught them and bound them, and all the sounds of the battle next day, had passed over him unheard. Then the Wood-elves had come to him, and bound him, and carried him away.

The feasting people were Wood-elves, of course. These are not wicked folk. If they have a fault it is distrust of strangers. Though their magic was strong, even in those days they were wary. They differed from the High Elves of the West, and were more dangerous and less wise. For most of them (together with their scattered relations in the hills and mountains) were descended from the ancient tribes that never went to Faerie in the West. There the Light-elves and the Deep-elves and the Sea-elves went and lived for ages, and grew fairer and wiser and more learned, and invented their magic and their cunning craft in the making of beautiful and marvellous things, before some came back into the Wide World. In the Wide World the Wood-elves lingered in the twilight of our Sun and Moon, but loved best the stars; and they wandered in the great forests that grew tall in lands that are now lost. They dwelt most often by the edges of the woods, from which they could escape at times to hunt, or to ride and run over the open lands by moonlight or starlight; and after the coming of Men they took ever more and more to the gloaming and the dusk. Still elves they were and remain, and that is Good People.

In a great cave some miles within the edge of Mirkwood on its eastern side there lived at this time their greatest king. Before his huge doors of stone a river ran out of the heights of the forest and flowed on and out into the marshes at the feet of the high

wooded lands. This great cave, from which countless smaller ones opened out on every side, wound
far underground and had many passages and wide
halls; but it was lighter and more wholesome than
any goblin-dwelling, and neither so deep nor so
dangerous. In fact the subjects of the king mostly
lived and hunted in the open woods, and had
houses or huts on the ground and in the branches.
The beeches were their favourite trees. The king's
cave was his palace, and the strong place of his
treasure, and the fortress of his people against their
enemies.

It was also the dungeon of his prisoners. So to the
cave they dragged Thorin—not too gently, for they
did not love dwarves, and thought he was an enemy.
In ancient days they had had wars with some of the
dwarves, whom they accused of stealing their treasure. It is only fair to say that the dwarves gave a different account, and said that they only took what was
their due, for the elf-king had bargained with them to
shape his raw gold and silver, and had afterwards
refused to give them their pay. If the elf-king had a
weakness it was for treasure, especially for silver and
white gems; and though his hoard was rich, he was
ever eager for more, since he had not yet as great a
treasure as other elf-lords of old. His people neither
mined nor worked metals or jewels, nor did they
bother much with trade or with tilling the earth. All
this was well known to every dwarf, though Thorin's
family had had nothing to do with the old quarrel I
have spoken of. Consequently Thorin was angry at
their treatment of him, when they took their spell off
him and he came to his senses; and also he was

determined that no word of gold or jewels should be dragged out of him.

The king looked sternly on Thorin, when he was brought before him, and asked him many questions. But Thorin would only say that he was starving.

"Why did you and your folk three times try to attack my people at their merrymaking?" asked the king.

"We did not attack them," answered Thorin; "we came to beg, because we were starving."

"Where are your friends now, and what are they doing?"

"I don't know, but I expect starving in the forest."

"What were you doing in the forest?"

"Looking for food and drink, because we were starving."

"But what brought you into the forest at all?" asked the king angrily.

At that Thorin shut his mouth and would not say another word.

"Very well!" said the king. "Take him away and keep him safe, until he feels inclined to tell the truth, even if he waits a hundred years."

Then the elves put thongs on him, and shut him in one of the inmost caves with strong wooden doors, and left him. They gave him food and drink, plenty of both, if not very fine; for Wood-elves were not goblins, and were reasonably well-behaved even to their worst enemies, when they captured them. The giant spiders were the only living things that they had no mercy upon.

There in the king's dungeon poor Thorin lay; and after he had got over his thankfulness for bread and meat and water, he began to wonder what had become of his unfortunate friends. It was not very long before he discovered; but that belongs to the next chapter and the beginning of another adventure in which the hobbit again showed his usefulness.

Chapter IX

BARRELS OUT OF BOND

The day after the battle with the spiders Bilbo and the dwarves made one last despairing effort to find a way out before they died of hunger and thirst. They got up and staggered on in the direction which eight out of the thirteen of them guessed to be the one in which the path lay; but they never found out if they were right. Such day as there ever was in the forest was fading once more into the blackness of night, when suddenly out sprang the light of many torches all round them, like hundreds of red stars. Out leaped Wood-elves with their bows and spears and called the dwarves to halt.

There was no thought of a fight. Even if the dwarves had not been in such a state that they were actually glad to be captured, their small knives, the only weapons they had, would have been of no use against the arrows of the elves that could hit a bird's eye in the dark. So they simply stopped dead and sat down and waited—all except Bilbo, who popped on his ring and slipped quickly to one side. That is why, when the elves bound the dwarves in a long line, one behind the other, and counted them, they never found or counted the hobbit.

Nor did they hear or feel him trotting along well behind their torch-light as they led off their prisoners into the forest. Each dwarf was blindfold, but that

did not make much difference, for even Bilbo with
the use of his eyes could not see where they were
going, and neither he nor the others knew where they
had started from anyway. Bilbo had all he could do
to keep up with the torches, for the elves were making
the dwarves go as fast as ever they could, sick and
weary as they were. The king had ordered them to
make haste. Suddenly the torches stopped, and the
hobbit had just time to catch them up before they
began to cross the bridge. This was the bridge that
led across the river to the king's doors. The water
flowed dark and swift and strong beneath; and at the
far end were gates before the mouth of a huge cave
that ran into the side of a steep slope covered with
trees. There the great beeches came right down to
the bank, till their feet were in the stream.

Across the bridge the elves thrust their prisoners,
but Bilbo hesitated in the rear. He did not at all like
the look of the cavern-mouth, and he only made up
his mind not to desert his friends just in time to scuttle
over at the heels of the last elves, before the great gates
of the king closed behind them with a clang.

Inside the passages were lit with red torch-light,
and the elf-guards sang as they marched along the
twisting, crossing, and echoing paths. These were not
like those of the goblin-cities; they were smaller, less
deep underground, and filled with a cleaner air. In a
great hall with pillars hewn out of the living stone sat
the Elvenking on a chair of carven wood. On his
head was a crown of berries and red leaves, for the
autumn was come again. In the spring he wore a
crown of woodland flowers. In his hand he held a
carven staff of oak.

.The ElvenKing's Gate.

The prisoners were brought before him; and though he looked grimly at them, he told his men to unbind them, for they were ragged and weary. "Besides they need no ropes in here," said he. "There is no escape from my magic doors for those who are once brought inside."

Long and searchingly he questioned the dwarves about their doings, and where they were going to, and where they were coming from; but he got little more news out of them than out of Thorin. They were surly and angry and did not even pretend to be polite.

"What have we done, O king?" said Balin, who was the eldest left. "Is it a crime to be lost in the forest, to be hungry and thirsty, to be trapped by spiders? Are the spiders your tame beasts or your pets, if killing them makes you angry?"

Such a question of course made the king angrier than ever, and he answered: "It is a crime to wander in my realm without leave. Do you forget that you were in my kingdom, using the road that my people made? Did you not three times pursue and trouble my people in the forest and rouse the spiders with your riot and clamour? After all the disturbance you have made I have a right to know what brings you here, and if you will not tell me now, I will keep you all in prison until you have learned sense and manners!"

Then he ordered the dwarves each to be put in a separate cell and to be given food and drink, but not to be allowed to pass the doors of their little prisons, until one at least of them was willing to tell him all he wanted to know. But he did not tell them that Thorin was also a prisoner with him. It was Bilbo who found that out.

Poor Mr. Baggins—it was a weary long time that he lived in that place all alone, and always in hiding, never daring to take off his ring, hardly daring to sleep, even tucked away in the darkest and remotest corners he could find. For something to do he took to wandering about the Elvenking's palace. Magic shut the gates, but he could sometimes get out, if he was quick. Companies of the Wood-elves, sometimes with the king at their head, would from time to time ride out to hunt, or to other business in the woods and in the lands to the East. Then if Bilbo was very nimble, he could slip out just behind them; though it was a dangerous thing to do. More than once he was nearly caught in the doors, as they clashed together when the last elf passed; yet he did not dare to march among them because of his shadow (altogether thin and wobbly as it was in torchlight), or for fear of being bumped into and discovered. And when he did go out, which was not very often, he did no good. He did not wish to desert the dwarves, and indeed he did not know where in the world to go without them. He could not keep up with the hunting elves all the time they were out, so he never discovered the ways out of the wood, and was left to wander miserably in the forest, terrified of losing himself, until a chance came of returning. He was hungry too outside, for he was no hunter; but inside the caves he could pick up a living of some sort by stealing food from store or table when no one was at hand.

"I am like a burglar that can't get away, but must

go on miserably burgling the same house day after day," he thought. "This is the dreariest and dullest part of all this wretched, tiresome, uncomfortable adventure! I wish I was back in my hobbit-hole by my own warm fireside with the lamp shining!" He often wished, too, that he could get a message for help sent to the wizard, but that of course was quite impossible; and he soon realized that if anything was to be done, it would have to be done by Mr. Baggins, alone and unaided.

Eventually, after a week or two of this sneaking sort of life, by watching and following the guards and taking what chances he could, he managed to find out where each dwarf was kept. He found all their twelve cells in different parts of the palace, and after a time he got to know his way about very well. What was his surprise one day to overhear some of the guards talking and to learn that there was another dwarf in prison too, in a specially deep dark place. He guessed at once, of course, that that was Thorin; and after a while he found that his guess was right. At last after many difficulties he managed to find the place when no one was about, and to have a word with the chief of the dwarves.

Thorin was too wretched to be angry any longer at his misfortunes, and was even beginning to think of telling the king all about his treasure and his quest (which shows how low-spirited he had become), when he heard Bilbo's little voice at his keyhole. He could hardly believe his ears. Soon however he made up his mind that he could not be mistaken, and he came to the door and had a long whispered talk with the hobbit on the other side.

So it was that Bilbo was able to take secretly
Thorin's message to each of the other imprisoned
dwarves, telling them that Thorin their chief was also
in prison close at hand, and that no one was to reveal
their errand to the king, not yet, nor before Thorin
gave the word. For Thorin had taken heart again
hearing how the hobbit had rescued his companions
from the spiders, and was determined once more not
to ransom himself with promises to the king of a
share in the treasure, until all hope of escaping in any
other way had disappeared; until in fact the remarkable Mr. Invisible Baggins (of whom he began to
have a very high opinion indeed) had altogether
failed to think of something clever.

The other dwarves quite agreed when they got the
message. They all thought their own shares in the
treasure (which they quite regarded as theirs, in spite
of their plight and the still unconquered dragon)
would suffer seriously if the Wood-elves claimed
part of it, and they all trusted Bilbo. Just what
Gandalf had said would happen, you see. Perhaps
that was part of his reason for going off and leaving
them.

Bilbo, however, did not feel nearly so hopeful as
they did. He did not like being depended on by
everyone, and he wished he had the wizard at hand.
But that was no use: probably all the dark distance of
Mirkwood lay between them. He sat and thought and
thought, until his head nearly burst, but no bright
idea would come. One invisible ring was a very fine
thing, but it was not much good among fourteen. But
of course, as you have guessed, he did rescue his
friends in the end, and this is how it happened.

One day, nosing and wandering about, Bilbo discovered a very interesting thing: the great gates were *not* the only entrance to the caves. A stream flowed under part of the lowest regions of the palace, and joined the Forest River some way further to the east, beyond the steep slope out of which the main mouth opened. Where this underground watercourse came forth from the hillside there was a water-gate. There the rocky roof came down close to the surface of the stream, and from it a portcullis could be dropped right to the bed of the river to prevent anyone coming in or out that way. But the portcullis was often open, for a good deal of traffic went out and in by the water-gate. If anyone had come in that way, he would have found himself in a dark rough tunnel leading deep into the heart of the hill; but at one point where it passed under the caves the roof had been cut away and covered with great oaken trapdoors. These opened upwards into the king's cellars. There stood barrels, and barrels, and barrels; for the Wood-elves, and especially their king, were very fond of wine, though no vines grew in those parts. The wine, and other goods, were brought from far away, from their kinsfolk in the South, or from the vineyards of Men in distant lands.

Hiding behind one of the largest barrels Bilbo discovered the trapdoors and their use, and lurking there, listening to the talk of the king's servants, he learned how the wine and other goods came up the rivers, or over land, to the Long Lake. It seemed a town of Men still throve there, built out on bridges far into the water as a protection against enemies of all sorts, and especially against the dragon of the Mountain. From Lake-town the barrels were brought

up the Forest River. Often they were just tied
together like big rafts and poled or rowed up the
stream; sometimes they were loaded on to flat boats.

When the barrels were empty the elves cast them
through the trapdoors, opened the water-gate, and
out the barrels floated on the stream, bobbing along,
until they were carried by the current to a place far
down the river where the bank jutted out, near to the
very eastern edge of Mirkwood. There they were collected and tied together and floated back to Lake-
town, which stood close to the point where the Forest
River flowed into the Long Lake.

For some time Bilbo sat and thought about this
water-gate, and wondered if it could be used for the
escape of his friends, and at last he had the desperate
beginnings of a plan.

The evening meal had been taken to the prisoners.
The guards were tramping away down the passages
taking the torchlight with them and leaving everything in darkness. Then Bilbo heard the king's butler
bidding the chief of the guards good-night.

"Now come with me," he said, "and taste the new
wine that has just come in. I shall be hard at work
tonight clearing the cellars of the empty wood, so let
us have a drink first to help the labour."

"Very good," laughed the chief of the guards. "I'll
taste with you, and see if it is fit for the king's table.
There is a feast tonight and it would not do to send
up poor stuff!"

When he heard this Bilbo was all in a flutter, for he
saw that luck was with him and he had a chance at

once to try his desperate plan. He followed the two
elves, until they entered a small cellar and sat down
at a table on which two large flagons were set. Soon
they began to drink and laugh merrily. Luck of an
unusual kind was with Bilbo then. It must be potent
wine to make a wood-elf drowsy; but this wine, it
would seem, was the heady vintage of the great
gardens of Dorwinion, not meant for his soldiers or
his servants, but for the king's feasts only, and for
smaller bowls not for the butler's great flagons.

Very soon the chief guard nodded his head, then
he laid it on the table and fell fast asleep. The butler
went on talking and laughing to himself for a while
without seeming to notice, but soon his head too
nodded to the table, and he fell asleep and snored
beside his friend. Then in crept the hobbit. Very
soon the chief guard had no keys, but Bilbo was trotting as fast as he could along the passages towards
the cells. The great bunch seemed very heavy to his
arms, and his heart was often in his mouth, in spite
of his ring, for he could not prevent the keys from
making every now and then a loud clink and clank,
which put him all in a tremble.

First he unlocked Balin's door, and locked it again
carefully as soon as the dwarf was outside. Balin was
most surprised, as you can imagine; but glad as he
was to get out of his wearisome little stone room, he
wanted to stop and ask questions, and know what
Bilbo was going to do, and all about it.

"No time now!" said the hobbit. "You just follow
me! We must all keep together and not risk getting
separated. All of us must escape or none, and this is
our last chance. If this is found out, goodness knows

where the king will put you next, with chains on your hands and feet too, I expect. Don't argue, there's a good fellow!"

Then off he went from door to door, until his following had grown to twelve—none of them any too nimble, what with the dark, and what with their long imprisonment. Bilbo's heart thumped every time one of them bumped into another, or grunted or whispered in the dark. "Drat this dwarvish racket!" he said to himself. But all went well, and they met no guards. As a matter of fact there was a great autumn feast in the woods that night, and in the halls above. Nearly all the king's folk were merrymaking.

At last after much blundering they came to Thorin's dungeon, far down in a deep place and fortunately not far from the cellars.

"Upon my word!" said Thorin, when Bilbo whispered to him to come out and join his friends, "Gandalf spoke true, as usual! A pretty fine burglar you make, it seems, when the time comes. I am sure we are all for ever at your service, whatever happens after this. But what comes next?"

Bilbo saw that the time had come to explain his idea, as far as he could; but he did not feel at all sure how the dwarves would take it. His fears were quite justified, for they did not like it a bit, and started grumbling loudly in spite of their danger.

"We shall be bruised and battered to pieces, and drowned too, for certain!" they muttered. "We thought you had got some sensible notion, when you managed to get hold of the keys. This is a mad idea!"

"Very well!" said Bilbo very downcast, and also rather annoyed. "Come along back to your nice cells,

and I will lock you all in again, and you can sit there
comfortably and think of a better plan—but I don't
suppose I shall ever get hold of the keys again, even
if I feel inclined to try."

That was too much for them, and they calmed
down. In the end, of course, they had to do just what
Bilbo suggested, because it was obviously impossible
for them to try and find their way into the upper
halls, or to fight their way out of gates that closed by
magic; and it was no good grumbling in the passages
until they were caught again. So following the hobbit,
down into the lowest cellars they crept. They passed
a door through which the chief guard and the butler
could be seen still happily snoring with smiles upon
their faces. The wine of Dorwinion brings deep and
pleasant dreams. There would be a different expression on the face of the chief guard next day, even
though Bilbo, before they went on, stole in and kind-
heartedly put the keys back on his belt.

"That will save him some of the trouble he is in
for," said Mr. Baggins to himself. "He wasn't a bad
fellow, and quite decent to the prisoners. It will
puzzle them all too. They will think we had a very
strong magic to pass through all those locked doors
and disappear. Disappear! We have got to get busy
very quick, if that is to happen!"

Balin was told off to watch the guard and the butler
and give warning if they stirred. The rest went into
the adjoining cellar with the trapdoors. There was
little time to lose. Before long, as Bilbo knew, some
elves were under orders to come down and help the
butler get the empty barrels through the doors into

the stream. These were in fact already standing in rows in the middle of the floor waiting to be pushed off. Some of them were wine-barrels, and these were not much use, as they could not easily be opened at the end without a deal of noise, nor could they easily be secured again. But among them were several others, which had been used for bringing other stuffs, butter, apples, and all sorts of things, to the king's palace.

They soon found thirteen with room enough for a dwarf in each. In fact some were too roomy, and as they climbed in the dwarves thought anxiously of the shaking and the bumping they would get inside, though Bilbo did his best to find straw and other stuff to pack them in as cosily as could be managed in a short time. At last twelve dwarves were stowed. Thorin had given a lot of trouble, and turned and twisted in his tub and grumbled like a large dog in a small kennel; while Balin, who came last, made a great fuss about his air-holes and said he was stifling, even before his lid was on. Bilbo had done what he could to close holes in the sides of the barrels, and to fix on all the lids as safely as could be managed, and now he was left alone again, running round putting the finishing touches to the packing, and hoping against hope that his plan would come off.

It had not been done a bit too soon. Only a minute or two after Balin's lid had been fitted on there came the sound of voices and the flicker of lights. A number of elves came laughing and talking into the cellars and singing snatches of song. They had left a merry feast in one of the halls and were bent on returning as soon as they could.

"Where's old Galion, the butler?" said one. "I haven't seen him at the tables tonight. He ought to be here now to show us what is to be done."

"I shall be angry if the old slowcoach is late," said another. "I have no wish to waste time down here while the song is up!"

"Ha, ha!" came a cry. "Here's the old villain with his head on a jug! He's been having a little feast all to himself and his friend the captain."

"Shake him! Wake him!" shouted the others impatiently.

Galion was not at all pleased at being shaken or wakened, and still less at being laughed at. "You're all late," he grumbled. "Here am I waiting and waiting down here, while you fellows drink and make merry and forget your tasks. Small wonder if I fall asleep from weariness!"

"Small wonder," said they, "when the explanation stands close at hand in a jug! Come give us a taste of your sleeping-draught before we fall to! No need to wake the turnkey yonder. He has had his share by the looks of it."

Then they drank once round and became mighty merry all of a sudden. But they did not quite lose their wits. "Save us, Galion!" cried some, "you began your feasting early and muddled your wits! You have stacked some full casks here instead of the empty ones, if there is anything in weight."

"Get on with the work!" growled the butler. "There is nothing in the feeling of weight in an idle toss-pot's arms. These are the ones to go and no others. Do as I say!"

"Very well, very well," they answered rolling the

barrels to the opening. "On your head be it, if the king's full buttertubs and his best wine is pushed into the river for the Lake-men to feast on for nothing!"

> Roll—roll—roll—roll,
> roll-roll-rolling down the hole!
> Heave ho! Splash plump!
> Down they go, down they bump!

So they sang as first one barrel and then another rumbled to the dark opening and was pushed over into the cold water some feet below. Some were barrels really empty, some were tubs neatly packed with a dwarf each; but down they all went, one after another, with many a clash and a bump, thudding on top of ones below, smacking into the water, jostling against the walls of the tunnel, knocking into one another, and bobbing away down the current.

It was just at this moment that Bilbo suddenly discovered the weak point in his plan. Most likely you saw it some time ago and have been laughing at him; but I don't suppose you would have done half as well yourselves in his place. Of course he was not in a barrel himself, nor was there anyone to pack him in, even if there had been a chance! It looked as if he would certainly lose his friends this time (nearly all of them had already disappeared through the dark trap-door), and get utterly left behind and have to stay lurking as a permanent burglar in the elf-caves for ever. For even if he could have escaped through the upper gates at once, he had precious small chance of ever finding the dwarves again. He did not know the way by land to the place where the barrels were collected.

He wondered what on earth would happen to them without him; for he had not had time to tell the dwarves all that he had learned, or what he had meant to do, once they were out of the wood.

While all these thoughts were passing through his mind, the elves being very merry began to sing a song round the river-door. Some had already gone to haul on the ropes which pulled up the portcullis at the water-gate so as to let out the barrels as soon as they were all afloat below.

> *Down the swift dark stream you go*
> *Back to lands you once did know!*
> *Leave the halls and caverns deep,*
> *Leave the northern mountains steep,*
> *Where the forest wide and dim*
> *Stoops in shadow grey and grim!*
> *Float beyond the world of trees*
> *Out into the whispering breeze,*
> *Past the rushes, past the reeds,*
> *Past the marsh's waving weeds,*
> *Through the mist that riseth white*
> *Up from mere and pool at night!*
> *Follow, follow stars that leap*
> *Up the heavens cold and steep;*
> *Turn when dawn comes over land,*
> *Over rapid, over sand,*
> *South away! and South away!*
> *Seek the sunlight and the day,*
> *Back to pasture, back to mead,*
> *Where the kine and oxen feed!*
> *Back to gardens on the hills*
> *Where the berry swells and fills*

Under sunlight, under day!
South away! and South away!
Down the swift dark stream you go
Back to lands you once did know!

Now the very last barrel was being rolled to the
doors! In despair and not knowing what else to do,
poor little Bilbo caught hold of it and was pushed
over the edge with it. Down into the water he fell,
splash! into the cold dark water with the barrel on
top of him.

He came up again spluttering and clinging to the
wood like a rat, but for all his efforts he could not
scramble on top. Every time he tried, the barrel
rolled round and ducked him under again. It was
really empty, and floated light as a cork. Though his
ears were full of water, he could hear the elves still
singing in the cellar above. Then suddenly the trapdoors fell to with a boom and their voices faded
away. He was in the dark tunnel floating in icy water,
all alone—for you cannot count friends that are all
packed up in barrels.

Very soon a grey patch came in the darkness
ahead. He heard the creak of the water-gate being
hauled up, and he found that he was in the midst of
a bobbing and bumping mass of casks and tubs all
pressing together to pass under the arch and get out
into the open stream. He had as much as he could do
to prevent himself from being hustled and battered to
bits; but at last the jostling crowd began to break up
and swing off, one by one, under the stony arch and
away. Then he saw that it would have been no good
even if he had managed to get astride his barrel, for

there was no room to spare, not even for a hobbit, between its top and the suddenly stooping roof where the gate was.

Out they went under the overhanging branches of the trees on either bank. Bilbo wondered what the dwarves were feeling and whether a lot of water was getting into their tubs. Some of those that bobbed along by him in the gloom seemed pretty low in the water, and he guessed that these had dwarves inside.

"I do hope I put the lids on tight enough!" he thought, but before long he was worrying too much about himself to remember the dwarves. He managed to keep his head above the water, but he was shivering with the cold, and he wondered if he would die of it before the luck turned, and how much longer he would be able to hang on, and whether he should risk the chance of letting go and trying to swim to the bank.

The luck turned all right before long: the eddying current carried several barrels close ashore at one point and there for a while they stuck against some hidden root. Then Bilbo took the opportunity of scrambling up the side of his barrel while it was held steady against another. Up he crawled like a drowned rat, and lay on the top spread out to keep the balance as best he could. The breeze was cold but better than the water, and he hoped he would not suddenly roll off again when they started off once more.

Before long the barrels broke free again and turned and twisted off down the stream, and out into the main current. Then he found it quite as difficult to stick on as he had feared; but he managed it somehow, though it was miserably uncomfortable. Luckily he was very light, and the barrel was a good big one and being rather leaky had now shipped a small amount of water. All the same it was like trying to ride, without bridle or stirrups, a round-bellied pony that was always thinking of rolling on the grass.

In this way at last Mr. Baggins came to a place where the trees on either hand grew thinner. He could see the paler sky between them. The dark river opened suddenly wide, and there it was joined to the main water of the Forest River flowing down in haste from the king's great doors. There was a dim sheet of water no longer overshadowed, and on its sliding surface there were dancing and broken reflections of clouds and of stars. Then the hurrying water of the Forest River swept all the company of casks and tubs away to the north bank, in which it had eaten out a wide bay. This had a shingly shore under hanging banks and was walled at the eastern end by a little jutting cape of hard rock. On the shallow shore most of the barrels ran aground, though a few went on to bump against the stony pier.

There were people on the look-out on the banks. They quickly poled and pushed all the barrels together into the shallows, and when they had counted them they roped them together and left them till the morning. Poor dwarves! Bilbo was not badly off now. He slipped from his barrel and waded ashore, and then sneaked along to some huts that he could see near the water's edge. He no longer thought twice about picking up a supper uninvited if he got the chance, he had been obliged to do it for so long, and he knew now only too well what it was to be really hungry, not merely politely interested in the dainties of a well-filled larder. Also he had caught a glimpse of a fire through the trees, and that appealed to him with his dripping and ragged clothes clinging to him cold and clammy.

There is no need to tell you much of his adventures that night, for now we are drawing near the end of the eastward journey and coming to the last and greatest adventure, so we must hurry on. Of course helped by his magic ring he got on very well at first, but he was given away in the end by his wet footsteps and the trail of drippings that he left wherever he went or sat; and also he began to snivel, and wherever he tried to hide he was found out by the terrific explosions of his suppressed sneezes. Very soon there was a fine commotion in the village by the riverside; but Bilbo escaped into the woods carrying a loaf and a leather bottle of wine and a pie that did not belong to him. The rest of the night he had to pass wet as he was and far from a fire, but the bottle helped him to do that, and he actually dozed a little on some dry leaves, even though the year was getting late and the air was chilly.

He woke again with a specially loud sneeze. It was already grey morning, and there was a merry racket down by the river. They were making up a raft of barrels, and the raft-elves would soon be steering it off down the stream to Lake-town. Bilbo sneezed again. He was no longer dripping but he felt cold all over. He scrambled down as fast as his stiff legs would take him and managed just in time to get on to the mass of casks without being noticed in the general bustle. Luckily there was no sun at the time to cast an awkward shadow, and for a mercy he did not sneeze again for a good while.

There was a mighty pushing of poles. The elves that were standing in the shallow water heaved and shoved. The barrels now all lashed together creaked and fretted.

"This is a heavy load!" some grumbled. "They float too deep—some of these are never empty. If they had come ashore in the daylight, we might have had a look inside," they said.

"No time now!" cried the raftman. "Shove off!"

And off they went at last, slowly at first, until they had passed the point of rock where other elves stood to fend them off with poles, and then quicker and quicker as they caught the main stream and went sailing away down, down towards the Lake.

They had escaped the dungeons of the king and were through the wood, but whether alive or dead still remains to be seen.

Chapter X

A WARM WELCOME

The day grew lighter and warmer as they floated along. After a while the river rounded a steep shoulder of land that came down upon their left. Under its rocky feet like an inland cliff the deepest stream had flowed lapping and bubbling. Suddenly the cliff fell away. The shores sank. The trees ended. Then Bilbo saw a sight:

The lands opened wide about him, filled with the waters of the river which broke up and wandered in a hundred winding courses, or halted in marshes and pools dotted with isles on every side; but still a strong water flowed on steadily through the midst. And far away, its dark head in a torn cloud, there loomed the Mountain! Its nearest neighbours to the North-East and the tumbled land that joined it to them could not be seen. All alone it rose and looked across the marshes to the forest. The Lonely Mountain! Bilbo had come far and through many adventures to see it, and now he did not like the look of it in the least.

As he listened to the talk of the raftmen and pieced together the scraps of information they let fall, he soon realized that he was very fortunate ever to have seen it at all, even from this distance. Dreary as had been his imprisonment and unpleasant as was his position (to say nothing of the poor dwarves underneath him) still, he had been more lucky than he had guessed. The talk was all of the trade that came and went on the waterways and the growth of the traffic on the river, as the roads out of the East towards Mirkwood vanished or fell into disuse; and of the bickerings of the Lake-men and the Wood-elves about the upkeep of the Forest River and the care of the banks. Those lands had changed much since the days when dwarves dwelt in the Mountain, days which most people now remembered only as a very shadowy tradition. They had changed even in recent years, and since the last news that Gandalf had had of them. Great floods and rains had swollen the waters that flowed east; and there had been an earthquake or two (which some were inclined to attribute to the dragon—alluding to him chiefly with a curse and an ominous nod in the direction of the Mountain). The marshes and bogs had spread wider and wider on either side. Paths had vanished, and many a rider and wanderer too, if they had tried to find the lost ways across. The elf-road through the wood which the dwarves had followed on the advice of Beorn now came to a doubtful and little used end at the eastern edge of the forest; only the river offered any longer a safe way from the skirts of Mirkwood in the North to the mountain-shadowed plains beyond, and the river was guarded by the Wood-elves' king.

So you see Bilbo had come in the end by the only road that was any good. It might have been some comfort to Mr. Baggins shivering on the barrels, if he had known that news of this had reached Gandalf far away and given him great anxiety, and that he was in fact finishing his other business (which does not come into this tale) and getting ready to come in search of Thorin's company. But Bilbo did not know it.

All he knew was that the river seemed to go on and on and on for ever, and he was hungry, and had a nasty cold in the nose, and did not like the way the Mountain seemed to frown at him and threaten him as it drew ever nearer. After a while, however, the river took a more southerly course and the Mountain receded again, and at last, late in the day the shores grew rocky, the river gathered all its wandering waters together into a deep and rapid flood, and they swept along at great speed.

The sun had set when turning with another sweep towards the East the forest-river rushed into the Long Lake. There it had a wide mouth with stony clifflike gates at either side whose feet were piled with shingles. The Long Lake! Bilbo had never imagined that any water that was not the sea could look so big. It was so wide that the opposite shores looked small and far, but it was so long that its northerly end, which pointed towards the Mountain, could not be seen at all. Only from the map did Bilbo know that away up there, where the stars of the Wain were already twinkling, the Running River came down into the lake from Dale and with the Forest River filled with deep waters what must once have been a great deep rocky valley. At the southern end the doubled waters poured out again over high waterfalls and ran away hurriedly to unknown lands. In the still evening air the noise of the falls could be heard like a distant roar.

Not far from the mouth of the Forest River was the strange town he heard the elves speak of in the king's cellars. It was not built on the shore, though there were a few huts and buildings there, but right out on the surface of the lake, protected from the swirl of the entering river by a promontory of rock which formed a calm bay. A great bridge made of wood ran out to where on huge piles made of forest trees was built a busy wooden town, not a town of elves but of Men, who still dared to dwell here under the shadow of the distant dragon-mountain. They still throve on the trade that came up the great river from the South and was carted past the falls to their town; but in the great days of old, when Dale in the North was rich and prosperous, they had been wealthy and powerful, and there had been fleets of boats on the waters, and some were filled with gold and some with warriors in armour, and there had been wars and deeds which were now only a legend. The rotting piles of a greater town could still be seen along the shores when the waters sank in a drought.

But men remembered little of all that, though some still sang old songs of the dwarf-kings of the Mountain, Thror and Thrain of the race of Durin, and of the coming of the Dragon, and the fall of the lords of Dale. Some sang too that Thror and Thrain would come back one day and gold would flow in rivers, through the mountain-gates, and all that land would be filled with new song and new laughter. But this pleasant legend did not much affect their daily business.

★   ★   ★

LAKE TOWN.

As soon as the raft of barrels came in sight boats rowed out from the piles of the town, and voices hailed the raft-steerers. Then ropes were cast and oars were pulled, and soon the raft was drawn out of the current of the Forest River and towed away round the high shoulder of rock into the little bay of Lake-town. There it was moored not far from the shoreward head of the great bridge. Soon men would come up from the South and take some of the casks away, and others they would fill with goods they had brought to be taken back up the stream to the Wood-elves' home. In the meanwhile the barrels were left afloat while the elves of the raft and the boatmen went to feast in Lake-town.

They would have been surprised, if they could have seen what happened down by the shore, after they had gone and the shades of night had fallen. First of all a barrel was cut loose by Bilbo and pushed to the shore and opened. Groans came from inside, and out crept a most unhappy dwarf. Wet straw was in his draggled beard; he was so sore and stiff, so bruised and buffeted he could hardly stand or stumble through the shallow water to lie groaning on the shore. He had a famished and a savage look like a dog that has been chained and forgotten in a kennel for a week. It was Thorin, but you could only have told it by his golden chain, and by the colour of his now dirty and tattered sky-blue hood with its tarnished silver tassel. It was some time before he would be even polite to the hobbit.

"Well, are you alive or are you dead?" asked Bilbo quite crossly. Perhaps he had forgotten that he had had at least one good meal more than the dwarves, and also the use of his arms and legs, not to speak of a greater allowance of air. "Are you still in prison, or are you free? If you want food, and if you want to go on with this silly adventure—it's yours after all and not mine—you had better slap your arms and rub your legs and try and help me get the others out while there is a chance!"

Thorin of course saw the sense of this, so after a few more groans he got up and helped the hobbit as well as he could. In the darkness floundering in the cold water they had a difficult and very nasty job finding which were the right barrels. Knocking outside and calling only discovered about six dwarves that could answer. These were unpacked and helped ashore where they sat or lay muttering and moaning; they were so soaked and bruised and cramped that they could hardly yet realize their release or be properly thankful for it.

Dwalin and Balin were two of the most unhappy, and it was no good asking them to help. Bifur and Bofur were less knocked about and drier, but they lay down and would do nothing. Fili and Kili, however, who were young (for dwarves) and had also been packed more neatly with plenty of straw into smaller casks, came out more or less smiling, with only a bruise or two and a stiffness that soon wore off.

"I hope I never smell the smell of apples again!" said Fili. "My tub was full of it. To smell apples everlastingly when you can scarcely move and are cold and sick with hunger is maddening. I could eat anything in the wide world now, for hours on end—but not an apple!"

With the willing help of Fili and Kili, Thorin and

Bilbo at last discovered the remainder of the company and got them out. Poor fat Bombur was asleep or senseless; Dori, Nori, Ori, Oin and Gloin were waterlogged and seemed only half alive; they all had to be carried one by one and laid helpless on the shore.

"Well! Here we are!" said Thorin. "And I suppose we ought to thank our stars and Mr. Baggins. I am sure he has a right to expect it, though I wish he could have arranged a more comfortable journey. Still—all very much at your service once more, Mr. Baggins. No doubt we shall feel properly grateful, when we are fed and recovered. In the meanwhile what next?"

"I suggest Lake-town," said Bilbo. "What else is there?"

Nothing else could, of course, be suggested; so leaving the others Thorin and Fili and Kili and the hobbit went along the shore to the great bridge. There were guards at the head of it, but they were not keeping very careful watch, for it was so long since there had been any real need. Except for occasional squabbles about river-tolls they were friends with the Wood-elves. Other folk were far away; and some of the younger people in the town openly doubted the existence of any dragon in the mountain, and laughed at the greybeards and gammers who said that they had seen him flying in the sky in their young days. That being so it is not surprising that the guards were drinking and laughing by a fire in their hut, and did not hear the noise of the unpacking of the dwarves or the footsteps of the four scouts. Their astonishment was enormous when Thorin Oakenshield stepped in through the door.

"Who are you and what do you want?" they shouted leaping to their feet and groping for weapons.

"Thorin son of Thrain son of Thror King under the Mountain!" said the dwarf in a loud voice, and he looked it, in spite of his torn clothes and draggled hood. The gold gleamed on his neck and waist; his eyes were dark and deep. "I have come back. I wish to see the Master of your town!"

Then there was tremendous excitement. Some of the more foolish ran out of the hut as if they expected the Mountain to go golden in the night and all the waters of the lake turn yellow right away. The captain of the guard came forward.

"And who are these?" he asked, pointing to Fili and Kili and Bilbo.

"The sons of my father's daughter," answered Thorin, "Fili and Kili of the race of Durin, and Mr. Baggins who has travelled with us out of the West."

"If you come in peace lay down your arms!" said the captain.

"We have none," said Thorin, and it was true enough: their knives had been taken from them by the wood-elves, and the great sword Orcrist too. Bilbo had his short sword, hidden as usual, but he said nothing about that. "We have no need of weapons, who return at last to our own as spoken of old. Nor could we fight against so many. Take us to your master!"

"He is at feast," said the captain.

"Then all the more reason for taking us to him," burst in Fili, who was getting impatient at these solemnities. "We are worn and famished after our long road and we have sick comrades. Now make haste and let us have no more words, or your master may have something to say to you."

"Follow me then," said the captain, and with six men about them he led them over the bridge through the gates and into the market-place of the town. This was a wide circle of quiet water surrounded by the tall piles on which were built the greater houses, and by long wooden quays with many steps and ladders going down to the surface of the lake. From one great hall shone many lights and there came the sound of many voices. They passed its doors and stood blinking in the light looking at long tables filled with folk.

"I am Thorin son of Thrain son of Thror King under the Mountain! I return!" cried Thorin in a loud voice from the door, before the captain could say anything.

All leaped to their feet. The Master of the town sprang from his great chair. But none rose in greater surprise than the raft-men of the elves who were sitting at the lower end of the hall. Pressing forward before the Master's table they cried:

"These are prisoners of our king that have escaped, wandering vagabond dwarves that could not give any good account of themselves, sneaking through the woods and molesting our people!"

"Is this true?" asked the Master. As a matter of fact he thought it far more likely than the return of the King under the Mountain, if any such person had ever existed.

"It is true that we were wrongfully waylaid by the Elvenking and imprisoned without cause as we journeyed back to our own land," answered Thorin. "But lock nor bar may hinder the home-coming spoken of old. Nor is this town in the Wood-elves' realm. I speak to the Master of the town of the Men of the Lake, not to the raft-men of the king."

Then the Master hesitated and looked from one to the other. The Elvenking was very powerful in those parts and the Master wished for no enmity with him, nor did he think much of old songs, giving his mind to trade and tolls, to cargoes and gold, to which habit he owed his position. Others were of different mind, however, and quickly the matter was settled without him. The news had spread from the doors of the hall like fire through all the town. People were shouting inside the hall and outside it. The quays were thronged with hurrying feet. Some began to sing snatches of old songs concerning the return of the King under the Mountain; that it was Thror's grandson not Thror himself that had come back did not bother them at all. Others took up the song and it rolled loud and high over the lake.

> *The King beneath the mountains,*
> *The King of carven stone,*
> *The lord of silver fountains*
> *Shall come into his own!*

> *His crown shall be upholden,*
> *His harp shall be restrung,*
> *His halls shall echo golden*
> *To songs of yore re-sung.*

The woods shall wave on mountains
And grass beneath the sun;
His wealth shall flow in fountains
And the rivers golden run.

The streams shall run in gladness,
The lakes shall shine and burn,
All sorrow fail and sadness
At the Mountain-king's return!

So they sang, or very like that, only there was a great deal more of it, and there was much shouting as well as the music of harps and of fiddles mixed up with it. Indeed such excitement had not been known in the town in the memory of the oldest grandfather. The Wood-elves themselves began to wonder greatly and even to be afraid. They did not know of course how Thorin had escaped, and they began to think their king might have made a serious mistake. As for the Master he saw there was nothing else for it but to obey the general clamour, for the moment at any rate, and to pretend to believe that Thorin was what he said. So he gave up to him his own great chair and set Fili and Kili beside him in places of honour. Even Bilbo was given a seat at the high table, and no explanation of where he came in—no songs had alluded to him even in the obscurest way—was asked for in the general bustle.

Soon afterwards the other dwarves were brought into the town amid scenes of astonishing enthusiasm. They were all doctored and fed and housed and pampered in the most delightful and satisfactory fashion. A large house was given up to Thorin and his company; boats and rowers were put at their service; and crowds sat outside and sang songs all day, or cheered if any dwarf showed so much as his nose.

Some of the songs were old ones; but some of them were quite new and spoke confidently of the sudden death of the dragon and of cargoes of rich presents coming down the river to Lake-town. These were inspired largely by the Master and they did not particularly please the dwarves, but in the meantime they were well contented and they quickly grew fat and strong again. Indeed within a week they were quite recovered, fitted out in fine cloth of their proper colours, with beards combed and trimmed, and proud steps. Thorin looked and walked as if his kingdom was already regained and Smaug chopped up into little pieces.

Then, as he had said, the dwarves' good feeling towards the little hobbit grew stronger every day. There were no more groans or grumbles. They drank his health, and they patted him on the back, and they made a great fuss of him; which was just as well, for he was not feeling particularly cheerful. He had not forgotten the look of the Mountain, nor the thought of the dragon, and he had besides a shocking cold. For three days he sneezed and coughed, and he could not go out, and even after that his speeches at banquets were limited to "Thag you very buch."

In the meanwhile the Wood-elves had gone back up the Forest River with their cargoes, and there was great excitement in the king's palace. I have never heard what happened to the chief of the guards and the butler. Nothing of course was ever said about keys or barrels while the dwarves stayed in Lake-town, and Bilbo was careful never to become invisible. Still, I daresay, more was guessed than was known, though doubtless Mr. Baggins remained a bit of a mystery. In any case the king knew now the dwarves' errand, or thought he did, and he said to himself:

"Very well! We'll see! No treasure will come back through Mirkwood without my having something to say in the matter. But I expect they will all come to a bad end, and serve them right!" He at any rate did not believe in dwarves fighting and killing dragons like Smaug, and he strongly suspected attempted burglary or something like it—which shows he was a wise elf and wiser than the men of the town, though not quite right, as we shall see in the end. He sent out his spies about the shores of the lake and as far northward towards the Mountain as they would go, and waited.

At the end of a fortnight Thorin began to think of departure. While the enthusiasm still lasted in the town was the time to get help. It would not do to let everything cool down with delay. So he spoke to the Master and his councillors and said that soon he and his company must go on towards the Mountain.

Then for the first time the Master was surprised and a little frightened; and he wondered if Thorin was after all really a descendant of the old kings. He had never thought that the dwarves would actually dare to approach Smaug, but believed they were frauds who would sooner or later be discovered and be turned out. He was wrong. Thorin, of course, was really the grandson of the King under the Mountain, and there is no knowing what a dwarf will not dare and do for revenge or the recovery of his own.

But the Master was not sorry at all to let them go. They were expensive to keep, and their arrival had turned things into a long holiday in which business was at a standstill. "Let them go and bother Smaug, and see how he welcomes them!" he thought. "Certainly, O Thorin Thrain's son Thror's son!" was what he said. "You must claim your own. The hour is at hand, spoken of old. What help we can offer shall be yours, and we trust to your gratitude when your kingdom is regained."

So one day, although autumn was now getting far on, and winds were cold, and leaves were falling fast, three large boats left Lake-town, laden with rowers, dwarves, Mr. Baggins, and many provisions. Horses and ponies had been sent round by circuitous paths to meet them at their appointed landing-place. The Master and his councillors bade them farewell from the great steps of the town-hall that went down to the lake. People sang on the quays and out of windows. The white oars dipped and splashed, and off they went north up the lake on the last stage of their long journey. The only person thoroughly unhappy was Bilbo.

Chapter XI

ON THE DOORSTEP

In two days going they rowed right up the Long Lake and passed out into the River Running, and now they could all see the Lonely Mountain towering grim and tall before them. The stream was strong and their going slow. At the end of the third day, some miles up the river, they drew in to the left or western bank and disembarked. Here they were joined by the horses with other provisions and necessaries and the ponies for their own use that had been sent to meet them. They packed what they could on the ponies and the rest was made into a store under a tent, but none of the men of the town would stay with them even for the night so near the shadow of the Mountain.

"Not at any rate until the songs have come true!" said they. It was easier to believe in the Dragon and less easy to believe in Thorin in these wild parts. Indeed their stores had no need of any guard, for all the land was desolate and empty. So their escort left them, making off swiftly down the river and the shoreward paths, although the night was already drawing on.

They spent a cold and lonely night and their spirits fell. The next day they set out again. Balin and Bilbo rode behind, each leading another pony heavily laden beside him; the others were some way ahead picking out a slow road, for there were no paths. They made north-west, slanting away from the River Running, and drawing ever nearer and nearer to a great spur of the Mountain that was flung out southwards towards them.

It was a weary journey, and a quiet and stealthy one. There was no laughter or song or sound of harps, and the pride and hopes which had stirred in their hearts at the singing of old songs by the lake died away to a plodding gloom. They knew that they were drawing near to the end of their journey, and that it might be a very horrible end. The land about them grew bleak and barren, though once, as Thorin told them, it had been green and fair. There was little grass, and before long there was neither bush nor tree, and only broken and blackened stumps to speak of ones long vanished. They were come to the Desolation of the Dragon, and they were come at the waning of the year.

They reached the skirts of the Mountain all the same without meeting any danger or any sign of the Dragon other than the wilderness he had made about his lair. The Mountain lay dark and silent before them and ever higher above them. They made their first camp on the western side of the great southern spur, which ended in a height called Ravenhill. On this there had been an old watch-post; but they dared not climb it yet, it was too exposed.

Before setting out to search the western spurs of the Mountain for the hidden door, on which all their hopes rested, Thorin sent out a scouting expedition to spy out the land to the South where the Front

Gate stood. For this purpose he chose Balin and Fili and Kili, and with them went Bilbo. They marched under the grey and silent cliffs to the feet of Ravenhill. There the river, after winding a wide loop over the valley of Dale, turned from the Mountain on its road to the Lake, flowing swift and noisily. Its bank was bare and rocky, tall and steep above the stream; and gazing out from it over the narrow water, foaming and splashing among many boulders, they could see in the wide valley shadowed by the Mountain's arms the grey ruins of ancient houses, towers, and walls.

"There lies all that is left of Dale," said Balin. "The mountain's sides were green with woods and all the sheltered valley rich and pleasant in the days when the bells rang in that town." He looked both sad and grim as he said this: he had been one of Thorin's companions on the day the Dragon came.

They did not dare to follow the river much further towards the Gate; but they went on beyond the end of the southern spur, until lying hidden behind a rock they could look out and see the dark cavernous opening in a great cliff-wall between the arms of the Mountain. Out of it the waters of the Running River sprang; and out of it too there came a steam and a dark smoke. Nothing moved in the waste, save the vapour and the water, and every now and again a black and ominous crow. The only sound was the sound of the stony water, and every now and again the harsh croak of a bird. Balin shuddered.

"Let us return!" he said. "We can do no good here! And I don't like these dark birds, they look like spies of evil."

. The Front Gate .

"The dragon is still alive and in the halls under the Mountain then—or I imagine so from the smoke," said the hobbit.

"That does not prove it," said Balin, "though I don't doubt you are right. But he might be gone away some time, or he might be lying out on the mountain-side keeping watch, and still I expect smokes and steams would come out of the gates: all the halls within must be filled with his foul reek."

With such gloomy thoughts, followed ever by croaking crows above them, they made their weary way back to the camp. Only in June they had been guests in the fair house of Elrond, and though autumn was now crawling towards winter that pleasant time now seemed years ago. They were alone in the perilous waste without hope of further help. They were at the end of their journey, but as far as ever, it seemed, from the end of their quest. None of them had much spirit left.

Now strange to say Mr. Baggins had more than the others. He would often borrow Thorin's map and gaze at it, pondering over the runes and the message of the moon-letters Elrond had read. It was he that made the dwarves begin the dangerous search on the western slopes for the secret door. They moved their camp then to a long valley, narrower than the great dale in the South where the Gates of the river stood, and walled with lower spurs of the Mountain. Two of these here thrust forward west from the main mass in long steep-sided ridges that fell ever downwards towards the plain. On this western side there were fewer signs of the dragon's marauding feet, and there was some grass for their ponies. From this western camp, shadowed all day by cliff and wall until the sun began to sink towards the forest, day by day they toiled in parties searching for paths up the mountainside. If the map was true, somewhere high above the cliff at the valley's head must stand the secret door. Day by day they came back to their camp without success.

But at last unexpectedly they found what they were seeking. Fili and Kili and the hobbit went back one day down the valley and scrambled among the tumbled rocks at its southern corner. About midday, creeping behind a great stone that stood alone like a pillar, Bilbo came on what looked like rough steps going upwards. Following these excitedly he and the dwarves found traces of a narrow track, often lost, often rediscovered, that wandered on to the top of the southern ridge and brought them at last to a still narrower ledge, which turned north across the face of the Mountain. Looking down they saw that they were at the top of the cliff at the valley's head and were gazing down on to their own camp below. Silently, clinging to the rocky wall on their right, they went in single file along the ledge, till the wall opened and they turned into a little steep-walled bay, grassy-floored, still and quiet. Its entrance which they had found could not be seen from below because of the overhang of the cliff, nor from further off because it was so small that it looked like a dark crack and no more. It was not a cave and was open to the sky above; but at its inner end a flat wall rose up that in the lower part, close to the ground, was as smooth and upright as masons' work, but without a joint or

crevice to be seen. No sign was there of post or lintel
or threshold, nor any sign of bar or bolt or key-hole;
yet they did not doubt that they had found the door
at last.

They beat on it, they thrust and pushed at it, they
implored it to move, they spoke fragments of broken
spells of opening, and nothing stirred. At last tired
out they rested on the grass at its feet, and then at
evening began their long climb down.

There was excitement in the camp that night. In the
morning they prepared to move once more. Only
Bofur and Bombur were left behind to guard the
ponies and such stores as they had brought with
them from the river. The others went down the
valley and up the newly found path, and so to the
narrow ledge. Along this they could carry no bundles
or packs, so narrow and breathless was it, with a fall
of a hundred and fifty feet beside them on to sharp
rocks below; but each of them took a good coil of
rope wound tight about his waist, and so at last
without mishap they reached the little grassy bay.

There they made their third camp, hauling up
what they needed from below with their ropes. Down
the same way they were able occasionally to lower
one of the more active dwarves, such as Kili, to
exchange such news as there was, or to take a share
in the guard below, while Bofur was hauled up to the
higher camp. Bombur would not come up either the
rope or the path.

"I am too fat for such fly-walks," he said. "I should
turn dizzy and tread on my beard, and then you
would be thirteen again. And the knotted ropes are

too slender for my weight." Luckily for him that was not true, as you will see.

In the meanwhile some of them explored the ledge beyond the opening and found a path that led higher and higher on to the mountain; but they did not dare to venture very far that way, nor was there much use in it. Out up there a silence reigned, broken by no bird or sound except that of the wind in the crannies of stone. They spoke low and never called or sang, for danger brooded in every rock. The others who were busy with the secret of the door had no more success. They were too eager to trouble about the runes or the moon-letters, but tried without resting to discover where exactly in the smooth face of the rock the door was hidden. They had brought picks and tools of many sorts from Lake-town, and at first they tried to use these. But when they struck the stone the handles splintered and jarred their arms cruelly, and the steel heads broke or bent like lead. Mining work, they saw clearly, was no good against the magic that had shut this door; and they grew terrified, too, of the echoing noise.

Bilbo found sitting on the doorstep lonesome and wearisome—there was not a doorstep, of course, really, but they used to call the little grassy space between the wall and the opening the "doorstep" in fun, remembering Bilbo's words long ago at the unexpected party in his hobbit-hole, when he said they could sit on the doorstep till they thought of something. And sit and think they did, or wandered aimlessly about, and glummer and glummer they became.

Their spirits had risen a little at the discovery of the path, but now they sank into their boots; and yet they would not give it up and go away. The hobbit was no longer much brighter than the dwarves. He would do nothing but sit with his back to the rock-face and stare away west through the opening, over the cliff, over the wide lands to the black wall of Mirkwood, and to the distances beyond, in which he sometimes thought he could catch glimpses of the Misty Mountains small and far. If the dwarves asked him what he was doing he answered:

"You said sitting on the doorstep and thinking would be my job, not to mention getting inside, so I am sitting and thinking." But I am afraid he was not thinking much of the job, but of what lay beyond the blue distance, the quiet Western Land and the Hill and his hobbit-hole under it.

A large grey stone lay in the centre of the grass and he stared moodily at it or watched the great snails. They seemed to love the little shut-in bay with its walls of cool rock, and there were many of them of huge size crawling slowly and stickily along its sides.

"Tomorrow begins the last week of autumn," said Thorin one day.

"And winter comes after autumn," said Bifur.

"And next year after that," said Dwalin, "and our beards will grow till they hang down the cliff to the valley before anything happens here. What is our burglar doing for us? Since he has got an invisible ring, and ought to be a specially excellent performer now, I am beginning to think he might go through the Front Gate and spy things out a bit!"

Bilbo heard this—the dwarves were on the rocks just above the enclosure where he was sitting—and "Good Gracious!" he thought, "so that is what they are beginning to think, is it? It is always poor me that has to get them out of their difficulties, at least since the wizard left. Whatever am I going to do? I might have known that something dreadful would happen to me in the end. I don't think I could bear to see the unhappy valley of Dale again, and as for that steaming gate!!!"

That night he was very miserable and hardly slept. Next day the dwarves all went wandering off in various directions; some were exercising the ponies down below, some were roving about the mountain-side. All day Bilbo sat gloomily in the grassy bay gazing at the stone, or out west through the narrow opening. He had a queer feeling that he was waiting for something. "Perhaps the wizard will suddenly come back today," he thought.

If he lifted his head he could see a glimpse of the distant forest. As the sun turned west there was a gleam of yellow upon its far roof, as if the light caught the last pale leaves. Soon he saw the orange ball of the sun sinking towards the level of his eyes. He went to the opening and there pale and faint was a thin new moon above the rim of Earth.

At that very moment he heard a sharp crack behind him. There on the grey stone in the grass was an enormous thrush, nearly coal black, its pale yellow breast freckled with dark spots. Crack! It had caught a snail and was knocking it on the stone. Crack! Crack!

Suddenly Bilbo understood. Forgetting all danger he stood on the ledge and hailed the dwarves, shouting and waving. Those that were nearest came tumbling over the rocks and as fast as they could along the ledge to him, wondering what on earth was the matter; the others shouted to be hauled up the ropes (except Bombur, of course: he was asleep).

Quickly Bilbo explained. They all fell silent: the hobbit standing by the grey stone, and the dwarves with wagging beards watching impatiently. The sun sank lower and lower, and their hopes fell. It sank into a belt of reddened cloud and disappeared. The dwarves groaned, but still Bilbo stood almost without moving. The little moon was dipping to the horizon. Evening was coming on. Then suddenly when their hope was lowest a red ray of the sun escaped like a finger through a rent in the cloud. A gleam of light came straight through the opening into the bay and fell on the smooth rock-face. The old thrush, who had been watching from a high perch with beady eyes and head cocked on one side, gave a sudden trill. There was a loud crack. A flake of rock split from the wall and fell. A hole appeared suddenly about three feet from the ground.

Quickly, trembling lest the chance should fade, the dwarves rushed to the rock and pushed—in vain.

"The key! The key!" cried Bilbo. "Where is Thorin?"

Thorin hurried up.

"The key!" shouted Bilbo. "The key that went with the map! Try it now while there is still time!"

Then Thorin stepped up and drew the key on its chain from round his neck. He put it to the hole. It fitted and it turned! Snap! The gleam went out, the sun sank, the moon was gone, and evening sprang into the sky.

Now they all pushed together, and slowly a part of the rock-wall gave way. Long straight cracks appeared and widened. A door five feet high and three broad was outlined, and slowly without a sound swung inwards. It seemed as if darkness flowed out like a vapour from the hole in the mountain-side, and deep darkness in which nothing could be seen lay before their eyes, a yawning mouth leading in and down.

Chapter XII

INSIDE INFORMATION

For a long time the dwarves stood in the dark before the door and debated, until at last Thorin spoke:

"Now is the time for our esteemed Mr. Baggins, who has proved himself a good companion on our long road, and a hobbit full of courage and resource far exceeding his size, and if I may say so possessed of good luck far exceeding the usual allowance—now is the time for him to perform the service for which he was included in our Company; now is the time for him to earn his Reward."

You are familiar with Thorin's style on important occasions, so I will not give you any more of it, though he went on a good deal longer than this. It certainly was an important occasion, but Bilbo felt impatient. By now he was quite familiar with Thorin too, and he knew what he was driving at.

"If you mean you think it is my job to go into the secret passage first, O Thorin Thrain's son Oakenshield, may your beard grow ever longer," he said crossly, "say so at once and have done! I might refuse. I have got you out of two messes already, which were hardly in the original bargain, so that I am, I think, already owed some reward. But 'third time pays for all' as my father used to say, and somehow I don't think I shall refuse. Perhaps I have begun to trust my luck more than I used to in the old days"—he meant last spring before he left his own house, but it seemed centuries ago—"but anyway I think I will go and have a peep at once and get it over. Now who is coming with me?"

He did not expect a chorus of volunteers, so he was not disappointed. Fili and Kili looked uncomfortable and stood on one leg, but the others made no pretence of offering—except old Balin, the lookout man, who was rather fond of the hobbit. He said he would come inside at least and perhaps a bit of the way too, ready to call for help if necessary.

The most that can be said for the dwarves is this: they intended to pay Bilbo really handsomely for his services; they had brought him to do a nasty job for them, and they did not mind the poor little fellow doing it if he would; but they would all have done their best to get him out of trouble, if he got into it, as they did in the case of the trolls at the beginning of their adventures before they had any particular reasons for being grateful to him. There it is: dwarves are not heroes, but calculating folk with a great idea of the value of money; some are tricky and treacherous and pretty bad lots; some are not, but are decent enough people like Thorin and Company, if you don't expect too much.

The stars were coming out behind him in a pale sky barred with black when the hobbit crept through the enchanted door and stole into the Mountain. It was far easier going than he expected. This was no goblin entrance, or rough wood-elves' cave. It was a passage made by dwarves, at the height of their wealth and skill: straight as a ruler, smooth-floored and smooth-sided,

going with a gentle never-varying slope direct—to some
distant end in the blackness below.

After a while Balin bade Bilbo "Good luck!" and
stopped where he could still see the faint outline of
the door, and by a trick of the echoes of the tunnel
hear the rustle of the whispering voices of the others
just outside. Then the hobbit slipped on his ring, and
warned by the echoes to take more than hobbit's care
to make no sound, he crept noiselessly down, down,
down into the dark. He was trembling with fear, but
his little face was set and grim. Already he was a very
different hobbit from the one that had run out
without a pocket-handkerchief from Bag-End long
ago. He had not had a pocket-handkerchief for ages.
He loosened his dagger in its sheath, tightened his
belt, and went on.

"Now you are in for it at last, Bilbo Baggins," he said
to himself. "You went and put your foot right in it
that night of the party, and now you have got to pull
it out and pay for it! Dear me, what a fool I was and
am!" said the least Tookish part of him. "I have
absolutely no use for dragon-guarded treasures, and
the whole lot could stay here for ever, if only I could
wake up and find this beastly tunnel was my own
front-hall at home!"

He did not wake up of course, but went still on and
on, till all sign of the door behind had faded away. He
was altogether alone. Soon he thought it was beginning to feel warm. "Is that a kind of a glow I seem to
see coming right ahead down there?" he thought.

It was. As he went forward it grew and grew, till
there was no doubt about it. It was a red light

steadily getting redder and redder. Also it was now undoubtedly hot in the tunnel. Wisps of vapour floated up and past him and he began to sweat. A sound, too, began to throb in his ears, a sort of bubbling like the noise of a large pot galloping on the fire, mixed with a rumble as of a gigantic tom-cat purring. This grew to the unmistakable gurgling noise of some vast animal snoring in its sleep down there in the red glow in front of him.

It was at this point that Bilbo stopped. Going on from there was the bravest thing he ever did. The tremendous things that happened afterwards were as nothing compared to it. He fought the real battle in the tunnel alone, before he ever saw the vast danger that lay in wait. At any rate after a short halt go on he did; and you can picture him coming to the end of the tunnel, an opening of much the same size and shape as the door above. Through it peeps the hobbit's little head. Before him lies the great bottommost cellar or dungeon-hall of the ancient dwarves right at the Mountain's root. It is almost dark so that its vastness can only be dimly guessed, but rising from the near side of the rocky floor there is a great glow. The glow of Smaug!

There he lay, a vast red-golden dragon, fast asleep; a thrumming came from his jaws and nostrils, and wisps of smoke, but his fires were low in slumber. Beneath him, under all his limbs and his huge coiled tail, and about him on all sides stretching away across the unseen floors, lay countless piles of precious things, gold wrought and unwrought, gems and jewels, and silver red-stained in the ruddy light.

Smaug lay, with wings folded like an immeasurable bat, turned partly on one side, so that the hobbit could see his underparts and his long pale belly crusted with gems and fragments of gold from his long lying on his costly bed. Behind him where the walls were nearest could dimly be seen coats of mail, helms and axes, swords and spears hanging; and there in rows stood great jars and vessels filled with a wealth that could not be guessed.

To say that Bilbo's breath was taken away is no description at all. There are no words left to express his staggerment, since Men changed the language that they learned of elves in the days when all the world was wonderful. Bilbo had heard tell and sing of dragon-hoards before, but the splendour, the lust, the glory of such treasure had never yet come home to him. His heart was filled and pierced with enchantment and with the desire of dwarves; and he gazed motionless, almost forgetting the frightful guardian, at the gold beyond price and count.

He gazed for what seemed an age, before drawn almost against his will, he stole from the shadow of the doorway, across the floor to the nearest edge of the mounds of treasure. Above him the sleeping dragon lay, a dire menace even in his sleep. He grasped a great two-handled cup, as heavy as he could carry, and cast one fearful eye upwards. Smaug stirred a wing, opened a claw, the rumble of his snoring changed its note.

Then Bilbo fled. But the dragon did not wake—not yet—but shifted into other dreams of greed and violence, lying there in his stolen hall while the little hobbit toiled back up the long tunnel. His heart was beating and a more fevered shaking was in his legs than when he was going down, but still he clutched the cup, and his chief thought was: "I've done it! This will show them. 'More like a grocer than a burglar' indeed! Well, we'll hear no more of that."

Nor did he. Balin was overjoyed to see the hobbit again, and as delighted as he was surprised. He picked Bilbo up and carried him out into the open air. It was midnight and clouds had covered the stars, but Bilbo lay with his eyes shut, gasping and taking pleasure in the feel of the fresh air again, and hardly noticing the excitement of the dwarves, or how they praised him and patted him on the back and put themselves and all their families for generations to come at his service.

The dwarves were still passing the cup from hand to hand and talking delightedly of the recovery of their treasure, when suddenly a vast rumbling woke in the mountain underneath as if it was an old volcano that had made up its mind to start eruptions once again. The door behind them was pulled nearly to, and blocked from closing with a stone, but up the long tunnel came the dreadful echoes, from far down in the depths, of a bellowing and a trampling that made the ground beneath them tremble.

Then the dwarves forgot their joy and their confident boasts of a moment before and cowered down in fright. Smaug was still to be reckoned with. It does not do to leave a live dragon out of your calculations, if you live near him. Dragons may not have much real use for all their wealth, but they know it to an ounce as a rule, especially after long possession; and Smaug was no exception. He had passed from an uneasy dream (in which a warrior, altogether insignificant in size but provided with a bitter sword and great courage, figured most unpleasantly) to a doze, and from a doze to wide waking. There was a breath of strange air in his cave. Could there be a draught from that little hole? He had never felt quite happy about it, though it was so small, and now he glared at it in suspicion and wondered why he had never blocked it up. Of late he had half fancied he had caught the dim echoes of a knocking sound from far above that came down through it to his lair. He stirred and stretched forth his neck to sniff. Then he missed the cup!

Thieves! Fire! Murder! Such a thing had not happened since first he came to the Mountain! His rage passes description—the sort of rage that is only seen when rich folk that have more than they can enjoy suddenly lose something that they have long had but have never before used or wanted. His fire belched forth, the hall smoked, he shook the mountain-roots. He thrust his head in vain at the little hole, and then coiling his length together, roaring like thunder underground, he sped from his deep lair through its great door, out into the huge passages of the mountain-palace and up towards the Front Gate.

To hunt the whole mountain till he had caught the thief and had torn and trampled him was his one thought. He issued from the Gate, the waters rose in fierce whistling steam, and up he soared blazing into the air and settled on the mountain-top in a spout of green and scarlet flame. The dwarves heard the awful rumour of his flight, and they crouched against the walls of the grassy terrace cringing under boulders, hoping somehow to escape the frightful eyes of the hunting dragon.

There they would have all been killed, if it had not been for Bilbo once again. "Quick! Quick!" he gasped. "The door! The tunnel! It's no good here."

Roused by these words they were just about to creep inside the tunnel when Bifur gave a cry: "My cousins! Bombur and Bofur—we have forgotten them, they are down in the valley!"

"They will be slain, and all our ponies too, and all our stores lost," moaned the others. "We can do nothing."

"Nonsense!" said Thorin, recovering his dignity. "We cannot leave them. Get inside Mr. Baggins and Balin, and you two Fili and Kili—the dragon shan't have all of us. Now you others, where are the ropes? Be quick!"

Those were perhaps the worst moments they had been through yet. The horrible sounds of Smaug's anger were echoing in the stony hollows far above; at any moment he might come blazing down or fly whirling round and find them there, near the perilous cliff's edge hauling madly on the ropes. Up came Bofur, and still all was safe. Up came Bombur, puffing and blowing while the ropes creaked, and still all was safe. Up came some tools and bundles of stores, and then danger was upon them.

A whirring noise was heard. A red light touched the points of standing rocks. The dragon came.

They had barely time to fly back to the tunnel, pulling and dragging in their bundles, when Smaug came hurtling from the North, licking the mountain-sides with flame, beating his great wings with a noise like a roaring wind. His hot breath shrivelled the grass before the door, and drove in through the crack they had left and scorched them as they lay hid. Flickering fires leaped up and black rock-shadows danced. Then darkness fell as he passed again. The ponies screamed with terror, burst their ropes and galloped wildly off. The dragon swooped and turned to pursue them, and was gone.

"That'll be the end of our poor beasts!" said Thorin. "Nothing can escape Smaug once he sees it. Here we are and here we shall have to stay, unless any one fancies tramping the long open miles back to the river with Smaug on the watch!"

It was not a pleasant thought! They crept further down the tunnel, and there they lay and shivered though it was warm and stuffy, until dawn came pale through the crack of the door. Every now and again through the night they could hear the roar of the flying dragon grow and then pass and fade, as he hunted round and round the mountain-sides.

He guessed from the ponies, and from the traces of the camps he had discovered, that men had come up from the river and the lake and had scaled the mountain-side from the valley where the ponies had been standing; but the door withstood his searching eye, and the little high-walled bay had kept out his fiercest flames. Long he had hunted in vain till the dawn chilled his wrath and he went back to his golden couch to sleep—and to gather new strength. He would not forget or forgive the theft, not if a thousand years turned him to smouldering stone, but he could afford to wait. Slow and silent he crept back to his lair and half closed his eyes.

When morning came the terror of the dwarves grew less. They realized that dangers of this kind were inevitable in dealing with such a guardian, and that it was no good giving up their quest yet. Nor could they get away just now, as Thorin had pointed out. Their ponies were lost or killed, and they would have to wait some time before Smaug relaxed his watch sufficiently for them to dare the long way on foot. Luckily they had saved enough of their stores to last them still for some time.

They debated long on what was to be done, but they could think of no way of getting rid of Smaug—which had always been a weak point in their plans, as Bilbo felt inclined to point out. Then as is the nature of folk that are thoroughly perplexed, they began to grumble at the hobbit, blaming him for what had at first so pleased them: for bringing away a cup and stirring up Smaug's wrath so soon.

"What else do you suppose a burglar is to do?" asked Bilbo angrily. "I was not engaged to kill dragons, that is warrior's work, but to steal treasure. I made the best beginning I could. Did you expect me to trot back with the whole hoard of Thror on my back? If there is any grumbling to be done, I think I might have a say. You ought to have brought five hundred burglars not one. I am sure it reflects great credit on your grandfather, but you cannot pretend that you ever made the vast extent of his wealth clear to me. I should want hundreds of years to bring it all up, if I was fifty times as big, and Smaug as tame as a rabbit."

After that of course the dwarves begged his pardon. "What then do you propose we should do, Mr. Baggins?" asked Thorin politely.

"I have no idea at the moment—if you mean about removing the treasure. That obviously depends entirely on some new turn of luck and the getting rid of Smaug. Getting rid of dragons is not at all in my line, but I will do my best to think about it. Personally I have no hopes at all, and wish I was safe back at home."

"Never mind that for the moment! What are we to do now, to-day?"

"Well, if you really want my advice, I should say we can do nothing but stay where we are. By day we can no doubt creep out safely enough to take the air. Perhaps before long one or two could be chosen to go back to the store by the river and replenish our supplies. But in the meanwhile everyone ought to be well inside the tunnel by night.

"Now I will make you an offer. I have got my ring and will creep down this very noon—then if ever Smaug ought to be napping—and see what he is up to. Perhaps something will turn up. 'Every worm has his weak spot,' as my father used to say, though I am sure it was not from personal experience."

Naturally the dwarves accepted the offer eagerly. Already they had come to respect little Bilbo. Now he had become the real leader in their adventure. He had begun to have ideas and plans of his own. When midday came he got ready for another journey down into the Mountain. He did not like it of course, but it was not so bad now he knew, more or less, what was in front of him. Had he known more about dragons and their wily ways, he might have been more frightened and less hopeful of catching this one napping.

The sun was shining when he started, but it was as dark as night in the tunnel. The light from the door, almost closed, soon faded as he went down. So silent was his going that smoke on a gentle wind could hardly have surpassed it, and he was inclined to feel a bit proud of himself as he drew near the lower door. There was only the very faintest glow to be seen.

"Old Smaug is weary and asleep," he thought. "He can't see me and he won't hear me. Cheer up Bilbo!" He had forgotten or had never heard about dragons' sense of smell. It is also an awkward fact that they can keep half an eye open watching while they sleep, if they are suspicious.

Smaug certainly looked fast asleep, almost dead and dark, with scarcely a snore more than a whiff of unseen steam, when Bilbo peeped once more from the entrance. He was just about to step out on to the floor when he caught a sudden thin and piercing ray of red from under the drooping lid of Smaug's left eye. He was only pretending to sleep! He was watching the tunnel entrance! Hurriedly Bilbo stepped back and blessed the luck of his ring. Then Smaug spoke.

"Well, thief! I smell you and I feel your air. I hear your breath. Come along! Help yourself again, there is plenty and to spare!"

But Bilbo was not quite so unlearned in dragon-lore as all that, and if Smaug hoped to get him to come nearer so easily he was disappointed. "No thank you, O Smaug the Tremendous!" he replied.

"I did not come for presents. I only wished to have a look at you and see if you were truly as great as tales say. I did not believe them."

"Do you now?" said the dragon somewhat flattered, even though he did not believe a word of it.

"Truly songs and tales fall utterly short of the reality, O Smaug the Chiefest and Greatest of Calamities," replied Bilbo.

"You have nice manners for a thief and a liar," said the dragon. "You seem familiar with my name, but I don't seem to remember smelling you before. Who are you and where do you come from, may I ask?"

"You may indeed! I come from under the hill, and under the hills and over the hills my paths led. And through the air. I am he that walks unseen."

"So I can well believe," said Smaug, "but that is hardly your usual name."

"I am the clue-finder, the web-cutter, the stinging fly. I was chosen for the lucky number."

"Lovely titles!" sneered the dragon. "But lucky numbers don't always come off."

"I am he that buries his friends alive and drowns them and draws them alive again from the water. I came from the end of a bag, but no bag went over me."

"These don't sound so creditable," scoffed Smaug.

"I am the friend of bears and the guest of eagles. I am Ringwinner and Luckwearer; and I am Barrel-rider," went on Bilbo beginning to be pleased with his riddling.

"That's better!" said Smaug. "But don't let your imagination run away with you!"

* * *

This of course is the way to talk to dragons, if you don't want to reveal your proper name (which is wise), and don't want to infuriate them by a flat refusal (which is also very wise). No dragon can resist the fascination of riddling talk and of wasting time trying to understand it. There was a lot here which Smaug did not understand at all (though I expect you do, since you know all about Bilbo's adventures to which he was referring), but he thought he understood enough, and he chuckled in his wicked inside.

"I thought so last night," he smiled to himself. "Lake-men, some nasty scheme of those miserable tub-trading Lake-men, or I'm a lizard. I haven't been down that way for an age and an age; but I will soon alter that!"

"Very well, O Barrel-rider!" he said aloud. "Maybe Barrel was your pony's name; and maybe not, though it was fat enough. You may walk unseen, but you did not walk all the way. Let me tell you I ate six ponies last night and I shall catch and eat all the others before long. In return for the excellent meal I will give you one piece of advice for your good: don't have more to do with dwarves than you can help!"

"Dwarves!" said Bilbo in pretended surprise.

"Don't talk to me!" said Smaug. "I know the smell (and taste) of dwarf—no one better. Don't tell me that I can eat a dwarf-ridden pony and not know it! You'll come to a bad end, if you go with such friends, Thief Barrel-rider. I don't mind if you go back and tell them so from me." But he did not tell Bilbo that there was one smell he could not make out at all, hobbit-smell; it was quite outside his experience and puzzled him mightily.

"I suppose you got a fair price for that cup last night?" he went on. "Come now, did you? Nothing at all! Well, that's just like them. And I suppose they are skulking outside, and your job is to do all the dangerous work and get what you can when I'm not looking—for them? And you will get a fair share? Don't you believe it! If you get off alive, you will be lucky."

Bilbo was now beginning to feel really uncomfortable. Whenever Smaug's roving eye, seeking for him in the shadows, flashed across him, he trembled, and an unaccountable desire seized hold of him to rush out and reveal himself and tell all the truth to Smaug. In fact he was in grievous danger of coming under the dragon-spell. But plucking up courage he spoke again.

"You don't know everything, O Smaug the Mighty," said he. "Not gold alone brought us hither."

"Ha! Ha! You admit the 'us'" laughed Smaug. "Why not say 'us fourteen' and be done with it, Mr. Lucky Number? I am pleased to hear that you had other business in these parts besides my gold. In that case you may, perhaps, not altogether waste your time.

"I don't know if it has occurred to you that, even if you could steal the gold bit by bit—a matter of a hundred years or so—you could not get it very far? Not much use on the mountain-side? Not much use in the forest? Bless me! Had you never thought of the catch? A fourteenth share, I suppose, or something like it, those were the terms, eh? But what about delivery? What about cartage? What about armed guards and tolls?" And Smaug laughed aloud. He had a wicked and a wily heart, and he knew his guesses were not far out, though he suspected that the Lake-men were at the back of the plans, and that most of the plunder was meant to stop there in the town by the shore that in his young days had been called Esgaroth.

You will hardly believe it, but poor Bilbo was really very taken aback. So far all his thoughts and energies had been concentrated on getting to the Mountain and finding the entrance. He had never bothered to wonder how the treasure was to be removed, certainly never how any part of it that might fall to his share was to be brought back all the way to Bag-End Under-Hill.

Now a nasty suspicion began to grow in his mind—had the dwarves forgotten this important point too, or were they laughing in their sleeves at him all the time? That is the effect that dragon-talk has on the inexperienced. Bilbo of course ought to have been on his guard; but Smaug had rather an overwhelming personality.

"I tell you," he said, in an effort to remain loyal to his friends and to keep his end up, "that gold was only an afterthought with us. We came over hill and under hill, by wave and wind, for *Revenge*. Surely, O Smaug the unassessably wealthy, you must realize that your success has made you some bitter enemies?"

Then Smaug really did laugh—a devastating sound which shook Bilbo to the floor, while far up in the tunnel the dwarves huddled together and imagined that the hobbit had come to a sudden and a nasty end.

"Revenge!" he snorted, and the light of his eyes lit the hall from floor to ceiling like scarlet lightning. "Revenge! The King under the Mountain is dead and where are his kin that dare seek revenge? Girion Lord of Dale is dead, and I have eaten his people like a wolf among sheep, and where are his sons' sons that dare approach me? I kill where I wish and none dare resist. I laid low the warriors of old and their like is not in the world today. Then I was but young and tender. Now I am old and strong, strong, strong, Thief in the Shadows!" he gloated. "My armour is like tenfold shields, my teeth are swords, my claws spears, the shock of my tail a thunderbolt, my wings a hurricane, and my breath death!"

"I have always understood," said Bilbo in a frightened squeak, "that dragons were softer underneath, especially in the region of the—er—chest; but doubtless one so fortified has thought of that."

The dragon stopped short in his boasting. "Your information is antiquated," he snapped. "I am armoured above and below with iron scales and hard gems. No blade can pierce me."

"I might have guessed it," said Bilbo. "Truly there can no-where be found the equal of Lord Smaug the Impenetrable. What magnificence to possess a waist-coat of fine diamonds!"

"Yes, it is rare and wonderful, indeed," said Smaug absurdly pleased. He did not know that the hobbit had already caught a glimpse of his peculiar under-covering on his previous visit, and was itching for a closer view for reasons of his own. The dragon rolled over. "Look!" he said. "What do you say to that?"

"Dazzlingly marvellous! Perfect! Flawless! Staggering!" exclaimed Bilbo aloud, but what he thought inside was: "Old fool! Why, there is a large patch in the hollow of his left breast as bare as a snail out of its shell!"

After he had seen that Mr. Baggins' one idea was to get away. "Well, I really must not detain Your Magnificence any longer," he said, "or keep you from much needed rest. Ponies take some catching, I believe, after a long start. And so do burglars," he added as a parting shot, as he darted back and fled up the tunnel.

It was an unfortunate remark, for the dragon spouted terrific flames after him, and fast though he sped up the slope, he had not gone nearly far enough to be comfortable before the ghastly head of Smaug was thrust against the opening behind. Luckily the whole head and jaws could not squeeze in, but the nostrils sent forth fire and vapour to pursue him, and he was nearly overcome, and stumbled blindly on in great pain and fear. He had been feeling rather pleased with the cleverness of his conversation with Smaug, but his mistake at the end shook him into better sense.

"Never laugh at live dragons, Bilbo you fool!" he said to himself, and it became a favourite saying of his later, and passed into a proverb. "You aren't nearly through this adventure yet," he added, and that was pretty true as well.

The afternoon was turning into evening when he came out again and stumbled and fell in a faint on the 'doorstep'. The dwarves revived him, and doctored his scorches as well as they could; but it was a long time before the hair on the back of his head and his heels grew properly again: it had all been singed and frizzled right down to the skin. In the meanwhile his friends did their best to cheer him up; and they were eager for his story, especially wanting to know why the dragon had made such an awful noise, and how Bilbo had escaped.

But the hobbit was worried and uncomfortable, and they had difficulty in getting anything out of him. On thinking things over he was now regretting some of the things he had said to the dragon, and was not eager to repeat them. The old thrush was sitting on a rock near by with his head cocked on one side, listening to all that was said. It shows what an ill temper Bilbo was in: he picked up a stone and threw it at the thrush, which merely fluttered aside and came back.

"Drat the bird!" said Bilbo crossly. "I believe he is listening, and I don't like the look of him."

"Leave him alone!" said Thorin. "The thrushes are good and friendly—this is a very old bird indeed, and is maybe the last left of the ancient breed that used to live about here, tame to the hands of my father and grandfather. They were a long-lived and magical race, and this might even be one of those that were alive then, a couple of hundreds of years or more ago. The Men of Dale used to have the trick of understanding their language, and used them for messengers to fly to the Men of the Lake and else-where."

"Well, he'll have news to take to Lake-town all right, if that is what he is after," said Bilbo; "though I

don't suppose there are any people left there that
trouble with thrush-language."

"Why what has happened?" cried the dwarves.
"Do get on with your tale!"

So Bilbo told them all he could remember, and he
confessed that he had a nasty feeling that the dragon
guessed too much from his riddles added to the
camps and the ponies. "I am sure he knows we came
from Lake-town and had help from there; and I have
a horrible feeling that his next move may be in that
direction. I wish to goodness I had never said that
about Barrel-rider; it would make even a blind rabbit
in these parts think of the Lake-men."

"Well, well! It cannot be helped, and it is difficult
not to slip in talking to a dragon, or so I have always
heard," said Balin anxious to comfort him. "I think
you did very well, if you ask me—you found out one
very useful thing at any rate, and got home alive, and
that is more than most can say who have had words
with the likes of Smaug. It may be a mercy and a
blessing yet to know of the bare patch in the old
Worm's diamond waistcoat."

That turned the conversation, and they all began
discussing dragon-slayings historical, dubious, and
mythical, and the various sorts of stabs and jabs and
undercuts, and the different arts devices and strata-
gems by which they had been accomplished. The
general opinion was that catching a dragon napping
was not as easy as it sounded, and the attempt to
stick one or prod one asleep was more likely to end
in disaster than a bold frontal attack. All the while
they talked the thrush listened, till at last when the
stars began to peep forth, it silently spread its wings

and flew away. And all the while they talked and the shadows lengthened Bilbo became more and more unhappy and his foreboding grew.

At last he interrupted them. "I am sure we are very unsafe here," he said, "and I don't see the point of sitting here. The dragon has withered all the pleasant green, and anyway the night has come and it is cold. But I feel it in my bones that this place will be attacked again. Smaug knows now how I came down to his hall, and you can trust him to guess where the other end of the tunnel is. He will break all this side of the Mountain to bits, if necessary, to stop up our entrance, and if we are smashed with it the better he will like it."

"You are very gloomy, Mr. Baggins!" said Thorin. "Why has not Smaug blocked the lower end, then, if he is so eager to keep us out? He has not, or we should have heard him."

"I don't know, I don't know—because at first he wanted to try and lure me in again, I suppose, and now perhaps because he is waiting till after tonight's hunt, or because he does not want to damage his bedroom if he can help it—but I wish you would not argue. Smaug will be coming out at any minute now, and our only hope is to get well in the tunnel and shut the door."

He seemed so much in earnest that the dwarves at last did as he said, though they delayed shutting the door—it seemed a desperate plan, for no one knew whether or how they could get it open again from the inside, and the thought of being shut in a place from which the only way out led through the dragon's lair was not one they liked. Also everything seemed quite quiet, both outside and down the tunnel. So for a longish while they sat inside not far down from the half-open door and went on talking.

The talk turned to the dragon's wicked words about the dwarves. Bilbo wished he had never heard them, or at least that he could feel quite certain that the dwarves now were absolutely honest when they declared that they had never thought at all about what would happen after the treasure had been won. "We knew it would be a desperate venture," said Thorin, "and we know that still; and I still think that when we have won it will be time enough to think what to do about it. As for your share, Mr. Baggins, I assure you we are more than grateful and you shall choose your own fourteenth, as soon as we have anything to divide. I am sorry if you are worried about transport, and I admit the difficulties are great—the lands have not become less wild with the passing of time, rather the reverse—but we will do whatever we can for you, and take our share of the cost when the time comes. Believe me or not as you like!"

From that the talk turned to the great hoard itself and to the things that Thorin and Balin remembered. They wondered if they were still lying there unharmed in the hall below: the spears that were made for the armies of the great King Bladorthin (long since dead), each had a thrice-forged head and their shafts were inlaid with cunning gold, but they were never delivered or paid for; shields made for warriors long dead; the great golden cup of Thror, two-handed, hammered and carven with birds and flowers whose eyes and petals were of jewels; coats of mail gilded and silvered and impenetrable; the necklace of Girion, Lord

of Dale, made of five hundred emeralds green as
grass, which he gave for the arming of his eldest son in
a coat of dwarf-linked rings the like of which had
never been made before, for it was wrought of pure
silver to the power and strength of triple steel. But
fairest of all was the great white gem, which the
dwarves had found beneath the roots of the Mountain,
the Heart of the Mountain, the Arkenstone of Thrain.

"The Arkenstone! The Arkenstone!" murmured
Thorin in the dark, half dreaming with his chin upon
his knees. "It was like a globe with a thousand facets;
it shone like silver in the firelight, like water in the
sun, like snow under the stars, like rain upon the
Moon!"

But the enchanted desire of the hoard had fallen
from Bilbo. All through their talk he was only half listening to them. He sat nearest to the door with one
ear cocked for any beginnings of a sound without, his
other was alert for echoes beyond the murmurs of
the dwarves, for any whisper of a movement from far
below.

Darkness grew deeper and he grew ever more
uneasy. "Shut the door!" he begged them, "I fear
that dragon in my marrow. I like this silence far less
than the uproar of last night. Shut the door before it
is too late!"

Something in his voice gave the dwarves an
uncomfortable feeling. Slowly Thorin shook off his
dreams and getting up he kicked away the stone that
wedged the door. Then they thrust upon it, and it
closed with a snap and a clang. No trace of a keyhole
was there left on the inside. They were shut in the
Mountain!

And not a moment too soon. They had hardly gone any distance down the tunnel when a blow smote the side of the Mountain like the crash of battering-rams made of forest oaks and swung by giants. The rock boomed, the walls cracked and stones fell from the roof on their heads. What would have happened if the door had still been open I don't like to think. They fled further down the tunnel glad to be still alive, while behind them outside they heard the roar and rumble of Smaug's fury. He was breaking rocks to pieces, smashing wall and cliff with the lashings of his huge tail, till their little lofty camping ground, the scorched grass, the thrush's stone, the snail-covered walls, the narrow ledge, and all disappeared in a jumble of smithereens, and an avalanche of splintered stones fell over the cliff into the valley below.

Smaug had left his lair in silent stealth, quietly soared into the air, and then floated heavy and slow in the dark like a monstrous crow, down the wind towards the west of the Mountain, in the hopes of catching unawares something or somebody there, and of spying the outlet to the passage which the thief had used. This was the outburst of his wrath when he could find nobody and see nothing, even where he guessed the outlet must actually be.

After he had let off his rage in this way he felt better and he thought in his heart that he would not be troubled again from that direction. In the meanwhile he had further vengeance to take. "Barrel-rider!" he snorted. "Your feet came from the waterside and up the water you came without a doubt. I don't know your smell, but if you are not

one of those men of the Lake, you had their help.
They shall see me and remember who is the real
King under the Mountain!"

He rose in fire and went away south towards the
Running River.

Chapter XIII

NOT AT HOME

In the meanwhile, the dwarves sat in darkness, and utter silence fell about them. Little they ate and little they spoke. They could not count the passing of time; and they scarcely dared to move, for the whisper of their voices echoed and rustled in the tunnel. If they dozed, they woke still to darkness and to silence going on unbroken. At last after days and days of waiting, as it seemed, when they were becoming choked and dazed for want of air, they could bear it no longer. They would almost have welcomed sounds from below of the dragon's return. In the silence they feared some cunning devilry of his, but they could not sit there for ever.

Thorin spoke: "Let us try the door!" he said. "I must feel the wind on my face soon or die. I think I would rather be smashed by Smaug in the open than suffocate in here!" So several of the dwarves got up and groped back to where the door had been. But they found that the upper end of the tunnel had been shattered and blocked with broken rock. Neither key nor the magic it had once obeyed would ever open that door again.

"We are trapped!" they groaned. "This is the end. We shall die here."

But somehow, just when the dwarves were most despairing, Bilbo felt a strange lightening of the heart, as if a heavy weight had gone from under his waist-coat.

"Come, come!" he said. "'While there's life there's hope!' as my father used to say, and 'Third time pays for all.' I am going *down* the tunnel once again. I have been that way twice, when I knew there was a dragon at the other end, so I will risk a third visit when I am no longer sure. Anyway the only way out is down. And I think this time you had better all come with me."

In desperation they agreed, and Thorin was the first to go forward by Bilbo's side.

"Now do be careful!" whispered the hobbit, "and as quiet as you can be! There may be no Smaug at the bottom, but then again there may be. Don't let us take any unnecessary risks!"

Down, down they went. The dwarves could not, of course, compare with the hobbit in real stealth, and they made a deal of puffing and shuffling which echoes magnified alarmingly; but though every now and again Bilbo in fear stopped and listened, not a sound stirred below. Near the bottom, as well as he could judge, Bilbo slipped on his ring and went ahead. But he did not need it: the darkness was complete, and they were all invisible, ring or no ring. In fact so black was it that the hobbit came to the opening unexpectedly, put his hand on air, stumbled forward, and rolled headlong into the hall!

There he lay face downwards on the floor and did not dare to get up, or hardly even to breathe. But nothing moved. There was not a gleam of light—unless, as it seemed to him, when at last he slowly raised his head, there was a pale white glint, above him and far off in the gloom. But certainly it was not a spark of dragon-fire, though the worm-stench was heavy in the place, and the taste of vapour was on his tongue.

At length Mr. Baggins could bear it no longer. "Confound you, Smaug, you worm!" he squeaked aloud. "Stop playing hide-and-seek! Give me a light, and then eat me, if you can catch me!"

Faint echoes ran round the unseen hall, but there was no answer.

Bilbo got up, and found that he did not know in what direction to turn.

"Now I wonder what on earth Smaug is playing at," he said. "He is not at home today (or tonight, or whatever it is), I do believe. If Oin and Gloin have not lost their tinder-boxes, perhaps we can make a little light, and have a look round before the luck turns."

"Light!" he cried. "Can anybody make a light?"

The dwarves, of course, were very alarmed when Bilbo fell forward down the step with a bump into the hall, and they sat huddled just where he had left them at the end of the tunnel.

"Sh! sh!" they hissed, when they heard his voice; and though that helped the hobbit to find out where they were, it was some time before he could get anything else out of them. But in the end, when Bilbo actually began to stamp on the floor, and screamed out "light!" at the top of his shrill voice, Thorin gave way, and Oin and Gloin were sent back to their bundles at the top of the tunnel.

After a while a twinkling gleam showed them

returning, Oin with a small pine-torch alight in his hand, and Gloin with a bundle of others under his arm. Quickly Bilbo trotted to the door and took the torch; but he could not persuade the dwarves to light the others or to come and join him yet. As Thorin carefully explained, Mr. Baggins was still officially their expert burglar and investigator. If he liked to risk a light, that was his affair. They would wait in the tunnel for his report. So they sat near the door and watched.

They saw the little dark shape of the hobbit start across the floor holding his tiny light aloft. Every now and again, while he was still near enough, they caught a glint and a tinkle as he stumbled on some golden thing. The light grew smaller as he wandered away into the vast hall; then it began to rise dancing into the air. Bilbo was climbing the great mound of treasure. Soon he stood upon the top, and still went on. Then they saw him halt and stoop for a moment; but they did not know the reason.

It was the Arkenstone, the Heart of the Mountain. So Bilbo guessed from Thorin's description; but indeed there could not be two such gems, even in so marvellous a hoard, even in all the world. Ever as he climbed, the same white gleam had shone before him and drawn his feet towards it. Slowly it grew to a little globe of pallid light. Now as he came near, it was tinged with a flickering sparkle of many colours at the surface, reflected and splintered from the wavering light of his torch. At last he looked down upon it, and he caught his breath. The great jewel shone before his feet of its own inner light, and yet, cut and fashioned by the dwarves, who had dug it from the heart of the mountain long ago, it took all light that fell upon it and changed it into ten thousand sparks of white radiance shot with glints of the rainbow.

Suddenly Bilbo's arm went towards it drawn by its enchantment. His small hand would not close about it, for it was a large and heavy gem; but he lifted it, shut his eyes, and put it in his deepest pocket.

"Now I am a burglar indeed!" thought he. "But I suppose I must tell the dwarves about it—some time. They did say I could pick and choose my own share; and I think I would choose this, if they took all the rest!" All the same he had an uncomfortable feeling that the picking and choosing had not really been meant to include this marvellous gem, and that trouble would yet come of it.

Now he went on again. Down the other side of the great mound he climbed, and the spark of his torch vanished from the sight of the watching dwarves. But soon they saw it far away in the distance again. Bilbo was crossing the floor of the hall.

He went on, until he came to the great doors at the further side, and there a draught of air refreshed him, but it almost puffed out his light. He peeped timidly through, and caught a glimpse of great passages and of the dim beginnings of wide stairs going up into the gloom. And still there was no sight nor sound of Smaug. He was just going to turn and go back, when a black shape swooped at him, and brushed his face. He squeaked and started, stumbled backwards and fell. His torch dropped head downwards and went out!

"Only a bat, I suppose and hope!" he said miserably. "But now what am I to do? Which is East, South, North, or West?"

"Thorin! Balin! Oin! Gloin! Fili! Kili!" he cried as loud as he could—it seemed a thin little noise in the wide blackness. "The light's gone out! Someone come and find me and help me!" For the moment his courage had failed altogether.

Faintly the dwarves heard his small cries, though the only word they could catch was "help!"

"Now what on earth or under it has happened?" said Thorin. "Certainly not the dragon, or he would not go on squeaking."

They waited a moment or two, and still there were no dragon-noises, no sound at all in fact but Bilbo's distant voice. "Come, one of you, get another light or two!" Thorin ordered. "It seems we have got to go and help our burglar."

"It is about our turn to help," said Balin, "and I am quite willing to go. Anyway I expect it is safe for the moment."

Gloin lit several more torches, and then they all crept out, one by one, and went along the wall as hurriedly as they could. It was not long before they met Bilbo himself coming back towards them. His wits had quickly returned as soon as he saw the twinkle of their lights.

"Only a bat and a dropped torch, nothing worse!" he said in answer to their questions. Though they were much relieved, they were inclined to be grumpy at being frightened for nothing; but what they would have said, if he had told them at that moment about the Arkenstone, I don't know. The mere fleeting glimpses of treasure which they had caught as they went along had rekindled all the fire of their dwarvish hearts; and when the heart of a dwarf, even the most respectable, is wakened by gold and by jewels, he grows suddenly bold, and he may become fierce.

The dwarves indeed no longer needed any urging. All were now eager to explore the hall while they had the chance, and willing to believe that, for the present, Smaug was away from home. Each now gripped a lighted torch; and as they gazed, first on one side and then on another, they forgot fear and even caution. They spoke aloud, and cried out to one another, as they lifted old treasures from the mound or from the wall and held them in the light, caressing and fingering them.

Fili and Kili were almost in merry mood, and finding still hanging there many golden harps strung with silver they took them and struck them; and being magical (and also untouched by the dragon, who had small interest in music) they were still in tune. The dark hall was filled with a melody that had long been silent. But most of the dwarves were more practical: they gathered gems and stuffed their pockets, and let what they could not carry fall back through their fingers with a sigh. Thorin was not least among these; but always he searched from side to side for something which he could not find. It was the Arkenstone; but he spoke of it yet to no one.

Now the dwarves took down mail and weapons from the walls, and armed themselves. Royal indeed did Thorin look, clad in a coat of gold-plated rings, with a silver-hafted axe in a belt crusted with scarlet stones.

"Mr. Baggins!" he cried. "Here is the first payment of your reward! Cast off your old coat and put on this!"

With that he put on Bilbo a small coat of mail, wrought for some young elf-prince long ago. It was of silver-steel, which the elves call *mithril*, and with it went a belt of pearls and crystals. A light helm of figured leather, strengthened beneath with hoops of steel, and studded about the brim with white gems, was set upon the hobbit's head.

"I feel magnificent," he thought; "but I expect I look rather absurd. How they would laugh on the Hill at home! Still I wish there was a looking-glass handy!"

All the same Mr. Baggins kept his head more clear of the bewitchment of the hoard than the dwarves did. Long before the dwarves were tired of examining the treasures, he became weary of it and sat down on the floor; and he began to wonder nervously what the end of it all would be. "I would give a good many of these precious goblets," he thought, "for a drink of something cheering out of one of Beorn's wooden bowls!"

"Thorin!" he cried aloud. "What next? We are armed, but what good has any armour ever been before against Smaug the Dreadful? This treasure is not yet won back. We are not looking for gold yet, but for a way of escape; and we have tempted luck too long!"

"You speak the truth!" answered Thorin, recovering his wits. "Let us go! I will guide you. Not in a thousand years should I forget the ways of this palace." Then he hailed the others, and they gathered together, and holding their torches above their heads they passed through the gaping doors, not without many a backward glance of longing.

Their glittering mail they had covered again with their old cloaks and their bright helms with their tattered hoods, and one by one they walked behind Thorin, a line of little lights in the darkness that halted often, listening in fear once more for any rumour of the dragon's coming.

Though all the old adornments were long mouldered or destroyed, and though all was befouled and blasted with the comings and goings of the monster, Thorin knew every passage and every turn. They climbed long stairs, and turned and went down wide echoing ways, and turned again and climbed yet more stairs, and yet more stairs again. These were smooth, cut out of the living rock broad and fair; and up, up, the dwarves went, and they met no sign of any living thing, only furtive shadows that fled from the approach of their torches fluttering in the draughts.

The steps were not made, all the same, for hobbit-legs, and Bilbo was just feeling that he could go on no longer, when suddenly the roof sprang high and far beyond the reach of their torch-light. A white glimmer could be seen coming through some opening far above, and the air smelt sweeter. Before them light came dimly through great doors, that hung twisted on their hinges and half burnt.

"This is the great chamber of Thror," said Thorin; "the hall of feasting and of council. Not far off now is the Front Gate."

They passed through the ruined chamber. Tables were rotting there; chairs and benches were lying there overturned, charred and decaying. Skulls and bones were upon the floor among flagons and bowls and broken drinking-horns and dust. As they came through yet more doors at the further end, a sound of water fell upon their ears, and the grey light grew suddenly more full.

"There is the birth of the Running River," said Thorin. "From here it hastens to the Gate. Let us follow it!"

Out of a dark opening in a wall of rock there issued a boiling water, and it flowed swirling in a narrow channel, carved and made straight and deep by the cunning of ancient hands. Beside it ran a stone-paved road, wide enough for many men abreast. Swiftly along this they ran, and round a wide-sweeping turn—and behold! before them stood the broad light of day. In front there rose a tall arch, still showing the fragments of old carven work within, worn and splintered and blackened though it was. A misty sun sent its pale light between the arms of the Mountain, and beams of gold fell on the pavement at the threshold.

A whirl of bats frightened from slumber by their smoking torches flurried over them; as they sprang forward their feet slithered on stones rubbed smooth and slimed by the passing of the dragon. Now before them the water fell noisily outward and foamed down towards the valley. They flung their pale torches to the ground, and stood gazing out with dazzled eyes. They were come to the Front Gate, and were looking out upon Dale.

"Well!" said Bilbo, "I never expected to be looking out of this door. And I never expected to be so pleased to see the sun again, and to feel the wind on my face. But, ow! this wind is cold!"

It was. A bitter easterly breeze blew with a threat of oncoming winter. It swirled over and round the arms of the Mountain into the valley, and sighed among the rocks. After their long time in the stewing depths of the dragon-haunted caverns, they shivered in the sun.

Suddenly Bilbo realized that he was not only tired but also very hungry indeed. "It seems to be late morning," he said, "and so I suppose it is more or less breakfast-time—if there is any breakfast to have. But I don't feel that Smaug's front doorstep is the safest place for a meal. Do let's go somewhere where we can sit quiet for a bit!"

"Quite right!" said Balin. "And I think I know which way we should go: we ought to make for the old look-out post at the South-West corner of the Mountain."

"How far is that?" asked the hobbit.

"Five hours march, I should think. It will be rough going. The road from the Gate along the left edge of the stream seems all broken up. But look down there! The river loops suddenly east across Dale in front of the ruined town. At that point there was once a bridge, leading to steep stairs that climbed up the right bank, and so to a road running towards Ravenhill. There is (or was) a path that left the road and climbed up to the post. A hard climb, too, even if the old steps are still there."

"Dear me!" grumbled the hobbit. "More walking and more climbing without breakfast! I wonder how many breakfasts, and other meals, we have missed inside that nasty clockless, timeless hole?"

As a matter of fact two nights and the day between

had gone by (and not altogether without food) since the dragon smashed the magic door, but Bilbo had quite lost count, and it might have been one night or a week of nights for all he could tell.

"Come, come!" said Thorin laughing—his spirits had begun to rise again, and he rattled the precious stones in his pockets. "Don't call my palace a nasty hole! You wait till it has been cleaned and redecorated!"

"That won't be till Smaug's dead," said Bilbo glumly. "In the meanwhile where is he? I would give a good breakfast to know. I hope he is not up on the Mountain looking down at us!"

That idea disturbed the dwarves mightily, and they quickly decided that Bilbo and Balin were right.

"We must move away from here," said Dori. "I feel as if his eyes were on the back of my head."

"It's a cold lonesome place," said Bombur. "There may be drink, but I see no sign of food. A dragon would always be hungry in such parts."

"Come on! Come on!" cried the others. "Let us follow Balin's path!"

Under the rocky wall to the right there was no path, so on they trudged among the stones on the left side of the river, and the emptiness and desolation soon sobered even Thorin again. The bridge that Balin had spoken of they found long fallen, and most of its stones were now only boulders in the shallow noisy stream; but they forded the water without much difficulty, and found the ancient steps, and climbed the high bank. After going a short way they struck the old road, and before long came to a deep dell sheltered among the rocks; there they rested for a while and had such a breakfast as they could, chiefly *cram* and water. (If you want to know what *cram* is, I can only say that I don't know the recipe; but it is biscuitish, keeps good indefinitely, is supposed to be sustaining, and is certainly not entertaining, being in fact very uninteresting except as a chewing exercise. It was made by the Lake-men for long journeys.)

After that they went on again; and now the road struck westwards and left the river, and the great shoulder of the south-pointing mountain-spur drew ever nearer. At length they reached the hill path. It scrambled steeply up, and they plodded slowly one behind the other, till at last in the late afternoon they came to the top of the ridge and saw the wintry sun going downwards to the West.

Here they found a flat place without a wall on three sides, but backed to the North by a rocky face in which there was an opening like a door. From that door there was a wide view East and South and West.

"Here," said Balin, "in the old days we used always to keep watchmen, and that door behind leads into a rockhewn chamber that was made here as a guardroom. There were several places like it round the Mountain. But there seemed small need for watching in the days of our prosperity, and the guards were made over comfortable, perhaps—otherwise we might have had longer warning of the coming of the dragon, and things might have been different. Still, here we can now lie hid and sheltered for a while, and can see much without being seen."

"Not much use, if we have been seen coming here," said Dori, who was always looking up towards the Mountain's peak, as if he expected to see Smaug perched there like a bird on a steeple.

"We must take our chance of that," said Thorin. "We can go no further to-day."

"Hear, hear!" cried Bilbo, and flung himself on the ground.

In the rock-chamber there would have been room for a hundred, and there was a small chamber further in, more removed from the cold outside. It was quite deserted; not even wild animals seemed to have used it in all the days of Smaug's dominion. There they laid their burdens; and some threw themselves down at once and slept, but the others sat near the outer door and discussed their plans. In all their talk they came perpetually back to one thing: where was Smaug? They looked West and there was nothing, and East there was nothing, and in the South there was no sign of the dragon, but there was a gathering of very many birds. At that they gazed and wondered; but they were no nearer understanding it, when the first cold stars came out.

Chapter XIV

FIRE AND WATER

Now if you wish, like the dwarves, to hear news of Smaug, you must go back again to the evening when he smashed the door and flew off in rage, two days before.

The men of the lake-town Esgaroth were mostly indoors, for the breeze was from the black East and chill, but a few were walking on the quays, and watching, as they were fond of doing, the stars shine out from the smooth patches of the lake as they opened in the sky. From their town the Lonely Mountain was mostly screened by the low hills at the far end of the lake, through a gap in which the Running River came down from the North. Only its high peak could they see in clear weather, and they looked seldom at it, for it was ominous and drear even in the light of morning. Now it was lost and gone, blotted in the dark.

Suddenly it flickered back to view; a brief glow touched it and faded.

"Look!" said one. "The lights again! Last night the watchmen saw them start and fade from midnight until dawn. Something is happening up there."

"Perhaps the King under the Mountain is forging gold," said another. "It is long since he went North. It is time the songs began to prove themselves again."

"Which king?" said another with a grim voice. "As like as not it is the marauding fire of the Dragon, the only king under the Mountain we have ever known."

"You are always foreboding gloomy things!" said the others. "Anything from floods to poisoned fish. Think of something cheerful!"

Then suddenly a great light appeared in the low place in the hills and the northern end of the lake turned golden. "The King beneath the Mountain!" they shouted. "His wealth is like the Sun, his silver like a fountain, his rivers golden run! The river is running gold from the Mountain!" they cried, and everywhere windows were opening and feet were hurrying.

There was once more a tremendous excitement and enthusiasm. But the grim-voiced fellow ran hotfoot to the Master. "The dragon is coming or I am a fool!" he cried. "Cut the bridges! To arms! To arms!"

Then warning trumpets were suddenly sounded, and echoed along the rocky shores. The cheering stopped and the joy was turned to dread. So it was that the dragon did not find them quite unprepared.

Before long, so great was his speed, they could see him as a spark of fire rushing towards them and growing ever huger and more bright, and not the most foolish doubted that the prophecies had gone rather wrong. Still they had a little time. Every vessel in the town was filled with water, every warrior was armed, every arrow and dart was ready, and the bridge to the land was thrown down and destroyed, before the roar of Smaug's terrible approach grew loud, and the lake rippled red as fire beneath the awful beating of his wings.

Amid shrieks and wailing and the shouts of men he came over them, swept towards the bridges and was foiled! The bridge was gone, and his enemies were on an island in deep water—too deep and dark and cool for his liking. If he plunged into it, a vapour and a steam would arise enough to cover all the land with a mist for days; but the lake was mightier than he, it would quench him before he could pass through.

Roaring he swept back over the town. A hail of dark arrows leaped up and snapped and rattled on his scales and jewels, and their shafts fell back kindled by his breath burning and hissing into the lake. No fireworks you ever imagined equalled the sights that night. At the twanging of the bows and the shrilling of the trumpets the dragon's wrath blazed to its height, till he was blind and mad with it. No one had dared to give battle to him for many an age; nor would they have dared now, if it had not been for the grim-voiced man (Bard was his name), who ran to and fro cheering on the archers and urging the Master to order them to fight to the last arrow.

Fire leaped from the dragon's jaws. He circled for a while high in the air above them lighting all the lake; the trees by the shores shone like copper and like blood with leaping shadows of dense black at their feet. Then down he swooped straight through the arrow-storm, reckless in his rage, taking no heed to turn his scaly sides towards his foes, seeking only to set their town ablaze.

Fire leaped from thatched roofs and wooden beam-ends as he hurtled down and past and round again, though all had been drenched with water

before he came. Once more water was flung by a
hundred hands wherever a spark appeared. Back
swirled the dragon. A sweep of his tail and the roof
of the Great House crumbled and smashed down.
Flames unquenchable sprang high into the night.
Another swoop and another, and another house and
then another sprang afire and fell; and still no arrow
hindered Smaug or hurt him more than a fly from
the marshes.

Already men were jumping into the water on every
side. Women and children were being huddled into
laden boats in the market-pool. Weapons were flung
down. There was mourning and weeping, where but a
little time ago the old songs of mirth to come had been
sung about the dwarves. Now men cursed their
names. The Master himself was turning to his great
gilded boat, hoping to row away in the confusion and
save himself. Soon all the town would be deserted and
burned down to the surface of the lake.

That was the dragon's hope. They could all get
into boats for all he cared. There he could have fine
sport hunting them, or they could stop till they
starved. Let them try to get to land and he would be
ready. Soon he would set all the shoreland woods
ablaze and wither every field and pasture. Just now
he was enjoying the sport of town-baiting more than
he had enjoyed anything for years.

But there was still a company of archers that held
their ground among the burning houses. Their
captain was Bard, grim-voiced and grim-faced,
whose friends had accused him of prophesying floods
and poisoned fish, though they knew his worth and

courage. He was a descendant in long line of Girion, Lord of Dale, whose wife and child had escaped down the Running River from the ruin long ago. Now he shot with a great yew bow, till all his arrows but one were spent. The flames were near him. His companions were leaving him. He bent his bow for the last time.

Suddenly out of the dark something fluttered to his shoulder. He started—but it was only an old thrush. Unafraid it perched by his ear and it brought him news. Marvelling he found he could understand its tongue, for he was of the race of Dale.

"Wait! Wait!" it said to him. "The moon is rising. Look for the hollow of the left breast as he flies and turns above you!" And while Bard paused in wonder it told him of tidings up in the Mountain and of all that it had heard.

Then Bard drew his bow-string to his ear. The dragon was circling back, flying low, and as he came the moon rose above the eastern shore and silvered his great wings.

"Arrow!" said the bowman. "Black arrow! I have saved you to the last. You have never failed me and always I have recovered you. I had you from my father and he from of old. If ever you came from the forges of the true king under the Mountain, go now and speed well!"

The dragon swooped once more lower than ever, and as he turned and dived down his belly glittered white with sparkling fires of gems in the moon—but not in one place. The great bow twanged. The black arrow sped straight from the string, straight for the hollow by the left breast where the foreleg was flung wide. In it smote and vanished, barb, shaft and feather, so fierce was its flight. With a shriek that deafened men, felled trees and split stone, Smaug shot spouting into the air, turned over and crashed down from on high in ruin.

Full on the town he fell. His last throes splintered it to sparks and gledes. The lake roared in. A vast steam leaped up, white in the sudden dark under the moon. There was a hiss, a gushing whirl, and then silence. And that was the end of Smaug and Esgaroth, but not of Bard.

The waxing moon rose higher and higher and the wind grew loud and cold. It twisted the white fog into bending pillars and hurrying clouds and drove it off to the West to scatter in tattered shreds over the marshes before Mirkwood. Then the many boats could be seen dotted dark on the surface of the lake, and down the wind came the voices of the people of Esgaroth lamenting their lost town and goods and ruined houses. But they had really much to be thankful for, had they thought of it, though it could hardly be expected that they should just then: three quarters of the people of the town had at least escaped alive; their woods and fields and pastures and cattle and most of their boats remained undamaged; and the dragon was dead. What that meant they had not yet realized.

They gathered in mournful crowds upon the western shores, shivering in the cold wind, and their first complaints and anger were against the Master, who had left the town so soon, while some were still willing to defend it.

"He may have a good head for business—especially his own business," some murmured, "but he is no good when anything serious happens!" And they praised the courage of Bard and his last mighty shot. "If only he had not been killed," they all said, "we would make him a king. Bard the Dragon-shooter of the line of Girion! Alas that he is lost!"

And in the very midst of their talk a tall figure stepped from the shadows. He was drenched with water, his black hair hung wet over his face and shoulders, and a fierce light was in his eyes.

"Bard is not lost!" he cried. "He dived from Esgaroth, when the enemy was slain. I am Bard, of the line of Girion; I am the slayer of the dragon!"

"King Bard! King Bard!" they shouted; but the Master ground his chattering teeth.

"Girion was lord of Dale, not king of Esgaroth," he said. "In the Lake-town we have always elected masters from among the old and wise, and have not endured the rule of mere fighting men. Let 'King Bard' go back to his own kingdom—Dale is now freed by his valour, and nothing hinders his return. And any that wish can go with him, if they prefer the cold stones under the shadow of the Mountain to the green shores of the lake. The wise will stay here and hope to rebuild our town, and enjoy again in time its peace and riches."

"We will have King Bard!" the people near at hand shouted in reply. "We have had enough of the old men and the money-counters!" And people further off took up the cry: "Up the Bowman, and down with Moneybags," till the clamour echoed along the shore.

"I am the last man to undervalue Bard the Bowman," said the Master warily (for Bard now stood close beside him). "He has tonight earned an eminent place in the roll of the benefactors of our town; and he is worthy of many imperishable songs. But, why O People?"—and here the Master rose to his feet and spoke very loud and clear—"Why do I get all your blame? For what fault am I to be deposed? Who aroused the dragon from his slumber, I might ask? Who obtained of us rich gifts and ample help, and led us to believe that old songs could come true? Who played on our soft hearts and our pleasant fancies? What sort of gold have they sent down the river to reward us? Dragon-fire and ruin! From whom should we claim the recompense of our damage, and aid for our widows and orphans?"

As you see, the Master had not got his position for nothing. The result of his words was that for the moment the people quite forgot their idea of a new king, and turned their angry thoughts towards Thorin and his company. Wild and bitter words were shouted from many sides; and some of those who had before sung the old songs loudest, were now heard as loudly crying that the dwarves had stirred the dragon up against them deliberately!

"Fools!" said Bard. "Why waste words and wrath on those unhappy creatures? Doubtless they perished first in fire, before Smaug came to us." Then even as he was speaking, the thought came into his heart of the fabled treasure of the Mountain lying without guard or owner, and he fell suddenly silent. He thought of the Master's words, and of Dale rebuilt, and filled with golden bells, if he could but find the men.

At length he spoke again: "This is no time for angry words, Master, or for considering weighty plans of change. There is work to do. I serve you still—though after a while I may think again of your words and go North with any that will follow me."

Then he strode off to help in the ordering of the camps and in the care of the sick and the wounded. But the Master scowled at his back as he went, and remained sitting on the ground. He thought much but said little, unless it was to call loudly for men to bring him fire and food.

Now everywhere Bard went he found talk running like fire among the people concerning the vast treasure that was now unguarded. Men spoke of the recompense for all their harm that they would soon get from it, and wealth over and to spare with which to buy rich things from the South; and it cheered them greatly in their plight. That was as well, for the night was bitter and miserable. Shelters could be contrived for few (the Master had one) and there was little food (even the Master went short). Many took ill of wet and cold and sorrow that night, and afterwards died, who had escaped uninjured from the ruin of the town; and in the days that followed there was much sickness and great hunger.

Meanwhile Bard took the lead, and ordered things as he wished, though always in the Master's name, and he had a hard task to govern the people and direct the preparations for their protection and housing. Probably most of them would have perished in the winter that now hurried after autumn, if help had not been to hand. But help came swiftly; for Bard at once had speedy messengers sent up the river to the Forest to ask the aid of the King of the Elves of the Wood, and these messengers had found a host already on the move, although it was then only the third day after the fall of Smaug.

The Elvenking had received news from his own messengers and from the birds that loved his folk, and already knew much of what had happened. Very great indeed was the commotion among all things with wings that dwelt on the borders of the Desolation of the Dragon. The air was filled with circling flocks, and their swift-flying messengers flew here and there across the sky. Above the borders of the Forest there was whistling, crying and piping. Far over Mirkwood tidings spread: "Smaug is dead!" Leaves rustled and startled ears were lifted. Even before the Elvenking rode forth the news had passed west right to the pinewoods of the Misty Mountains; Beorn had heard it in his wooden house, and the goblins were at council in their caves.

"That will be the last we shall hear of Thorin Oakenshield, I fear," said the king. "He would have done better to have remained my guest. It is an ill wind, all the same," he added, "that blows no one any good." For he too had not forgotten the legend of the wealth of Thror. So it was that Bard's messengers found him now marching with many spearmen and bowmen; and crows were gathered thick above him, for they thought that war was awakening again, such as had not been in those parts for a long age.

But the king, when he received the prayers of Bard, had pity, for he was the lord of a good and kindly people; so turning his march, which had at first been direct towards the Mountain, he hastened

now down the river to the Long Lake. He had not
boats or rafts enough for his host, and they were
forced to go the slower way by foot; but great store
of goods he sent ahead by water. Still elves are light-
footed, and though they were not in these days much
used to the marches and the treacherous lands
between the Forest and the Lake, their going was
swift. Only five days after the death of the dragon
they came upon the shores and looked on the ruins
of the town. Their welcome was good, as may be
expected, and the men and their Master were ready
to make any bargain for the future in return for the
Elvenking's aid.

Their plans were soon made. With the women and
the children, the old and the unfit, the Master
remained behind; and with him were some men of
crafts and many skilled elves; and they busied themselves felling trees, and collecting the timber sent
down from the Forest. Then they set about raising
many huts by the shore against the oncoming winter;
and also under the Master's direction they began the
planning of a new town, designed more fair and large
even than before, but not in the same place. They
removed northward higher up the shore; for ever
after they had a dread of the water where the dragon
lay. He would never again return to his golden bed,
but was stretched cold as stone, twisted upon the
floor of the shallows. There for ages his huge bones
could be seen in calm weather amid the ruined piles
of the old town. But few dared to cross the cursed
spot, and none dared to dive into the shivering water
or recover the precious stones that fell from his
rotting carcase.

But all the men of arms who were still able, and the most of the Elvenking's array, got ready to march north to the Mountain. It was thus that in eleven days from the ruin of the town the head of their host passed the rock-gates at the end of the lake and came into the desolate lands.

Chapter XV

THE GATHERING OF THE CLOUDS

Now we will return to Bilbo and the dwarves. All night one of them had watched, but when morning came they had not heard or seen any sign of danger. But ever more thickly the birds were gathering. Their companies came flying from the South; and the crows that still lived about the Mountain were wheeling and crying unceasingly above.

"Something strange is happening," said Thorin. "The time has gone for the autumn wanderings; and these are birds that dwell always in the land; there are starlings and flocks of finches; and far off there are many carrion birds as if a battle were afoot!"

Suddenly Bilbo pointed: "There is that old thrush again!" he cried. "He seems to have escaped, when Smaug smashed the mountain-side, but I don't suppose the snails have!"

Sure enough the old thrush was there, and as Bilbo pointed, he flew towards them and perched on a stone near by. Then he fluttered his wings and sang; then he cocked his head on one side, as if to listen; and again he sang, and again he listened.

"I believe he is trying to tell us something," said Balin; "but I cannot follow the speech of such birds, it is very quick and difficult. Can you make it out Baggins?"

"Not very well," said Bilbo (as a matter of fact, he

could make nothing of it at all); "but the old fellow seems very excited."

"I only wish he was a raven!" said Balin.

"I thought you did not like them! You seemed very shy of them, when we came this way before."

"Those were crows! And nasty suspicious-looking creatures at that, and rude as well. You must have heard the ugly names they were calling after us. But the ravens are different. There used to be great friendship between them and the people of Thror; and they often brought us secret news, and were rewarded with such bright things as they coveted to hide in their dwellings.

"They live many a year, and their memories are long, and they hand on their wisdom to their children. I knew many among the ravens of the rocks when I was a dwarf-lad. This very height was once named Ravenhill, because there was a wise and famous pair, old Carc and his wife, that lived here above the guard-chamber. But I don't suppose that any of that ancient breed linger here now."

No sooner had he finished speaking than the old thrush gave a loud call, and immediately flew away.

"We may not understand him, but that old bird understands us, I am sure," said Balin. "Keep watch now, and see what happens!"

Before long there was a fluttering of wings, and back came the thrush; and with him came a most decrepit old bird. He was getting blind, he could hardly fly, and the top of his head was bald. He was an aged raven of great size. He alighted stiffly on the ground before them, slowly flapped his wings, and bobbed towards Thorin.

"O Thorin son of Thrain, and Balin son of Fundin," he croaked (and Bilbo could understand what he said, for he used ordinary language and not bird-speech). "I am Roäc son of Carc. Carc is dead, but he was well known to you once. It is a hundred years and three and fifty since I came out of the egg, but I do not forget what my father told me. Now I am the chief of the great ravens of the Mountain. We are few, but we remember still the king that was of old. Most of my people are abroad, for there are great tidings in the South— some are tidings of joy to you, and some you will not think so good.

"Behold! the birds are gathering back again to the Mountain and to Dale from South and East and West, for word has gone out that Smaug is dead!"

"Dead! Dead?" shouted the dwarves. "Dead! Then we have been in needless fear—and the treasure is ours!" They all sprang up and began to caper about for joy.

"Yes, dead," said Roäc. "The thrush, may his feathers never fall, saw him die, and we may trust his words. He saw him fall in battle with the men of Esgaroth the third night back from now at the rising of the moon."

It was some time before Thorin could bring the dwarves to be silent and listen to the raven's news. At length when he had told all the tale of the battle he went on:

"So much for joy, Thorin Oakenshield. You may go back to your halls in safety; all the treasure is yours—for the moment. But many are gathering hither beside the birds. The news of the death of the guardian has already gone far and wide, and the legend of the wealth of Thror has not lost in the telling during many years; many are eager for a share of the spoil. Already a host of the elves is on the way, and carrion birds are with them hoping for battle and slaughter. By the lake men murmur that their sorrows are due to the dwarves; for they are homeless and many have died, and Smaug has destroyed their town. They too think to find amends from your treasure, whether you are alive or dead.

"Your own wisdom must decide your course; but thirteen is small remnant of the great folk of Durin that once dwelt here, and now are scattered far. If you will listen to my counsel, you will not trust the Master of the Lake-men, but rather him that shot the dragon with his bow. Bard is he, of the race of Dale, of the line of Girion; he is a grim man but true. We would see peace once more among dwarves and men and elves after the long desolation; but it may cost you dear in gold. I have spoken."

Then Thorin burst forth in anger: "Our thanks, Roäc Carc's son. You and your people shall not be forgotten. But none of our gold shall thieves take or the violent carry off while we are alive. If you would earn our thanks still more, bring us news of any that draw near. Also I would beg of you, if any of you are still young and strong of wing, that you would send messengers to our kin in the mountains of the North, both west from here and east, and tell them of our plight. But go specially to my cousin Dain in the Iron Hills, for he has many people well-armed, and dwells nearest to this place. Bid him hasten!"

"I will not say if this counsel be good or bad," croaked Roäc, "but I will do what can be done." Then off he slowly flew.

"Back now to the Mountain!" cried Thorin. "We have little time to lose."

"And little food to use!" cried Bilbo, always practical on such points. In any case he felt that the adventure was, properly speaking, over with the death of the dragon—in which he was much mistaken—and he would have given most of his share of the profits for the peaceful winding up of these affairs.

"Back to the Mountain!" cried the dwarves as if they had not heard him; so back he had to go with them.

As you have heard some of the events already, you will see that the dwarves still had some days before them. They explored the caverns once more, and found, as they expected, that only the Front Gate remained open; all the other gates (except, of course, the small secret door) had long ago been broken and blocked by Smaug, and no sign of them remained. So now they began to labour hard in fortifying the main entrance, and in making a new path that led from it. Tools were to be found in plenty that the miners and quarriers and builders of old had used; and at such work the dwarves were still very skilled.

As they worked the ravens brought them constant tidings. In this way they learned that the Elvenking had turned aside to the Lake, and they still had a breathing space. Better still, they heard that three of their ponies had escaped and were wandering wild far down the banks of the Running River, not far from where the rest of their stores had been left. So while the others went on with their work, Fili and Kili were sent, guided by a raven, to find the ponies and bring back all they could.

They were four days gone, and by that time they knew that the joined armies of the Lake-men and the Elves were hurrying toward the Mountain. But now their hopes were higher; for they had food for some weeks with care—chiefly *cram*, of course, and they were very tired of it; but *cram* is much better than nothing—and already the gate was blocked with a wall of squared stones laid dry, but very thick and high, across the opening. There were holes in the wall through which they could see (or shoot), but no entrance. They climbed in or out with ladders, and hauled stuff up with ropes. For the issuing of the stream they had contrived a small low arch under the new wall; but near the entrance they had so altered the narrow bed that a wide pool stretched from the mountain-wall to the head of the fall over which the stream went towards Dale. Approach to the Gate was now only possible, without swimming, along a narrow ledge of the cliff, to the right as one looked outwards from the wall. The ponies they had brought only to the head of the steps above the old bridge, and unloading them there had bidden them return to their masters and sent them back riderless to the South.

There came a night when suddenly there were many lights as of fires and torches away south in Dale before them.

"They have come!" called Balin. "And their camp is

very great. They must have come into the valley under the cover of dusk along both banks of the river."

That night the dwarves slept little. The morning was still pale when they saw a company approaching. From behind their wall they watched them come up to the valley's head and climb slowly up. Before long they could see that both men of the lake armed as if for war and elvish bowmen were among them. At length the foremost of these climbed the tumbled rocks and appeared at the top of the falls; and very great was their surprise to see the pool before them and the Gate blocked with a wall of new-hewn stone.

As they stood pointing and speaking to one another Thorin hailed them: "Who are you," he called in a very loud voice, "that come as if in war to the gates of Thorin son of Thrain, King under the Mountain, and what do you desire?"

But they answered nothing. Some turned swiftly back, and the others after gazing for a while at the Gate and its defences soon followed them. That day the camp was moved to the east of the river, right between the arms of the Mountain. The rocks echoed then with voices and with song, as they had not done for many a day. There was the sound, too, of elven-harps and of sweet music; and as it echoed up towards them it seemed that the chill of the air was warmed, and they caught faintly the fragrance of woodland flowers blossoming in spring.

Then Bilbo longed to escape from the dark fortress and to go down and join in the mirth and feasting by the fires. Some of the younger dwarves were moved in their hearts, too, and they muttered that they wished things had fallen out otherwise and that they might welcome such folk as friends; but Thorin scowled.

Then the dwarves themselves brought forth harps and instruments regained from the hoard, and made music to soften his mood; but their song was not as elvish song, and was much like the song they had sung long before in Bilbo's little hobbit-hole.

> *Under the Mountain dark and tall*
> *The King has come unto his hall!*
> *His foe is dead, the Worm of Dread,*
> *And ever so his foes shall fall.*
>
> *The sword is sharp, the spear is long,*
> *The arrow swift, the Gate is strong;*
> *The heart is bold that looks on gold;*
> *The dwarves no more shall suffer wrong.*
>
> *The dwarves of yore made mighty spells,*
> *While hammers fell like ringing bells*
> *In places deep, where dark things sleep,*
> *In hollow halls beneath the fells.*
>
> *On silver necklaces they strung*
> *The light of stars, on crowns they hung*
> *The dragon-fire, from twisted wire*
> *The melody of harps they wrung.*
>
> *The mountain throne once more is freed!*
> *O! wandering folk, the summons heed!*
> *Come haste! Come haste! across the waste!*
> *The king of friend and kin has need.*

Now call we over mountains cold,
'Come back unto the caverns old'!
Here at the Gates the king awaits,
His hands are rich with gems and gold.

The king is come unto his hall
Under the Mountain dark and tall.
The Worm of Dread is slain and dead,
And ever so our foes shall fall!

This song appeared to please Thorin, and he smiled again and grew merry; and he began reckoning the distance to the Iron Hills and how long it would be before Dain could reach the Lonely Mountain, if he had set out as soon as the message reached him. But Bilbo's heart fell, both at the song and the talk: they sounded much too warlike.

The next morning early a company of spearmen was seen crossing the river, and marching up the valley. They bore with them the green banner of the Elvenking and the blue banner of the Lake, and they advanced until they stood right before the wall at the Gate.

Again Thorin hailed them in a loud voice: "Who are you that come armed for war to the gates of Thorin son of Thrain, King under the Mountain?" This time he was answered.

A tall man stood forward, dark of hair and grim of face, and he cried: "Hail Thorin! Why do you fence yourself like a robber in his hold? We are not yet foes, and we rejoice that you are alive beyond our hope. We came expecting to find none living here;

yet now that we are met there is matter for a parley and a council."

"Who are you, and of what would you parley?"

"I am Bard, and by my hand was the dragon slain and your treasure delivered. Is that not a matter that concerns you? Moreover I am by right descent the heir of Girion of Dale, and in your hoard is mingled much of the wealth of his halls and towns, which of old Smaug stole. Is not that a matter of which we may speak? Further in his last battle Smaug destroyed the dwellings of the men of Esgaroth, and I am yet the servant of their Master. I would speak for him and ask whether you have no thought for the sorrow and misery of his people. They aided you in your distress, and in recompense you have thus far brought ruin only, though doubtless undesigned."

Now these were fair words and true, if proudly and grimly spoken; and Bilbo thought that Thorin would at once admit what justice was in them. He did not, of course, expect that any one would remember that it was he who discovered all by himself the dragon's weak spot; and that was just as well, for no one ever did. But also he did not reckon with the power that gold has upon which a dragon has long brooded, nor with dwarvish hearts. Long hours in the past days Thorin had spent in the treasury, and the lust of it was heavy on him. Though he had hunted chiefly for the Arkenstone, yet he had an eye for many another wonderful thing that was lying there, about which were wound old memories of the labours and the sorrows of his race.

"You put your worst cause last and in the chief place," Thorin answered. "To the treasure of my people no man has a claim, because Smaug who stole it from us also robbed him of life or home. The treasure was not his that his evil deeds should be amended with a share of it. The price of the goods and the assistance that we received of the Lake-men we will fairly pay—in due time. But *nothing* will we give, not even a loaf's worth, under threat of force. While an armed host lies before our doors, we look on you as foes and thieves.

"It is in my mind to ask what share of their inheritance you would have paid to our kindred, had you found the hoard unguarded and us slain."

"A just question," replied Bard. "But you are not dead, and we are not robbers. Moreover the wealthy may have pity beyond right on the needy that befriended them when they were in want. And still my other claims remain unanswered."

"I will not parley, as I have said, with armed men at my gate. Nor at all with the people of the Elvenking, whom I remember with small kindness. In this debate they have no place. Begone now ere our arrows fly! And if you would speak with me again, first dismiss the elvish host to the woods where it belongs, and then return, laying down your arms before you approach the threshold."

"The Elvenking is my friend, and he has succoured the people of the Lake in their need, though they had no claim but friendship on him," answered Bard. "We will give you time to repent your words. Gather your wisdom ere we return!" Then he departed and went back to the camp.

Ere many hours were past, the banner-bearers returned, and trumpeters stood forth and blew a blast:

"In the name of Esgaroth and the Forest," one cried, "we speak unto Thorin Thrain's son Oakenshield, calling himself the King under the Mountain, and we bid him consider well the claims that have been urged, or be declared our foe. At the least he shall deliver one twelfth portion of the treasure unto Bard, as the dragon-slayer, and as the heir of Girion. From that portion Bard will himself contribute to the aid of Esgaroth; but if Thorin would have the friendship and honour of the lands about, as his sires had of old, then he will give also somewhat of his own for the comfort of the men of the Lake."

Then Thorin seized a bow of horn and shot an arrow at the speaker. It smote into his shield and stuck there quivering.

"Since such is your answer," he called in return, "I declare the Mountain besieged. You shall not depart from it, until you call on your side for a truce and a parley. We will bear no weapons against you, but we leave you to your gold. You may eat that, if you will!"

With that the messengers departed swiftly, and the dwarves were left to consider their case. So grim had Thorin become, that even if they had wished, the others would not have dared to find fault with him; but indeed most of them seemed to share his mind—except perhaps old fat Bombur and Fili and Kili. Bilbo, of course, disapproved of the whole turn of affairs. He had by now had more than enough of the Mountain, and being besieged inside it was not at all to his taste.

"The whole place still stinks of dragon," he grumbled to himself, "and it makes me sick. And *cram* is beginning simply to stick in my throat."

Chapter XVI

A THIEF IN THE NIGHT

Now the days passed slowly and wearily. Many of the dwarves spent their time piling and ordering the treasure; and now Thorin spoke of the Arkenstone of Thrain, and bade them eagerly to look for it in every corner.

"For the Arkenstone of my father," he said, "is worth more than a river of gold in itself, and to me it is beyond price. That stone of all the treasure I name unto myself, and I will be avenged on anyone who finds it and withholds it."

Bilbo heard these words and he grew afraid, wondering what would happen, if the stone was found—wrapped in an old bundle of tattered oddments that he used as a pillow. All the same he did not speak of it, for as the weariness of the days grew heavier, the beginnings of a plan had come into his little head.

Things had gone on like this for some time, when the ravens brought news that Dain and more than five hundred dwarves, hurrying from the Iron Hills, were now within about two days' march of Dale, coming from the North-East.

"But they cannot reach the Mountain unmarked," said Roäc, "and I fear lest there be battle in the valley. I do not call this counsel good. Though they are a grim folk, they are not likely to overcome the host that besets you; and even if they did so, what

will you gain? Winter and snow is hastening behind
them. How shall you be fed without the friendship
and goodwill of the lands about you? The treasure is
likely to be your death, though the dragon is no
more!"

But Thorin was not moved. "Winter and snow will
bite both men and elves," he said, "and they may
find their dwelling in the waste grievous to bear.
With my friends behind them and winter upon them,
they will perhaps be in softer mood to parley with."

That night Bilbo made up his mind. The sky was
black and moonless. As soon as it was full dark, he
went to a corner of an inner chamber just within the
gate and drew from his bundle a rope, and also the
Arkenstone wrapped in a rag. Then he climbed to
the top of the wall. Only Bombur was there, for it
was his turn to watch, and the dwarves kept only one
watchman at a time.

"It is mighty cold!" said Bombur. "I wish we could
have a fire up here as they have in the camp!"

"It is warm enough inside," said Bilbo.

"I daresay; but I am bound here till midnight,"
grumbled the fat dwarf. "A sorry business altogether.
Not that I venture to disagree with Thorin, may his
beard grow ever longer; yet he was ever a dwarf with
a stiff neck."

"Not as stiff as my legs," said Bilbo. "I am tired of
stairs and stone passages. I would give a good deal
for the feel of grass at my toes."

"I would give a good deal for the feel of a strong
drink in my throat, and for a soft bed after a good
supper!"

"I can't give you those, while the siege is going on.

But it is long since I watched, and I will take your turn for you, if you like. There is no sleep in me tonight."

"You are a good fellow, Mr. Baggins, and I will take your offer kindly. If there should be anything to note, rouse me first, mind you! I will lie in the inner chamber to the left, not far away."

"Off you go!" said Bilbo. "I will wake you at midnight, and you can wake the next watchman."

As soon as Bombur had gone, Bilbo put on his ring, fastened his rope, slipped down over the wall, and was gone. He had about five hours before him. Bombur would sleep (he could sleep at any time, and ever since the adventure in the forest he was always trying to recapture the beautiful dreams he had then); and all the others were busy with Thorin. It was unlikely that any, even Fili or Kili, would come out on the wall until it was their turn.

It was very dark, and the road after a while, when he left the newly made path and climbed down towards the lower course of the stream, was strange to him. At last he came to the bend where he had to cross the water, if he was to make for the camp, as he wished. The bed of the stream was there shallow but already broad, and fording it in the dark was not easy for the little hobbit. He was nearly across when he missed his footing on a round stone and fell into the cold water with a splash. He had barely scrambled out on the far bank, shivering and spluttering, when up came elves in the gloom with bright lanterns and searched for the cause of the noise.

"That was no fish!" one said. "There is a spy about. Hide your lights! They will help him more than us, if it is that queer little creature that is said to be their servant."

"Servant, indeed!" snorted Bilbo; and in the middle of his snort he sneezed loudly, and the elves immediately gathered towards the sound.

"Let's have a light!" he said. "I am here, if you want me!" and he slipped off his ring, and popped from behind a rock.

They seized him quickly, in spite of their surprise. "Who are you? Are you the dwarves' hobbit? What are you doing? How did you get so far past our sentinels?" they asked one after another.

"I am Mr. Bilbo Baggins," he answered, "companion of Thorin, if you want to know. I know your king well by sight, though perhaps he doesn't know me to look at. But Bard will remember me, and it is Bard I particularly want to see."

"Indeed!" said they, "and what may be your business?"

"Whatever it is, it's my own, my good elves. But if you wish ever to get back to your own woods from this cold cheerless place," he answered shivering, "you will take me along quick to a fire, where I can dry—and then you will let me speak to your chiefs as quick as may be. I have only an hour or two to spare."

That is how it came about that some two hours after his escape from the Gate, Bilbo was sitting beside a warm fire in front of a large tent, and there sat too, gazing curiously at him, both the Elvenking and Bard. A hobbit in elvish armour, partly wrapped in an old blanket, was something new to them.

"Really you know," Bilbo was saying in his best business manner, "things are impossible. Personally I am tired of the whole affair. I wish I was back in the West in my own home, where folk are more reasonable. But I have an interest in this matter—one fourteenth share, to be precise, according to a letter, which fortunately I believe I have kept." He drew from a pocket in his old jacket (which he still wore over his mail), crumpled and much folded, Thorin's letter that had been put under the clock on his mantelpiece in May!

"A share in the *profits*, mind you," he went on. "I am aware of that. Personally I am only too ready to consider all your claims carefully, and deduct what is right from the total before putting in my own claim. However you don't know Thorin Oakenshield as well as I do now. I assure you, he is quite ready to sit on a heap of gold and starve, as long as you sit here."

"Well, let him!" said Bard. "Such a fool deserves to starve."

"Quite so," said Bilbo. "I see your point of view. At the same time winter is coming on fast. Before long you will be having snow and what not, and supplies will be difficult—even for elves I imagine. Also there will be other difficulties. You have not heard of Dain and the dwarves of the Iron Hills?"

"We have, a long time ago; but what has he got to do with us?" asked the king.

"I thought as much. I see I have some information you have not got. Dain, I may tell you, is now less than two days' march off, and has at least five hundred grim dwarves with him—a good many of them have had experience in the dreadful dwarf and goblin wars, of which you have no doubt heard. When they arrive there may be serious trouble."

"Why do you tell us this? Are you betraying your friends, or are you threatening us?" asked Bard grimly.

"My dear Bard!" squeaked Bilbo. "Don't be so hasty! I never met such suspicious folk! I am merely trying to avoid trouble for all concerned. Now I will make you an offer! !"

"Let us hear it!" they said.

"You may see it!" said he. "It is this!" and he drew forth the Arkenstone, and threw away the wrapping.

The Elvenking himself, whose eyes were used to things of wonder and beauty, stood up in amazement. Even Bard gazed marvelling at it in silence. It was as if a globe had been filled with moonlight and hung before them in a net woven of the glint of frosty stars.

"This is the Arkenstone of Thrain," said Bilbo, "the Heart of the Mountain; and it is also the heart of Thorin. He values it above a river of gold. I give it to you. It will aid you in your bargaining." Then Bilbo, not without a shudder, not without a glance of longing, handed the marvellous stone to Bard, and he held it in his hand, as though dazed.

"But how is it yours to give?" he asked at last with an effort.

"O well!" said the hobbit uncomfortably. "It isn't exactly; but, well, I am willing to let it stand against all my claim, don't you know. I may be a burglar—or so they say: personally I never really felt like one— but I am an honest one, I hope, more or less. Anyway I am going back now, and the dwarves can do what they like to me. I hope you will find it useful."

The Elvenking looked at Bilbo with a new wonder. "Bilbo Baggins!" he said. "You are more worthy to wear the armour of elf-princes than many that have looked more comely in it. But I wonder if Thorin Oakenshield will see it so. I have more knowledge of dwarves in general than you have perhaps. I advise you to remain with us, and here you shall be honoured and thrice welcome."

"Thank you very much I am sure," said Bilbo with a bow. "But I don't think I ought to leave my friends like this, after all we have gone through together. And I promised to wake old Bombur at midnight, too! Really I must be going, and quickly."

Nothing they could say would stop him; so an escort was provided for him, and as he went both the king and Bard saluted him with honour. As they passed through the camp an old man, wrapped in a dark cloak, rose from a tent door where he was sitting and came towards them.

"Well done! Mr. Baggins!" he said, clapping Bilbo on the back. "There is always more about you than anyone expects!" It was Gandalf.

For the first time for many a day Bilbo was really delighted. But there was no time for all the questions that he immediately wished to ask.

"All in good time!" said Gandalf. "Things are drawing towards the end now, unless I am mistaken. There is an unpleasant time just in front of you; but keep your heart up! You *may* come through all right. There is news brewing that even the ravens have not heard. Good night!"

Puzzled but cheered, Bilbo hurried on. He was guided to a safe ford and set across dry, and then he said farewell to the elves and climbed carefully back towards the Gate. Great weariness began to come over him; but it was well before midnight when he clambered up the rope again—it was still where he had left it. He untied it and hid it, and then he sat down on the wall and wondered anxiously what would happen next.

At midnight he woke up Bombur; and then in turn rolled himself up in his corner, without listening to the old dwarf's thanks (which he felt he had hardly earned). He was soon fast asleep forgetting all his worries till the morning. As a matter of fact he was dreaming of eggs and bacon.

Chapter XVII

THE CLOUDS BURST

Next day the trumpets rang early in the camp. Soon a single runner was seen hurrying along the narrow path. At a distance he stood and hailed them, asking whether Thorin would now listen to another embassy, since new tidings had come to hand, and matters were changed.

"That will be Dain!" said Thorin when he heard. "They will have got wind of his coming. I thought that would alter their mood! Bid them come few in number and weaponless, and I will hear," he called to the messenger.

About midday the banners of the Forest and the Lake were seen to be borne forth again. A company of twenty was approaching. At the beginning of the narrow way they laid aside sword and spear, and came on towards the Gate. Wondering, the dwarves saw that among them were both Bard and the Elvenking, before whom an old man wrapped in cloak and hood bore a strong casket of iron-bound wood.

"Hail Thorin!" said Bard. "Are you still of the same mind?"

"My mind does not change with the rising and setting of a few suns," answered Thorin. "Did you come to ask me idle questions? Still the elf-host has not departed as I bade! Till then you come in vain to bargain with me."

"Is there then nothing for which you would yield any of your gold?"

"Nothing that you or your friends have to offer."

"What of the Arkenstone of Thrain?" said he, and at the same moment the old man opened the casket and held aloft the jewel. The light leapt from his hand, bright and white in the morning.

Then Thorin was stricken dumb with amazement and confusion. No one spoke for a long while.

Thorin at length broke the silence, and his voice was thick with wrath. "That stone was my father's, and is mine," he said. "Why should I purchase my own?" But wonder overcame him and he added: "But how came you by the heirloom of my house—if there is need to ask such a question of thieves?"

"We are not thieves," Bard answered. "Your own we will give back in return for our own."

"How came you by it?" shouted Thorin in gathering rage.

"I gave it to them!" squeaked Bilbo, who was peering over the wall, by now in a dreadful fright.

"You! You!" cried Thorin, turning upon him and grasping him with both hands. "You miserable hobbit! You undersized—burglar!" he shouted at a loss for words, and he shook poor Bilbo like a rabbit.

"By the beard of Durin! I wish I had Gandalf here! Curse him for his choice of you! May his beard wither! As for you I will throw you to the rocks!" he cried and lifted Bilbo in his arms.

"Stay! Your wish is granted!" said a voice. The old man with the casket threw aside his hood and cloak. "Here is Gandalf! And none too soon it seems. If you don't like my Burglar, please don't damage him.

Put him down, and listen first to what he has to say!"

"You all seem in league!" said Thorin dropping Bilbo on the top of the wall. "Never again will I have dealings with any wizard or his friends. What have you to say, you descendant of rats?"

"Dear me! Dear me!" said Bilbo. "I am sure this is all very uncomfortable. You may remember saying that I might choose my own fourteenth share? Perhaps I took it too literally—I have been told that dwarves are sometimes politer in word than in deed. The time was, all the same, when you seemed to think that I had been of some service. Descendant of rats, indeed! Is this all the service of you and your family that I was promised, Thorin? Take it that I have disposed of my share as I wished, and let it go at that!"

"I will," said Thorin grimly. "And I will let you go at that—and may we never meet again!" Then he turned and spoke over the wall. "I am betrayed," he said. "It was rightly guessed that I could not forbear to redeem the Arkenstone, the treasure of my house. For it I will give one fourteenth share of the hoard in silver and gold, setting aside the gems; but that shall be accounted the promised share of this traitor, and with that reward he shall depart, and you can divide it as you will. He will get little enough, I doubt not. Take him, if you wish him to live; and no friendship of mine goes with him.

"Get down now to your friends!" he said to Bilbo, "or I will throw you down."

"What about the gold and silver?" asked Bilbo.

"That shall follow after, as can be arranged," said he. "Get down!"

"Until then we keep the stone," cried Bard.

"You are not making a very splendid figure as King under the Mountain," said Gandalf. "But things may change yet."

"They may indeed," said Thorin. And already, so strong was the bewilderment of the treasure upon him, he was pondering whether by the help of Dain he might not recapture the Arkenstone and withhold the share of the reward.

And so Bilbo was swung down from the wall, and departed with nothing for all his trouble, except the armour which Thorin had given him already. More than one of the dwarves in their hearts felt shame and pity at his going.

"Farewell!" he cried to them. "We may meet again as friends."

"Be off!" called Thorin. "You have mail upon you, which was made by my folk, and is too good for you. It cannot be pierced by arrows; but if you do not hasten, I will sting your miserable feet. So be swift!"

"Not so hasty!" said Bard. "We will give you until tomorrow. At noon we will return, and see if you have brought from the hoard the portion that is to be set against the stone. If that is done without deceit, then we will depart, and the elf-host will go back to the Forest. In the meanwhile farewell!"

With that they went back to the camp; but Thorin sent messengers by Roäc telling Dain of what had passed, and bidding him come with wary speed.

That day passed and the night. The next day the wind shifted west, and the air was dark and gloomy. The morning was still early when a cry was heard in the camp. Runners came in to report that a host of dwarves had appeared round the eastern spur of the Mountain and was now hastening to Dale. Dain had come. He had hurried on through the night, and so had come upon them sooner than they had expected. Each one of his folk was clad in a hauberk of steel mail that hung to his knees, and his legs were covered with hose of a fine and flexible metal mesh, the secret of whose making was possessed by Dain's people. The dwarves are exceedingly strong for their height, but most of these were strong even for dwarves. In battle they wielded heavy two-handed mattocks; but each of them had also a short broad sword at his side and a roundshield slung at his back. Their beards were forked and plaited and thrust into their belts. Their caps were of iron and they were shod with iron, and their faces were grim.

Trumpets called men and elves to arms. Before long the dwarves could be seen coming up the valley at a great pace. They halted between the river and the eastern spur; but a few held on their way, and crossing the river drew near the camp; and there they laid down their weapons and held up their hands in sign of peace. Bard went out to meet them, and with him went Bilbo.

"We are sent from Dain son of Nain," they said when questioned. "We are hastening to our kinsmen in the Mountain, since we learn that the kingdom of old is renewed. But who are you that sit in the plain as foes before defended walls?" This, of course, in the polite and rather old-fashioned language of such occasions, meant simply: "You have no business here. We are going on, so make way or we shall fight you!" They meant to push on between the Mountain and the loop of the river; for the narrow land there did not seem to be strongly guarded.

Bard, of course, refused to allow the dwarves to go straight on to the Mountain. He was determined to wait until the gold and silver had been brought out in exchange for the Arkenstone; for he did not believe that this would be done, if once the fortress was manned with so large and warlike a company. They had brought with them a great store of supplies; for the dwarves can carry very heavy burdens, and nearly all of Dain's folk, in spite of their rapid march, bore huge packs on their backs in addition to their weapons. They would stand a siege for weeks, and by that time yet more dwarves might come, and yet more, for Thorin had many relatives. Also they would be able to reopen and guard some other gate, so that the besiegers would have to encircle the whole mountain; and for that they had not sufficient numbers.

These were, in fact, precisely their plans (for the raven-messengers had been busy between Thorin and Dain); but for the moment the way was barred, so after angry words the dwarf-messengers retired muttering in their beards. Bard then sent messengers at once to the Gate; but they found no gold or payment. Arrows came forth as soon as they were within shot, and they hastened back in dismay. In the camp all was now astir, as if for battle; for the dwarves of Dain were advancing along the eastern bank.

"Fools!" laughed Bard, "to come thus beneath the Mountain's arm! They do not understand war above ground, whatever they may know of battle in the mines. There are many of our archers and spearmen now hidden in the rocks upon their right flank. Dwarf-mail may be good, but they will soon be hard put to it. Let us set on them now from both sides, before they are fully rested!"

But the Elvenking said: "Long will I tarry, ere I begin this war for gold. The dwarves cannot pass us, unless we will, or do anything that we cannot mark. Let us hope still for something that will bring reconciliation. Our advantage in numbers will be enough, if in the end it must come to unhappy blows."

But he reckoned without the dwarves. The knowledge that the Arkenstone was in the hands of the besiegers burned in their thoughts; also they guessed the hesitation of Bard and his friends, and resolved to strike while they debated.

Suddenly without a signal they sprang silently forward to attack. Bows twanged and arrows whistled; battle was about to be joined.

Still more suddenly a darkness came on with dreadful swiftness! A black cloud hurried over the sky. Winter thunder on a wild wind rolled roaring up and rumbled in the Mountain, and lightning lit its peak. And beneath the thunder another blackness could be seen whirling forward; but it did not come with the wind, it came from the North, like a vast cloud of birds, so dense that no light could be seen between their wings.

"Halt!" cried Gandalf, who appeared suddenly, and stood alone, with arms uplifted, between the advancing dwarves and the ranks awaiting them. "Halt!" he called in a voice like thunder, and his staff blazed forth with a flash like the lightning. "Dread has come upon you all! Alas! it has come more swiftly than I guessed. The Goblins are upon you! Bolg* of the North is coming, O Dain! whose father you slew in Moria. Behold! the bats are above his army like a sea of locusts. They ride upon wolves and Wargs are in their train!"

Amazement and confusion fell upon them all. Even as Gandalf had been speaking the darkness grew. The dwarves halted and gazed at the sky. The elves cried out with many voices.

"Come!" called Gandalf. "There is yet time for council. Let Dain son of Nain come swiftly to us!"

So began a battle that none had expected; and it was called the Battle of Five Armies, and it was very terrible. Upon one side were the Goblins and the Wild Wolves, and upon the other were Elves and Men and Dwarves. This is how it fell out. Ever since the fall of the Great Goblin of the Misty Mountains the hatred of their race for the dwarves had been rekindled to fury. Messengers had passed to and fro between all their cities, colonies and strongholds; for they resolved now to win the dominion of the North. Tidings they had gathered in secret ways; and in all the mountains there was a forging and an arming. Then they marched and gathered by hill and valley, going ever by tunnel or under dark, until around and beneath the great mountain Gundabad of the North, where was their capital, a vast host was assembled ready to sweep down in time of storm unawares

* Son of Azog. See p.30

upon the South. Then they learned of the death of Smaug, and joy was in their hearts; and they hastened night after night through the mountains, and came thus at last on a sudden from the North hard on the heels of Dain. Not even the ravens knew of their coming until they came out in the broken lands which divided the Lonely Mountain from the hills behind. How much Gandalf knew cannot be said, but it is plain that he had not expected this sudden assault.

This is the plan that he made in council with the Elven-king and with Bard; and with Dain, for the dwarf-lord now joined them: the Goblins were the foes of all, and at their coming all other quarrels were forgotten. Their only hope was to lure the goblins into the valley between the arms of the Mountain; and themselves to man the great spurs that struck south and east. Yet this would be perilous, if the goblins were in sufficient numbers to overrun the Mountain itself, and so attack them also from behind and above; but there was no time to make any other plan, or to summon any help.

Soon the thunder passed, rolling away to the South-East; but the bat-cloud came, flying lower, over the shoulder of the Mountain, and whirled above them shutting out the light and filling them with dread.

"To the Mountain!" called Bard. "To the Mountain! Let us take our places while there is yet time!"

On the Southern spur, in its lower slopes and in the rocks at its feet, the Elves were set; on the Eastern spur were men and dwarves. But Bard and some of the nimblest of men and elves climbed to the height of the Eastern shoulder to gain a view to the North. Soon they could see the lands before the Mountain's feet black with a hurrying multitude. Ere long the vanguard swirled round the spur's end and came rushing into Dale. These were the swiftest wolf-riders, and already their cries and howls rent the air afar. A few brave men were strung before them to make a feint of resistance, and many there fell before the rest drew back and fled to either side. As Gandalf had hoped, the goblin army had gathered behind the resisted vanguard, and poured now in rage into the valley, driving wildly up between the arms of the Mountain, seeking for the foe. Their banners were countless, black and red, and they came on like a tide in fury and disorder.

It was a terrible battle. The most dreadful of all Bilbo's experiences, and the one which at the time he hated most—which is to say it was the one he was most proud of, and most fond of recalling long afterwards, although he was quite unimportant in it. Actually I may say he put on his ring early in the business, and vanished from sight, if not from all danger. A magic ring of that sort is not a complete protection in a goblin charge, nor does it stop flying arrows and wild spears; but it does help in getting out of the way, and it prevents your head from being specially chosen for a sweeping stroke by a goblin swordsman.

The elves were the first to charge. Their hatred for the goblins is cold and bitter. Their spears and swords shone in the gloom with a gleam of chill flame, so deadly was the wrath of the hands that held them. As soon as the host of their enemies was dense in the valley, they sent against it a shower of arrows, and each flickered as it fled as if with stinging fire. Behind the arrows a thousand of their spearmen leapt down and charged. The yells were deafening. The rocks were stained black with goblin blood.

Just as the goblins were recovering from the onslaught and the elf-charge was halted, there rose from across the valley a deep-throated roar. With cries of "Moria!" and "Dain, Dain!" the dwarves of the Iron Hills plunged in, wielding their mattocks, upon the other side; and beside them came the men of the Lake with long swords.

Panic came upon the Goblins; and even as they turned to meet this new attack, the elves charged again with renewed numbers. Already many of the goblins were flying back down the river to escape from the trap; and many of their own wolves were turning upon them and rending the dead and the wounded. Victory seemed at hand, when a cry rang out on the heights above.

Goblins had scaled the Mountain from the other side and already many were on the slopes above the Gate, and others were streaming down recklessly, heedless of those that fell screaming from cliff and precipice, to attack the spurs from above. Each of these could be reached by paths that ran down from the main mass of the Mountain in the centre; and the defenders had too few to bar the way for long. Victory now vanished from hope. They had only stemmed the first onslaught of the black tide.

Day drew on. The goblins gathered again in the valley. There a host of Wargs came ravening and with them came the bodyguard of Bolg, goblins of

huge size with scimitars of steel. Soon actual darkness was coming into a stormy sky; while still the
great bats swirled about the heads and ears of elves
and men, or fastened vampire-like on the stricken.
Now Bard was fighting to defend the Eastern spur,
and yet giving slowly back; and the elf-lords were at
bay about their king upon the southern arm, near to
the watch-post on Ravenhill.

Suddenly there was a great shout, and from the
Gate came a trumpet call. They had forgotten
Thorin! Part of the wall, moved by levers, fell
outward with a crash into the pool. Out leapt the
King under the Mountain, and his companions
followed him. Hood and cloak were gone; they were
in shining armour, and red light leapt from their
eyes. In the gloom the great dwarf gleamed like gold
in a dying fire.

Rocks were hurled down from on high by the
goblins above; but they held on, leapt down to the
falls' foot, and rushed forward to battle. Wolf and
rider fell or fled before them. Thorin wielded his axe
with mighty strokes, and nothing seemed to harm
him.

"To me! To me! Elves and Men! To me! O my
kinsfolk!" he cried, and his voice shook like a horn in
the valley.

Down, heedless of order, rushed all the dwarves of
Dain to his help. Down too came many of the Lake-
men, for Bard could not restrain them; and out upon
the other side came many of the spearmen of the
elves. Once again the goblins were stricken in the
valley; and they were piled in heaps till Dale was dark
and hideous with their corpses. The Wargs were

scattered and Thorin drove right against the body-guard of Bolg. But he could not pierce their ranks.

Already behind him among the goblin dead lay many men and many dwarves, and many a fair elf that should have lived yet long ages merrily in the wood. And as the valley widened his onset grew ever slower. His numbers were too few. His flanks were unguarded. Soon the attackers were attacked, and they were forced into a great ring, facing every way, hemmed all about with goblins and wolves returning to the assault. The bodyguard of Bolg came howling against them, and drove in upon their ranks like waves upon cliffs of sand. Their friends could not help them, for the assault from the Mountain was renewed with redoubled force, and upon either side men and elves were being slowly beaten down.

On all this Bilbo looked with misery. He had taken his stand on Ravenhill among the Elves—partly because there was more chance of escape from that point, and partly (with the more Tookish part of his mind) because if he was going to be in a last desper-ate stand, he preferred on the whole to defend the Elvenking. Gandalf, too, I may say, was there, sitting on the ground as if in deep thought, preparing, I suppose, some last blast of magic before the end.

That did not seem far off. "It will not be long now," thought Bilbo, "before the goblins win the Gate, and we are all slaughtered or driven down and captured. Really it is enough to make one weep, after all one has gone through. I would rather old Smaug had been left with all the wretched treasure, than that these vile creatures should get it, and poor old Bombur, and Balin and Fili and Kili and all the rest come to a bad end; and Bard too, and the Lake-men and the merry elves. Misery me! I have heard songs of many battles, and I have always understood that defeat may be glorious. It seems very uncomfortable, not to say distressing. I wish I was well out of it."

The clouds were torn by the wind, and a red sunset slashed the West. Seeing the sudden gleam in the gloom Bilbo looked round. He gave a great cry: he had seen a sight that made his heart leap, dark shapes small yet majestic against the distant glow.

"The Eagles! The Eagles!" he shouted. "The Eagles are coming!"

Bilbo's eyes were seldom wrong. The eagles were coming down the wind, line after line, in such a host as must have gathered from all the eyries of the North.

"The Eagles! the Eagles!" Bilbo cried, dancing and waving his arms. If the elves could not see him they could hear him. Soon they too took up the cry, and it echoed across the valley. Many wondering eyes looked up, though as yet nothing could be seen except from the southern shoulders of the Mountain.

"The Eagles!" cried Bilbo once more, but at that moment a stone hurtling from above smote heavily on his helm, and he fell with a crash and knew no more.

Chapter XVIII

THE RETURN JOURNEY

When Bilbo came to himself, he was literally by himself. He was lying on the flat stones of Ravenhill, and no one was near. A cloudless day, but cold, was broad above him. He was shaking, and as chilled as stone, but his head burned with fire.

"Now I wonder what has happened?" he said to himself. "At any rate I am not yet one of the fallen heroes; but I suppose there is still time enough for that!"

He sat up painfully. Looking into the valley he could see no living goblins. After a while as his head cleared a little, he thought he could see elves moving in the rocks below. He rubbed his eyes. Surely there was a camp still in the plain some distance off; and there was a coming and going about the Gate? Dwarves seemed to be busy removing the wall. But all was deadly still. There was no call and no echo of a song. Sorrow seemed to be in the air.

"Victory after all, I suppose!" he said, feeling his aching head. "Well, it seems a very gloomy business."

Suddenly he was aware of a man climbing up and coming towards him.

"Hullo there!" he called with a shaky voice. "Hullo there! What news?"

"What voice is it that speaks among the stones?"

said the man halting and peering about him not far from where Bilbo sat.

Then Bilbo remembered his ring! "Well I'm blessed!" said he. "This invisibility has its drawbacks after all. Otherwise I suppose I might have spent a warm and comfortable night in bed!"

"It's me, Bilbo Baggins, companion of Thorin!" he cried, hurriedly taking off the ring.

"It is well that I have found you!" said the man striding forward. "You are needed and we have looked for you long. You would have been numbered among the dead, who are many, if Gandalf the wizard had not said that your voice was last heard in this place. I have been sent to look here for the last time. Are you much hurt?"

"A nasty knock on the head, I think," said Bilbo. "But I have a helm and a hard skull. All the same I feel sick and my legs are like straws."

"I will carry you down to the camp in the valley," said the man, and picked him lightly up.

The man was swift and sure-footed. It was not long before Bilbo was set down before a tent in Dale; and there stood Gandalf, with his arm in a sling. Even the wizard had not escaped without a wound; and there were few unharmed in all the host.

When Gandalf saw Bilbo, he was delighted. "Baggins!" he exclaimed. "Well I never! Alive after all—I *am* glad! I began to wonder if even your luck would see you through! A terrible business, and it nearly was disastrous. But other news can wait. Come!" he said more gravely. "You are called for;" and leading the hobbit he took him within the tent.

"Hail! Thorin," he said as he entered. "I have brought him."

There indeed lay Thorin Oakenshield, wounded with many wounds, and his rent armour and notched axe were cast upon the floor. He looked up as Bilbo came beside him.

"Farewell, good thief," he said. "I go now to the halls of waiting to sit beside my fathers, until the world is renewed. Since I leave now all gold and silver, and go where it is of little worth, I wish to part in friendship from you, and I would take back my words and deeds at the Gate."

Bilbo knelt on one knee filled with sorrow. "Farewell, King under the Mountain!" he said. "This is a bitter adventure, if it must end so; and not a mountain of gold can amend it. Yet I am glad that I have shared in your perils—that has been more than any Baggins deserves."

"No!" said Thorin. "There is more in you of good than you know, child of the kindly West. Some courage and some wisdom, blended in measure. If more of us valued food and cheer and song above hoarded gold, it would be a merrier world. But sad or merry, I must leave it now. Farewell!"

Then Bilbo turned away, and he went by himself, and sat alone wrapped in a blanket, and, whether you believe it or not, he wept until his eyes were red and his voice was hoarse. He was a kindly little soul. Indeed it was long before he had the heart to make a joke again. "A mercy it is," he said at last to himself, "that I woke when I did. I wish Thorin were living, but I am glad that we parted in kindness. You are a fool, Bilbo Baggins, and you made a great mess

of that business with the stone; and there was a
battle, in spite of all your efforts to buy peace and
quiet, but I suppose you can hardly be blamed for
that."

All that had happened after he was stunned, Bilbo
learned later; but it gave him more sorrow than joy,
and he was now weary of his adventure. He was
aching in his bones for the homeward journey. That,
however, was a little delayed, so in the meantime I
will tell something of events. The Eagles had long
had suspicion of the goblins' mustering; from their
watchfulness the movements in the mountains could
not be altogether hid. So they too had gathered in
great numbers, under the great Eagle of the Misty
Mountains; and at length smelling battle from afar
they had come speeding down the gale in the nick of
time. They it was who dislodged the goblins from the
mountain-slopes, casting them over precipices, or
driving them down shrieking and bewildered among
their foes. It was not long before they had freed the
Lonely Mountain, and elves and men on either side
of the valley could come at last to the help of the
battle below.

But even with the Eagles they were still outnum-
bered. In that last hour Beorn himself had appeared—
no one knew how or from where. He came alone, and
in bear's shape; and he seemed to have grown almost
to giant-size in his wrath.

The roar of his voice was like drums and guns; and
he tossed wolves and goblins from his path like
straws and feathers. He fell upon their rear, and
broke like a clap of thunder through the ring. The

dwarves were making a stand still about their lords upon a low rounded hill. Then Beorn stooped and lifted Thorin, who had fallen pierced with spears, and bore him out of the fray.

Swiftly he returned and his wrath was redoubled, so that nothing could withstand him, and no weapon seemed to bite upon him. He scattered the body-guard, and pulled down Bolg himself and crushed him. Then dismay fell on the Goblins and they fled in all directions. But weariness left their enemies with the coming of new hope, and they pursued them closely, and prevented most of them from escaping where they could. They drove many of them into the Running River, and such as fled south or west they hunted into the marshes about the Forest River; and there the greater part of the last fugitives perished, while those that came hardly to the Wood-elves' realm were there slain, or drawn in to die deep in the trackless dark of Mirkwood. Songs have said that three parts of the goblin warriors of the North perished on that day, and the mountains had peace for many a year.

Victory had been assured before the fall of night; but the pursuit was still on foot, when Bilbo returned to the camp; and not many were in the valley save the more grievously wounded.

"Where are the Eagles?" he asked Gandalf that evening, as he lay wrapped in many warm blankets.

"Some are in the hunt," said the wizard, "but most have gone back to their eyries. They would not stay here, and departed with the first light of morning. Dain has crowned their chief with gold, and sworn friendship with them forever."

"I am sorry. I mean, I should have liked to see them again," said Bilbo sleepily; "perhaps I shall see them on the way home. I suppose I shall be going home soon?"

"As soon as you like," said the wizard.

Actually it was some days before Bilbo really set out. They buried Thorin deep beneath the Mountain, and Bard laid the Arkenstone upon his breast.

"There let it lie till the Mountain falls!" he said. "May it bring good fortune to all his folk that dwell here after!"

Upon his tomb the Elvenking then laid Orcrist, the elvish sword that had been taken from Thorin in captivity. It is said in songs that it gleamed ever in the dark if foes approached, and the fortress of the dwarves could not be taken by surprise. There now Dain son of Nain took up his abode, and he became King under the Mountain, and in time many other dwarves gathered to his throne in the ancient halls. Of the twelve companions of Thorin, ten remained. Fili and Kili had fallen defending him with shield and body, for he was their mother's elder brother. The others remained with Dain; for Dain dealt his treasure well.

There was, of course, no longer any question of dividing the hoard in such shares as had been planned, to Balin and Dwalin, and Dori and Nori and Ori, and Oin and Gloin, and Bifur and Bofur and Bombur—or to Bilbo. Yet a fourteenth share of all the silver and gold, wrought and unwrought, was given up to Bard; for Dain said: "We will honour the agreement of the dead, and he has now the Arkenstone in his keeping."

Even a fourteenth share was wealth exceedingly great, greater than that of many mortal kings. From that treasure Bard sent much gold to the Master of Lake-town; and he rewarded his followers and friends freely. To the Elvenking he gave the emeralds of Girion, such jewels as he most loved, which Dain had restored to him.

To Bilbo he said: "This treasure is as much yours as it is mine; though old agreements cannot stand, since so many have a claim in its winning and defence. Yet even though you were willing to lay aside all your claim, I should wish that the words of Thorin, of which he repented, should not prove true: that we should give you little. I would reward you most richly of all."

"Very kind of you," said Bilbo. "But really it is a relief to me. How on earth should I have got all that treasure home without war and murder all along the way, I don't know. And I don't know what I should have done with it when I got home. I am sure it is better in your hands."

In the end he would only take two small chests, one filled with silver, and the other with gold, such as one strong pony could carry. "That will be quite as much as I can manage," said he.

At last the time came for him to say good-bye to his friends. "Farewell, Balin!" he said; "and farewell, Dwalin; and farewell Dori, Nori, Ori, Oin, Gloin, Bifur, Bofur, and Bombur! May your beards never grow thin!" And turning towards the Mountain he added: "Farewell Thorin Oakenshield! And Fili and Kili! May your memory never fade!"

Then the dwarves bowed low before their Gate, but words stuck in their throats. "Good-bye and good luck, wherever you fare!" said Balin at last. "If ever you visit us again, when our halls are made fair once more, then the feast shall indeed be splendid!"

"If ever you are passing my way," said Bilbo, "don't wait to knock! Tea is at four; but any of you are welcome at any time!"

Then he turned away.

The elf-host was on the march; and if it was sadly lessened, yet many were glad, for now the northern world would be merrier for many a long day. The dragon was dead, and the goblins overthrown, and their hearts looked forward after winter to a spring of joy.

Gandalf and Bilbo rode behind the Elvenking, and beside them strode Beorn, once again in man's shape, and he laughed and sang in a loud voice upon the road. So they went on until they drew near to the borders of Mirkwood, to the north of the place where the Forest River ran out. Then they halted, for the wizard and Bilbo would not enter the wood, even though the king bade them stay a while in his halls. They intended to go along the edge of the forest, and round its northern end in the waste that lay between it and the beginning of the Grey Mountains. It was a long and cheerless road, but now that the goblins were crushed, it seemed safer to them than the dreadful pathways under the trees. Moreover Beorn was going that way too.

"Farewell! O Elvenking!" said Gandalf. "Merry be the greenwood, while the world is yet young! And merry be all your folk!"

"Farewell! O Gandalf!" said the king. "May you ever appear where you are most needed and least expected! The oftener you appear in my halls the better shall I be pleased!"

"I beg of you," said Bilbo stammering and standing on one foot, "to accept this gift!" and he brought out a necklace of silver and pearls that Dain had given him at their parting.

"In what way have I earned such a gift, O hobbit?" said the king.

"Well, er, I thought, don't you know," said Bilbo rather confused, "that, er, some little return should be made for your, er, hospitality. I mean even a burglar has his feelings. I have drunk much of your wine and eaten much of your bread."

"I will take your gift, O Bilbo the Magnificent!" said the king gravely. "And I name you elf-friend and blessed. May your shadow never grow less (or stealing would be too easy)! Farewell!"

Then the elves turned towards the Forest, and Bilbo started on his long road home.

He had many hardships and adventures before he got back. The Wild was still the Wild, and there were many other things in it in those days beside goblins; but he was well guided and well guarded—the wizard was with him, and Beorn for much of the way—and he was never in great danger again. Anyway by midwinter Gandalf and Bilbo had come all the way back, along both edges of the Forest, to the doors of Beorn's house; and there for a while they both stayed. Yule-tide was warm and merry there; and men came from far and wide to feast at Beorn's bidding. The goblins of the Misty Mountains were now few and terrified, and hidden in the deepest holes they could find; and the Wargs had vanished from the woods, so that men went abroad without fear. Beorn indeed became a great chief afterwards in those regions and ruled a wide land between the mountains and the wood; and it is said that for many generations the men of his line had the power of taking bear's shape, and some were grim men and bad, but most were in heart like Beorn, if less in size and strength. In their day the last goblins were hunted from the Misty Mountains and a new peace came over the edge of the Wild.

It was spring, and a fair one with mild weathers and a bright sun, before Bilbo and Gandalf took their leave at last of Beorn, and though he longed for home, Bilbo left with regret, for the flowers of the gardens of Beorn were in springtime no less marvellous than in high summer.

At last they came up the long road, and reached the very pass where the goblins had captured them before. But they came to that high point at morning, and looking backward they saw a white sun shining over the outstretched lands. There behind lay Mirkwood, blue in the distance, and darkly green at the nearer edge even in the spring. There far away was the Lonely Mountain on the edge of eyesight. On its highest peak snow yet unmelted was gleaming pale.

"So comes snow after fire, and even dragons have their ending!" said Bilbo, and he turned his back on his adventure. The Tookish part was getting very tired, and the Baggins was daily getting stronger. "I wish now only to be in my own arm-chair!" he said.

Chapter XIX

THE LAST STAGE

It was on May the First that the two came back at last to the brink of the valley of Rivendell, where stood the Last (or the First) Homely House. Again it was evening, their ponies were tired, especially the one that carried the baggage; and they all felt in need of rest. As they rode down the steep path, Bilbo heard the elves still singing in the trees, as if they had not stopped since he left; and as soon as the riders came down into the lower glades of the wood they burst into a song of much the same kind as before. This is something like it:

> *The dragon is withered,*
> *His bones are now crumbled;*
> *His armour is shivered,*
> *His splendour is humbled!*
> *Though sword shall be rusted,*
> *And throne and crown perish*
> *With strength that men trusted*
> *And wealth that they cherish,*
> *Here grass is still growing,*
> *And leaves are yet swinging,*
> *The white water flowing,*
> *And elves are yet singing*
> > *Come! Tra-la-la-lally!*
> > *Come back to the valley!*

The stars are far brighter
Than gems without measure,
The moon is far whiter
Than silver in treasure;
The fire is more shining
On hearth in the gloaming
Than gold won by mining,
So why go a-roaming?
O! Tra-la-la-lally
Come back to the Valley.

O! Where are you going,
So late in returning?
The river is flowing,
The stars are all burning!
O! Whither so laden,
So sad and so dreary?
Here elf and elf-maiden
Now welcome the weary
With Tra-la-la-lally
Come back to the Valley,
Tra-la-la-lally
Fa-la-la-lally
Fa-la!

Then the elves of the valley came out and greeted them and led them across the water to the house of Elrond. There a warm welcome was made them, and there were many eager ears that evening to hear the tale of their adventures. Gandalf it was who spoke, for Bilbo was fallen quiet and drowsy. Most of the tale he knew, for he had been in it, and had himself told much of it to the wizard on their homeward way or in the house of Beorn; but every now and again he would open one eye, and listen, when a part of the story which he did not yet know came in.

It was in this way that he learned where Gandalf had been to; for he overheard the words of the wizard to Elrond. It appeared that Gandalf had been to a great council of the white wizards, masters of lore and good magic; and that they had at last driven the Necromancer from his dark hold in the south of Mirkwood.

"Ere long now," Gandalf was saying, "the Forest will grow somewhat more wholesome. The North will be freed from that horror for many long years, I hope. Yet I wish he were banished from the world!"

"It would be well indeed," said Elrond; "but I fear that will not come about in this age of the world, or for many after."

When the tale of their journeyings was told, there were other tales, and yet more tales, tales of long ago, and tales of new things, and tales of no time at all, till Bilbo's head fell forward on his chest, and he snored comfortably in a corner.

He woke to find himself in a white bed, and the moon shining through an open window. Below it many elves were singing loud and clear on the banks of the stream.

> *Sing all ye joyful, now sing all together!*
> *The wind's in the tree-top, the wind's in the heather;*
> *The stars are in blossom, the moon is in flower,*
> *And bright are the windows of Night in her tower.*

Dance all ye joyful, now dance all together!
Soft is the grass, and let foot be like feather!
The river is silver, the shadows are fleeting;
Merry is May-time, and merry our meeting.

Sing we now softly, and dreams let us weave him!
Wind him in slumber and there let us leave him!
The wanderer sleepeth. Now soft be his pillow!
Lullaby! Lullaby! Alder and Willow!

Sigh no more Pine, till the wind of the morn!
  Fall Moon! Dark be the land!
  Hush! Hush! Oak, Ash, and Thorn!
Hushed be all water, till dawn is at hand!

"Well, Merry People!" said Bilbo looking out. "What time by the moon is this? Your lullaby would waken a drunken goblin! Yet I thank you."

"And your snores would waken a stone dragon—yet we thank you," they answered with laughter. "It is drawing towards dawn, and you have slept now since the night's beginning. Tomorrow, perhaps, you will be cured of weariness."

"A little sleep does a great cure in the house of Elrond," said he; "but I will take all the cure I can get. A second good night, fair friends!" And with that he went back to bed and slept till late morning.

Weariness fell from him soon in that house, and he had many a merry jest and dance, early and late, with the elves of the valley. Yet even that place could not long delay him now, and he thought always of his own home. After a week, therefore, he said farewell to Elrond, and giving him such small gifts as he would accept, he rode away with Gandalf.

Even as they left the valley the sky darkened in the West before them, and wind and rain came up to meet them.

"Merry is May-time!" said Bilbo, as the rain beat into his face. "But our back is to legends and we are coming home. I suppose this is the first taste of it."

"There is a long road yet," said Gandalf.

"But it is the last road," said Bilbo.

They came to the river that marked the very edge of the borderland of the Wild, and to the ford beneath the steep bank, which you may remember. The water was swollen both with the melting of the snows at the approach of summer, and with the daylong rain; but they crossed with some difficulty, and pressed forward, as evening fell, on the last stage of their journey.

This was much as it had been before, except that the company was smaller, and more silent; also this time there were no trolls. At each point on the road Bilbo recalled the happenings and the words of a year ago—it seemed to him more like ten—so that, of course, he quickly noted the place where the pony had fallen in the river, and they had turned aside for their nasty adventure with Tom and Bert and Bill.

Not far from the road they found the gold of the trolls, which they had buried, still hidden and untouched. "I have enough to last me my time," said Bilbo, when they had dug it up. "You had better take this, Gandalf. I daresay you can find a use for it."

"Indeed I can!" said the wizard. "But share and

share alike! You may find you have more needs than you expect."

So they put the gold in bags and slung them on the ponies, who were not at all pleased about it. After that their going was slower, for most of the time they walked. But the land was green and there was much grass through which the hobbit strolled along contentedly. He mopped his face with a red silk handkerchief—no! not a single one of his own had survived, he had borrowed this one from Elrond—for now June had brought summer, and the weather was bright and hot again.

As all things come to an end, even this story, a day came at last when they were in sight of the country where Bilbo had been born and bred, where the shapes of the land and of the trees were as well known to him as his hands and toes. Coming to a rise he could see his own Hill in the distance, and he stopped suddenly and said:

> Roads go ever ever on,
>   Over rock and under tree,
> By caves where never sun has shone,
>   By streams that never find the sea;
> Over snow by winter sown,
>   And through the merry flowers of June,
> Over grass and over stone,
>   And under mountains in the moon.
>
> Roads go ever ever on
>   Under cloud and under star,
> Yet feet that wandering have gone
>   Turn at last to home afar.

Eyes that fire and sword have seen
And horror in the halls of stone
Look at last on meadows green
And trees and hills they long have known.

Gandalf looked at him. "My dear Bilbo!" he said. "Something is the matter with you! You are not the hobbit that you were."

And so they crossed the bridge and passed the mill by the river and came right back to Bilbo's own door.

"Bless me! What's going on?" he cried. There was a great commotion, and people of all sorts, respectable and unrespectable, were thick round the door, and many were going in and out—not even wiping their feet on the mat, as Bilbo noticed with annoyance.

If he was surprised, they were more surprised still. He had arrived back in the middle of an auction! There was a large notice in black and red hung on the gate, stating that on June the Twenty-second Messrs Grubb, Grubb, and Burrowes would sell by auction the effects of the late Bilbo Baggins Esquire, of Bag-End, Underhill, Hobbiton. Sale to commence at ten o'clock sharp. It was now nearly lunchtime, and most of the things had already been sold, for various prices from next to nothing to old songs (as is not unusual at auctions). Bilbo's cousins the Sackville-Bagginses were, in fact, busy measuring his rooms to see if their own furniture would fit. In short Bilbo was "Presumed Dead", and not everybody that said so was sorry to find the presumption wrong.

The return of Mr. Bilbo Baggins created quite a disturbance, both under the Hill and over the Hill, and across the Water; it was a great deal more than a nine days' wonder. The legal bother, indeed, lasted for years. It was quite a long time before Mr. Baggins was in fact admitted to be alive again. The people who had got specially good bargains at the Sale took a deal of convincing; and in the end to save time Bilbo had to buy back quite a lot of his own furniture. Many of his silver spoons mysteriously disappeared and were never accounted for. Personally he suspected the Sackville-Bagginses. On their side they never admitted that the returned Baggins was genuine, and they were not on friendly terms with Bilbo ever after. They really had wanted to live in his nice hobbit-hole so very much.

Indeed Bilbo found he had lost more than spoons—he had lost his reputation. It is true that for ever after he remained an elf-friend, and had the honour of dwarves, wizards, and all such folk as ever passed that way; but he was no longer quite respectable. He was in fact held by all the hobbits of the neighbourhood to be 'queer'—except by his nephews and nieces on the Took side, but even they were not encouraged in their friendship by their elders.

I am sorry to say he did not mind. He was quite content; and the sound of the kettle on his hearth was ever after more musical than it had been even in the quiet days before the Unexpected Party. His sword he hung over the mantelpiece. His coat of mail was arranged on a stand in the hall (until he lent it to a Museum). His gold and silver was largely spent in presents, both useful and extravagant—which to a certain extent accounts for the affection of his nephews and his nieces. His magic ring he kept a great secret, for he chiefly used it when unpleasant callers came.

He took to writing poetry and visiting the elves; and though many shook their heads and touched their foreheads and said "Poor old Baggins!" and though few believed any of his tales, he remained very happy to the end of his days, and those were extraordinarily long.

One autumn evening some years afterwards Bilbo was sitting in his study writing his memoirs—he thought of calling them "There and Back Again, a Hobbit's Holiday"—when there was a ring at the door. It was Gandalf and a dwarf; and the dwarf was actually Balin.

"Come in! Come in!" said Bilbo, and soon they were settled in chairs by the fire. If Balin noticed that Mr. Baggins' waistcoat was more extensive (and had real gold buttons), Bilbo also noticed that Balin's beard was several inches longer, and his jewelled belt was of great magnificence.

They fell to talking of their times together, of course, and Bilbo asked how things were going in the lands of the Mountain. It seemed they were going very well. Bard had rebuilt the town in Dale and men had gathered to him from the Lake and from South and West, and all the valley had become tilled again and rich, and the desolation was now filled with birds and blossoms in spring and fruit and feasting in autumn. And Lake-town was refounded and was more prosperous than ever, and much wealth went up and down the Running River; and there was

The Hall at Bag-End, Residence of B. Baggins Esquire

friendship in those parts between elves and dwarves and men.

The old Master had come to a bad end. Bard had given him much gold for the help of the Lake-people, but being of the kind that easily catches such disease he fell under the dragon-sickness, and took most of the gold and fled with it, and died of starvation in the Waste, deserted by his companions.

"The new Master is of wiser kind," said Balin, "and very popular, for, of course, he gets most of the credit for the present prosperity. They are making songs which say that in his day the rivers run with gold."

"Then the prophecies of the old songs have turned out to be true, after a fashion!" said Bilbo.

"Of course!" said Gandalf. "And why should not they prove true? Surely you don't disbelieve the prophecies, because you had a hand in bringing them about yourself? You don't really suppose, do you, that all your adventures and escapes were managed by mere luck, just for your sole bene-fit? You are a very fine person, Mr. Baggins, and I am very fond of you; but you are only quite a little fellow in a wide world after all!"

"Thank goodness!" said Bilbo laughing, and handed him the tobacco-jar.

If you are interested in Hobbits you will learn a lot more about them in The Lord of the Rings:

1. THE FELLOWSHIP OF THE RING
2. THE TWO TOWERS
3. THE RETURN OF THE KING

THE LORD OF THE RINGS

BY

J.R.R. TOLKIEN

The following pages contain the first chapter
of *The Fellowship of the Ring*, the first part
of J.R.R. Tolkien's epic adventure
The Lord of the Rings.

In a sleepy village in the Shire, young
Frodo Baggins finds himself faced with an
immense task, as his elderly cousin Bilbo
entrusts the Ring to his care. Frodo must leave
his home and make a perilous journey across
Middle-earth to the Cracks of Doom, there
to destroy the Ring and foil the Dark Lord
in his evil purpose.

Chapter I

A LONG-EXPECTED PARTY

When Mr. Bilbo Baggins of Bag End announced that he would shortly be celebrating his eleventy-first birthday with a party of special magnificence, there was much talk and excitement in Hobbiton.

Bilbo was very rich and very peculiar, and had been the wonder of the Shire for sixty years, ever since his remarkable disappearance and unexpected return. The riches he had brought back from his travels had now become a local legend, and it was popularly believed, whatever the old folk might say, that the Hill at Bag End was full of tunnels stuffed with treasure. And if that was not enough for fame, there was also his prolonged vigour to marvel at. Time wore on, but it seemed to have little effect on Mr. Baggins. At ninety he was much the same as at fifty. At ninety-nine they began to call him *well-preserved*; but *unchanged* would have been nearer the mark. There were some that shook their heads and thought this was too much of a good thing; it seemed unfair that anyone should possess (apparently) perpetual youth as well as (reputedly) inexhaustible wealth.

'It will have to be paid for,' they said. 'It isn't natural, and trouble will come of it!'

But so far trouble had not come; and as Mr. Baggins was generous with his money, most people were willing to forgive him his oddities and his good

fortune. He remained on visiting terms with his relatives (except, of course, the Sackville-Bagginses), and
he had many devoted admirers among the hobbits of
poor and unimportant families. But he had no close
friends, until some of his younger cousins began to
grow up.

The eldest of these, and Bilbo's favourite, was
young Frodo Baggins. When Bilbo was ninety-nine he
adopted Frodo as his heir, and brought him to live at
Bag End; and the hopes of the Sackville- Bagginses
were finally dashed. Bilbo and Frodo happened to
have the same birthday, September 22nd. 'You had
better come and live here, Frodo my lad,' said Bilbo
one day; 'and then we can celebrate our birthday-
parties comfortably together.' At that time Frodo was
still in his *tweens*, as the hobbits called the irresponsible
twenties between childhood and coming of age at
thirty-three.

Twelve more years passed. Each year the Bagginses
had given very lively combined birthday-parties at Bag
End; but now it was understood that something quite
exceptional was being planned for that autumn. Bilbo
was going to be *eleventy-one*, 111, a rather curious
number, and a very respectable age for a hobbit (the
Old Took himself had only reached 130); and Frodo
was going to be *thirty-three*, 33, an important number:
the date of his 'coming of age'.

Tongues began to wag in Hobbiton and Bywater;
and rumour of the coming event travelled all over the
Shire. The history and character of Mr. Bilbo Baggins
became once again the chief topic of conversation; and
the older folk suddenly found their reminiscences in
welcome demand.

No one had a more attentive audience than old Ham Gamgee, commonly known as the Gaffer. He held forth at *The Ivy Bush*, a small inn on the Bywater road; and he spoke with some authority, for he had tended the garden at Bag End for forty years, and had helped old Holman in the same job before that. Now that he was himself growing old and stiff in the joints, the job was mainly carriedon by his youngest son, Sam Gamgee. Both father and son were on very friendly terms with Bilbo and Frodo. They lived on the Hill itself, in Number 3 Bagshot Row just below Bag End.

'A very nice well-spoken gentlehobbit is Mr. Bilbo, as I've always said,' the Gaffer declared. With perfect truth: for Bilbo was very polite to him, calling him 'Master Hamfast', and consulting him constantly upon the growing of vegetables – in the matter of 'roots', especially potatoes, the Gaffer was recognized as the leading authority by all in the neighbourhood (including himself).

'But what about this Frodo that lives with him?' asked Old Noakes of Bywater. 'Baggins is his name, but he's more than half a Brandybuck, they say. It beats me why any Baggins of Hobbiton should go looking for a wife away there in Buckland, where folks are so queer.'

'And no wonder they're queer,' put in Daddy Twofoot (the Gaffer's next-door neighbour), 'if they live on the wrong side of the Brandywine River, and right agin the Old Forest. That's a dark bad place, if half the tales be true.'

'You're right, Dad!' said the Gaffer. 'Not that the Brandybucks of Buckland live *in* the Old Forest; but they're a queer breed, seemingly. They fool about with

boats on that big river – and that isn't natural. Small
wonder that trouble came of it, I say. But be that as it
may, Mr. Frodo is as nice a young hobbit as you
could wish to meet. Very much like Mr. Bilbo, and in
more than looks. After all his father was a Baggins. A
decent respectable hobbit was Mr. Drogo Baggins;
there was never much to tell of him, till he was
drownded.'

'Drownded?' said several voices. They had heard
this and other darker rumours before, of course; but
hobbits have a passion for family history, and they
were ready to hear it again.

'Well, so they say,' said the Gaffer. 'Yousee: Mr.
Drogo, he married poor Miss Primula Brandybuck.
She was our Mr. Bilbo's first cousin on the mother's
side (her mother being the youngest of the Old Took's
daughters); and Mr. Drogo was his second cousin. So
Mr. Frodo is his first *and* second cousin, once removed
either way, as the saying is, if you follow me. And Mr.
Drogo was staying at Brandy Hall with his father-in-
law, old Master Gorbadoc, as he often did after his
marriage (him being partial to his vittles, and old
Gorbadoc keeping a mighty generous table); and he
went out *boating* on the Brandywine River; and he and
his wife were drownded, and poor Mr. Frodo only a
child and all.'

'I've heard they went on the water after dinner in
the moonlight,'said Old Noakes; 'and it was Drogo's
weight as sunk the boat.'

'And *I* heard she pushed him in, and he pulled her
in after him,' said Sandyman, the Hobbiton miller.

'You shouldn't listen to all you hear, Sandyman,'
said the Gaffer, who did not much like the miller.
'There isn't no call to go talking of pushing and

pulling. Boats are quite tricky enough for those that sit still without looking further for the cause of trouble. Anyway: there was this Mr. Frodo left an orphan and stranded, as you might say, among those queer Bucklanders, being brought up anyhow in Brandy Hall. A regular warren, by all accounts. Old Master Gorbadoc never had fewer than a couple of hundred relations in the place. Mr. Bilbo never did a kinder deed than when he brought the lad back to live among decent folk.

'But I reckon it was a nasty knock for those Sackville-Bagginses. They thought they were going to get Bag End, that time when he went off and was thought to be dead. And then he comes back and orders them off; and he goes on living and living, and never looking a day older, bless him! And suddenly he produces an heir, and has all the papers made out proper. The Sackville-Bagginses won't never see the inside of Bag End now, or it is to be hoped not.'

'There's a tidy bit of money tucked away up there, I hear tell,' said a stranger, a visitor on business from Michel Delving in the Westfarthing. 'All the top of your hill is full of tunnels packed with chests of gold and silver, *and* jools, by what I've heard.'

'Then you've heard more than I can speak to,' answered the Gaffer. 'I know nothing about *jools*. Mr. Bilbo is free with his money, and there seems no lack of it; but I know of no tunnel-making. I saw Mr. Bilbo when he came back, a matter of sixty years ago, when I was a lad. I'd not long come prentice to old Holman (him being my dad's cousin), but he had me up at Bag End helping him to keep folks from trampling and trapessing all over the garden while the sale was on. And in the middle of it all Mr. Bilbo comes up the Hill with a pony and some mighty big bags and a couple of chests. I don't doubt they were mostly full of treasure he had picked up in foreign parts, where there be mountains of gold, they say; but there wasn't enough to fill tunnels. But my lad Sam will know more about that. He's in and out of Bag End. Crazy about stories of the old days, he is, and he listens to all Mr. Bilbo's tales. Mr. Bilbo has learned him his letters – meaning no harm, mark you, and I hope no harm will come of it.

'*Elves and Dragons!* I says to him. *Cabbages and potatoes are better for me and you. Don't go getting mixed up in the business of your betters, or you'll land in trouble too big for you*, I says to him. And I might say it to others,' he added with a look at the stranger and the miller.

But the Gaffer did not convince his audience. The legend of Bilbo's wealth was now too firmly fixed in the minds of the younger generation of hobbits.

'Ah, but he has likely enough been adding to what he brought at first,' argued the miller, voicing common opinion. 'He's often away from home. And look at the outlandish folk that visit him: dwarves coming at night, and that old wandering conjuror, Gandalf, and all. You can say what you like, Gaffer, but Bag End's a queer place, and its folk are queerer.'

'And you can say what *you* like, about what you know no more of than you do of boating, Mr. Sandyman,' retorted the Gaffer, disliking the miller even more than usual. 'If that's being queer, then we could do with a bit more queerness in these parts. There's some not far away that wouldn't offer a pint of beer to a friend, if they lived in a hole with golden walls. But they do things proper at Bag End. Our Sam says that *everyone's* going to be invited to the party, and there's going to be presents, mark you, presents for all – this very month as is.'

That very month was September, and as fine as you could ask. A day or two later a rumour (probably started by the knowledgeable Sam) was spread about that there were going to be fireworks – fireworks, what is more, such as had not been seen in the Shire for nigh on a century, not indeed since the Old Took died.

Days passed and The Day drew nearer. An odd-looking waggon laden with odd-looking packages rolled into Hobbiton one evening and toiled up the Hill to Bag End. The startled hobbits peered out of lamplit doors to gape at it. It was driven by outlandish folk, singing strange songs: dwarves with long beards and deep hoods. A few of them remained at Bag End. At the end of the second week in September a cart came in through Bywater from the direction of Brandywine Bridge in broad daylight. An old man was driving it all alone. He wore a tall pointed blue hat, a long grey cloak, and a silver scarf. He had a long white beard and bushy eyebrows that stuck out beyond the brim of his hat. Small hobbit-children ran after the cart all through Hobbiton and right up the hill. It had a cargo of fireworks, as they rightly guessed. At Bilbo's front door the old man began to unload: there were great bundles of fireworks of all sorts and shapes, each labelled with a large red G ᚷ and the elf-rune, ᚹ .

That was Gandalf's mark, of course, and the old man was Gandalf the Wizard, whose fame in the Shire was due mainly to his skill with fires, smokes, and lights. His real business was far more difficult and dangerous, but the Shire-folk knew nothing about it. To them he was just one of the 'attractions' at the Party. Hence the excitement of the hobbit-children. 'G for

Grand!' they shouted, and the old man smiled. They knew him by sight, though he only appeared in Hobbiton occasionally and never stopped long; but neither they nor any but the oldest of their elders had seen one of his firework displays – they now belonged to a legendary past.

When the old man, helped by Bilbo and some dwarves, had finished unloading, Bilbo gave a few pennies away; but not a single squib or cracker was forthcoming, to the disappointment of the onlookers.

'Run away now!' said Gandalf. 'You will get plenty when the time comes.' Then he disappeared inside with Bilbo, and the door was shut. The young hobbits stared at the door in vain for a while, and then made off, feeling that the day of the party would never come.

Inside Bag End, Bilbo and Gandalf were sitting at the open window of a small room looking out west on to the garden. The late afternoon was bright and peaceful. The flowers glowed red and golden: snapdragons and sunflowers, and nasturtians trailing all over the turf walls and peeping in at the round windows.

'How bright your garden looks!' said Gandalf.

'Yes,' said Bilbo. 'I am very fond indeed of it, and of all the dear old Shire; but I think I need a holiday.'

'You mean to go on with your plan then?'

'I do. I made up my mind months ago, and I haven't changed it.'

'Very well. It is no good saying any more. Stick to your plan – your whole plan, mind – and I hope it will turn out for the best, for you, and for all of us.'

'I hope so. Anyway I mean to enjoy myself on Thursday, and have my little joke.'

'Who will laugh, I wonder?' said Gandalf, shaking his head.

'We shall see,' said Bilbo.

The next day more carts rolled up the Hill, and still more carts. There might have been some grumbling about 'dealing locally', but that very week orders began to pour out of Bag End for every kind of provision, commodity, or luxury that could be obtained in Hobbiton or Bywater or anywhere in the neighbourhood. People became enthusiastic; and they began to tick off the days on the calendar; and they watched eagerly for the postman, hoping for invitations.

Before long the invitations began pouring out, and the Hobbiton post-office was blocked, and the Bywater post-office was snowed under, and voluntary assistant postmen were called for. There was a constant stream of them going up the Hill, carrying hundreds of polite variations on *Thank you, I shall certainly come.*

A notice appeared on the gate at Bag End: NO ADMITTANCE EXCEPT ON PARTY BUSINESS. Even those who had, or pretended to have Party Business were seldom allowed inside. Bilbo was busy: writing invitations, ticking off answers, packing up presents, and making some private preparations of his own. From the time of Gandalf's arrival he remained hidden from view.

One morning the hobbits woke to find the large field, south of Bilbo's front door, covered with ropes and poles for tents and pavilions. A special entrance was cut into the bank leading to the road, and wide steps and a large white gate were built there. The three hobbit-families of Bagshot Row, adjoining the field, were intensely interested and generally envied. Old

Gaffer Gamgee stopped even pretending to work in his garden.

The tents began to go up. There was a specially large pavilion, so big that the tree that grew in the field was right inside it, and stood proudly near one end, at the head of the chief table. Lanterns were hung on all its branches. More promising still (to the hobbits' mind): an enormous open-air kitchen was erected in the north corner of the field. A draught of cooks, from every inn and eating-house for miles around, arrived to supplement the dwarves and other odd folk that were quartered at Bag End. Excitement rose to its height.

Then the weather clouded over. That was on Wednesday the eve of the Party. Anxiety was intense. Then Thursday, September the 22nd, actually dawned. The sun got up, the clouds vanished, flags were unfurled and the fun began.

Bilbo Baggins called it a *party*, but it was really a variety of entertainments rolled into one. Practically everybody living near was invited. A very few were overlooked by accident, but as they turned up all the same, that did not matter. Many people from other parts of the Shire were also asked; and there were even a few from outside the borders. Bilbo met the guests (and additions) at the new white gate in person. He gave away presents to all and sundry – the latter were those who went out again by a back way and came in again by the gate. Hobbits give presents to other people on their own birthdays. Not very expensive ones, as a rule, and not so lavishly as on this occasion; but it was not a bad system. Actually in Hobbiton and Bywater every day in the year was somebody's birthday, so that every hobbit in those parts had a fair chance of at least one present at least once a week. But they never got tired of them.

On this occasion the presents were unusually good. The hobbit-children were so excited that for a while they almost forgot about eating. There were toys the like of which they had never seen before, all beautiful and some obviously magical. Many of them had indeed been ordered a year before, and had come all the way from the Mountain and from Dale, and were of real dwarf-make.

When every guest had been welcomed and was finally inside the gate, there were songs, dances, music, games, and, of course, food and drink. There were three official meals: lunch, tea, and dinner (or supper). But lunch and tea were marked chiefly by the fact that at those times all the guests were sitting down and eating together. At other times there were merely lots of people eating and drinking – continuously from elevenses until six-thirty, when the fireworks started.

The fireworks were by Gandalf: they were not only brought by him, but designed and made by him; and the special effects, set pieces, and flights of rockets were let off by him. But there was also a generous distribution of squibs, crackers, backarappers, sparklers, torches, dwarf-candles, elf-fountains, goblin-barkers and thunderclaps. They were all superb. The art of Gandalf improved with age.

There were rockets like a flight of scintillating birds singing with sweet voices. There were green trees with trunks of dark smoke: their leaves opened like a whole spring unfolding in a moment, and their shining branches dropped glowing flowers down upon the astonished hobbits, disappearing with a sweet scent just before they touched their upturned faces. There were fountains of butterflies that flew glittering into the trees; there were pillars of coloured fires that rose and turned into eagles, or sailing ships, or a phalanx of flying swans; there was a red thunderstorm and a shower of yellow rain; there was a forest of silver spears that sprang suddenly into the air with a yell like an embattled army, and came down again into the Water with a hiss like a hundred hot snakes. And there was also one last surprise, in honour of Bilbo, and it startled the hobbits exceedingly, as Gandalf intended. The lights went out. A great smoke went up. It shaped itself like a mountain seen in the distance, and began to glow at the summit. It spouted green and scarlet flames. Out flew a red-golden dragon – not life-size, but terribly life-like: fire came from his jaws, his eyes glared down; there was a roar, and he whizzed three times over the heads of the crowd. They all ducked, and many fell flat on their faces. The dragon passed like an express train, turned a somersault, and burst over Bywater with a deafening explosion.

That is the signal for supper!' said Bilbo. The pain and alarm vanished at once, and the prostrate hobbits leaped to their feet. There was a splendid supper for everyone; for everyone, that is, except those invited to the special family dinner-party. This was held in the great pavilion with the tree. The invitations were limited to twelve dozen (a number also called by the hobbits one Gross, though the word was not considered proper to use of people); and the guests were selected from all the families to which Bilbo and Frodo were related, with the addition of a few special unrelated friends (such as Gandalf). Many young hobbits were included, and present by parental permission; for hobbits were easy-going with their children in the matter of sitting up late, especially when there was a chance of getting them a free meal. Bringing up young hobbits took a lot of provender.

There were many Bagginses and Boffins, and also many Tooks and Brandybucks; there were various Grubbs (relations of Bilbo Baggins' grandmother), and various Chubbs (connexions of his Took grandfather); and a selection of Burrowses, Bolgers, Bracegirdles, Brockhouses, Goodbodies, Hornblowers and Proudfoots. Some of these were only very distantly connected with Bilbo, and some had hardly ever been in Hobbiton before, as they lived in remote corners of the Shire. The Sackville-Bagginses were not forgotten. Otho and his wife Lobelia were present. They disliked Bilbo and detested Frodo, but so magnificent was the invitation card, written in golden ink, that they had felt it was impossible to refuse. Besides, their cousin, Bilbo, had been specializing in food for many years and his table had a high reputation.

All the one hundred and forty-four guests expected a pleasant feast; though they rather dreaded the after-dinner speech of their host (an inevitable item). He was liable to drag in bits of what he called poetry; and sometimes, after a glass or two, would allude to the absurd adventures of his mysterious journey. The guests were not disappointed: they had a *very* pleasant feast, in fact an engrossing entertainment: rich, abundant, varied, and prolonged. The purchase of provisions fell almost to nothing throughout the district in the ensuing weeks; but as Bilbo's catering had depleted the stocks of most of the stores, cellars and warehouses for miles around, that did not matter much.

After the feast (more or less) came the Speech. Most of the company were, however, now in a tolerant

mood, at that delightful stage which they called 'filling
up the corners'. They were sipping their favourite
drinks, and nibbling at their favourite dainties, and
their fears were forgotten. They were prepared to
listen to anything, and to cheer at every full stop.

My dear People, began Bilbo, rising in his place.
'Hear! Hear! Hear!' they shouted, and kept on repeat-
ing it in chorus, seeming reluctant to follow their own
advice. Bilbo left his place and went and stood on a
chair under the illuminated tree. The light of the
lanterns fell on his beaming face; the golden buttons
shone on his embroidered silk waistcoat. They could
all see him standing, waving one hand in the air, the
other was in his trouser-pocket.

My dear Bagginses and Boffins, he began again; *and
my dear Took and Brandybucks, and Grubbs, and
Chubbs, and Burrowses, and Hornblowers, and Bolgers,
Bracegirdles, Goodbodies, Brockhouses and Proudfoots.*
'ProudFEET!' shouted an elderly hobbit from the back
of the pavilion. His name, of course, was Proudfoot,
and well merited; his feet were large, exceptionally
furry, and both were on the table.

Proudfoots, repeated Bilbo. *Also my good Sackville-
Bagginses that I welcome back at last to Bag End. Today
is my one hundred and eleventh birthday: I am eleventy-
one today!* 'Hurray! Hurray! Many Happy Returns!'
they shouted, and they hammered joyously on the
tables. Bilbo was doing splendidly. This was the sort
of stuff they liked: short and obvious.

I hope you are all enjoying yourselves as much as I am.
Deafening cheers. Cries of *Yes* (and *No*). Noises of
trumpets and horns, pipes and flutes, and other musical
instruments. There were, as has been said, many young
hobbits present. Hundreds of musical crackers had been

pulled. Most of them bore the mark DALE on them; which did not convey much to most of the hobbits, but they all agreed they were marvellous crackers. They contained instruments, small, but of perfect make and enchanting tones. Indeed, in one corner some of the young Tooks and Brandybucks, supposing Uncle Bilbo to have finished (since he had plainly said all that was necessary), now got up an impromptu orchestra, and began a merry dance-tune. Master Everard Took and Miss Melilot Brandybuck got on a table and with bells in their hands began to dance the Springle-ring: a pretty dance, but rather vigorous.

But Bilbo had not finished. Seizing a horn from a youngster nearby, he blew three loud hoots. The noise subsided. *I shall not keep you long*, he cried. Cheers from all the assembly. *I have called you all together for a Purpose.* Something in the way that he said this made an impression. There was almost silence, and one or two of the Tooks pricked up their ears.

Indeed, for Three Purposes! First of all, to tell you that I am immensely fond of you all, and that eleventy-one years is too short a time to live among such excellent and admirable hobbits. Tremendous outburst of approval.

I don't know half of you half as well as I should like; and I like less than half of you half as well as you deserve. This was unexpected and rather difficult. There was some scattered clapping, but most of them were trying to work it out and see if it came to a compliment.

Secondly, to celebrate my birthday. Cheers again. *I should say: OUR birthday. For it is, of course, also the birthday of my heir and nephew, Frodo. He comes of age and into his inheritance today.* Some perfunctory clapping by the elders; and some loud shouts of 'Frodo! Frodo! Jolly old Frodo,' from the juniors. The

Sackville-Bagginses scowled, and wondered what was meant by 'coming into his inheritance'.

Together we score one hundred and forty-four. Your numbers were chosen to fit this remarkable total: One Gross, if I may use the expression. No cheers. This was ridiculous. Many of the guests, and especially the Sackville-Bagginses, were insulted, feeling sure they had only been asked to fill up the required number, like goods in a package. 'One Gross, indeed! Vulgar expression.'

It is also, if I may be allowed to refer to ancient history, the anniversary of my arrival by barrel at Esgaroth on the Long Lake; though the fact that it was my birthday slipped my memory on that occasion. I was only fifty-one then, and birthdays did not seem so important. The banquet was very splendid, however, though I had a bad cold at the time, I remember, and could only say 'thag you very buch'. I now repeat it more correctly: Thank you very much for coming to my little party. Obstinate silence. They all feared that a song or some poetry was now imminent; and they were getting bored. Why couldn't he stop talking and let them drink his health? But Bilbo did not sing or recite. He paused for a moment.

Thirdly and finally, he said, *I wish to make an ANNOUNCEMENT.* He spoke this last word so loudly and suddenly that everyone sat up who still could. *I regret to announce that – though, as I said, eleventy-one years is far too short a time to spend among you – this is the END. I am going. I am leaving NOW. GOOD-BYE!*

He stepped down and vanished. There was a blinding flash of light, and the guests all blinked. When they opened their eyes Bilbo was nowhere to be seen.

One hundred and forty-four flabbergasted hobbits sat back speechless. Old Odo Proudfoot removed his feet from the table and stamped. Then there was a dead silence, until suddenly, after several deep breaths, every Baggins, Boffin, Took, Brandybuck, Grubb, Chubb, Burrows, Bolger, Bracegirdle, Brockhouse, Goodbody, Hornblower, and Proudfoot began to talk at once.

It was generally agreed that the joke was in very bad taste, and more food and drink were needed to cure the guests of shock and annoyance.

'He's mad. I always said so,' was probably the most popular comment. Even the Tooks (with a few exceptions) thought Bilbo's behaviour was absurd. For the moment most of them took it for granted that his disappearance was nothing more than a ridiculous prank.

But old Rory Brandybuck was not so sure. Neither age nor an enormous dinner had clouded his wits, and he said to his daughter-inlaw, Esmeralda: 'There's something fishy in this, my dear! I believe that mad Baggins is off again. Silly old fool. But why worry? He hasn't taken the vittles with him.' He called loudly to Frodo to send the wine round again.

Frodo was the only one present who had said nothing. For some time he had sat silent beside Bilbo's empty chair, and ignored all remarks and questions. He had enjoyed the joke, of course, even though he had been in the know. He had difficulty in keeping from laughter at the indignant surprise of the guests. But at the same time he felt deeply troubled: he realized suddenly that he loved the old hobbit dearly. Most of the guests went on eating and drinking and discussing Bilbo Baggins' oddities, past and present; but the Sackville-Bagginses had already departed in wrath. Frodo did not want to have any more to do with the party. He gave orders for more wine to be served; then he got up and drained his own glass silently to the health of Bilbo, and slipped out of the pavilion.

As for Bilbo Baggins, even while he was making his speech, he had been fingering the golden ring in his pocket: his magic ring that he had kept secret for so many years. As he stepped down he slipped it on his finger, and he was never seen by any hobbit in Hobbiton again.

He walked briskly back to his hole, and stood for a moment listening with a smile to the din in the pavilion, and to the sounds of merrymaking in other parts of the field. Then he went in. He took off his party clothes, folded up and wrapped in tissue-paper his embroidered silk waistcoat, and put it away. Then he put on quickly some old untidy garments, and fastened round his waist a worn leather belt. On it he hung a short sword in a battered black-leather scabbard. From a locked drawer, smelling of moth-balls, he took out an old cloak and hood. They had been locked up as if they were very precious, but they were so patched and weatherstained that their original colour could hardly be guessed: it might have been dark green. They were rather too large for him. He then went into his study, and from a large strong-box took out a bundle wrapped in old cloths, and a leather-bound manuscript; and also a large bulky envelope. The book and bundle he stuffed into the top of a heavy bag that was standing there, already nearly full. Into the envelope he slipped his golden ring, and its fine chain, and then sealed it, and addressed it to Frodo. At first he put it on the mantelpiece, but suddenly he removed it and stuck it in his pocket. At that moment the door opened and Gandalf came quickly in.

'Hullo!' said Bilbo. 'I wondered if you would turn up.'

'I am glad to find you visible,' replied the wizard, sitting down in a chair, 'I wanted to catch you and have a few final words. I suppose you feel that everything has gone off splendidly and according to plan?'

'Yes, I do,' said Bilbo. 'Though that flash was surprising: it quite startled me, let alone the others. A little addition of your own, I suppose?'

'It was. You have wisely kept that ring secret all these years, and it seemed to me necessary to give your guests something else that would seem to explain your sudden vanishment.'

'And would spoil my joke. You are an interfering old busybody,' laughed Bilbo, 'but I expect you know best, as usual.'

'I do – when I know anything. But I don't feel too sure about this whole affair. It has now come to the final point. You have had your joke, and alarmed or offended most of your relations, and given the whole Shire something to talk about for nine days, or ninety-nine more likely. Are you going any further?'

'Yes, I am. I feel I need a holiday, a very long holiday, as I have told you before. Probably a permanent holiday: I don't expect I shall return. In fact, I don't mean to, and I have made all arrangements.

'I am old, Gandalf. I don't look it, but I am beginning to feel it in my heart of hearts. *Well-preserved* indeed!' he snorted. 'Why, I feel all thin, sort of *stretched*, if you know what I mean: like butter that has been scraped over too much bread. That can't be right. I need a change, or something.'

Gandalf looked curiously and closely at him. 'No, it does not seem right,' he said thoughtfully. 'No, after all I believe your plan is probably the best.'

'Well, I've made up my mind, anyway. I want to see mountains again, Gandalf – *mountains*; and then find somewhere where I can *rest*. In peace and quiet, without a lot of relatives prying around, and a string of confounded visitors hanging on the bell. I might find somewhere where I can finish my book. I have thought of a nice ending for it: *and he lived happily ever after to the end of his days.*'

Gandalf laughed. 'I hope he will. But nobody will read the book, however it ends.'

'Oh, they may, in years to come. Frodo has read some already, as far as it has gone. You'll keep an eye on Frodo, won't you?'

'Yes, I will – two eyes, as often as I can spare them.'

'He would come with me, of course, if I asked him. In fact he offered to once, just before the party. But he does not really want to, yet. I want to see the wild country again before I die, and the Mountains; but he is still in love with the Shire, with woods and fields and little rivers. He ought to be comfortable here. I am leaving everything to him, of course, except a few oddments. I hope he will be happy, when he gets used to being on his own. It's time he was his own master now.'

'Everything?' said Gandalf. 'The ring as well? You agreed to that, you remember.'

'Well, er, yes, I suppose so,' stammered Bilbo.

'Where is it?'

'In an envelope, if you must know,' said Bilbo impatiently. 'There on the mantelpiece. Well, no! Here it is in my pocket!' He hesitated. 'Isn't that odd now?' he said softly to himself. 'Yet after all, why not? Why shouldn't it stay there?'

Gandalf looked again very hard at Bilbo, and there was a gleam in his eyes. 'I think, Bilbo,' he said quietly, 'I should leave it behind. Don't you want to?'

'Well yes – and no. Now it comes to it, I don't like parting with it at all, I may say. And I don't really see why I should. Why do you want me to?' he asked, and a curious change came over his voice. It was sharp with suspicion and annoyance. 'You are always badgering me about my ring; but you have never bothered me about the other things that I got on my journey.'

'No, but I had to badger you,' said Gandalf. 'I wanted the truth. It was important. Magic rings are – well, magical; and they are rare and curious. I was professionally interested in your ring, you may say; and I still am. I should like to know where it is, if you go wandering again. Also I think *you* have had it quite long enough. You won't need it any more, Bilbo, unless I am quite mistaken.'

Bilbo flushed, and there was an angry light in his eyes. His kindly face grew hard. 'Why not?' he cried. 'And what business is it of yours, anyway, to know what I do with my own things? It is my own. I found it. It came to me.'

'Yes, yes,' said Gandalf. 'But there is no need to get angry.'

'If I am it is your fault,' said Bilbo. 'It is mine, I tell you. My own. My Precious. Yes, my Precious.'

The wizard's face remained grave and attentive, and only a flicker in his deep eyes showed that he was startled and indeed alarmed. 'It has been called that before,' he said, 'but not by you.'

'But I say it now. And why not? Even if Gollum said the same once. It's not his now, but mine. And I shall keep it, I say.'

Gandalf stood up. He spoke sternly. 'You will be a fool if you do, Bilbo,' he said. 'You make that clearer with every word you say. It has got far too much hold on you. Let it go! And then you can go yourself, and be free.'

'I'll do as I choose and go as I please,' said Bilbo obstinately.

'Now, now, my dear hobbit!' said Gandalf. 'All your long life we have been friends, and you owe me something. Come! Do as you promised: give it up!'

'Well, if you want my ring yourself, say so!' cried Bilbo. 'But you won't get it. I won't give my Precious away, I tell you.' His hand strayed to the hilt of his small sword.

Gandalf's eyes flashed. 'It will be my turn to get angry soon,' he said. 'If you say that again, I shall. Then you will see Gandalf the Grey uncloaked.' He took a step towards the hobbit, and he seemed to grow tall and menacing; his shadow filled the little room.

Bilbo backed away to the wall, breathing hard, his hand clutching at his pocket. They stood for a while facing one another, and the air of the room tingled. Gandalf's eyes remained bent on the hobbit. Slowly his hands relaxed, and he began to tremble.

'I don't know what has come over you, Gandalf,' he said. 'You have never been like this before. What is it all about? It is mine isn't it? I found it, and Gollum would have killed me, if I hadn't kept it. I'm not a thief, whatever he said.'

'I have never called you one,' Gandalf answered. 'And I am not one either. I am not trying to rob you, but to help you. I wish you would trust me, as you used.' He turned away, and the shadow passed. He seemed to dwindle again to an old grey man, bent and troubled.

Bilbo drew his hand over his eyes. 'I am sorry,' he said. 'But I felt so queer. And yet it would be a relief in a way not to be bothered with it any more. It has been so growing on my mind lately. Sometimes I have felt it was like an eye looking at me. And I am always wanting to put it on and disappear, don't you know; or wondering if it is safe, and pulling it out to make sure. I tried locking it up, but I found I couldn't rest without it in my pocket. I don't know why. And I don't seem able to make up my mind.'

'Then trust mine,' said Gandalf. 'It is quite made up. Go away and leave it behind. Stop possessing it. Give it to Frodo, and I will look after him.'

Bilbo stood for a moment tense and undecided. Presently he sighed. 'All right,' he said with an effort. 'I will.' Then he shrugged his shoulders, and smiled rather ruefully. 'After all that's what this party business was all about, really: to give away lots of birthday presents, and somehow make it easier to give it away at the same time. It hasn't made it any easier in the end, but it would be a pity to waste all my preparations. It would quite spoil the joke.'

'Indeed it would take away the only point I ever saw in the affair,' said Gandalf.

'Very well,' said Bilbo, 'it goes to Frodo with all the rest.' He drew a deep breath. 'And now I really must be starting, or somebody else will catch me. I have said good-bye, and I couldn't bear to do it all over again.' He picked up his bag and moved to the door.

'You have still got the ring in your pocket,' said the wizard.

'Well, so I have!' cried Bilbo. 'And my will and all the other documents too. You had better take it and deliver it for me. That will be safest.'

'No, don't give the ring to me,' said Gandalf. 'Put it on the mantelpiece. It will be safe enough there, till Frodo comes. I shall wait for him.'

Bilbo took out the envelope, but just as he was about to set it by the clock, his hand jerked back, and the packet fell on the floor. Before he could pick it up, the wizard stooped and seized it and set it in its place. A spasm of anger passed swiftly over the hobbit's face again. Suddenly it gave way to a look of relief and a laugh.

'Well, that's that,' he said. 'Now I'm off !'

They went out into the hall. Bilbo chose his favourite stick from the stand; then he whistled. Three dwarves came out of different rooms where they had been busy.

'Is everything ready?' asked Bilbo. 'Everything packed and labelled?'

'Everything,' they answered.

'Well, let's start then!' He stepped out of the front-door. It was a fine night, and the black sky was dotted with stars. He looked up, sniffing the air. 'What fun! What fun to be off again, off on the Road with dwarves! This is what I have really been longing for, for years! Good-bye!' he said, looking at his old home and bowing to the door. 'Good-bye, Gandalf!'

'Good-bye, for the present, Bilbo. Take care of your-self! You are old enough, and perhaps wise enough.'

'Take care! I don't care. Don't you worry about me! I am as happy now as I have ever been, and that is saying a great deal. But the time has come. I am being swept off my feet at last,' he added, and then in a low voice, as if to himself, he sang softly in the dark:

> The Road goes ever on and on
> Down from the door where it began.
> Now far ahead the Road has gone,
> And I must follow, if I can,
> Pursuing it with eager feet,
> Until it joins some larger way
> Where many paths and errands meet.
> And whither then? I cannot say.

He paused, silent for a moment. Then without another word he turned away from the lights and voices in the field and tents, and followed by his three companions went round into his garden, and trotted down the long sloping path. He jumped over a low place in the hedge at the bottom, and took to the meadows, passing into the night like a rustle of wind in the grass.

Gandalf remained for a while staring after him into the darkness. 'Good-bye, my dear Bilbo – until our next meeting!' he said softly and went back indoors.

Frodo came in soon afterwards, and found him sitting in the dark, deep in thought. 'Has he gone?' he asked.

'Yes,' answered Gandalf, 'he has gone at last.'

'I wish – I mean, I hoped until this evening that it was only a joke,' said Frodo. 'But I knew in my heart that he really meant to go. He always used to joke about serious things. I wish I had come back sooner, just to see him off.'

'I think really he preferred slipping off quietly in the end,' said Gandalf. 'Don't be too troubled. He'll be all right – now. He left a packet for you. There it is!'

Frodo took the envelope from the mantelpiece, and glanced at it, but did not open it.

'You'll find his will and all the other documents in there, I think,' said the wizard. 'You are the master of Bag End now. And also, I fancy, you'll find a golden ring.'

'The ring!' exclaimed Frodo. 'Has he left me that? I wonder why. Still, it may be useful.'

'It may, and it may not,' said Gandalf. 'I should not make use of it, if I were you. But keep it secret, and keep it safe! Now I am going to bed.'

As master of Bag End Frodo felt it his painful duty to say good-bye to the guests. Rumours of strange events had by now spread all over the field, but Frodo would only say *no doubt everything will be cleared up in the morning*. About midnight carriages came for the important folk. One by one they rolled away, filled with full but very unsatisfied hobbits. Gardeners came by arrangement, and removed in wheelbarrows those that had inadvertently remained behind.

Night slowly passed. The sun rose. The hobbits rose rather later. Morning went on. People came and began (by orders) to clear away the pavilions and the tables and the chairs, and the spoons and knives and bottles and plates, and the lanterns, and the flowering shrubs in boxes, and the crumbs and cracker-paper, the forgotten bags and gloves and handkerchiefs, and the uneaten food (a very small item). Then a number of other people came (without orders): Bagginses, and

Boffins, and Bolgers, and Tooks, and other guests that lived or were staying near. By mid-day, when even the best-fed were out and about again, there was a large crowd at Bag End, uninvited but not unexpected.

Frodo was waiting on the step, smiling, but looking rather tired and worried. He welcomed all the callers, but he had not much more to say than before. His reply to all inquiries was simply this: 'Mr. Bilbo Baggins has gone away; as far as I know, for good.' Some of the visitors he invited to come inside, as Bilbo had left 'messages' for them.

Inside in the hall there was piled a large assortment of packages and parcels and small articles of furniture. On every item there was a label tied. There were several labels of this sort:

For ADELARD TOOK, for his VERY OWN, from Bilbo; on an umbrella. Adelard had carried off many unlabelled ones.

For DORA BAGGINS in memory of a LONG correspondence, with love from Bilbo; on a large waste-paper basket. Dora was Drogo's sister and the eldest surviving female relative of Bilbo and Frodo; she was ninety-nine, and had written reams of good advice for more than half a century.

For MILO BURROWS, hoping it will be useful, from B.B.; on a gold pen and ink-bottle. Milo never answered letters.

For ANGELICA'S use, from Uncle Bilbo; on a round convex mirror. She was a young Baggins, and too obviously considered her face shapely.

For the collection of HUGO BRACEGIRDLE, from a contributor; on an (empty) book-case. Hugo was a great borrower of books, and worse than usual at returning them.

For LOBELIA SACKVILLE-BAGGINS, as a PRESENT; on a case of silver spoons. Bilbo believed that she had acquired a good many of his spoons, while he was away on his former journey. Lobelia knew that quite well. When she arrived later in the day, she took the point at once, but she also took the spoons.

This is only a small selection of the assembled presents. Bilbo's residence had got rather cluttered up with things in the course of his long life. It was a tendency of hobbit-holes to get cluttered up: for which the custom of giving so many birthday-presents was largely responsible. Not, of course, that the birthday-presents were always *new*; there were one or two old *mathoms* of forgotten uses that had circulated all around the district; but Bilbo had usually given new presents, and kept those that he received. The old hole was now being cleared a little.

Every one of the various parting gifts had labels, written out personally by Bilbo, and several had some point, or some joke. But, of course, most of the things were given where they would be wanted and welcome. The poorer hobbits, and especially those of Bagshot Row, did very well. Old Gaffer Gamgee got two sacks of potatoes, a new spade, a woollen waistcoat, and a bottle of ointment for creaking joints. Old Rory Brandybuck, in return for much hospitality, got a dozen bottles of Old Winyards: a strong red wine from the Southfarthing, and now quite mature, as it had been laid down by Bilbo's father. Rory quite forgave Bilbo, and voted him a capital fellow after the first bottle.

There was plenty of everything left for Frodo. And, of course, all the chief treasures, as well as the books, pictures, and more than enough furniture, were left in his possession. There was, however, no sign nor mention of money or jewellery: not a penny-piece or a glass bead was given away.

Frodo had a very trying time that afternoon. A false rumour that the whole household was being distributed free spread like wildfire; and before long the place was packed with people who had no business there, but could not be kept out. Labels got torn off and mixed, and quarrels broke out. Some people tried to do swaps and deals in the hall; and others tried to make off with minor items not addressed to them, or with anything that seemed unwanted or unwatched. The road to the gate was blocked with barrows and handcarts.

In the middle of the commotion the Sackville-Bagginses arrived. Frodo had retired for a while and left his friend Merry Brandybuck to keep an eye on things. When Otho loudly demanded to see Frodo, Merry bowed politely.

'He is indisposed,' he said. 'He is resting.'

'Hiding, you mean,' said Lobelia. 'Anyway we want to see him and we mean to see him. Just go and tell him so!'

Merry left them a long while in the hall, and they had time to discover their parting gift of spoons. It did not improve their tempers. Eventually they were shown into the study. Frodo was sitting at a table with a lot of papers in front of him. He looked indisposed – to see Sackville-Bagginses at any rate; and he stood up, fidgeting with something in his pocket. But he spoke quite politely.

The Sackville-Bagginses were rather offensive. They began by offering him bad bargain-prices (as between friends) for various valuable and unlabelled

things. When Frodo replied that only the things specially directed by Bilbo were being given away, they
said the whole affair was very fishy.

'Only one thing is clear to me,' said Otho, 'and that
is that you are doing exceedingly well out of it. I insist
on seeing the will.'

Otho would have been Bilbo's heir, but for the
adoption of Frodo. He read the will carefully and
snorted. It was, unfortunately, very clear and correct
(according to the legal customs of hobbits, which
demand among other things seven signatures of wit-
nesses in red ink).

'Foiled again!' he said to his wife. 'And after waiting
sixty years. Spoons? Fiddlesticks!' He snapped his fingers
under Frodo's nose and stumped off. But Lobelia was
not so easily got rid of. A little later Frodo came out of
the study to see how things were going on, and found
her still about the place, investigating nooks and corners,
and tapping the floors. He escorted her firmly off the
premises, after he had relieved her of several small (but
rather valuable) articles that had somehow fallen inside
her umbrella. Her face looked as if she was in the throes
of thinking out a really crushing parting remark; but all
she found to say, turning round on the step, was:

'You'll live to regret it, young fellow! Why didn't
you go too? You don't belong here; you're no Baggins
– you – you're a Brandybuck!' 'Did you hear that,
Merry? That was an insult, if you like,' said Frodo as
he shut the door on her.

'It was a compliment,' said Merry Brandybuck, 'and
so, of course, not true.'

Then they went round the hole, and evicted three
young hobbits (two Boffins and a Bolger) who were

knocking holes in the walls of one of the cellars. Frodo also had a tussle with young Sancho Proudfoot (old Odo Proudfoot's grandson), who had begun an excavation in the larger pantry, where he thought there was an echo. The legend of Bilbo's gold excited both curiosity and hope; for legendary gold (mysteriously obtained, if not positively ill-gotten), is, as everyone knows, anyone's for the finding – unless the search is interrupted.

When he had overcome Sancho and pushed him out, Frodo collapsed on a chair in the hall. 'It's time to close the shop, Merry,' he said. 'Lock the door, and don't open it to anyone today, not even if they bring a battering ram.' Then he went to revive himself with a belated cup of tea.

He had hardly sat down, when there came a soft knock at the front-door. 'Lobelia again most likely,' he thought. 'She must have thought of something really nasty, and have come back again to say it. It can wait.'

He went on with his tea. The knock was repeated, much louder, but he took no notice. Suddenly the wizard's head appeared at the window.

'If youdon't let me in, Frodo, I shall blow your door right down your hole and out through the hill,' he said.

'My dear Gandalf! Half a minute!' cried Frodo, running out of the room to the door. 'Come in! Come in! I thought it was Lobelia.'

'Then I forgive you. But I saw her some time ago, driving a ponytrap towards Bywater with a face that would have curdled new milk.'

'She had already nearly curdled me. Honestly, I nearly tried on Bilbo's ring. I longed to disappear.'

'Don't do that!' said Gandalf, sitting down. 'Do be

careful of that ring, Frodo! In fact, it is partly about that that I have come to say a last word.'

'Well, what about it?'

'What do you know already?'

'Only what Bilbo told me. I have heard his story: how he found it, and how he used it: on his journey, I mean.'

'Which story, I wonder,' said Gandalf.

'Oh, not what he told the dwarves and put in his book,' said Frodo. 'He told me the true story soon after I came to live here. He said you had pestered him till he told you, so I had better know too. "No secrets between us, Frodo," he said; "but they are not to go any further. It's mine anyway." '

'That's interesting,' said Gandalf. 'Well, what did you think of it all?'

'If you mean, inventing all that about a "present", well, I thought the true story much more likely, and I couldn't see the point of altering it at all. It was very unlike Bilbo to do so, anyway; and I thought it rather odd.'

'So did I. But odd things may happen to people that have such treasures – if they use them. Let it be a warning to you to be very careful with it. It may have other powers than just making you vanish when you wish to.'

'I don't understand,' said Frodo.

'Neither do I,' answered the wizard. 'I have merely begun to wonder about the ring, especially since last night. No need to worry. But if you take my advice you will use it very seldom, or not at all. At least I beg you not to use it in any way that will cause talk or rouse suspicion. I say again: keep it safe, and keep it secret!'

'You are very mysterious! What are you afraid of?'

'I am not certain, so I will say no more. I may be able to tell you something when I come back. I am going off at once: so this is good-bye for the present.' He got up.

'At once!' cried Frodo. 'Why, I thought you were staying on for at least a week. I was looking forward to your help.'

'I did mean to – but I have had to change my mind. I may be away for a good while; but I'll come and see you again, as soon as I can. Expect me when you see me! I shall slip in quietly. I shan't often be visiting the Shire openly again. I find that I have become rather unpopular. They say I am a nuisance and a disturber of the peace. Some people are actually accusing me of spiriting Bilbo away, or worse. If you want to know, there is supposed to be a plot between you and me to get hold of his wealth.'

'Some people!' exclaimed Frodo. 'You mean Otho and Lobelia. How abominable! I would give them Bag End and everything else, if I could get Bilbo back and go off tramping in the country with him. I love the Shire. But I begin to wish, somehow, that I had gone too. I wonder if I shall ever see him again.'

'So do I,' said Gandalf. 'And I wonder many other things. Goodbye now! Take care of yourself! Look out for me, especially at unlikely times! Good-bye!'

Frodo saw him to the door. He gave a final wave of his hand, and walked off at a surprising pace; but Frodo thought the old wizard looked unusually bent, almost as if he was carrying a great weight. The evening was closing in, and his cloaked figure quickly vanished into the twilight. Frodo did not see him again for a long time.